PURGATORIUM

JOSH DEERE

Cover design by Erin New

Proofreading and formatting by Nicola Lovick

ACKNOWLEDGEMENTS

For Brittany, my first and biggest fan. The best part about this project has been our long talks late at night or in the car about story, characters, the genre, etc. Sharing this experience with you has made it fun, and your love and loyalty have kept me going. After all, I'm really just a boy who wrote a book to try and impress a girl. I love you.

For my boys, Joshua, Wyatt and Jack. You're my reason for getting out of bed every morning, and for laughing almost every day (not to mention a few extra gray hairs). I'm so proud for the honor of getting to be your father.

For mom for always telling me that I can be anything and go anywhere I want, and for dad for teaching me how to work to get there.

For my brothers - Monte for being my example, Mike for being my protector, and Jason for teaching us how to dream.

Also, thanks to Dylan for telling me to shut up and start telling my story.

And finally, thanks to Kevin, Ana, Michelle, and Ricky for your selfless support and encouragement while this project took flight.

Leave a Review!

After you finish reading, please leave a review for Purgatorium at:

https://www.amazon.com/dp/0578600668

https://www.goodreads.com/book/show/48750981-purgatorium

https://www.barnesandnoble.com/w/purgatorium-josh-deere/1134947188?ean=9780578600666

Thank you!

"There is no place so dark that light cannot lead the way."

— Slade Combs, The Choice: Death Is Just The Beginning

Prologue

In an instant, Sophie's mind fractured into a billion pieces. Excruciating pain tore through her like magmatic, electrical currents. She saw only severe and blinding whiteness. A shrill cry burst from within, as if it did not belong to her. Her mind then snapped back like a rubber band, into a sudden state of hyper-awareness, yet her body was unable to move. For a moment, time froze.

And then, as quickly as her body petrified, her muscles were liberated, and her body crashed to the earth. She watched it collapse beneath her like a mound of limp rags. Yet somehow her awareness hovered above, stunned to see her own lifeless body crumpled in a heap.

Sophie extended her two trembling hands. She recognized them as hers only by their familiar shape, but they felt completely foreign. Her silky skin was gone, replaced by steel-gray flesh. She dragged her fingers across her arm and felt almost nothing, so she dug her fingernails in deep and watched as a smoky vapor rippled beneath her almost transparent skin.

The sallow, ashen appendage that hovered before her didn't even seem to be a part of her. Rage coursed through her as she forced herself to her knees and slammed her palm into the ground, while hunching over her cadaver. "Noooooooooooooooo!" she howled, momentarily drowning out the ghostly chorus of cries filling the night air. Her physical sensations were dulled, but the emotions —the terror, the nauseating sorrow, the despair—were exponentially worse than anything she had felt before, at least not since her father died.

Please, no. Please. I cannot be…

Dead.

Please.

Chapter One

"Hi, Daddy. What's happenin'?" Sophie sat, legs crossed, in the grass next to her father. She didn't look directly toward him, instead staring at the ground as she ran fingers through the soft grass. She plucked the occasional clover leaf and rolled it between her fingers before flicking it away in the breeze. The vibrant green blades of grass juxtaposed perfectly against her crimson fingernails.

She wasn't sure why she was nervous; she'd been coming to chat with her father at least once a month for years. But this time was different.

"I, uh…I've come to ask forgiveness, and I hope you're not upset." She knew it was stupid to even bring it up, and she was certain how he would respond. But she felt she at least owed it to him to offer an explanation. "It's been nine years since I promised you that I'd come see you every month and tell you everything that's going on, and I've never missed a month."

She liked to sit next to him, but always gave him some space. For her, it was a sign of respect. She loved and respected this man more than anyone in the world.

"But, listen!" Her eyes opened wide as she leaned in. "Remember when I told you I was denied the scholarship to go and intern at the museum in Switzerland? I mean, you know I've wanted to go there for years, ever since you told me about it and the Witz collection." Her heart raced as she wondered what he was thinking.

"And you know Mom can't afford to send me…although she'd never admit that." Sophie knew her father was just as excited as she was when she received the acceptance letter to the intern program, and that his heart broke just like hers when she was turned down for the scholarship.

"Well," she allowed herself a small grin as she wiped away a tear, "they called a few days ago and said one of the other scholarship recipients dropped out at the last minute and they have an opening! They're covering almost everything! Tuition. My apartment. Even some supplies!" Her voice raced faster and faster as she buzzed through the details. But he always loved how her voice spun out of control when she was truly excited. "I'll be there for the whole semester, and will get to associate with the head curator. I've heard that if I do well, there may even be a chance at a full-time position after I graduate.

"I really will live cheap, Daddy. I mean, it shouldn't cost much 'cause I'll want to spend all my time at the museum." She looked down at her black Chuck Taylors and wiped off some of the morning dew. "I mean, when am I ever going to have another opportunity like this?" She had always been Daddy's little girl, and he was a complete sucker for her in every way. She learned at a very young age to take full advantage of that early and often.

She stopped, closed her eyes, and waited patiently for an answer, as she often did. She adjusted her Red Sox cap, hoping her father would notice her sporting his favorite team. *Their* favorite team.

"And…" She took a deep breath, "I leave today! This morning, in fact. That's why I came so early. And yes, Mom is okay with it. I mean, she's nervous, and hasn't shut up about all the horrible things that can happen to me in Europe. Right now, she's parked over there with Kevin in the back seat, probably talking his ear off. I'm sorry she wouldn't come and talk to you herself, but you know how she's been since you left. I hope you'll forgive her for that someday, if you haven't already." In truth, Sophie's mother was an absolute mess. Yet she somehow managed to carry on, albeit with a ton of help from her twenty-year-old daughter. "I'd be lying if I said I wasn't a little worried about how she's going to get along while I'm gone." She shrugged. "She'll probably survive, but I'm not so sure about Kevin. He'll probably live off video games and Lucky Charms. Probably won't do one minute of homework. Heck, that's probably an eleven-year-old's dream. But I promise I'll call and check in on them, every day if necessary. And Aunt Janette is just down the road if they need her."

Sophie scooted closer to her father, and then stretched out her legs. Her shoes squeaked like church mice as she rubbed the soles together. Then she leaned back on her arms, tilted her head back, and closed her eyes. She sat silently for a few minutes and took in the morning breeze. She tried to fight back tears, but not for long. This made her look away. She never wanted her father to see her unhappy.

"Oh, and look. I'm taking your brush." She slid the worn, frayed paintbrush out of her back pocket and showed it to him. When she was little, she would watch him run the dry bristles over the prints of his favorite paintings on their walls. He would dramatically trace the strokes of the master artists while teaching their techniques to Sophie, her azure eyes fixed on her hero and his seemingly magic brush. Then he would lie next to her in bed and gently run it over her face as she fell asleep. "If I get a chance when nobody's looking, I promise to trace a Witz painting for you. And I shall come back and tell you all about it.

"You know I love you more than anything. I would never break a promise to you under any other circumstances, and I will never do it again." She wiped another tear as she got as close to him as possible. "But I just couldn't imagine you'd get mad about this. It's like I'm fulfilling a dream that we've *both* had forever! And you know I'd give *anything, anything* in the world, if you could just come with me."

She paused for a moment, allowing herself to hope that maybe, just maybe, she would hear him say, "Of course I'll go, Sophie. Let me get my things." But instead she leaned over, touched her forehead to the cold headstone and said, "I miss you so much."

Just then, her mother honked. "Great timing, Mom."

She traced the letters of her father's name with her finger. "JOHN GABRIEL CALDWELL". A tear rolled down her cheek as she read the inscription below his name: "HE DREAMED OF PAINTING THE WORLD, BUT HIS GREATEST WORK WAS HIS FAMILY. AN AMAZING FRIEND, AN EVEN BETTER HUSBAND...." She then traced the last part with her finger. "AND THE BEST FATHER EVER." As she always did, she pushed her fiercely against the curve of the final "R", causing a half-heart-shaped indention to appear on the tip of her finger. One day she would see him again, and her broken heart would be fixed.

"Bye, Daddy! Give me four months, *four months*, and I'll come back and tell you all about it."

Chapter Two

The unnerving silence of the blistering Iraqi afternoon was pierced by the buttery-smooth vibrato of the unseen voice resonating across the dusty rooftops. The first time he heard it, Alasdair "Alie" Quin of the 22nd SAS British Special Forces Regiment thought the Muslim call to prayer was the creepiest sound he had ever heard. But numerous tours later, it had become a welcome break from their otherwise typically monotonous afternoons.

Sure, there were firefights, and moments of intense brutality, but those moments were few and far between the more common hours of watching and waiting. But he was a soldier, and he knew this came with the territory. And he loved it. Not because he came from generations of decorated veterans. Not even close. In reality, he came from generations of alcoholic, wife-beating losers. But he was a fighter, and that was just about all he was. The story goes that he was given the name Alasdair—Gaelic for "defender of mankind"—by a grandfather who he never met, and who spent half his time drinking in local pubs, and the other half sleeping it off behind bars.

His first time in combat, Alie convinced himself he was there to defend freedom, or fight for the "little man", or represent the honor of the queen, or something like that. But it didn't take long until he was just a soldier, fighting simply because that's what he was trained to do. And what he was good at.

Most soldiers have moments every now and then when they are shaken out of the monotony. Like having to promise a buddy that you will tell his wife and kids they were his everything as his eyes roll back in his head. Or taking a minute to stare at a picture of a loved one back home. But Alie didn't have any loved ones back home. No family to speak of, and very few friends. Sure, he had a dog and a few old school mates, and there was a bartender he was quite fond of at the neighborhood pub. But they all got along just fine without him when he was gone, and he wasn't too preoccupied with their wellbeing either.

Unlike most, Alie didn't look forward to returning home, and didn't even think too much about survival. He just lived day to day. Hour to hour. Minute to minute. He kept his mind on the next mission, the next task, the next target, and didn't let much get to him.

His one major annoyance, however, was the sand in his teeth. It was a constant since his first day there. Every time he closed his mouth, several grains of sand crunched between his teeth. He wondered how much he had actually swallowed in his thirty-one months in Iraq. An X-ray of his colon would probably look like an hourglass.

Staring out over the sea of sand, and the matching, monochromatic buildings, reminded him that he was a long way from his hometown of Birmingham, England. He never understood why people in a barren, monotonous landscape would build buildings that were also completely void of color. Yet people in beautiful, lush places like Scotland's coastal villages or the Austrian alps built multi-colored structures. It seemed backwards.

These were the kinds of random thoughts that bounced around his mind while sitting in the blistering Iraqi sun, waiting to finally return to base for the evening. On this peach of a day in particular, he and his three best SAS buddies were spread across the rooftop of an obscenely inadequate building in the lovely Anbar Province—a place where British and American soldiers tended to die with more frequency than usual. Alie leaned against the short wall that lined the roof's edge, which was the only thing between him and the wanna-be snipers peering through some blinds a half-click to the north. The holy warriors believed themselves to be hidden, but Alie and his guys spotted them hours before.

Alie could easily go to work with his C8 Carbine and eviscerate cheap plastic blinds masking the insurgents' hiding place, and then dissect the dilapidated walls. But in the few city blocks separating Alie from the insurgents, a team of American Marines were going door to door snuffing out a rumored al Qaeda weapons stash. Alie's mission was to provide bird's-eye support so the Americans didn't get jumped by any resident uglies looking for a fight. Unlike the insurgents across the way, Alie was under no illusion that he and his mates were hidden. Tucked behind a wall, sure. But not hidden. He figured, however, that like most Iraqis, these guys recognized Special Forces by their bearded faces, and would much rather perform a dirty hit-and-run on some hapless Marines than tangle with the bearded guys.

As Alie rested against the half-wall, he traced the sizzling hot serial number on his rifle. "Big, ugly, clumsy piece of metal," he thought. Despite his ability to work magic with a rifle, Alie would much rather lay the guns down and go mano a mano with the puny extremist nut jobs. Or, even better, in Alie's opinion, a razor-sharp steel sword.

He had practiced martial arts relentlessly since age nine. He earned his black belt in Tae Kwon Do by thirteen, and dominated several tournaments along the way. But by fourteen, he began pursuing more brutal, punishing techniques. He lost interest in scoring points and winning trophies. Alie wanted to know how to dismantle and cripple an opponent.

He had been raised by a despondent mother and a vile, alcoholic stepfather. He never met his biological father. By fifteen, Alie was just waiting, hoping for his stepfather to lay a hand on him, sure that he could cripple the miserable asshole, perhaps permanently. But his stepfather went out one night with some friends, and never returned. He didn't take anything with him, not even his clothes. He just disappeared. After crying, cursing and drinking for about a week, his mother never spoke of the man again, and neither did Alie.

By nineteen, Alie had gained regional notoriety as a prodigy in Muay Thai and Krav Maga. But he was most passionate about the arts related to the sword. He studied Battojutsu and Kenjutsu religiously. It was his escape. He often got lost for hours at the studio, soaking up as much knowledge and skill as his teachers could give. Many nights, after the studio shut down, he would continue in his bedroom long after midnight.

In many ways, martial arts saved him. His disdain for authority eventually gave way to his immense respect for his instructors. He felt oddly freed by the intense discipline. Strength, but with restraint. Ferocious, but precise. Deadly, but at the right time. All characteristics that benefited him as a soldier, and gave him a substantial advantage over other recruits.

After enlisting, Alie soon earned a reputation as a close-range combat wizard. In initial hand-to-hand training, he embarrassed the instructor badly. And when it came time for close-quarters weapons—

usually wooden swords and knifes—he was downright scary. After common training, Alie was recommended to Special Forces, where he found a home among other elite warriors. He didn't care too much for accolades and awards. He preferred the anonymity of the Special Forces, and found he had much more respect for his contemporaries. But he couldn't help thinking he was born a few centuries too late. He belonged in an era when men met on the battlefield, armed with swords, not hiding in upstairs rooms waiting take cowardly pot shots at the enemy.

Alie tried to be patient in the late-afternoon heat. But he was becoming mildly annoyed at how long the Americans were taking. This was no place for picnics. The longer they waited, the lower the sun sank in the sky and he knew they did not want to stick around and check out the nightlife. He felt relatively confident that if they were up on that roof, the insurgents would keep their cool. But he also knew that all bets were off at night. So he decided to give it five more minutes, and then he would have to have a chat with the Americans.

His plans were cut short when a white van and two makeshift armored trucks, each with mounted 14.5mm heavy machine guns, came zipping down the street directly below them packed to the brim with pissed off rebel fighters, armed to the teeth. The trucks staked out positions in the intersections below them and pointed their guns down the streets toward the Marines. In a matter of seconds, they had pinned the Americans in on both sides. The van then screeched to a halt between the armed trucks, directly below Alie. The sliding door flew open, and armed men poured out like ants.

After a glance and a nod from his mates, Alie tossed a grenade over the wall. He then immediately followed the explosion with a spray of rounds into the scattering crowd of insurgents. But almost instantly bullets slapped the side of the half-wall, forcing him to duck as shards of plaster exploded behind him. The wannabe snipers were pinning him down while the insurgents set out after the Marines. He knew the Americans could fight like hell, but he also knew that more insurgent fighters were likely on their way, looking to lock horns with the Western infidels. He also knew that under heavy fire like this, the half-wall behind him wouldn't last long.

"Diggs, do you have a visual on the snipers?"

"Negative," shouted Lance-Corporal Allen Diggs. "But I can make an educated guess." Diggs took out a small mirror attached to a thin metal rod and extended it slightly above the wall. With a loud ping, the mirror shattered, but not before Diggs got a look.

"I didn't see anything coming from the loft, but there are at least two more snipers, one to the east and one to the west."

"This is the last time I let the Americans give me orders," Alie snapped.

"Well, at least they invited us to the party!" Diggs shouted, then smirked.

Alie had to think quickly. They were pinned down, and it was just a matter of time until grenades started coming over that wall. Alie knew they could disappear quickly if necessary. But a quick exit would mean leaving the Americans to die in an ambush. And as irritated as he was with them, he liked the Americans, and was bloody delighted they were on his side.

"Harris! Can you hear me?" Sporadic gunfire rattled below as the Americans yelled out commands in the distance.

"Talk to me, sergeant!" replied Corporal Jaden Harris, their demolitions expert.

"How's your payload?" Bullets zinged overhead as Alie worked on putting a plan together.

"Getting a little heavy, corporal," Harris grinned. "I wouldn't mind offloading some of it."

"Well, you're about to get your chance. Rig it on a delay and toss it across the street to the other side."

"Brilliant thinking, Quin." Harris opened his pack and started giving life to several packs of explosives.

"Diggs, Redwine. I need a couple of seconds of suppressive fire on 'go'. After that, makes sure nothing comes through that door," Alie yelled, a bit anxious about the door jutting up from the roof three meters from them. They had come through the same door a few hours earlier, and there was no reason their enemies couldn't do the same. "And watch for grenades coming over those walls!"

"What are you up to, Quin?" yelled Diggs, looking worried.

"I've got to get behind that door," Alie replied while tossing two smoke grenades. "We need eyes on those snipers, or we'll never get out of here."

Whap-whap-whap-whap. Shards of concrete showered their helmets as bullets tore at the half-wall.

"Alie, maybe you should hang on a sec—"

"GO!" screamed Alie as he tucked into a crouch, ready to pounce. Diggs and Redwine led with their rifles, generously spraying rounds into the shadowy windows across the way. Alie dashed toward the door, ducking behind it just as several bullets pinged against the metal.

"I'm checking comms to see what kind of support we've got!" Alie yelled as he removed his Bowman radio from his pack. Within seconds, he was communicating with American Intelligence, who were apparently watching the scene unfold on satellite.

"You part of that mess down there?" came the American voice.

"Roger," Alie returned. "Do we have anything in the area?"

"Yes, sir. A gunship's headed your way. First priority are those technicals, then what appears to be a white van."

"Affirmative," responded Alie. "The white van was the primary transport. They were packed in there like sardines. Although the two taller buildings to the north and east are packed with snipers."

"Copy that," said the American. "We'll get those on the second pass."

"Light 'em up, sir." Forget any irritation Alie had with the Americans. They had big, big guns, and that engendered a lot of love at a time like this.

"Look alive, mates," Alie yelled. "Big bird's coming!"

"You think it's safe to watch the show from up here?" asked Redwine.

"Good point. Harris, chuck that payload. I'll get the door!" shouted Alie.

"How chivalrous of you," chirped Harris as he heaved the explosives backwards, high over the wall. They landed with a thud on the pavement below, followed by pure chaos from the insurgents. Tick...tick...

An ear-splitting explosion rocked the street below them. Seconds later, dense smoke crawled up the building's face and then lifted skyward, creating a black curtain that obscured them temporarily from the opportunistic snipers across the way. Alie and his crew wasted no time barreling into the rooftop doorway. They found themselves at the top of a dark stairwell, where a dangling light bulb flickered above, intermittently illuminating crumbling walls. They maneuvered down two flights of stairs with theirs guns raised and ready for any lurking threats. Alie had expected to encounter Al Qaeda inside the building, or at least some terrified Iraqi families, but it was empty. The Iraqis had lived with war long enough to know when it was time to disappear.

Redwine's boot made short work of a door leading to a second-story apartment, revealing the meager living space inside. Alie and his men peered at the insurgents below through curtains that hung from north-facing windows. Several were dragging bloodied fighters—some dead, some still hanging on—into the white van. Others peered aimlessly through their rifle sites toward the rooftop. After a few seconds, the sliding door slammed shut, and the van buzzed off down the street to the west.

"Fellas, we'd probably better back away from those windows," said Redwine.

Then, just as an insurgent fighter aimed an RPG toward the top of the building, fire rained down from the sky. Hundreds of 40mm-rounds cut a swathe down the middle of the street, nearly splitting the two armored pickups in half. The concrete on the street churned and spit upwards as if it were in a blender. One of the apartment windows shattered as rubble came flying through. Screams filled the block below, followed by panicked commands in Arabic. Over the horrified shouting, Alie heard the rumbling AC-130 circling for another pass.

The remaining holy warriors sprinted down the street to the west, running through pieces of what used to be their comrades, and disappeared around a corner. Alie and Diggs peered through the curtains, eager to get a quick look before the gunship unleashed the sequel. As they carefully surveyed the scene, something caught Alie's eye. Through the rising smoke, he made out a white van two blocks away. But it was not the same van used by the insurgents. Alie raised his binoculars for a better look

Through thick smoke, he could see that the van's windshield was shattered, and its roof torn partly open. He watched an Iraqi man climb out onto the hood as he and his frantic wife struggled to tear out the rest of the windshield. Two young boys leapt from the van, bloodied and hysterical. Their father pleaded with them to get back in the van.

"You've got to be joking," whispered Alie. He instantly realized that when the gunship made its second run, it would likely mistake the white van for the one belonging to the insurgents, and it would become their primary target. The Iraqi family stood no chance.

Alie screamed into his radio to call off the strike, but there was no response. Harris began screaming at the family from the upstairs window, waiving his arm wildly to get off the road. But his desperate cries only made the parents work faster as the roar of the AC-130 grew even closer. Against his better judgment, Alie bolted out the apartment door and down the hallway to the stairs.

Alie briefly surveyed the street for insurgents, but they were long gone. He then dashed down the street toward the family. He cleared several piles of rubble while screaming "Haraba!", which he understood to mean "run away!"

The frightened mother jerked one of the boys back into the van, while the father turned toward Alie. They stared at one another for several seconds, frozen. Alie could tell the man was confused, not knowing who or what to fear. He just wanted to escape with his family. Alie stopped in the street and again waived his arms and yelled, "Haraba!"

The man looked inquisitively at Alie, and toward the sky. As he turned his gaze back, Alie could see that he suddenly understood.

"No," whispered Alie.

The street again began to churn just beyond the van. Alie dove into the doorway of a flower shop. By the time he hit the ground, the 40-mm rounds had torn down the street to the west and were gone. He stumbled to his feet and ran out into the smoky street. He could hear Diggs and Redwine yelling as they ran toward him.

"I'm okay!" screamed Alie. "Come help! Hurry!"

As he ran, he fumbled for his radio to try and call off any more strikes. He tripped several times over chunks of concrete as he choked through the smoke. But he stopped as the twisted remains of what had been a van appeared through the haze. The flicker of flames peeked through the ruins as he dropped his pack and rifle. Alie had experienced countless scenes of carnage during his days in Iraq, but this was something different. It was the ultimate case of being in the wrong place at the wrong time…and in the wrong van. Alie was there on purpose. So were the Americans, and the insurgents. But this Iraqi father was just trying to escape with his family, and made a wrong turn.

Alie stared at the mutilated father, strewn across the street in front of the van. Inside, he could see the mother lying motionless on the older boy, their clothes soaked in deep red.

Alie whipped his hand back and forth, trying to clear the smoke. Then he heard a gasp, followed by a gurgled cry.

"Get over here!" he yelled while running to the back of the van. He could a delicate head of wet black hair. A number 3 on the soccer jersey on the boy's back rose and fell sporadically as he fought for life. Alie reached through the window and gently scooped the boy up, who he cried out in pain.

Alie held the boy and looked into his eyes. The boy's round black eyes stared penetratingly at Alie as his little body shivered. He was no older than five, with a wiry, bony frame. He had the same look of terror his father had only moments before. The boy opened his mouth to speak, but only blood came out. As Alie knelt to the ground, the boy grabbed Alie's vest and squeezed until his knuckles whitened.

"Don't die, little dude," Alie choked out.

"Hey, mate, he's gutted wide—"

"I know, mate!" Alie snapped. "Shut up. I know."

The boy continued staring at Alie as his breaths became more and more shallow. His lungs were filling with blood, and Alie watched as tears traced a path through the dust and blood on the boy's face. Alie couldn't talk to him; he could only nod his head, trying to reassure him that everything would be okay, knowing that it would soon be over.

Life slipped out of the boy while Alie held him. His legs dangled as his grip loosened on Alie's vest. Then his neck went limp and his head drooped backward. But his eyes did not close.

Several American Marines came jogging toward them, chattering excitedly as they greeted the Brits. Diggs waived at them, motioning them to be quiet. The Marines stared inquisitively as Alie looked into the boy's eyes for a few seconds more, and then gently reached up and shut the boy's eyes. Alie looked at Diggs, who put his hand on Alie's shoulder.

"Little guy got to me, brother," whispered Alie. "Don't know why."

"It's alright, Alie," answered Diggs. "You're still human."

"You sure?" said Alie.

He laid the boy's body down softly next to the van. He stood up and stared at the body once more. He thought about how cold he had become, so void of emotion. He had felt so little in years. It almost felt good to mourn a tiny stranger's death, if even for a minute. It was at least a sign that he was still alive.

Alie turned and walked past the Marines toward his backpack and his gun. He bent over and picked them up, then looked back to the Marines and said, "You're welcome."

Chapter Three

"Virgil, keep your voice down, please," Rikku pleaded. "Not everyone has to hear you."

"Well, Rik, perhaps if I shout loud enough, *somebody* in this Godforsaken place will listen for once!" Virgil's grumbling ricocheted down the metallic tunnels of the Hadron Collider facility.

Rikku Laine looked past Virgil's irritated face to the group of tourists marching like ducklings behind their tour guide. They plodded along the sterile catwalks with cheap translator headsets tucked beneath cherry-red hard hats. Rikku shot the guide a brief, exasperated look, and she quickly shuttled the gawking herd down an adjacent tunnel.

"Never mind the tourists, Rik," Virgil lectured, wagging his finger inches from Rikku's nose. "We're talking about the potential for a disaster that could wipe out millions, maybe more!"

"Virgil…." Rikku shook his head and opened the door to a small office before pushing Virgil inside. Before Rikku could shut the door, Virgil continued his protest. "Virgil," Rikku cut him off, "you know I like and respect you."

"If you respected me, you would listen to what I'm saying—"

"Virgil, you must…"

"And if you liked me, you wouldn't shove me into tiny, cramped offices to shut me up!" Virgil's eyed darted to the jumbled diagrams and sci-fi posters tacked to the wall. "Whose pathetic little office is this anyway?"

"I don't know, and don't care. Now listen to me." Rikku was a Finnish physicist turned bureaucratic financier. A better money magnet than a scientist, Rikku made a name for himself bouncing between global philanthropic organizations. He'd managed to navigate the awkwardly juxtaposed worlds of science and philanthropy for a very lucrative decade before being snatched up by CERN, the French "Conseil Européen pour la Recherche Nucléaire", or European Council for Nuclear Research.

CERN was arguably the biggest and most powerful scientific organization in the Western world. Since its founding in 1954, CERN had pushed the boundaries of nuclear physics research, primarily at its mega-laboratory spanning the border between Switzerland and France, near the city of Geneva. It revolutionized nuclear physics in 1959 as the first to achieve proton acceleration. Over the next five decades, CERN scientists continued to build and operate boldly innovative, yet astonishingly expensive accelerators, synchrotrons and colliders, which succeeded time and time again in achieving some of the grandest nucleophysical discoveries of our time.

In 2008, CERN lapped the field when it debuted the Large Hadron Collider—the "LHC"— a 16.8-mile circular tunnel 300 feet below the surface of the French-Swiss border, jam-packed with 9,300 magnets that are super-cooled to -456.25 degrees Fahrenheit. The project cost $4.75 billion to build, and billions more every year to operate. And all of this to search for one sub-atomic particle known as the "Higgs boson" particle. The Higgs boson, or "God particle" to some, was the theoretical glue that held the universe together. The particle, however, is so unbelievably small and elusive that it existed only in theory in the minds of the world's greatest nuclear physicists, that is until the LHC succeeded in "finding" it in 2012 by repeatedly and violently ramming sub-atomic particles together at velocities approaching the speed of light. The result was a series of manifestations that, in essence, hinted that the Higgs boson did, in fact, exist as scientists predicted.

CERN enticed Rikku in 2007 by almost doubling his already sizeable income. He would receive additional incentives if he continued his streak of rounding up generous donations from big-wig donors and large contributing universities and governments. Rikku did not disappoint.

But with his success came an increasing ego, or at least in Virgil's opinion. CERN hired Virgil the year before Rikku, but the two had little reason to interact until the higher-ups tasked Rikku with reining in Virgil's radical interactions with the outside world, which they feared would threaten CERN's fundraising capacities. Despite these concerns, Rikku and Virgil learned to respect one another, and eventually became friends.

Born in Lithuania as Virgilijus Andrius, Virgil gained distinction in the '90s as an abstract astrophysicist. But his favorable reputation as a scientist was almost eclipsed by the infamy created by his book, *Nucleo Angelis: The Intersection of Nuclear Physics and Spirituality*. In just over 1,000 pages, Virgil hypothesized that the scientific world's obsession with sub-atomic discoveries on an increasingly smaller and smaller scale to disprove the existence of, or need for a god, would eventually lead science to the opposite conclusion: that there must be a god, or at least some spiritual or sub-dimensional world beyond our own. And he criticized most of the world's leading nuclear and astrophysicists in the process.

But appeasing others was the last thing on Virgil's mind. He cut and combed his stringy white hair about once a year and trimmed his bushy mustache even less. He usually wore a thin, stained gray sweatshirt under a tweed sports coat, and showered sparingly between obsessive all-nighters at the laboratory. But despite his eccentricities, no one doubted Virgil's brilliance. CERN followed Virgil's career from afar for years, eventually deciding that having him onboard made more sense than worrying that he would outfox them somewhere else.

Rikku begged Virgil to take a seat on a small pleather-backed chair inside the tiny office. Virgil remained standing. "Virgil, your continued stay at this facility is aided greatly by your impeccable credentials and reputation." Rikku leaned against the desk and rubbed his eyes. "But the administration's admiration for your work is occasionally harmed by our unease at your coinciding reputation as a conspiracy theorist, with a mild obsession with the supernatural."

At that, Virgil stopped squabbling and asked, "What exactly do you mean, Rik?"

"Oh, don't play coy with me, Virgil. It's no secret you like to mix in a ghost story or two amongst your brilliant, albeit winded discourses on—"

"My spiritual convictions have absolutely nothing to do with my work," snapped Virgil.

"Of course they don't," Rikku responded, "except when your ludicrous theories of world disaster get in the way of your work, and mine."

"You must listen to me, Rik!" Virgil's Baltic accent thickened as he intensified. "I have been watching these readings for months and, given some time, I'm confident I can prove it. But I'm afraid we don't *have* much time at all if we continue to operate an unstable collider."

"Virgil, do you have any idea what it took to obtain approval for this facility, and the bureaucratic nightmare we go through monthly just to keep it afloat? We're on the heels of one of the greatest, if not *the* greatest discovery in science history, with much more on the way."

"Don't patronize me, Rik. Of course I know. I watched and waited for years for it to open——"

"Then quit trying to screw it up!" Rikku's blue eyes stared at Virgil, then beyond him again as the tour group obliviously shuffled past.

Virgil sighed, removed his wiry, crooked glasses, and wiped his forehead. "Rik, something very bad is coming," he pleaded, his voice just above a whisper. "The collider is a marvel and a wonder. Hell, it may be the greatest facility ever constructed in the name of science. But no amount of discovery and excitement is worth the colossal disaster that could take place if we don't shut it down and figure this out. And it could be back up in six months, Rik. Six months!"

"It's never gonna happen, Virgil. I'm sorry, but that's reality…a concept which you may need to look into sooner or later."

"But, Rik——"

"Like I said, I've liked and respected you for years, Virgil, but I'm not talking to you as your friend right now. I have no choice but to tell you that any more talk of this monstrous disaster of yours, or whatever it is you think is going to happen…" Rikku shrugged and then sighed, "Well, Virgil, then there will no longer be a place for you here." The two stared at each other in silence for an uncomfortable moment.

Virgil took a deep breath. "Rik, if we've come to the point where we care more about bureaucracy and politics…and money, than we do people, then I'm afraid you're right. There is no longer a place for me here." Rik shook his head and started to backtrack, but Virgil cut him off. "I will clear out my things and go peacefully on one condition: You deliver my report to the panel, one copy to each member."

"Virgil, I can't——"

"Then the sin is on your head, Rik my boy." Virgil reached out and clasped his hand on Rikku's shoulder, nodded, and then walked out of the office. Rikku couldn't decide if he had just made a huge mistake, or saved the project a ton of money. He chose to convince himself that it was the latter.

Chapter Four

Sophie slowly slid her English—French Dictionary into her backpack, followed by her English—German Dictionary, as she strolled past the shops in Geneva's airport. She had read all about how Switzerland had four official languages: French, German, Italian, and some local dialect called Rumantsch, which she had no plan of even attempting. She had made cheat sheets and note cards to navigate her way to the baggage claim, and then to the hotel. So, she felt a bit disappointed when most shops' signs were in English. If it weren't for the medley of languages spoken by people whizzing by her, she could easily have mistaken this for an airport in the U.S.

Sophie eyed a middle-aged man on a bench reading a newspaper. Its headline said "Visite Présidentielle", so she flipped through her assortment of French index cards. As she stood awkwardly gazing at the man, trying to muster up the courage to ask him, "Je m'excuse, où puis-je trouver le train?" she realized just how alone she really was, pretending to be brave all by herself in another hemisphere, in a country where they spoke four official languages, none of which were her own. She slid her hand into her jeans pocket and felt her father's weathered paint brush. "I can do this, Dad. I got this."

She briskly rolled her suitcase right up to the tips of the man's loafers and clumsily exclaimed, "Jay, may, eksoozay…uhhhh…jay, may…tro-vayr." The man peered over the newspaper and cocked an eyebrow. This was not going well.

"Ummm, sorry," stumbled Sophie. "Le train? Le train?"

The man grinned slightly and said, with a slight, unknown accent, "Where exactly is it that you are going?"

"Oh, I'm so sorry!" Sophie's face was burning beet red. "I just thought, since your newspaper…."

"Welcome to Europe," he quipped, "where we speak a few languages, even English sometimes." He stood up, folded his paper, and pointed. "Do you see that sign past the baggage carousel? The one that says 'TRAIN'? That's where you'll find the train."

Sophie hunched her shoulders and scratched her head, feeling stupid. "Sorry, sir. Thank you."

"Nothing to be sorry about, miss. Enjoy your trip."

. . . .

Sophie was quite certain that she would, in fact, enjoy Geneva, but maybe not for the same reasons most travelers do. Geneva is a world-class city that sits on the far southwest end of the breathtaking Lake Geneva, where the Rhône River escapes the lake before abandoning Switzerland for France. The impressive French Alps dominate the southern horizon, while the smaller, forest-covered Jura mountains span the skyline to the north.

Her first view of the city from the plane surprised her. Compared to other major European cities, Geneva is relatively small. But for its size, the city plays a major role in international affairs. It was home to one of the main offices of the United Nations, as well as the headquarters of the International Red Cross.

The city itself is an elegant fusion of modern with picturesque historical beauty. The Old Town sits on one side of the lake beneath the towering spires of the one-thousand-year-old St. Pierre's cathedral. The opposite shore is dotted with grand hotels and expensive restaurants. And bursting 140 meters high in the middle of the lake is the Jet d'Eau, the world's highest fountain.

Geneva is packed full of shops ranging from small tourist traps to showcases for world-class fashion designers, as well as quaint cafes, lush greenways and parks, dazzling lakeside promenades, and plenty of side-street exploration. It is also a cultural melting pot with more than thirty museums of all varieties. Sophie planned to visit them all, of course, but was most excited about the next four months that she would spend as an apprentice curator at the Musée d'Art et d'Histoire (Museum of Art and History).

While most high school girls were caught up in shopping, social media, and partying, Sophie had spent most of her teenage years studying the Renaissance and French Impressionism. Now in college, she still mostly steered clear of bars, football games, sororities, and, of course, boys. She was, however, a sucker for baseball, and attended many Red Sox games by herself in Fenway Park's cheap seats. She especially loved day games, where she would pass the time reading a book with her legs crossed in her green-back chair, her T-shirt sleeves rolled up to soak in the muggy, lazy Massachusetts sun.

She wasn't necessarily anti-social; she had her core group of friends with whom she shared many late nights laughing heartily inside the Bald Barista coffee shop just off the campus of Emmanuel College. And it certainly wasn't a lack of looks that kept Sophie away from the college boys. She was strikingly beautiful, although she did very little to show it. Sophie had golden hair that she rarely styled, but that naturally spun itself into silky, dangling curls. But more often than not, she stuffed her blond locks under a ball cap.

She usually hid her deep midnight blue eyes behind frumpy black-rimmed glasses that were entirely too masculine for her slender face. Sophie wore almost no make-up. Her skin was pale like ivory, but nearly flawless, a fact that she appreciated not because it was beautiful, but because it was low maintenance. It was this simple nature that allowed her to pack relatively lightly compared to most college-aged girls. After all, she had no aspirations of impressing anyone in Switzerland other than the museum's head curator.

Standing on the platform of Geneva's Cornavin Station, she stared at her reflection in the trains' windows as they whirred past. She realized just how much like a tourist she looked, with her fleece tied around her waist, her left arm leaning on the handle of her rolling suitcase, and her plaid backpack draped over her shoulder. She had left Boston the day before, changed planes in New York, and then touched down briefly in Istanbul, Turkey, before landing in Geneva twenty-one hours later. She had a fierce yearning to crash in a soft hotel bed, but not quite as fierce as her excitement to explore Geneva and, especially, the museum. If she hurried, she hoped to meet the curator briefly before it closed.

Sophie snaked through the crowd as she pulled her suitcase down the long train platform. She made her way down the escalator into a bustling corridor of shops and newspaper stands, now all in French. Sophie could tell by the store fronts and moving billboards that the Swiss are, as advertised, very proud of their watches and clocks.

On the ride to the hotel she stared with wide-eyed excitement at the city's French château architecture and sculptures. The friendly cab driver spoke to her in broken English, mostly emphasizing several touristy landmarks which Sophie knew from travel books. She was so eager to begin exploring that she almost forgot to pay the cab driver when they arrived at her hotel until he interjected a garish "AHEM!", to which she responded by pulling a scrunched, colorful Swiss Franc bill from her pocket and handed it to him. She had not yet mastered the exchange rate and, therefore, wasn't sure if she had given him enough. But when he darted off without another word, she guessed that he was satisfied.

Sophie saw her hotel room only long enough to drop off her suitcase, and to feel the pillows to make sure they were soft for later. She would only spend one night there before checking into her dorm the next day.

The doorman eyed her curiously as she zipped past him only minutes after checking in. She gave him a nod and a nervous, two-fingered salute, which she immediately thought must have looked very nerdy. But her embarrassment disappeared as soon as she stepped onto the sidewalk of the famed Rue du Mont Blanc—Geneva's busiest and trendiest street. She was actually there, by herself, in Geneva, Switzerland! For a brief moment, she closed her eyes and inhaled a mixture of fresh flowers, coffee, and diesel fumes from the passing buses. But she came to quickly as crowds of people brushed hastily by.

From where she stood, she could see no less than ten masterfully crafted Swish clocks adorning store fronts, crowning buildings, and perched atop street posts, all displaying the exact time. She was aware that the museum closed in only eighteen minutes, and she was several blocks away. So for now, she ignored the store windows with their Swiss chocolates, pastries, and very, very expensive clothing, and half-walked, half-jogged toward the museum. She passed numerous cafes that were filling up with people at the end of the workday. She couldn't help but notice the contrast between the frantic chaos of the streets and sidewalks, and the incredibly relaxed patrons sipping coffee in the outdoor cafes. She watched as their demeanors morphed magically as they sat at the wrought-iron patio tables and laughed with their friends. She hoped to do the same over the next few months, but had no time for that now.

In hindsight, she should have hailed a taxi. But on her map, the museum didn't appear too far from her hotel, and she opted to avoid another awkward chat with another French-speaking cab driver. Plus, she was on a tight budget, and planned to do a lot of walking to save as much as possible. So, instead, she hurried even more with her eyes fixed down the street toward the museum, looking down only occasionally at her watch. She panicked when she was still a block away as her watch read 4:55 p.m. She had no expectations of exploring the entire museum that night, but hoped to at least make a good impression by quickly introducing herself to the head curator before they closed.

As she passed the last row of French château-style buildings that obstructed her view, the full grandeur of the Musée d'Art et d'Histoire came into view. It was magnificent. The museum was certainly not the largest Sophie had visited—New York's Metropolitan Museum of Art dwarfed it many times over. But there was something regal about the way it dominated an already extraordinary city block that took Sophie's breath away, if only for a second before she sprinted across the bridge on the Rue Charles-Galland and up the front steps. As she reached for the ornate iron door handle, she met the gaze of a portly security guard peering through the glass as he turned the key to lock up for the night. She looked at her watch: 4:59 p.m. She raised her wrist desperately to show the guard. He nodded and smiled politely before turning his back and disappearing into the darkness. She had read that the Swiss were sticklers about punctuality. Apparently, this was true.

Sophie scratched her head as she turned her back to the museum. No longer in a hurry, she allowed herself to admire the towering pillars of the museum's façade, which she had seen many times in the grainy picture of her parents that hung above her bed. She dodged a few cars crossing the Rue Charles-Galland and stepped onto the sidewalk on the other side of the street next to the beautifully manicured lawn across from the museum. She did her best to stand in the spot where her parents had once stood when some passer-by agreed to snap an impromptu photograph that would later become one of Sophie's treasures. She took out her phone and extended her arm to take a selfie with her back to the museum to send to her mom. Click. Then she turned back to the museum, put her hand in her back pocket and grasped the old brush.

"I made it, Daddy," she whispered. "And, just like you said, it's awesome."

She took the time to inspect the front of the museum, this time in detail, including the immaculate Paul Amlehn sculptures towering over the entrance, as well as the others standing watch on each corner of the building. Then she stepped back onto the soft emerald grass and took a seat. Her mind slowed down for the first time all day as a yawn reminded her how exhausted she really was. She knew that if she laid back on the grass, she would fall asleep. So she got to her feet and began to retrace her steps back toward the Rue du Mont-Blanc and her hotel.

On the way, Sophie passed by several more cafes, each one more enticing than the last. She couldn't wait to curl up in the feathery hotel bed and sleep off her travels. But as she sauntered along, she found herself suddenly mesmerized by one particularly charming cafe. An empty table outside was nestled perfectly between two overflowing window boxes. Hungry, and eager to try her first Swiss hot chocolate, Sophie took a seat.

For the next hour, Sophie sipped on a decadently sinful cup of chocolate and scarfed down a piece of spinach pie, completely entertained by the people passing by on the street. She wondered why everyone on earth didn't do this every evening. As she sat with her legs propped up, several young men passing by slowed and smiled at her with cocky nods.

Europeans, she thought.

Chapter Five

"Aaaahh, Brutha. It's the only way to fly!" Redwine belly-laughed and slapped Harris on the thigh.

"Gack. I hate this," Harris mumbled into an air sickness bag. Flying in the hulking C-130 Hercules was like being tossed around inside a giant churning clothes dryer during an earthquake.

Diggs smiled as he closed his eyes and grasped the restraint harness that crisscrossed his chest. "You think he'll ever get used to this?" he whispered to Alie. The better part of him hoped Harris wouldn't puke, as the smell made the already jarring trip in the C-130 even worse. But, man, it was funny when he did.

"After seven years in, you'd think so. Maybe one day…" Alie started with a whisper, but then deliberately elevated to a shout, "…he'll STOP BEING A PUSSY AND GROW SOME NUTS!" At that, Redwine howled and elbowed Harris.

"Pussy? Really, mate?" Harris peeked over the top of the paper bag, deadly serious. "I'll peel the scalp of every Mujahideen by myself with a butter knife." Harris' eyes rolled as he took a deep breath and steadied himself. "But when the war's over, I'd rather walk home to England than ride in one of these bloody…" The plane suddenly lurched downward through a patch of rough air, and he stuffed his face back in the bag.

"And after you bloody this butter knife of yours, you can suck their slurpy brains down the back of your throat like an oyster," Redwine shouted to Harris, eyes wide with giddy anticipation that Harris would finally blow. "Don't toss your cookies, mate."

Harris took several deep breaths, then dropped the puke sack and turned and heaved directly at Redwine's chest. Redwine snapped his head back frantically, but nothing came out of Harris except a labored chuckle. Redwine looked like he had seen a ghost as he reached out and shoved Harris' face the other direction.

"Atta kid," Diggs encouraged Harris. "You're gonna be alright after all."

Diggs often joked that his primary duty was to babysit Redwine and Harris. Even their superiors referred to Diggs and Alie as the big brothers, and Redwine and Harris as "The Tweedles" (as in Tweedle Dee and Tweedle Dum). Harris was a walking dichotomy; there was "on-the-clock Harris" and "off-the-clock Harris", as they lovingly referred to him. One was gravely serious and laser-focused. But off the clock, Harris was loud, brash, and loved a good prank almost as much as he loved a stout pint.

Redwine, on the other hand, was completely off his trolley every waking moment—a walking, breathing party wrapped in a tall, rock-solid frame. He had absolutely zero regard for danger, and would crack jokes—mostly filthy ones—throughout the entirety of even the most intense firefights. He loved to shoot the bird to enemy fighters during battle, and once even mooned a particularly pissed-off group of al Qaedas out the window of a moving Humvee while screaming, "You like that, you sandy twits?"

But when it came time to get to work, Alie wouldn't trade these guys for anyone in the world. They were his brothers, and there wasn't an ounce of blood in his veins that he wouldn't spill for every single one of them. But with these guys around, there really wasn't much danger of spilling any blood at all. Goofy as hell like the Tweedles, or painfully serious like Diggs, each of them was downright scary with a loaded C8 Carbine. They were the finest Her Majesty's Armed Forces had to offer, and it irked Alie that they were wasting precious time on this trip to Geneva.

Two days after the American gunship obliterated the Iraqi family's van, the four of them were summoned to UNOG (the United Nations Office at Geneva) to report on the incident. It turned out that the father was some sort of Iraqi dignitary, which several media organizations were exploiting into an international travesty. Alie had been assured that their trip was nothing more than a stunt—a good-faith gesture to demonstrate Britain's commitment to diplomatic relations with a very unstable Iraq. But Alie wondered if they were lambs being thrown to the wolves, scapegoats in a scheme to divert blame from the Brits in what really was a blameless situation.

But the four of them would show up and put on their best show, all for the good of the Crown, and hope to return to their real jobs as soon as possible. Alie was disheartened to learn that they had been placed on a brief leave in Geneva after the "debriefing", partially to get some "R&R" that Alie didn't particularly want, and partially to make sure they were available for additional diplomatic brown-nosing if needed.

Alie glanced at Diggs, who was flipping through pictures of his wife and kids on his iPhone. Diggs had considered flying them in from London to Geneva while he was there. But worried that the length of stay was unpredictable, so it might not be worth it.

"Your kids are getting big, man," Alie said. "Good thing they look like their mum."

"No kidding, right," snickered Diggs, his eyes fixed on the iPod. "If I were a good father, I'd give up this insanity and go home."

"You *are* a really good father, Diggs. There are few kids in the world who get to look up to a father like you." Alie loved them all like brothers, but he respected Diggs like no one else. He swore that one day he would tell Diggs' kids, face to face, just how lucky they really were. He just hoped that conversation wouldn't take place at Diggs' funeral.

"You know, Quin, you've never shown me any photos of your family."

Alie sat silent for a few seconds, stroking the brushed silver of his own iPod. "That's 'cause I don't have any."

"Aw, come on, man, you gotta have some kind of family," Diggs pressed. "I've heard you mention them."

"Yeah, there's some family, just no pictures," said Alie.

Alie turned on his iPod and start flipping through multiple photos of cars. A black 1967 Plymouth GTX. A red 1990 Ferrari F40. A white 1965 Austin Healey 3000 MKIII.

"Those won't keep you warm on a cold English night," smiled Diggs.

Alie chuckled. "Probably not, mate. Now sod off and leave me alone." Alie slid his headphones into his ears and cranked Flogging Molly until his ears hurt. He had become accustomed to falling asleep to the thunderous roar of the C-130 engines, but that night sleep wouldn't come. He tried to stop thinking about the Iraqi boy who had died in his arms just two days earlier. It was not the gruesome way the boy and his family died; Alie had seen more than his fair share of carnage. And it was not the fact that the kid died in Alie's arms. But those last moments with a boy he knew nothing about, and who was not really any different than any other Iraqi street kids, impacted Alie in a way he never saw coming.

Alie had never believed in God. He found it ludicrous, downright embarrassing in fact, that sane people still held on to the idea that some nebulous, all-powerful super-being was floating around space demanding servitude from a bunch of measly earthlings. He could comprehend no rational explanation for mankind's insistence that we are destined to someday turn into ghosts and walk through walls. Alie found it curious that people would trade logic for a ridiculous fairy tale just to avoid dealing with dying and all the finality that comes with it. Alie had seen plenty of bodies blown to bits, and found them to be pretty damn final. Like a car, the human body tends to cease functioning when disassembled. It was just that simple.

Perhaps it was that Alie couldn't think of much in this life that he would want to continue into the hereafter. Life had not exactly been kind to Alie, and if it took death to put an end to a rather miserable and meaningless existence, then so be it. He didn't necessarily want to die, at least not yet. He had a powerful survival instinct that had saved his life more than once, and he hoped it would continue to do so. But when his time finally came, he would quite sure he'd be just fine with a death that was just the end and nothing more. He had never given a second thought to what came after. At least, not until two days ago.

What Alie pulled from the van and what he laid on the street were two very different things. From the van, Alie had pulled a writhing, desperate and completely terrified life, entirely aware of the horror going on around him. But what he left behind was a lifeless heap of bones and skin, a hunk of clay that only somewhat resembled what had once been a boy. In the few minutes in between, Alie had watched the young life distance itself from his frail, broken body. The boy's darting eyes had begged Alie to help him. But he was powerless. Alie tried to comfort him in a language he didn't understand, but the boy listened anyway. His tiny fingers clung to Alie's vest with the last bit of fight left in him. But it was the boy's final seconds that shook Alie to the core.

Just as the boy gagged and exhaled for the last time, he rolled his head away and appeared to fix his gaze down the street. Then the boy relaxed and released his grip on Alie's vest. For a moment, he seemed to lean slightly toward whatever he was looking at, his eyes suddenly still and transfixed on who knows what. And then he died. No more breath. No more struggle. No more pain. He was just gone. Body or no body, the boy simply was no longer there.

Alie had spent the next forty-eight hours wondering if he had imagined it all. Was the boy just experiencing the final firing synapses of a dying brain? Or was he actually seeing something, or someone, that calmed him and made him want to leave? Alie would never know, but he couldn't ignore the dramatic absence he felt when the boy was gone. Alie cursed himself for even considering it, and even more so for allowing it to affect him so profoundly. He did not usually give in to such distractions, and did not intend to do so now. So, at 30,000 feet, somewhere over the Mediterranean Sea, he swore to himself that he had thought about it for the last time.

Chapter Six

"Oops. Excuse me." Sophie flattened herself against the wall of the stairwell of the seven-story dorm building, otherwise known as "Les Epinettes." Students poured past her on their semester-ending mass exodus, carrying boxes, bean bags, guitar cases, and other typical dorm room items. A few hesitated on the stairs above her with curious glances, likely wondering why she was lugging her suitcase *up* the stairs while they were moving out. But apparently none cared enough to stop and ask, much less help. So Sophie continued lugging until she reached the landing with a large "4" on the wall.

Sophie's past 24 hours had been filled with glorious architecture and charming buildings. Les Epinettes was definitely not one of those buildings. It was a seven-story monument to the drab and uninspired. The building sported a light-tan exterior, with a slightly lighter-tan interior, with all the decorative styling of a modern prison. With a grunt, she hauled open the heavy metal door to the fourth floor. The hallway was empty, but loud electronica music escaped from one of the doors down the hall.

Please don't be my roommates, she thought. She hated electronica, or any other kind of techno music for that matter. For the thousandth time, Sophie prayed she wouldn't be stuck with roommates who would ruin her time in Geneva.

Just as Sophie parked her suitcase to dig into her backpack for her room key, the door to 4-J swung open and a tall, picturesque girl with obscenely long legs and short shorts stood holding a glass of wine and looking startled. Never having had a roommate, and with no idea how to break the ice, Sophie stuck out her hand and awkwardly said, "Hi, I think I'm Sophie, your roommate."

"You *think* you're Sophie?" The long-legged beauty looked at her as if she were crazy.

"I mean, I know my name is Sophie, but I think I am your roommate...I think." Sophie's face was burning as she fumbled through her backpack for her registration papers. "Did I find the right room?"

A blonde ponytail poked between the legged one and the door frame and said, "Boston?"

"Huh?" asked Sophie.

"You're the girl from Boston?" She pushed aside her much taller roommate and stepped into full view.

"Yes, I'm from Boston," Sophie answered apologetically.

"Excuse my extremely rude friend," said the one with the ponytail and an overly perky grin. "She pretty much sucks, but we've been friends since kindergarten, so we had to bring her."

"Suck it, Cammie," the tall brunette quipped as she turned and escaped down the short hallway. "Nice to meet you, Boston," she said unconvincingly as she shut the door behind her.

"Don't worry about her. She's the perfect mixture of sweetheart and bitch," laughed Cammie. As they semi-shouted pleasantries over the blaring music, Sophie tried not to let on how uncomfortable she felt with Cammie standing there nursing a beer bottle in nothing but underwear and a skimpy Roxy tank top. Cammie obviously felt no such discomfort. She was maybe five feet tall with tan, muscular legs and the athletic physique of a gymnast or cheerleader. Her platinum-blonde ponytail bounced when she talked, which she did loudly and confidently. Cammie spun suddenly and snatched another bottle from the counter.

"How rude of me! Wanna beer?" Before Sophie could respond, Cammie popped the cap and handed it to Sophie, then bounced down the hallway and banged on a door. "Hey, come meet the new roommate!"

Sophie hated beer, especially before noon. She set the full bottle down next to four empty ones and a wine bottled scattered across the counter. Her dream of a peaceful European experience was disappearing before her eyes.

"Dude, what's up?" The fourth roommate bounded into the kitchen and wrapped her arms around Sophie. "I'm Liz, and it looks like you're stuck rooming with me for a few months." She was of Asian descent with perfect skin and every bit as athletic as Cammie. She, however, was fully clothed, which Sophie rather appreciated. "Come chill for a bit on the couch," she said as she went into the living room and turned off the music—possibly the first sensible thing Sophie had witnessed since arriving.

Sophie spent the next hour chatting with Cammie and Liz, with the occasional appearance and then abrupt departure of Bridgette—the rude one with legs up to her neck. Sophie learned they were from Simi Valley, California, which was apparently a suburb of Los Angeles. They had grown up in the same neighborhood, and had been best friends most of their lives. Their high school experience basically consisted of expensive cars, Daddy's credit cards, and wild weekends that followed them to UC Santa Barbara, where Cammie and Liz were cheerleaders, and Bridgette maintained a C average. At first blush, Liz seemed to have twice the brains of Bridgette and Cammie combined. But Sophie was surprised to learn that between weekend exploits, Cammie managed a 3.8 GPA. Sophie felt a bit guilty for judging the bubbly sprite by her cover.

For Sophie, the most disappointing detail revealed was that the three girls had no intention of doing anything remotely constructive while in Europe. They made it clear that they were there on their parents' dime, and were eagerly in search of Geneva's finest dance clubs, and the European men who frequented them.

The conversation eventually turned to Sophie and her plans for the semester…and then ended as soon as Sophie began explaining the museum and its offerings. Sophie knew her new friends weren't likely to be visiting the museum any time soon, which was quite alright with her.

Despite their clearly diverging interests, Sophie decided she liked her new flatmates, or at least two of them. And she decided not to dislike Bridgette until she actually had a conversation with her, whenever that might be.

"Hey, Sophie," Liz hopped on the bed as Sophie was starting to unpack. "Got plans for the night?"

The next thing she knew, Sophie was sitting by herself, miserable, atop an uncomfortable barstool in some generic club while her roommates sucked face with half the dance floor. Venturing more than a foot away from her stool meant sliding into a mob of sweat-drenched bodies gyrating to the pulsating throbs of some sorry excuse for music. So Sophie stayed put, sipping a club soda—which she hated—and hoping that she would go unnoticed in the hazy darkness. She was frighteningly unimpressed by the whole scene, only agreeing to come along as a friendly gesture. But if she could help it, her first venture into Geneva's night life would be her last.

Chapter Seven

"Seven-and-a-half," Redwine pronounced, his head cocked analytically.

"You're crazy," answered Harris. "Six at best."

"Six?" Redwine was disgusted. "How can your taste *possibly* be that fussy after five months in the desert?"

The brunette lying on a blanket in the park suddenly looked up at them and glared.

"Is that really necessary?" Diggs snapped, clearly embarrassed.

"What?" inquired Redwine. "Looking at girls?"

"No, wanker, announcing to the world that you're a shallow prick by noisily rating every girl in Geneva." Diggs simulated disgust, but Alie knew he was secretly grateful for the entertainment provided by Redwine and Harris and their juvenile exploits.

"Sod off, you munch. Just because you're hitched you pretend not to notice?" Redwine snickered.

"Look but don't touch, right, Diggsy?" Harris added. Alie chuckled, but kept to himself. The four of them prowled the streets of Geneva, with Redwine and Harris eagerly taking the lead, and Alie and Diggs strolling behind. In between pub stops, Harris and Redwine plotted which dance clubs they would hunt that night. Geneva's remarkable culture and beauty were completely lost on these four, except, that is, for its female population.

"I see nothing wrong with being picky," Harris added while surveying the sunbathers sprawled across the lawn across from the Musée d'Art et d'Histoire.

"Listen, Harris, right now I don't really care if you pick up the ugliest girl in Switzerland; I'm just sick of walking," Diggs said. It was abnormally hot and Diggs, being faithfully married, was done tailing Harris and Redwine and their pursuit of lady companionship. "Look at that fancy building over there," Diggs pointed at the museum across the Rue Charles-Galland. "Can't we go relax in some air conditioning?

Plus, you never know, maybe there are some beauties in the museum," Diggs added jokingly.

"Right, right," Alie sneered, "I'm sure you'll find *tons* of hot chicks in there."

. . . .

Sophie stood just inside the museum's entrance and struggled to catch her breath. She stared across the lobby at the towering, arched stained-glass window. She felt overwhelmed, with no idea where to begin. But then her grin turned to a large smile as she realized this was the moment she had waited for.

"Puis-je vous aider?"

Sophie managed to shake her stupor to focus on the voice coming from the reception desk.

"Bienvenue. Maintenant comment puis-je vous aider?" An ash-haired woman peered through thick, horn-rimmed glasses perched on the end of her nose. The only word Sophie recognized was "bienvenue"—French for "welcome"—which Sophie found to be ironic considering the greeter's clear irritation at Sophie's presence.

"Huh?" That was the best Sophie could muster. "I mean…je suis désolé." Sophie struggled. "Je suis…ici…pour voir—"

"Please don't block the doorway," the woman interrupted, in English, with almost no accent. "Here's a very helpful map of the museum, so please move along." She slid a pamphlet across the counter and didn't look up again.

"But I'm here to see Curator Martineau. I'm the—"

"Here's your map. It's easy to follow," the receptionist grumbled, showing only the top of her head.

Sophie considered trying to break the ice, knowing she would see the icy woman almost daily for the next several months. But she decided that could wait for another day and, as commanded, moved along. She followed the map up a long ivory staircase dissected by crimson carpet tread. This time she had arrived about an hour before closing time—not enough time to experience the whole museum, but hopefully enough to meet the curator and make a good impression. On the upper level, she passed works by Van Gogh and Renoir, and fell deeper and deeper in love with every step. It was every bit as incredible as she had imagined.

Her nose was buried deep in the pamphlet when she turned a corner and smacked into the back of a plump, sweaty man sporting an orange golf shirt. He spun and glared at her from under the brim of a straw, perspiration-ringed fedora. She blurted out an uncomfortably loud "sorry" just as she realized he was part of a large guided tour, all of which were noticeably annoyed.

"Sorry," she grimaced, this time in a whisper, doing her best to squeeze past the irritated tourists and disappear around a corner. As she shuffled past, however, she made unintended eye contact with the tour guide, and noticed that she was none other than the head curator herself, Simone Martineau. What a first impression, thought Sophie. Ms. Martineau stared at Sophie with eyebrows raised, as if to say, "Are you done yet?" She was a heavy-set woman with audaciously red lipstick, but not one piece of jewelry. She sported large sunglasses poking out of her bushy, black hair, and had a small coffee stain on her otherwise clean, white blouse.

Sophie began to second-guess her goal of meeting Ms. Martineau that day, hoping Ms. Martineau would somehow forget her face before she started the internship on Monday. However, she now desperately wanted to listen to Ms. Martineau's tour, so she decided instead to follow from a distance, as inconspicuously as possible. Detached from the group, Sophie could only make out portions of Ms. Martineau's lecture, but she was intrigued nonetheless. The rest of the crowd seemed oblivious to Sophie's eavesdropping, but Ms. Martineau's occasional glances let Sophie know she was well aware. But if Ms. Martineau was bothered by Sophie's presence, she didn't let it show.

The group trudged from one masterpiece to the next, paying them the same regard they would a collection of t-shirts at a corner gift shop. This infuriated Sophie. She wanted to stop at each one—Cézanne, Modigliani, Jean-Baptiste-Camille Corot—and spend hours taking them in. Her father had taught her that God's most beautiful work was mankind, and mankind's most beautiful works were their artistic masterpieces. So, to Sophie, these canvases were more than just paintings; they were reflections of the divine. They had been sprinkled down through history to remind the world of true, heavenly beauty. They were the best we, as people, had to offer.

"Now, ladies and gentleman," Ms. Martineau urged them forward, "we move on to our collection of Konrad Witz, an artist who…" Sophie spun around at the mention of Witz and focused on the wall just past the group. And it was there she saw it: her father's favorite painting, the *Miraculous Draught of Fishes*, hanging just past Ms. Martineau's outstretched hand. She had seen it a million times before, or at least print versions of it. But now she stood only feet away from the original. She had longed to experience it in person since she was eight years old, when her father took down his version from the wall and laid it on the kitchen table. He allowed her to gently trace the images in the painting with his brush: the elegant Christ figure draped in a crimson robe, the shocked expressions of the disciples as they recognized their master, and the peculiarly European landscape that formed the scene's backdrop. Her father explained that Witz was seen as a radical during his time. Instead of painting Christ and his disciples on the Sea of Galilee, as described in the Bible, Witz placed them only a short distance away on the shores of Lake Geneva, with Mont Blanc and the snow-capped Alps in the distance. To the drably close-minded people of his time, Witz's art challenged tradition. But to her father, Witz's vision and ingenuity simply made sense.

The *Miraculous Draught of Fishes* hung directly next to another Witz masterpiece, *The Liberation of St. Peter*, and was surrounded by several others. Sophie was in awe of Witz's bold, emotional reds, and his natural panoramas that longed to escape the lifeless art that dominated his medieval era. She methodically inspected each one, but returned repeatedly to her father's favorite. She choked back tears, feeling even closer to her father at that moment than while visiting his grave.

Sophie eventually realized that the tour group had moved on without her noticing. She peeked around the corner, but saw no one. She was alone, just her and Mr. Witz. She stood in front of the *Miraculous Draught of Fishes*, this time closer than before, and cautiously withdrew her father's brush from her back pocket. She fought back tears as she raised the brush, just inches from the canvas, and began gracefully tracing the contours of Witz's great masterpiece. She paused occasionally, wondering at his motivations for creating such a beautiful, yet peculiar scene. She was so entranced that she did not hear Ms. Martineau enter behind her.

"Please, mademoiselle! Do NOT touch!"

Sophie let out a shriek and dropped the brush. "Oh, I wuh…I would never…" she stuttered as she quickly bent over to snatch up the brush.

"I certainly hope not." Ms. Martineau spoke with a thick accent, but with a full command of English. She was not particularly beautiful, but had a fierce confidence that made her strangely attractive nonetheless.

"No, you see, I just trace the images in the air, like this," Sophie defended herself as she waived the brush clumsily, feeling quite foolish.

"Do you fancy yourself a painter or something?" inquired Ms. Martineau, not taking her eyes off Sophie.

"Well, yes, sometimes," answered Sophie, "but I don't think I'm very good. I really love to study art though." She then thrust out her hand. "In fact, I'm Sophie Caldwell, your intern."

"Mmmm, I thought so," Ms. Martineau did not offer her hand in return. "You have some strange habits: air painting, stalking tour groups.…" She stared down her nose at Sophie. "Am I going to regret choosing you for the internship?"

"No, no," Sophie pleaded. "I'm so sorry if you have that impression. I'm very excited to be here, and I've wanted to come here for years…actually most of my life. I promise you won't."

"Well, I hope not," Ms. Martineau interrupted. "I will see you Monday morning, bright and early." She folded her arms across her hefty bosom and scowled at Sophie. Sophie nodded quickly and made her way out of the room, gratefully, away from Ms. Martineau.

"Ms. Caldwell!" Ms. Martineau snapped just as Sophie was about to escape. Sophie turned back nervously and found Ms. Martineau still standing, arms folded menacingly.

"Yes?" Sophie squeaked.

Ms. Martineau raised an eyebrow and stood silent for a few very long seconds, then smiled slightly. "I'm glad you're here. We're going to have a great time together." Sophie had to consciously keep her jaw from dropping. "But don't touch my paintings!" With that, Ms. Martineau spun and charged out of the room.

Sophie stood bewildered for a moment, then she made her way around the Witz room one last time. She then started down the stairway toward the lobby, where she passed by the front desk and tried, unsuccessfully, to make the grouchy receptionist smile.

Chapter Eight

Please, no! Sophie thought. She tried her best to appear grateful for the invitation, but couldn't quite conceal her horror at the thought of spending another night in some awful club.

"Come on, Sophie," pleaded Cammie. "When's the next time you're gonna have access to so many hot European guys in one place?"

"Please Cammie," Sophie pleaded. "I promise it's not you. Clubbing just really isn't my thing. Plus, I did a lot of walking today and I'm exhausted."

"Boston!" Cammie looked even more determined as she scowled playfully through the putrid green face mask slathered all over her face. She leaned on one leg against the wall, with the other propped horizontally across the hallway blocking Sophie from passing. "I am bound and determined…no, downright HELL BENT on seeing you have fun while you're here. Fate has brought you all the way across the Atlantic…no Pacific…no, no, the Atlantic, to live with the three most fun girls on earth." Liz had been reading on the couch and not paying attention. But as Cammie pressed on with her rousing speech, Liz became amused.

"Cammie, I don't doubt for a minute that you're the most fun girl in the—" Sophie's words didn't even register with Cammie. She just grabbed Sophie's arm and pulled her into the kitchen. Then she swung open the refrigerator and pulled out a large white cake with pink words scribbled across the top.

"Do you know what this is, Bos-TON? It's a freaking BIRTHDAY cake! B-I-R-T-H-D-A-freaking-Y!"

"Birthday?" This wasn't going well for Sophie. "Whose birthday?"

"Your own freaking roommate," Cammie replied.

Sophie turned to Liz. "Seriously, Liz?"

"'Fraid so," Liz admitted.

Sophie felt a bit guilty, though she wasn't sure why. "Happy birthday. Why didn't you say anything before?"

"'Cause it's no big deal," answered Liz.

"No big deal?" screeched Cammie. "No big deal? Are you freaking kidding me?"

"Soon you'll learn that if Cammie wants something, there's no point in resisting. It's gonna happen. Sorry, but you're going out tonight whether you like it or not," said Bridgette, dryly, from the hallway. Sophie wondered from where she'd appeared.

"Yeah, Boston!" Cammie was even more energized now that she had an ally. "Whether you like it or not!" She stuck out her finger and smeared a large swath of white frosting on Sophie's nose. She smiled an extra-large smile and sauntered off, licking frosting off her finger. Sophie reached up and wiped the frosting from her nose into her mouth. Somehow, she was going clubbing again.

. . . .

The first hour at the club was a repeat of last time, with Sophie sitting on an uncomfortable bar stool while the others tore up the dance floor. In between fending off the advances of sweaty guys, Sophie wondered how long she had to stick around before she could leave without offending her roommates. Every other song or so, Cammie would come over and pull Sophie onto the dance floor. Sophie would begrudgingly join her for long enough for Cammie's attention to shift to someone else, then Sophie would quickly find her seat again. *This will all be over soon*, Sophie kept telling herself.

Just as Sophie mustered up enough courage to leave, the three girls stumbled out of the mass of gyrating bodies and converged on Sophie. Liz was wearing a cheap birthday cone hat, and Bridgette, oddly enough, was smiling and acting like she was actually happy to see Sophie.

"Okay, roomie," Liz said while trying to steady herself. At the apartment, Liz easily came off as the most sensible and studious of the three. But at the club, all bets were off, and Liz could easily keep pace with the other two. "You have to give me at least one dance on my birthday. That's only common courte—"

"Holy heavenly angels from on high!" Cammie blurted. "Do you see what I see?"

Liz and Bridgette chimed in with highly inappropriate expressions of awe, lust, and indulgence. Sophie spun on her barstool in time to observe four guys walking in, who appeared to be dripping with ego. She immediately realized that, like the other men in the club, they were not her type, although she had no idea what her type actually was. However, they just might be the distraction she needed to justify her exit.

As Sophie waited for the opportune moment to escape, she watched Bridgette and Liz plunge back into the crowd like prowling lions. Three of the four guys had already found the dance floor, and Bridgette and Liz were in pursuit. Cammie, oddly enough, stayed sitting next to Sophie. Sophie observed curiously as Cammie stared past the pulsating strobe lights with a rather mischievous look on her face, her eyes fixed on a pleathery corner booth where the last of the four sat alone, draped in shadows, slowly sipping a beer.

"I want that one," Cammie said without breaking her stare.

"Oh dear," Sophie said, "you're acting all determined again."

Cammie stared for a few more seconds. Then, in one fluid motion, she declared, "It's on," and set out toward the loner in the booth. At only five feet tall, she walked like she owned the dance club. Amazingly, despite being presented with the perfect opportunity to sneak away, Sophie couldn't take her eyes off what was about to happen. Instead, she watched, fascinated, as Cammie descended upon this poor chap who had no idea what he was in for.

Sophie couldn't make out the guy's face, but could tell Cammie was doing most, if not all, of the talking. While she was silly and a bit obnoxious, Cammie was also very pretty, athletic, and a walking bundle of charisma. She was wearing a very short, black dress that must have cost more than all of Sophie's clothes combined. When it came to guys, Sophie was sure that Cammie had the pick of the litter, so it was clearly just a matter of time until this one was hers as well. But, surprisingly, after a few minutes, Cammie nodded quickly at the obscure stranger and gave a curt wave, then started back toward Sophie. Cammie appeared shell-shocked, looking as if she'd just been turned down for the first time in her life.

"What happened?" Sophie asked delicately.

"He's gay," Cammie answered, staring at the floor.

"Wait, what?" Sophie blurted out in disbelief.

"You heard me. He's freakin' gay," Cammie said, shaking her head.

"No, he's not!" Sophie looked again toward the figure in the dark booth. She couldn't see his face, but could tell he was starting right back at them as he continued to take tugs from his bottle.

"Boston, I'm telling you, he made it very clear that he's gay," Cammie continued. "Very, very hot, but apparently very gay." Cammie stirred her drink with the straw.

"Sorry to break it to you, Cammie, but that guy is *not* gay," Sophie had to tread lightly, as Cammie's impenetrable ego was, perhaps, facing its first moment of vulnerability.

"How do you know?" Cammie looked at Sophie as if to say, *How dare you even suggest such a thing.*

Sophie leaned forward on her stool, trying to get a better look. "I can just tell by looking at him, Cammie."

"You can't tell if a guy's gay by looking at him," Cammie exclaimed.

"I can," countered Sophie.

"I thought I could too," Cammie said, "until I spent a summer in New York. I kept meeting all kinds of super-hot guys, but they were gay. I guess I've lost my ability."

"Well, I don't know about New York guys," said Sophie, "but that guy is not gay. I'd bet my life on it."

"Well if he's not gay, then what is he?"

"He's an ass, that's what," Sophie answered, now feeling indignant and strangely protective.

"But why would he lie to me?" Cammie said, still trying to grasp what happened.

Sophie suddenly felt like a parent struggling to comfort an angst-ridden teenager. "Think about it: A hot guy walks in a bar with three friends, then sits down by himself with a scowl on his face drinking a beer while his buddies walk around sticking their tongues down girls' throats, and you're surprised he's making up an alternative lifestyle just to be left alone? He's obviously some kind of psycho loner and is probably better left alone."

"Wow," Cammie looked his way longingly, "that almost makes him even more intriguing."

"Oh my, Cammie," Sophie grinned, "you're amazing."

"Well, obviously he doesn't think so." Cammie turned to Sophie.

"Am I really that hideous?"

"My goodness, no," Sophie insisted. "You're gorgeous, and I'd be all over you if I were him. I think he's the hideous one."

"Hideous? Um, can you not see what I see?"

"I mean a hideous person, or in a hideous mood. To reject you, I mean."

"Or maybe he's gay," said Cammie, somewhat under her breath.

"He's not gay."

"Oh yeah? Prove it!" Cammie stared her down, issuing the challenge.

"Are you serious?" Sophie was horrified. "No way, not a chance!"

"Boston, he just knocked me flat on my ass; if you have any sense of loyalty as my friend, you'll do this for me. Go get him!" Cammie pushed Sophie off her barstool and slapped her hard on the butt. Once again, what Cammie wants, she apparently gets.

Not only was Sophie at a club listening to loud, horrific music—again—she was now about to walk up and fake hit on an apparently dreadful person who had absolutely no desire to be hit on. Sophie trudged slowly across the floor toward the corner booth, with no idea whatsoever how this type of thing was supposed to go. Once again, she found herself wondering what the absolute least amount of time she had to endure this horrible experience was before Cammie would be satisfied. As she neared the booth, she opted for the direct approach, especially since she had no aspiration to impress this idiot.

"You're not gay."

"What?" the voice came from a face hidden by a dark shadow.

"I said, you're not gay," Sophie answered with all the confidence she could muster.

He leaned forward out of the dark, revealing penetrating blue eyes that bore deeply into her. "I'm not?"

She tried to stay tough, but couldn't help but notice his outstanding British accent. She didn't want to admit to being shallow enough to be so impressed by an accent but, damn, it was cute.

"No, you're not," she said, suddenly realizing how ridiculous she must sound.

"Prove it."

Sophie laughed out loud, trying to sound insulted. "Wow, you're a choice one.”

"How do you know?” he responded. "We've just met.”

"Let's just say I'm observant.”

"Or judgmental. Very judgmental.”

"Well, you lied to my roommate about being gay.” She was still trying to look outraged, and yes, probably even a little judgmental. She did everything she could to banter with him without fixing upon all the things about him that were begging to distract her. He wore a white button-down shirt with several buttons undone. When he leaned forward, she fought herself to not peek down at his chiseled chest that bore a tattooed inscription she couldn't make out.

"How do you know it's a lie?” he persisted.

"Well, are you gay?” she insisted.

"No.”

Sophie laughed out loud again. "Then why did you shoot down my friend so quickly? She's obviously very pretty.”

"Very…” he responded.

"And a sublimely sweet girl, might I add.”

"I'm sure.” He slid his beer bottle aside and leaned in, yet again. She couldn't remember if she had seen him blink. His smile was playful, but his stare was intense, like a wolf peering from the dark recesses of a primeval forest.

"Then why did you dismiss her so quickly?” she wondered.

"Disappointment, I guess,” he replied with a smirk.

"Disappointment?”

"What's your favorite food?” he said, shifting gears suddenly.

"Excuse me?”

"Your favorite food? What is it?”

Sophie was perplexed. So, he's crazy then, she thought.

"Do you have a favorite food?” he pressed.

"Uh…what kind of question is that?”

"Not a bad one if you'd give an answer.” He was either nuts, or was playing with her…or both.

"Strawberries,” answered Sophie, having no idea if that really was her favorite food.

"Seriously? Strawberries? Rather clichéd, isn't it?”

"Clichéd? I can't like strawberries?”

"Do you like blueberries?" he asked.

"Um…yeah, I guess," she answered, cocking her head as she tried to figure him out.

"But not as much as strawberries?"

"No," she responded. "Why on earth are you—?"

"So, if I offered you some blueberries you'd take them?"

"If I wanted some blueberries at the time, I suppose."

"But if I had blueberries and strawberries, and gave you the blueberries but held back the strawberries, you'd be disappointed, right?"

Sophie nodded, not quite sure what to say.

"Well, your friend, she's the blueberries," he said, and then sat back, his face again disappearing into the shadow.

Sophie felt as if she had been punched in the gut. She tried to say something—anything—but nothing came out. She was both insulted and smitten at the same time. She stared at him uncomfortably for what seemed like forever. He calmly sipped on his bottle as she tried to gather herself. What an arrogant jerk. Intriguing, and gorgeous, with an amazing accent, but a jerk nonetheless. Through all the chaos and confusion inside her, she found herself staring at the muscles and tendons in his forearm that rippled when he gripped his bottle. He was truly a beautiful specimen, she thought. But he very well could be insane as well.

"Well, Mr. Fruit…cake," she finally managed to squeak out.

"Mr. Fruitcake?"

Sophie stood frozen for a few more seconds, then turned abruptly and walked back to Cammie.

"Told you," Cammie said proudly as Sophie sat down.

"What, that he's gay?" Sophie asked while peering back toward the corner booth.

"Yep."

"He's definitely not gay," Sophie responded.

"Wait, seriously?" Cammie was amazed. "But then—"

"He likes strawberries," said Sophie, still staring.

"He likes strawberries?" Cammie looked at her, completely confused.

"Apparently."

"You guys talked about strawberries?"

Chapter Nine

The morning sun brought a hint of warmth as it peeked over the rooftops above Sophie's balcony. It felt amazing, but it wasn't enough. She got up and slipped back through the sliding glass door in search of coffee. It was nothing compared to the gourmet blends found at Geneva's streetside cafes. But it was warmth, not quality, Sophie was after.

Like most days, Sophie was the first one awake. She valued her time alone in the mornings, which she usually spent on the balcony watching and listening to the city wake up. If she was up early enough, she could hear the distant trumpet of swans on the lake, soon to be drowned out by the morning commute. On Saturdays such as this, the city would take a little longer to come alive, but it was still just a matter of time.

As she stood barefoot on the cold linoleum stirring her coffee, the door swung open to Bridgett's and Cammie's room. Sophie was surprised when the person who appeared was not Bridgett or Cammie, but a brawny male wearing only a low-hanging pair of jeans. He stopped when he saw Sophie and offered a cheerful, "Oh, morning." Sophie suddenly felt very uncomfortable. He, apparently, did not as he sprung up and sat on the counter.

"Is there any of that coffee to share?" he grinned, paying no mind to her obvious discomfort. His British accent reminded her of the night before and the bizarre conversation with the mysterious corner booth guy. Like the shadowy stranger, this surprise house guest was noticeably chiseled with tightly buzzed hair and a tattooed forearm. In fact, she thought the insignia might match the one on the corner booth guy.

"Um, I have no idea who you are," Sophie said. He laughed, much too loudly for the early morning. "And I'm hoping one of my roommates at least knows your name."

He smiled, looking a little too proud of himself. "I'm Jaden Harris. And who might you be?"

She ignored his question. "Are you military of some sort?"

"Maybe," he answered. "Why do you ask?"

"You and your friends from last night?" Sophie wasn't sure he was one of them, but thought she'd take a crack at it anyway.

"How do you know about them?" He looked both puzzled and entertained. "I don't remember seeing you there."

Before she could answer, Bridgette peeked around the corner wearing only a sheet. Bridgette looked dryly at Sophie and said, with a shrewd smile, "Sorry to interrupt. Jason, can you come here? I need to show you something."

"Um, it's Jaden," he said uncomfortably, and hopped off the counter and followed the flowing sheet back down the hallway.

Sophie was curious to know more, but realized her inquisitive banter couldn't compete with what Bridgette had to offer. So, she resigned herself back to the balcony, this time warmed by the coffee mug in her hand. But as she started to slide the balcony door, she was startled by a stiff knock at the front door. She couldn't imagine who might be knocking so early, unless it was Cammie or Liz at the end of a walk of shame. That is, of course, assuming they felt any shame.

Sophie cracked the door just open enough. When she saw who was standing on the other side, she almost collapsed.

"Morning."

He had traded the button-down for a plain black t-shirt, perhaps a size too small. But the eyes gave him away; the shadowy corner booth guy with the wolf stare—the one she tried not to think about while falling asleep last night, and again when she woke up this morning. There he stood, at her door first thing in the morning, and she couldn't even begin to imagine why.

"Hang on," she said, and gracelessly slammed the door. The polite next step would have been to undo the chain and let him in, but her mind was racing between "why is he here?" and "is he following me?" to "I can't believe how amazing the word 'morning' can sound". As she bounced between giddiness and sheer panic, she hardly even noticed the second knock until she realized that Bridgette and her shirtless beau were watching in bewilderment.

"Well, are you going to let him in?" said Bridgette, barely holding back a laugh.

"Let who in?" Sophie answered, not grasping the absurdity of her response. They had obviously heard the knock and, even worse, apparently witnessed some of the panic attack that followed.

"It's Alie," said Harris, both amused and irritated.

"Yes, it's Alie," came the voice through the door.

"Who's Alie?" Sophie knew the answer, but was too busy making a fool of herself to put two and two together. When Bridgette and her cohort shot her a look of disbelief rather than an answer, Sophie decided that opening the door couldn't be any less comfortable than what she was experiencing. So, she slowly unhitched the chain and cracked the door. And there he was, piercing blue eyes and all, sporting the same roguish grin from the night before during their brief but strange conversation about fruit.

"I believe my colleagues may be here," he said with a bit of humor, "possibly…visiting with your roommates?" So, there are more than one, Sophie wondered. She had not yet seen Cammie or Liz, so there could be ten for all she knew.

"Um, sure, come in." As he entered the apartment, she considered making a break for it into the hall and down the stairs. She couldn't have made any bigger fool of herself than she already had, so why not? But instead, Sophie forced herself to inhale and exhale with a great amount of effort, and she gave him the best smile she could muster.

Alie nodded to Harris, sized up Bridgette and her salacious sheet, and asked, "Well now, are we well-rested?" Bridgette chuckled and then retreated to her room, with very little concern for the amount of skin she exposed in the process.

"Morning to you too, mate," quipped Harris. "I'll get Reddy," and he turned and shouted, "Up and at 'em, Reddy!" as he closed the bedroom door behind him.

"You didn't want to join the sleepover? I've got three roommates, you know," Sophie wanted to make it clear that it wasn't an invitation.

"No, that's not my style," replied Alie, looking a bit nervous himself. He leaned against the wall with his hands shoved deep into his jeans pockets. Sophie again noticed the ripples in his chiseled, tan forearms, and the insignia tattooed a few inches above his wrist. For a few moments they stood in silence, with her mostly staring at the floor in between timid glances at his sun-weathered face. He, however, did not take his eyes off her.

"Would you like to sit?" she finally asked.

But before he could answer, the bedroom door flew open and Harris and another beefy, buzzed chap barreled out of the room, both barking promises about when they would call again and thanks for the great night and anything else that would fill the awkward seconds before they made it out the door. Neither Bridgette nor Cammie emerged from the room.

Alie followed them to the door, but paused before exiting and glanced back at Sophie. He looked her up and down, and she was again reminded of just how dreadful she must look so early in the morning. As he stood with his arm extended, holding open the door, the other two urged him to hurry up.

"Sorry, I'd better go," he said, still staring. "Oh, and those are for you." He pointed at a small white box on the breakfast table. Sophie had not noticed him put it there, and was immediately curious to find out what was inside. When she looked back to the door, he was gone.

She snatched the box off the table and ran her finger under the lid, severing the small piece of tape that separated her from whatever was inside. She found six plump, ruby-red strawberries. She looked around as if there should be a great audience to witness such a moment, but it was just her and the strawberries. So she stood, by herself, with her hands leaning on the flimsy table, transfixed on the contents of the box. How did he know where to find her? And why did he track her down? The act of finding and bringing strawberries to her so early in the morning took some effort. Was this just his way of teasing her, and would she never see him again? Or could it possibly be that he was actually interested in her? Part of her wanted to run after him and pepper him with questions to unravel this mystery. But she fought the temptation.

Sophie spent the next hour back on the balcony with her feet tucked beneath her savoring, one by one, the sweetest strawberries she had ever tasted as the world passed beneath her. She marveled at how six small pieces of fruit in a white box could suddenly make her trip to Geneva much, much more interesting.

Chapter Ten

The train from Geneva to Lyon, France, is just under two hours, and Sophie planned to take advantage of every minute to recharge. She had managed to avoid spending the night before clubbing again with her roommates. But come Sunday morning, she still needed a break from their revelry, so she decided to cross Lyon off her list of must-see destinations.

While waiting for the train to depart, Sophie reviewed the notes on Lyon she had compiled over the years in her European guidebook. There was more to see in Lyon than she could hope to see in a month, much less a Sunday. Among the sights to see were the Amphithéatre des Trois Gaules, where the ancient Romans martyred St. Blandine and several other early Christians, and the lush Parc de la Tete d'Or. And, of course, she looked forward not only to Lyon's Museum of Fine Arts, but also the numerous exquisite pieces of street art adorning many of Lyon's buildings.

Confident in her plan, Sophie tucked her notes back into her backpack and laid her head against the headrest. She closed her eyes and thought about her mom and brother, and just how chaotic the house must be by now. She adored her mother, but often wondered how she managed to make it to the grocery store and back, much less raise two kids. She knew her mother needed regular doses of reassurance and encouragement, so she decided that on the way back, she would call home and have one of those mushy mother—daughter talks she'd been avoiding. She would fill her mother in on all the details of the trip so far, minus, of course, the part about the cute British guy from the corner booth.

Somewhere in between the hiss of the train engine and drifting off to thoughts of strawberries, Sophie was jostled abruptly by a bumbling, portly man who smelled like stale cheese and mothballs. She opened her eyes just in time to behold his brown corduroy pockets just inches from her face as he squeezed past while repeatedly apologizing, "Sorry, excuse me, je suis désolé, pardon me," in an Eastern European accent that she couldn't quite place. He crashed into the seat next to her, weighed down by an armful of what looked like rolled-up blueprints and a heavy leather satchel overflowing with coffee-stained notebooks and a flurry of paper. Once seated, he struggled between grunts and mumbles to stuff his cargo under his seat, mostly unsuccessfully. Sophie's prospects for a peaceful train ride had just drastically diminished.

After a long, deep sigh, the man turned and peered at Sophie with raised eyebrows resembling silver caterpillars. He removed a peach-colored newsboy cap and smoothed back several strands of thinning white hair. From underneath a snowy, unkempt moustache, he let out an emphatic "My, my! Aren't you a beauty?" He leaned in closer and whispered, "This should make our trip much more pleasant!"

Sophie thought that if he were a bit younger and a tad less haphazard, she might find his opening observations to be a little creepy. Instead, she thought him to be completely harmless, and rather amusing. He looked sort of like a comic book version of David Crosby, and talked like a slightly inebriated Dracula. He donned the tweed jacket of a distinguished, scholarly gentleman, but wore it over a thin, discolored, hooded sweatshirt that made it clear that he really couldn't care less what others thought about him.

"I am Virgil," he said. "Please pardon my overabundance of carry-ons; I am working."

"Oh, it's fine," answered Sophie. "You're no bother at all." She in no way wanted to add to his chaos.

"I won't bore you with the details of my labors," he offered, "no matter how dreadfully important they may be." With that, he looked at her as if he were waiting for her to beg for details. What an odd comment, she thought. She decided not to respond at all, not exactly sure the extent of his sanity.

"What is a beautiful American girl doing by herself on a train to Lyon?" Sophie blushed. "And do shy American girls not like to tell old Lithuanian men their names?" Ah, so the accent was Lithuanian. She was not likely to have guessed that.

"Pardon me. I am Sophie Caldwell," she said.

"Oh, my, I get a last name as well," he shot back with a hearty, stained-tooth grin. "Very well then, I will one-up you. I am Virgilijus

Jonas Andrius, originally from Kaunas, Lithuania, but most recently of Geneva, Switzerland." He nodded in a very chivalrous fashion. He was strangely charming despite himself.

Sophie nodded back and extended her hand, "And I, sir, am Sophia Marie Caldwell of Dedham, Massachusetts, a suburb of Boston." He took her hand and kissed it playfully, and she giggled. She was starting to enjoy him more and more with every passing minute. "Are you familiar with Boston, Mr.…." She paused, trying to not obliterate the pronunciation of his name.

"Please, Sophie, we shall address one another by our first names. To you, I am Virgil." He peered at her over his thick spectacles. "Do I know Boston? Very well, yes. I love Boston. I have lectured there many times."

"Lectured?" Sophie was impressed. "Do you mind if I ask on what?"

"Sure, you may ask. But I warn you, that may venture into the details of my work, with which I promised not to bore you."

"Nonsense," shot Sophie. "I'm all ears."

"Well, you asked for it." Virgil proceeded to recount his adventures in Astrophysics, including the particulars of his recent work at the massive Hadron Collider facility. Sophie was certainly not well-versed in Astrophysics, or any science for that matter, but she managed to understand most of what he said. He explained that he had been hired by a large and extremely well-funded organization called CERN, which had built an enormous underground testing facility, apparently shaped like a donut, which used giant magnets to accelerate sub-atomic particles to extremely fast speeds that, if pushed fast enough, would collide with enough force to create an extremely rare phenomenon called a "Higgs boson" particle…or something like that. Virgil said these miniature explosions mimicked the infinitesimally small interactions that happened in the instants just before the Big Bang that created the universe. And in 2012, the CERN scientists had apparently succeeded in proving the existence of this theoretical particle, which was considered one of the greatest scientific discoveries in history. Virgil carried on with talk of protons, accelerated particles, black holes, strangelets, and many other invisible, yet very powerful things that, to Sophie, sounded like science fiction.

Virgil had been contracted to oversee a field of study called Abstract Astrophysics, which involved as much theoretical science as actual, hands-on application. His hiring was apparently rather controversial because he had dared to intermingle topics that were well accepted within his field with discussions of God and the divine. He insisted that he never allowed his faith to cloud his adherence to sound, empirical principles of science. But, unfortunately, his way of thinking proved too much for CERN's bureaucracy, which led to his departure.

Sophie told Virgil that she was sorry he had lost his job. "Agh! Who cares?" he grumbled. "They're a bunch of imbeciles, and I would have eventually left anyway. I just wish someone there would have listened to me before it's too late." Virgil seemed sad as he turned to watch the French countryside whiz by.

"What do you mean by 'before it's too late'?" asked Sophie. "Is it something about your theories on God?"

"No, no, not that." He shook his head. "That's for everyone to figure out for themselves. I'm talking about a potential global disaster." He glared at Sophie with a startling gaze. His accent thickened as he spoke more forcefully. "It could cause the end of the world, but nobody seems to want to talk about that, so I'll just go on shutting my mouth." He ran his fingers across his mouth, pretending to zip his lips, then looked back out the window.

Sophie considered shutting down the conversation at that point. She wasn't sure that she wanted to engage a scraggly scientist in a discussion of apocalyptic doomsday theories. But then again, whether what was coming was a prophetic diatribe, or simply the paranoid ramblings of a madman, it was bound to be entertaining.

"Come on, Virgil!" she pushed whimsically, yet respectfully. "You can't leave a girl hanging like that."

"What do you mean?" He eyed her warily.

"Well, you can't mention global catastrophe, and then just clam up." His defenses were up, but his eagerness obviously outweighed his skepticism. She elbowed him playfully to try and engender some trust, then sat back and listened as the floodgates opened.

"You see, Sophie, the miniature explosions caused by this Hadron Collider, or particle accelerator, or whatever you want to call it, can be so powerful that they could destabilize our existence to the point that it could literally come apart at the seams." By this point, he was talking so fast that his words were stumbling over themselves. "Or even worse…"

"Or even worse?" Sophie repeated, wondering how much worse it could get.

"Well, from a scientific perspective…you know." No, she did not know, but didn't want to stop now. "Even worse, the sudden subversion of the Higgs boson could create an instant black hole, causing everything on earth to be sucked into oblivion."

"Wow," said Sophie. "That's heavy."

"Heavy? Yes, exactly! Very, very heavy! In fact, everything on Earth would instantly become a singularity—a lump of matter with almost infinite density," he explained, his arms flailing around as he spoke.

"So, if this really is as dangerous as you say, Virgil, how come nobody wants to listen?"

"Good question, my girl," Virgil barely broke stride. "One would think that those responsible for such an incredibly historic scientific discovery would feel a great responsibility to make sure it is safe." He paused, sighing sorrowfully, "but that is not the case."

"Why not?"

"Unfortunately, the powers that be are more concerned with public relations and fundraising than with the potential repercussions of what they are doing." He again looked very sad. "I showed them my research, and begged them to shut it down until we could be sure. Instead, they commissioned studies by several 'independent' researchers," he flashed sarcastic air quotes with his fingers, which almost made Sophie laugh out loud. "And those researchers produced bogus reports that drastically downplayed any possibility of catastrophe."

"But you disagree?" Sophie asked.

"Of course I disagree!" he shouted, drawing stares from other gawking passengers. Virgil didn't even notice. "These so-called researchers spent only a couple of weeks in our extremely complex facility, and then came up with exactly the right data needed to keep our benefactors' checkbooks open."

"It's all about the money," Sophie said under her breath.

"That's it, exactly," Virgil agreed enthusiastically. "Money, money, money. The root of all evil."

"Sounds like it," added Sophie. "So, they refuse to shut it down, even for a little bit?"

"No." Virgil wagged his finger at Sophie. "After they discovered the particle, they decided to shut it down in December of 2012."

"Well, that's great news then, right?"

"Not at all. They shut it down so they could tweak the accelerator to make the particles even faster and the collisions even bigger!" Virgil made a large explosion-like motion with his hands. "They have managed to shorten the space between the proton bunches to the point of potentially doubling or tripling the force of the explosions."

"Whoa, that doesn't sound good," said Sophie.

"I'm afraid you may be correct."

Virgil paused for the first time in a while, and Sophie pondered everything he had said. She wasn't so sure that she believed it, but it certainly made an impression. She had never even heard of the Hadron Collider, or a "god particle" for that matter. But wouldn't it be just her luck to choose the epicenter of global disaster to spend a semester? Her mind started filling with all kinds of outrageous thoughts, like if the world suddenly collapsed into a pea-sized black hole, would it hurt? Or if it happened during her flight back to Boston, would the Earth just disappear underneath, leaving the plane to hurling aimlessly through space?

"Sophie? Have I caused you to be alarmed?" Virgil looked sympathetic, evidently mistaking her silence as she humored herself with outlandish daydreams for deep-rooted concern.

"Virgil, I'm curious," Sophie started, "if you are so convinced that we are facing a massive catastrophe, why don't you travel as far away from Geneva as possible?"

He again sighed deeply, as if he had pondered this same question before. "That's a good question, my dear," he responded. "And I'm afraid the answer is rather complicated." He went on to explain that his life had not been an easy one, full of sadness and regrets. He had never been satisfied with his personal life, which he had sacrificed in pursuit of his work. Most, if not all of his relationships with family and friends had suffered greatly as a result.

"I had a daughter once," he confessed, "and you remind me very much of her." Virgil seemed suddenly very uncomfortable. "Her hair was blonde, just like yours. And she was very smart, like you."

"Thank you, Virgil," said Sophie. "I don't know what to say." She did not want to pry, but sincerely wanted to know what happened to her. "Was she…did…what happened to her?"

"Oh, don't worry, she is fine," he assured her with a smile. "The last I heard she lives in Prague and has two daughters."

"Well, it sounds like you are well traveled," Sophie plodded on. "You should visit her."

"Oh, no. That ship has long since sailed," he said, still managing a melancholy grin. "It has been too long, and she has no interest in me. And for good reason; I was not a great father."

"But, Virgil, it's never too late to be a father, especially for a sweet old guy like you," Sophie said with a sweet smile.

"No, no, she is better off without me. She was the most beautiful thing to ever come into my life, and I was a fool. I could contemplate the deepest recesses of space, and the smallest particles known to mankind, but I was completely blind to this magnificent creature that God entrusted to me, so I lost her."

"I am so sorry, Virgil," Sophie whispered, nearly choking up.

"It is of no matter, girl," he replied, suddenly perking up. "And I suppose I still haven't answered your question."

"Which question is that?" she asked.

"That of why I am still here," he responded. "Other than the fact that Geneva is a very pleasant town, I suppose that since I concluded that the Collider presents a very serious danger, I have actually found myself, for the first time in a long while, enjoying the beautiful things of the world again." He pointed out the window and leaned back to give her a better view. "You see that beautiful row of trees there? They are called plane trees."

"Oh, I am very familiar with those," Sophie answered. "I adore them. They are very romantic."

"You are right," he nodded in agreement. "But until recently, I only saw them as *Platanus occidentalis,* a regenerative molecular structure that demonstrates remarkable atypical 5S rDNA intergenetic spacer sequences that produce significant inter-individual polymorphism."

"Whoa," laughed Sophie, "don't we all?" She was pretty sure that was English, but… "I…I'm not sure I follow."

Virgil thought for a minute, then said, "Let me see your camera." Sophie removed her camera from the carrying case looped around her wrist and handed it to him. He studied it momentarily, and then said, "Tell me what comes to your mind when you look at it."

She wasn't sure exactly where he was going with this, but she played along. "Pictures, I guess. I like to take pictures."

"Come on now, young lady," he pushed her. "You can do better than that. Be more specific. What does this camera represent to you?"

Sophie pondered again, this time determined to give a more meaningful answer. "Well, for me it's a window to the world; a way to capture fleeting beauty and try to hold onto it in some tangible way. It's a way to turn a passing moment into a timeless piece of art."

"That's exactly what I thought you'd say," Virgil responded, clearly satisfied. "You know what I see? Gears, molded plastic, aluminum mounts, metal oxides and light-alloy fluorides. And, of course, the way that engineering and the laws of physics allow it to work."

"Aw, Virgil, that's kind of sad," Sophie said, patting him on the shoulder with a lighthearted grin.

"To you, maybe. But they are just two different ways of seeing the world. When I see a radio, I want to tear it apart and see how it works. You, however, probably see it and want to hear beautiful music. You want to capture beauty with a camera, I want to dissect it on my tool bench. Neither one is right nor wrong, just different." He looked again out the window, this time through the camera's viewfinder. While still squinting, he muttered, "but you know, it never once occurred to me to take the camera out into the world and simply take a beautiful picture." Then he handed the camera back to Sophie and added, "That is, not until now."

"Now? What has changed?" Sophie asked.

"Well, I suppose there's something about the potential end of the world that changes the way you look at things," Virgil answered while twirling his moustache thoughtfully.

They sat in silence for several minutes, Sophie reflecting on everything he said. She still wasn't sure what to think of his doomsday theories. Frankly, she didn't have an opinion either way. But she had never before considered that her way of viewing the world was substantially different than anyone else's. Perhaps she should take the time now and then to consider things from a different perspective, to ponder the spectacular way things are put together. And perhaps it would do some good for an old, jaded guy like Virgil to see some of the most beautiful things the world has to offer.

"Virgil, I would like to invite you to be my guest at the museum," Sophie nodded emphatically as she explained her internship. She was excited by the prospect of introducing Virgil to Konrad Witz and all the museum's other legendary artists.

"Really? A date with the most beautiful American girl in Geneva? How can I resist?"

Sophie laughed and gave him another playful jab of the elbow. "Yes, and I with the most handsome Lithuanian scientist in Geneva."

Virgil chuckled as well and said, "Well played, girl. Very well played."

As the train slowed to a halt in Lyon, the two of them planned to meet on Tuesday at the museum, where she would give him the grand tour. Sophie thanked him earnestly for a perfectly delightful conversation, and kissed him on the cheek before leaving the train. She was unexpectedly grateful that her voyage next to the disheveled, mothball-smelling old man, which certainly could have been a complete disaster, had turned out to be both fascinating and altogether lovely. She ventured off into Lyon, looking forward to Tuesday.

Chapter Eleven

As she sat waiting for Virgil near the entrance of the museum, Sophie couldn't help but laugh at her peculiar situation. While at the clubs with her roommates, she consistently repelled the advances of young, attractive men without a second thought. Yet there she sat on her lunch break, anxiously awaiting the arrival of an eccentric, odd-smelling old man. She certainly didn't find him attractive, but their conversation on the train was quite compelling, even if he did come across as somewhat of a bizarre conspiracy theorist. She wasn't sure if it was the intrigue of the unfamiliar "god particle" concept, or his talk of apocalyptic demise, or just that he showed some interest in discovering art for the first time. Whatever it was, it was enough to make her look forward to their noon meeting.

At twenty-six minutes after the hour, Sophie glanced at the clock one last time, then accepted that she had actually been stood up by the old man. Sophie forced a final, unreciprocated smile to the blistery cold front desk lady, and then made her way to the lawn across the street to eat one of the two sandwiches she had packed for lunch.

The rest of Sophie's day was rather routine—taking inventory, assisting tour groups, and researching for a blog that Ms. Martineau kept threatening to start. But, unlike other days, Sophie was distracted, her mind drifting frequently to the Hadron Collider and the devastation foretold by Virgil. It wasn't that she necessarily believed it; she actually found it silly that one kooky old guy would know better than the greatest scientists on the planet. But it was fascinating nevertheless, like a cross between a fireside ghost story and a science-fiction movie, except that it was apparently happening—or at least according to this Virgil character—only a few miles away.

Sophie considered all the things she loved that would disappear if there really were a cataclysmic, earth-swallowing black hole. She could do without football, chicken potpies…and probably Bridgette. But the universe would also lose Monet, Pissarro, Michelangelo and Witz, all sucked up in a massive, or tiny, black hole caused by some giant underground scientific superstructure that Sophie didn't even know existed until the day before. Even if the catastrophe didn't destroy the entire earth, a small localized explosion, or implosion, or whatever, would likely at least take out Witz's *The Miraculous Draught of Fishes*, and possibly even reach as far as the Louvre in Paris—Mecca for art lovers. This was near sacrilege to Sophie. So, with nothing better to do, Sophie decided, in a tongue-in-cheek sort of way, to investigate the matter a little further.

Sophie walked a few blocks to a small bookstore, where she asked the scrawny clerk behind the counter, with his face full of random piercings, if they carried anything on the Hadron Collider. He rolled his eyes and sighed, but when he looked up and saw Sophie, his annoyance quickly turned to intrigue. "So, which are you," he started in a heavy French accent, "one of those science-geek tourists or a doomsdayer?"

Sophie laughed and said she was neither, just curious. "Well then, I have a deal for you," he said, cocking an eyebrow. "How about I show you a good book on the Collider, and you let me take you out for dinner?" It was everything Sophie could do to keep from laughing out loud, but she realized that this might be an opportune moment to speed up her research.

"Sure, why not?" she answered playfully. The clerk bounded off, leading Sophie through several dusty aisles of books, with very little appearance of organization. He stopped at a small science section and pulled out what looked more like a kiddy picture book than anything truly useful. He then stood rigid, like a dog anxious for a treat, as she thumbed the book's scarce pages. When she asked if that was all they had, he answered yes, obviously waiting for something more. She then handed the book back to him and started toward the door with the boy and his abundantly perforated face in tow. As she reached for the door handle, he protested, clearly insulted that she still had not provided a way for him to get in touch for their date. Sophie thanked him for his service, then started down the Rue de la Madeleine, grinning as he hurled French cuss words at her from the store front.

The library at the University of Geneva provided more literature on the Hadron Collider than Sophie would ever want to read, about a third of which were in English. She scanned various books and articles on the

Collider, CERN, and the history of the project. She managed to find a few pieces on the potential dangers of the Collider, and even a mention of Virgil and his infamous ramblings. After about an hour-and-a-half of perusing through mostly uninteresting babble about sub-atomic physics, Sophie was convinced that this stuff was much, much more interesting coming from Virgil than from a bunch of books in a stuffy old library. So her education in the workings of this great underground science thingy ended almost as quickly as it began, and she slipped out into the cool evening in search of another delicious hot chocolate before heading home for the night.

Chapter Twelve

Sophie flicked the ballpoint pen against her teeth out of habit while gazing at a collection of twelfth-century armor. She still wasn't clear what her task for the day was, which Ms. Martineau had scratched on a piece of paper in her characteristically indecipherable hieroglyphics. But Sophie figured that walking from room to room holding a clipboard would at least buy her some time until Ms. Martineau returned from her morning meeting.

Sophie was jotting down nonsensical notes on the clipboard when a half-whispered voice snuck up behind her. "Excuse me, mademoiselle," his voice was cautious and soft, but immediately recognizable. "I was wondering if I could try on one of those suits of armor." Sophie looked over her shoulder apprehensively, and saw Alie leaning, arms folded, against the door frame. He wore dark blue jeans, worn leather boots, and a faded green cord around his neck that disappeared underneath a plain black t-shirt. Like before, he eyed Sophie with that look that made her feel a bit uncomfortable, but not in a bad way, and in a way that she wasn't sure she had ever felt before.

"Well, sir, I don't think they would fit." Sophie liked his friskiness and decided to play along. "Plus, they are entirely too expensive—"

"For a poor bloke like me," Alie interrupted.

"Oh, I didn't mean that," Sophie muttered. She suddenly realized she was wearing her horrifyingly unflattering black-rimmed glasses and jerked them from her face.

"No, put them back on," Alie insisted. He took two cautious steps toward her before stopping abruptly and shoving his hands deep into his pockets, just as he had done the morning he knocked on her door. Sophie wondered if this was a sort of nervous habit, although his face and eyes still looked astoundingly calm and reassured. Plus, she couldn't believe that she could actually make someone as strikingly beautiful as he was feel nervous.

"You've got to be kidding me," she uttered. She considered

dropping them on the floor and stepping on them so that there was no chance he would ever see her in them again.

"I like them," Alie said as he stepped even closer. He gently removed the glasses from her hand and placed them on her face. "They make you look—"

"Nerdy?"

"No," Alie responded, "decisive."

Once again, Sophie didn't know how to respond. She had engaged in just three short conversations with this guy, and at some point during each one he said something that left her speechless. It was as if with a single, simple response, he could cause a world of chaos and passion to swirl within her. With little effort, it was as if he knew how to reach deep inside her lungs and suck the air out, giving her no choice but to just stare. And so she stood, staring, like a complete idiot, wholly and completely exposed by him.

"What exactly are you doing here anyway?" he asked.

"Huh? Why?" Great response, Sophie. "I mean, what?"

"No, 'what' is what I asked you," Alie said. "Okay, we'll go with 'why'. WHY…" With a long pause and a strong emphasis on the "why", he grinned and proceeded, "…are you here?"

"Now you are making fun of me," Sophie protested and poked him squarely in the chest.

"I would never…" he said as his grin widened.

Sophie explained the semester internship at the museum, and just how incredible the opportunity was, and that it was made possible only by scholarships. She then launched into a rather academic discussion about the museum's exhibits, with added emphasis on the Witz pieces and why they were her favorites. She continued, flipping between flirting and playing the tour guide as she led through the museum. She was consciously aware that she was blabbing on about things that most likely didn't interest him, but he just stayed quiet, pretending to be fascinated by everything she said.

"So why Geneva?" he asked. "Why this museum? Why not the Louvre, or the National Gallery in London?"

"Well, I suppose you could blame my father," she laughed.

"Why? Did he force you to come here?"

"No. He died when I was twelve," she answered.

"Oh, man. I'm sorry," he fumbled. "I didn't know."

"No, of course not," she said. "How could you? He was an artist, an amazing one. I used to fall asleep on an old ugly green couch watching him paint in our basement. And he would carry me up to my bed, and then the next morning I would run down the stairs to see what he had created. It was like Christmas morning every time I woke up."

"How did he die?"

"Car accident," Sophie replied. "It was winter, and he left to buy some firewood for our old iron stove, and then the phone rang about ten minutes later and my mom started screaming," Sophie's fell silent. Alie again shoved his hands into his pockets as his arms stiffened, showcasing his rock-hard forearms. He looked as if he wanted to say something, but instead just stood next to her as they stared at a painting neither of them really saw. She felt embarrassed getting so personal with someone she barely knew, but for some reason sharing this with him was easy.

"Come on," she broke the silence. "I want to show you something." She led him through a few more doorways into the small space that housed the Witz paintings. "This one is called *The Miraculous Draught of Fishes*."

"Cool," Alie said.

"No, not just cool. It's a masterpiece." Sophie explained Witz's unique style and use of dramatic colors. But Alie just stood, arms folded, nodding politely. "You really don't care, do you?"

"Sorry, I guess I just don't get it," Alie shrugged. "To me, it's just someone coloring stuff on paper. I left that behind in grade school."

Sophie let out an exaggerated gasp, and Alie laughed. She was fully aware that few people shared her fascination with art, but she was determined to at least try and make an impression on him. "You're telling me that you don't see any difference between this and a child's scribbling? You have no appreciation for the way he shows Christ—"

"I don't believe in God," Alie interjected, rather forcefully.

"Um, okay…" Sophie responded, curious at his apparent need to make his atheism clear. "But I don't think it's necessary to—"

"Does that bother you?" Alie interrupted.

"What, that you don't believe in God?"

"Yeah," he answered, watching her intently as if her response could change the future of their association. Sophie suddenly felt like she was under the spotlight.

"No, I suppose not. Not nearly as much as your lack of appreciation for true beauty," she while again directing his attention to another Witz painting.

"Oh, I never said I don't appreciate true beauty," Alie said while stepping closer to her, closer than he ever had before. His eyes narrowed again, this time with a sly grin.

There he goes again, Sophie thought, saying something that made her completely lose her senses. She slid her hand into her back pocket and touched her father's paint brush, like she often did when she felt nervous or uncomfortable. He was suddenly uncomfortably close, yet she did not want him to move away. A tidal wave of anxiety rushed over her in that moment of silence. Surely he wouldn't be bold enough to actually try and kiss her there, in the museum, during the first real conversation they had ever had. That would be highly inappropriate for a million different reasons, yet there wasn't a chance she was moving an inch, either toward him or away from him. She didn't notice his arm move toward hers, but she jumped like a startled alley cat when he touched her elbow. Her hand jerked out of her back pocket, and with it the paintbrush dropped to the floor. Smooth, Sophie, really smooth.

Before she could react, Alie bent down and picked up the brush. He began to study it, but Sophie snatched it from his hand.

"Easy there, tiger," he teased. "I promise I was going to give it back. It's just a brush."

"No, it's not *just* a brush," Sophie said. "It belonged to my father."

"Oh, wow. Sorry," said Alie. "Is that the one he used when you watched him paint?"

"No, he never painted with this one, at least not with actual paint." She turned and walked back to *The Miraculous Draught of Fishes*. "He called it ghost painting," her voice softened as she raised the brush to within a few inches from the canvas and began to gracefully trace images in the air. "He would stand in front of his favorite prints and meticulously mimic the artist in the air, without ever touching the painting itself. He said it made him a better painter, and that it was how he learned to truly love the paintings; to appreciate the artist's mastery. I don't think it has made me any better—I'm really not very good. But I do it all the time anyway. It makes me feel very…connected to him."

She paused for a moment. "You should try it," she said. "Maybe that would help you appreciate the art a little."

"If you insist." Alie took the brush and made several barbaric swipes through the air.

"You have all the grace of a drunk rhinoceros," Sophie laughed heartily, loud enough to echo down the corridor. Just as the cackle escaped, she realized that flirting extensively with Alie while tour groups wandered guideless through the museum may not bode well with Ms. Martineau. She promptly slipped the brush back into her pocket and peered down the hall to see if anyone was around.

"Hey," griped Alie. "That's it? That's the end of my art lesson?"

"Sorry, but if I get caught…if my boss sees me goofing around with you, I could get…"

"You might get the sack?" Alie cut in.

Sophie's eyes widened with surprise. "What?" she exclaimed.

"You know, get sacked? Lose your job?"

"Oh, you mean get fired?" Sophie laughed. "Apparently the 'sack' carries a completely different meaning in England."

"Apparently." Alie turned back to the painting and extended an open hand toward Sophie. "May I?" She handed him the brush, and he again began tracing images clumsily in the air. Sophie chuckled. "Yeah, thanks a lot, Sophie."

"Sorry, but you paint like a soldier," she mocked.

"Well, I bet you fight like an artist." She stepped closer and attempted to give a few pointers. But not long after, Alie shook his head and handed the brush to her. "Here, I'd rather watch you."

Sophie blushed and took the brush. She peeked again around the corner to make sure they were alone, then continued her lecture as she traced the strokes in the air. She looked back several times to find him leaning against a wall in a dark corner. Each time it was obvious that his eyes were not on the painting. Sure that he was paying no attention to her lecture, she stopped talking, but continued tracing the brush through the air. The museum was quieter than she ever remembered it. She knew he was behind her, partially obscured by shadow, observing her every move, but she could only hear herself breathe.

After several uncomfortable, yet surreal minutes, Sophie turned and said, "Well, what do you think now?"

"Beautiful." His response was simple, and yet again breathtaking. Her face was on fire, and she had no idea what to do next. She was torn between disappointment and relief when she heard Ms. Martineau's booming voice herding a group of tourists their way. Sophie struggled to compose herself as the group rounded the corner and filled the small room, separating her from Alie. They jabbered loudly, with Ms. Martineau almost screaming to be heard over them. Ms. Martineau's eyes connected with Sophie's and she seemed relieved to find an ally.

"Sophie, is everything okay?" Ms. Martineau inquired.

"What?"

"Are you OK?" Ms. Martineau insisted. "You look like you've seen a ghost."

Sophie snapped her gaze back to the corner where Alie had been standing, and it was empty. She looked around frantically for a few seconds, but saw only tourists. Ms. Martineau asked again if she was okay.

"Sorry, Ms. Martineau," Sophie took a deep breath and forced herself to focus. "Yes, I'm fine. Perhaps just a bit tired today."

"Okay, if you're sure…" She peered at Sophie suspiciously, and Sophie did her best to look composed. "If that's the case, can you finish up the tour for me? I have a few things I must tend to before we close for the evening." With that, Ms. Martineau strode out of the room and left Sophie to take over.

Sophie was certain that she gave a rather underwhelming finale to the tour, but she was too distracted to care. Sophie thanked the group for coming and escorted them out the museum's front door, locking it behind them. The lobby was empty; no more visitors, no security guards, no grumpy old lady behind the receptionist desk. She started toward Ms. Martineau's office, but detoured instead up the stairs and to the Witz room where she had last seen Alie. She found herself again in front of *The Miraculous Draught of Fishes* with brush in hand. As she lifted her arm, her reflection in the nearby window caught her eye. She observed her silhouette ghost painting in the window as raindrops began to gently tap the glass. As she watched herself, she wondered if she looked as ridiculous when Alie was watching her. No wonder he disappeared, she thought, and wondered if she would ever see him again.

. . . .

Alie stood on the sidewalk, staring up at the museum's second-floor window as raindrops pelted his scalp. The streetlights flickered on as sundown gave way to darkness. The soft light of the window perfectly framed her unmistakable silhouette as her brush stirred the air. At one point she looked toward the window, and Alie's heart skipped in anticipation that she might see him. But instead she turned back to the painting, and he continued to watch from below as the rain soaked his clothes. He wondered if he would ever see her again.

Chapter Thirteen

The morning began with what had become an all-too-familiar scene: Sophie in the kitchen making coffee, Bridgette wrapped in nothing but a sheet, and one of the chiseled British soldiers standing in the kitchen waiting for coffee, half-dressed and scratching himself in places where only guys scratch. Sophie felt like she was working for tips at a roadside diner, except that her customers wore almost no clothes, and there were no tips. She would admit, though, that she had had some interesting conversations with the Brits while the coffee brewed, ranging from Iraq to music, to politics, and just about everything except Sophie's roommates. Apparently, they kept coming back for the nightly revelry with Bridgette, Cammie and Liz and then Sophie's conversation and coffee in the morning. That didn't seem to bother her roommates one bit.

"So, things getting pretty *serious* between you and…well, one of my roommates?" Sophie jabbed sarcastically. He ignored the comment completely.

"What about you, Sophie?" asked the one named Jaden. "What of your romantic…*affiliations*?"

"I don't suppose I have any," Sophie answered, avoiding eye contact.

"You don't *suppose*?" He wrapped *suppose* in sarcastic air quotes. "Meaning you don't fancy anyone?" He grinned over the top of his coffee mug. "No one in particular comes to mind?"

"Wow, what are we, ten?" Sophie pretended to nonchalantly clean the countertops, hoping he would lose interest and move on. He did not.

"Come on, Sophie. Can you honestly say there is no one you've met here in Geneva who even remotely interests you?"

"Sorry…Jaden, right?" she responded. "I didn't come here to party, or to meet guys, so I'm sorry but the answer is no." She tried her best to be convincing, but the truth was that thoughts of Alie hadn't stopped racing through her mind since he disappeared from the museum a few nights before. He was like an itch that she had to scratch, but couldn't figure out how. She desperately wanted him to come back to the

museum, or to run into him on her walk home. Last night she'd laid in bed for hours wondering where he was from, what he was like, where he was at that
particular moment, and how in the world he could melt her insides with a single word. But her pride kept her from letting on that she even knew who he was. Pride, and fear that she had officially and completely scared him away for good with her ghost painting. But there must have been a reason he showed up at the museum in the first place. Surely if he had any interest in her, he would have come around again by now, right?

"You know, Sophie, I've been known to be a pretty intuitive guy...." Oh, here we go, Sophie thought, "and I'm pretty sure I noticed a connection between you and Alie."

Sophie nearly spit out her coffee. "Who?"

"Oh, come on. Don't act like you don't know who I'm taking about."

"Alie?" Sophie thought she might hyperventilate. "Is that one of your friends? Which one is he?"

Just then Bridgette emerged from the hallway, sheet and all, and rested her chin on his shoulder. She was sporting a mischievous grin, clearly amused by Jaden's line of questioning. Like a shark with blood in the water, Bridgette sensed Sophie's discomfort and wanted to take part in the feast.

"You know perfectly well who Alie is," insisted Bridgette. Sophie couldn't believe her nerve, as if she and Bridgette had ever had a conversation about anything, much less Alie. Sophie wanted to tear her head off, but instead continued to feign disinterest in the topic.

"I think so, but I'm not sure," Sophie offered.

"Well, too bad, Sophie," Jaden cut in, "'cause I think he may kinda fancy you a bit." Sophie froze. She wanted to know everything, every possible reason why Jaden might think Alie was interested in her. But she needed to play it cool.

"Look, Jaden, isn't that cute?" Bridgette said while running her fingers through his buzz cut. "She's trying so hard to act like she doesn't care, but she just can't hide it, can she?"

Was it really that obvious? Sophie thought.

"I've seen you when he's around," Jaden persisted as he slid past

Sophie and started digging through the refrigerator in search of breakfast. "Plus, he's a good guy. It wouldn't hurt you to have a little fun, you know."

"Like I said, that's not why I'm here," Sophie insisted with as much sincerity as she could muster up.

"Alright, if you say so," Jaden laughed from inside the fridge. "Then I suppose you have no interest in knowing that your roommates and I are meeting up with him tomorrow night at the Cottage Café for dinner."

"Of course she's not, babe," said Bridgette. "Remember, that's not why she's here."

Sophie shot Bridgette a nasty glare, which Bridgette met with a treacherous grin. She was obviously very proud of herself. "I don't mean to be rude, Jaden, but I have to take this opportunity seriously," explained Sophie. "I didn't come here to hook up with anyone."

"I came here to hook up with that," Bridgette chimed while pointing at Jaden's butt. She then slapped his backside, causing his head to clank against the inside of the refrigerator, before sashaying back to her bedroom.

"Look, Sophie," added Jaden as he emerged from the refrigerator clutching several eggs and a jar of something, "it can't hurt to stop by after work. Just come hang out, and maybe he'll be there too. And maybe, just maybe, you'll enjoy yourself."

Sophie carefully considered her response, trying to cipher a billion swirling thoughts. She decided to keep it simple: "Maybe. We'll see."

. . . .

It's funny how "Maybe" and "We'll see" can turn into the inability to think about anything else all day long. Sophie watched the clock most of the day, with every minute passing like an eternity. Just under an hour before closing, Sophie and Ms. Martineau were reviewing a stack of brochures at the front desk when an abundantly furry man with greasy hair and a gold chain approached and said, in broken English, "I am very much interested in having a tour." Sophie looked desperately at Ms. Martineau, who returned a look that made it quite clear that there was no way Sophie was getting out of this. Sophie panicked. Tours could last well over an hour, and she had already been trying to think of an excuse to leave early. Plus, this guy had not taken his eyes off Sophie since walking in the front door. Ms. Martineau handed him a pamphlet, told him he had come to the right place, and patted Sophie on the back before disappearing down the hallway.

The tour was nothing short of pathetic; Sophie skipped half of the usual stops, and gave incoherent descriptions of the others. When he requested to visit a medieval furniture exhibit in the basement, she apologetically said the basement was closed for renovation, which was a complete lie. It didn't really matter, however, because he was clearly only interested in one thing, and it had nothing to do with art. Over the course of fifty-eight minutes, he complimented Sophie's beauty four times, asked for her phone number twice, invited her to dinner, and even invited her to his parents' house in Slovakia for the weekend. Even on a normal day, she wouldn't have been tempted by any of his offers. But on that particular day, his advances were beyond hopeless.

Sophie all but pushed the Slovakian Casanova out the front door at 5:02 p.m. Then she dashed to the bathroom reapply her make-up, brush her hair and give herself a pep talk. Do *not* act like an idiot, Sophie! Deep breaths. It's just a dinner with friends.

Once she was able to quell her panic, if only for a minute, Sophie passed by Ms. Martineau's office to sign out for the day. Ms. Martineau was busy indexing a stack of cards, but stopped when Sophie entered. "Have a seat, Sophie. I would like to chat for a minute."

Sophie's stomach tied itself into a knot as her face started to flush. "I uh…I'm really in sort of a hurry." But Ms. Martineau was not the kind of woman to whom you said no, and Sophie reconsidered and took a seat.

"Ms. Caldwell," that was the first time Ms. Martineau had ever called her that. "I believe you are extremely bright and that you can be an asset to a curator's staff, if…if you are on task and not distracted." Ms. Martineau's sky-blue office chair creaked like an old ship as she leaned back and folded her arms. Ms. Martineau went on to lecture Sophie for several minutes about how amazing this opportunity was, and just how difficult it was to get a foot in the door of the curatorial profession. Sophie did her best to look terribly concerned and not check the clock on the wall. Then Ms. Martineau paused for a moment and said something that stunned Sophie.

"What's his name?"

"What?"

Ms. Martineau, who was far wiser and more perceptive than Sophie gave her credit for, said, "Come on now, girl."

Sophie was speechless.

"You think I don't know everything that goes on inside my museum," continued Ms. Martineau. "You don't think I saw you with that fellow with the soldier's haircut who was a few days ago?"

Sophie had no idea how to react. She wasn't sure if she was being teased or reprimanded. Either way, she desperately wanted to escape.

"Not to mention, Ms. Caldwell, I have been around the block a time or three, you know. I know that look on your face all too well." With that, Ms. Martineau paused and raised one of her eyebrows.

"I…I'm sorry to have disappointed you, Ms. M—"

"*Tais toi!* You're a young, beautiful girl in Europe. Art is wonderful, but it's not everything." Ms. Martineau shook a finger at Sophie. "Let your hair down a bit. Have some fun. If you have met a man, then so what? Live it up." She leaned forward in her chair with a slight grunt, "But just hurry up and get it over with and then leave it at home. I need your help around here and, right now, you're not much good to me. Now, stand up!"

Sophie sat frozen like a school kid in the principal's office. "On your feet, I said!" Ms. Martineau snapped like a drill sergeant, and Sophie sprang to her feet. "Now, get out of here, Ms. Caldwell." Ms. Martineau grabbed Sophie and spun her around, pointing her toward the door, then swatted her vigorously on the butt. Sophie let out a startled yelp.

. . . .

Within minutes Sophie was striding across the Pont du Mont Blanc that spanned the Rhône River. The plan was to meet at the Cottage Café at 5:30 p.m., and it was now eleven minutes until 6:00. The Cottage Café was a quaint, Parisian-style eatery with a simple, yet elegant ambiance and black dinette tables that spilled over onto the sidewalk beneath tall chestnut trees. It was expertly run by a perky and cheerful woman named Nicole, who greeted Sophie and her roommates by name each time they stopped in. The locale had become a favorite of Sophie and her roommates, along with the small, manicured park just across the sidewalk.

Sophie stopped to catch her breath before turning onto *ADHÉMAR FABRI, THE STREET WHERE THE CAFE WAS LOCATED.* She desperately hoped they had not decided to leave her behind, but absolutely did not want to appear to be in too much of a hurry. As she rounded the corner at a make-believe relaxed pace, Sophie heard Cammie's unmistakably rowdy laugh, and then saw her roommates at a table with three guys. She anxiously counted the three tightly buzzed heads at the table: she could make out Jaden—despite him being fully clothed—as well as the other crazy one who tended to stagger, most mornings, half-awake from Cammie's room. Sophie wasn't sure, but thought she recognized the third guy from the club. What she was certain of was that he was not Alie, and her heart sunk. Had she freaked him out at the museum, as she feared, to the point that he had no interest in seeing her again?

"It's about time!" chimed Cammie, who appeared to have already emptied several glasses of wine. Sophie took a seat, but said nothing. She did her best to act like she didn't notice Alie's absence, while covertly scanning the neighboring park for some sign of him. After several moments, she noticed that everyone at the table were silently staring at her.

"Ah, man," said Jaden, shaking his head slowly.

"Ah, man, what?" responded Sophie.

"Yeah, it's bad," said Liz, flashing a conspicuous grin.

"What are you talking about," shot Sophie nervously. "What's bad? What's going on?"

"Who you lookin' for?" asked Cammie with delight.

"I'm not looking for—" Sophie stopped abruptly. Over Liz's shoulder, Sophie noticed a small white dog darting across the grass, barking wildly at several panicking geese. On the heels of the dog was a giggling boy carrying an empty leash. And there was Alie, jogging just behind the boy, with a wide grin. He and the boy were engaged in enthusiastic chatter, or clever planning even, aimed at corralling the dog. Sophie spent the next several minutes completely entertained by Alie's antics, and ignoring the snickering remarks from the table. Then, with almost no effort, Alie took several strides past the boy and snatched up the puppy, and helped the boy fasten the leash to its collar. He escorted the boy and the yipping dog to a nearby bench where an elderly woman, probably the boy's grandmother, received them both with a grateful nod. Alie shook the woman's hand, playfully ruffled the boy's hair, then turned and jogged toward the cafe.

"Your white knight approaches, madam," joked Diggs, tipping his glass in Sophie's direction.

"This should be fun," said Bridgette.

Sophie flashed an unnerved glare at all of them. "I swear on everything that is holy that I will end your lives if you make this awkward."

"Too late," chuckled Redwine.

Sophie caught Alie's eye as he was approaching, and he nodded with an uncomfortable smile. He sat on the opposite side of the table from Sophie, and she pretended not to care.

"Glad you came back, hero?" said Diggs.

"Just thought I'd join the party," answered Alie.

"Funny, mate," Redwine piped in, "you were awfully anti-social before she showed up. You were perfectly content playing with ducks and puppies."

Alie leaned somberly over the table. "Well, Mr. Redwine...you, mate, are a repulsive wanker. And most of these lovely ladies are repulsive for having bedded down with you, so sod off to all of you." Redwine punched him square in the arm, and the table burst with laughter. Alie continued, "Miss Sophie here is tolerable because she's the only one who hasn't been tainted by the likes of you blokes."

Sophie cocked her head toward Alie and said, "I'm happy to hear that you find me 'tolerable'." Alie watched her over the top of his glass and took a long, slow sip. The corners of his mouth turned up in a grin as he drank. Sophie's roommates and the soldiers mercifully relented their teasing and moved on to more trivial matters. The rest of dinner was dominated by crude stories, obnoxious laughter, and excessive alcohol. Sophie tried to pretend to be interested in the banter, and to only occasionally sneak glances at Alie. Several times she caught Alie glancing back, and they would quickly look away as if it did not happen. It was the sort of painfully awkward, middle school-ish back-and-forth that makes one both terrified and exhilarated.

Sophie suddenly wanted everyone to disappear—her roommates, Alie's friends, the waiters, the people at the other tables, even the passers-by on the sidewalk—everyone but her and Alie. She wanted the playful awkwardness between the two of them to give way to a long, real conversation. She desired to know more about him, to find out what was beneath his mysterious, hushed mannerisms. She wanted to find out if he was as intriguing as she thought he might be, and to fast-forward past all the preliminary trivialities that tend to wedge their way into the dawn of a romance. But they were still there—her roommates, his friends, the people on the sidewalk and in the park—and she simply had to be patient. So she just sat, and waited, and hoped.

The conversation inevitably turned to hitting the clubs, which turned Sophie's stomach as always. She rolled her eyes predictably, and her roommates predictably insisted that she come along. Despite her obvious disdain for Geneva's club scene—or any city's for that matter—going along that night might at least mean she would get to spend more time with Alie, albeit in a place where they would struggle to have an actual conversation. But, she decided, she would take what she could get.

Alie, however, flatly announced that he was tired and had a headache, and the last place he wanted to be was in another vile discothèque. And with that, he stood up, slapped Diggs on the shoulder, bid a quick and generic farewell, and walked away along with Sophie's hopes for the evening. She tried, but failed miserably, to hide her disappointment.

The table fell silent as Sophie stared past the crowds and toward the distant waterfront, which was starting to glow from the first signs of a fading sun. No one dared mention the club again, and Cammie suddenly insisted on paying for Sophie's dinner over Sophie's feeble protests. Sophie felt fragile as she stood up and wished them a fun evening before starting the long walk to their dorm building. During the walk, she reminded herself over and over that she only came to Switzerland to spend a semester at the museum, and that there was no room in her plans for trivial distractions, especially English soldier boys. With a little more effort, Sophie was sure she could convince herself that this was true.

She made her way up four flights of Les Epinettes' stale staircase and hauled open the bulky metal door to her hallway. She walked down the hall with her nose buried in the chaotic innards of her backpack as she rummaged for her keys. She managed to dig out the keys, but dropped a tube of lipstick in the process. She bent to pick it up, but froze when something out of place caught her eye down the hall. There, sitting in the hallway, leaning his back against her door, was Alie. He nodded at her timidly and said, "I wasn't quite as tired as I made out."

Somehow, Sophie managed to whisper, "me neither," which she immediately realized made no sense.

"Good, 'cause I want to show you something," Alie said, and got to his feet.

. . . .

Sophie felt like she floated down the staircase and along the boulevard next to Alie. He wouldn't tell her where he was taking her, but she didn't really care. In fact, he said almost nothing; he just took her gently by the hand and led her to a street corner, where he flagged a taxi. To Sophie's surprise, he delivered some instructions to the driver in French, and off they went.

"Is it far?" Sophie managed, knowing what the answer would be.

"You'll see." Just as she thought.

The taxi darted frantically past cars on the Quai de Cologny, a busy highway that runs along the south-eastern shore of Lake Geneva. Every few minutes, Alie would lean forward and say something quietly in French to the driver, after which the driver would speed up just a little. Sophie sat quietly, occasionally glancing at Alie. But Alie just stared quietly out the window toward the lake. The glow of sunset snuck between the gaps in the extravagant lakeside châteaus that dotted the lake shore. Sophie badly wanted Alie to look her way and take her hand again, but he just kept staring out the window.

The long row of houses finally gave way to a substantial stretch of green that sloped hurriedly to the lake shore. Alie quickly tapped the driver on the shoulder and said, "*Arrêtez-vous ici se il vous plait*," after which a brief argument ensued between the two of them. After a few seconds of silence, the driver sighed heavily, then pulled over on the narrow shoulder. After Alie tossed some bills at him, they found themselves standing on the busy roadside as cars whipped by.

"This is what you wanted to show me?"

"Not quite," Alie laughed, "but we're close." Alie firmly took Sophie by the hand and the two of them dashed across the roadway, not slowing down until they reached the bottom of the hill, just a few feet from the water's edge.

The mossy ground squished beneath them before giving way to a gritty, charcoal-colored beach. The coarse sand caught humble waves as they washed ashore. A pair of panicked ducks, startled by their approach, protested noisily as their wingtips beat the surface of the water before disappearing into the golden channel of sunlight that cut across the lake's surface. The horizon beyond the north-western shore smoldered with every shade of orange and red, then red and purple, and then the most profound purples and blues that Sophie could ever remember seeing. The departure of the noisy ducks brought silence, interrupted only by the lapping of the waves. Sophie and Alie stood together, staring across the blackening water. Sophie was completely absorbed by the most perfect silence, but, at the same time, was desperate for a word from him. She turned and watched him, for the first time not caring how obvious it was; but his eyes remained fixed on the magnificent sunset that stretched before them.

Who was this guy, anyway? Sophie knew almost nothing about him. In just a few short days he had turned her world upside down, yet all she really knew of him was that he was in the British military, that he was quiet and a bit out of place in a crowd, and that he was fiercely loyal to his friends, two of which were his animalistic, polar opposites. He was never in a hurry to say anything, and when he did, it was brief and definite. But with just a few words he could spin Sophie into a cyclone of unfamiliar exhilaration, apprehension, insecurity, and desire. She usually took pride in her level-headed predictability. Yet here she was, alone with an almost complete stranger, on edge in anticipation of the possibility that he might, just might, kiss her before the night was over. At the risk of ruining the perfect moment, she decided to break the silence. "Alie," she whispered, "tell me…"

"Do you still have that paintbrush?" Alie cut her off as he met her gaze directly. His face was partially washed in the golden glow. He leaned in, his face only inches from hers. Sophie could not speak. He slid his hand slowly down her back as Sophie trembled. His fingers paused at the top of her jeans, then crawled a few more inches over her back pockets to the end of her shirt. His steady breaths tickled the intersection where her ear met her cheek. He lifted her shirt slightly and traced several inches of her lower back with his finger. She allowed herself to close her eyes as she fell completely into him. For a moment, their chests rose and fell simultaneously. Then he pulled away.

Sophie held her breath and opened her eyes, wondering what was wrong. Alie's eyes remained locked onto hers, but lifted his hand between their faces, and in it was the paintbrush. He smiled softly, clearly proud of himself. Sophie was amused, curious, and a bit disappointed that such a moment had to end. He offered the brush to her, and she took it. Then he gently took her by the shoulders and turned her toward the lake and the multicolored display that reached across to the opposite bank. Alie stepped behind Sophie, slid his right hand down her arm and grasped her wrist. His left hand brushed her hair back over her left ear, and again she could feel his breath on her cheek. Then he raised her arm to her eye level and began to move it in sweeping motions through the air. And, suddenly, Sophie understood. Their breathing synchronized once again, and their bodies moved together as she ghost-painted the sunset. The brush methodically traced the rolling Jura mountains that formed the blackening horizon, the disappearing outline of the distant shoreline, and the spectral kaleidoscopic of colors that transformed dramatically with every passing minute that the sun sank further and further into the night's oblivion.

Sophie closed her eyes again, allowing Alie to move her arm. He buried his nose deep into the back of her head, and she felt him draw in a long breath. Her heart pounded inside her, and she no longer cared how ridiculous or audacious she might seem. All she knew at that moment was that she was either going to kiss him, or she was going to pass out, and she considered kissing him to be just slightly less outlandish than keeling over. So she withdrew the brush and started to turn. But before she could make it all the way around, he grabbed her shoulder with his left hand, put his right hand on her left cheek, then slid it back until it cradled the back of her neck. She could see the sunset's fiery reflection in his eyes as he pulled her closer. She drew in one last breath, and then he kissed her.

He kissed her like every girl dreams of being kissed. It was at the same time sweet and tender, but also full of every bit of the fire and intensity that had exploded across that evening's sky. She could no longer feel the ground beneath her, or the lakefront's humid breeze. She could only feel him. She felt like every part of her that touched him would melt, leaving behind deep scars that she hoped would never go away. And just as she wished the kiss would go on and on until the sun rose the next morning, he again pulled slightly away and raised the brush. But this time he held her firmly against his body with one hand as he gently traced every curve of her face with the brush's soft bristles. She closed her moistened eyes as he brushed the last remaining remnants of sunlight from her eyelids.

. . . .

The morning sun crept gradually across Sophie's pillow until it reached her face. She struggled to pry apart her eyelashes as her dreams faded into semi-consciousness. For a moment, she did not recognize the pillow, the bed, or the curtains that hung thinly before her. It took a few minutes to make sense of where she was, but as her thoughts thickened into rationality, she remembered that she was in Alie's hotel room. The memories of the night before came rushing back, and she couldn't help but smile at the unbelievable perfection of it all.

She hesitated to roll over, partially because she did not want to wake Alie, but more because she did not want this to end. She remained perfectly still, listening for the sound of Alie breathing behind her, but there was nothing. When she finally got the nerve, she gently turned to face him, but found that she was alone.

Sophie got out of bed, parted the curtains to check the balcony, and found that it was empty. She then went to the bathroom door, but it was open with the light off. There was nowhere left to look; Alie was not there. Sophie scanned the hotel room for a note or some other sign of where he might have gone, but found nothing more than two neatly packed suitcases sitting side by side near the window.

She sat perplexed on the end of the bed; she didn't even want to consider the possibility that she had just been a victim of her first one-night stand, especially not under these circumstances. But yet there she was, alone in a hotel room, wondering if she was just naively wanting the night before to be more than it was. After all, she was just some simple American girl falling quickly and foolishly for a British soldier after less than two weeks. Was she really so stupid to think that he was all that different from his womanizing buddies? Perhaps the only difference was that Sophie was a less-willing target, at least up until last night, which she would no doubt hear about from her roommates the rest of the semester. That settled it; she had to get out of there. Perhaps, with a little luck, she would make it home before her roommates woke up and could avoid the questioning that would follow. Her frantic deliberating was interrupted by the chirping rings of her phone. It was Cammie. Crap. So much for sneaking into the apartment undetected.

Sophie ignored the call and instead flipped on the bathroom light to check the mirror. Bad idea. No makeup other than smudged mascara, and no way to tame the snarled bird's nest on top of her head. Maybe it was a good thing Alie wasn't there after all.

She fought the urge to hyper-analyze what last night did or didn't mean. For the moment, she just wanted to make it back to her apartment without overthinking herself to death.

Chirp chirp. Another call from Cammie. Sophie absolutely did not want to have that conversation, at least not yet. The only thing worse than trying to explain last night with Alie was trying to explain this morning without him.

Sophie slowly opened the door to the hallway as the phone rang a third time. Cammie's persistence was legendary. "Hello," Sophie answered.

"Jeez, dude! Where the heck are you? And why aren't you answering?"

"Hey, Cammie," Sophie said, backing into the hallway while taking extra care to close the hotel room door quietly.

"What do you mean 'Hey, Cammie', doofus? Where are you?" Cammie did sound a bit worried, but much more intrigued. "Are you really where I think you are?"

"What? Where would you think I am?"

Cammie's mischievous giggles mixed with others in the background. She was clearly not alone. "Well, I can tell you that there are two very fine soldier boys sitting here grinning because they think they know where their mate Alie was last night. Any chance you have some insight on that?"

Oh, great. Here it comes, thought Sophie. She turned toward the elevators to make her escape. She wondered if she was actually starting her first official walk of shame. "Look, Cammie, I'll be home in—"

"Don't leave!" The shout came from behind her. She turned to see Alie jogging toward her carrying a bouquet of wildflowers. "Please,

82

don't leave."

Sophie stood, vulnerable and speechless. "What's going on, Sophie? Hey!" Cammie's voice echoed desperately from the phone.

"I gotta call you back," Sophie whispered into the phone as it slid down her cheek.

"No, wait! Sophie, you'd better..." Sophie hung up and stuffed the phone into her pocket. She thought she should say something, but nothing came out.

"I'm sorry, really," Alie pleaded. "I just went to get these. I should have—"

"No, it's okay. I just thought you were, you know—"

"I know. I should've left a note." He extended the flowers. "Do you have to go?"

"Well no, but look at me." She was suddenly horrified as she regained her senses. "I look horrible, and I don't have a toothbrush. That's just downright gross."

Alie laughed loudly, then draped his arms over her shoulders. "You look amazing, better than I've ever seen you." He pulled her close and kissed her deeply. She dropped the flowers to her side, upside down, as several blossoms spilled onto the carpet.

Chapter Fourteen

Rikku Laine sat in what used to be Virgil's chair, staring blankly at what used to be Virgil's desk. The mint-green vinyl desktop was barren except for a stack of fourteen reports—one for each panel member. Rikku removed the top copy and began thumbing the pages. The document began with a brief, one-paragraph summary of Virgil's findings, followed by an even shorter, but highly inflammatory paragraph full of dire warnings of the disasters that could be caused by the Hadron Collider. The next eighty-three pages formed a mosaic of graphs, equations, charts and diagrams, intermingled among highly technical rationalizations supporting Virgil's hypotheses.

Rikku skimmed the highlights of the report, but already knew what it contained. He had heard Virgil's ominous warnings many times. In fact, because Rikku shared an odd sort of friendship with Virgil, he had been tasked by the rest of the panel members with keeping Virgil "on task", or in other words, steering Virgil's away from publicly declaring his prophetic warnings, and toward the quality scientific research that brought him here in the first place. But despite Rikku's best diplomatic efforts, Virgil's insistence that the Collider was dangerously unstable continued to a fever pitch, well beyond what was tolerable to the panel.

Virgil's departure from CERN was little more than a passing event to the organization's higher-ups. He had become a relatively significant annoyance; but once he was gone, he was essentially forgotten within the organization, and it was business as usual. Rikku, however, was left with a fair share of guilt for how things ended, and a nagging feeling that maybe there was something to Virgil's forewarnings. After all, what if this colossal superstructure really did explode, or implode, or whatever, and took half of Europe with it, or even worse? Rikku had convinced himself on more than one occasion that Virgil was simply too kooky to be taken seriously, but doing so required Rikku to ignore Virgil's staggering brilliance and all he had accomplished. The truth was that if anyone's research at CERN concerning the potential for a crisis should be taken seriously, it was Virgil. However, siding with Virgil on this issue would have been career suicide for Rikku, not to mention utterly futile. Even if Rikku had gone to bat for Virgil, the only difference would have been that Rikku would have joined Virgil on the job hunt. So Rikku decided to keep his mouth shut and play the game, like he had always done.

When Rikku entered Virgil's office that day, he made sure no one saw him, and then locked the door behind him. He had deliberately neglected to turn in Virgil's key after his departure. Instead, Rikku kept it until he had time to investigate whatever Virgil may have left behind, which turned out to be the reports. Virgil tried to get Rikku to promise to deliver them to the panel, but Rikku had dodged making any such commitment. As Rikku sat in the cramped remains of Virgil's office, he deliberated for the final time whether the reports should ever find their way to the panel members, or anyone else outside of that office.

"Sorry, Virgil," Rikku whispered. "But the choice is not mine to make." Rikku removed the binder clips from each of the reports and began to slide the 1,176 pages into the shredder.

Chapter Fifteen

The bathrooms in Les Epinettes are laughably tiny, especially when meant to serve four girls in their early twenties. There was barely enough room for one to get ready, so it was nothing short of a miracle when Sophie's roommates stuffed themselves inside with Sophie as she prepped herself for the night. With Cammie perched on the toilet like a hawk, and Liz and Bridgette sharing the minuscule bathtub, they peppered Sophie with questions. She had managed to avoid interrogation since failing to come home a few nights before. But when she let it slip that she was going out with Alie that night, they surrounded her like slobbering hyenas on a baby gazelle.

"Where's he taking you?"

"What's he like?"

"How did you guys kiss the first time?"

"Does he have any tattoos?"

"Are you guys, like, falling in…"

Sophie rolled her eyes. "He says he wants to take me somewhere to show me *real* art."

"Oh great," smirked Bridgette, "not another art nerd."

"Hardly," said Sophie. "I'm quite certain he doesn't know the first thing about art."

"Then what does he mean?" asked Liz.

"No idea," shrugged Sophie. She had asked herself that question a million times since he brought it up.

"Oh I bet I have an idea, if you know what I mean!" Cammie cackled.

"I swear you guys are twenty-one going on twelve," Sophie said before checking herself one last time in the mirror.

"Listen here, young lady."

"I want you home at a decent hour, or else…" Cammie laughed and slapped Sophie on the butt as Sophie turned to escape.

. . . .

"Ho-ly crap, that's good," sighed Sophie as she licked a stream of melting chocolate ice cream dribbling over her thumb. "You were right, this *is* real art."

Alie belted out a loud laugh. "The ice cream isn't quite the art I was referring to; but you're right, it's exceptional."

"You mean you plan to show me something more exquisite than this?" Sophie scoffed. "Good luck." They strolled carelessly down the Rue du Rhône, one of Geneva's—and Europe's for that matter—most remarkably luxurious shopping districts. They passed storefronts selling $100,000 watches and some of the most expensive clothing in the world.

"Well, I for one wouldn't trade this cone for any one of those stupidly expensive watches," said Sophie. "Unless, of course, I could trade the watch for ten thousand scoops of this." At the suggestion of the concierge at Alie's hotel, they had hunted down *MÖVENPICK,* the famously chic and sinfully indulgent ice cream boutique. Alie opted for the special edition Vanilla & Macadamia. But Sophie considered it blasphemous to be in Switzerland and get anything other than chocolate—the Chocolate & Tonka truffle, to be precise.

"If I lived here, I'd weigh 400 pounds."

"And you'd still be lovely," Alie responded before dabbing a drop of chocolate off of Sophie's chin, and stealing a quick kiss. "Never underestimate a girl and her chocolate," he grinned.

"Truer words were never spoken," she answered. "I really liked you before," Sophie raised her cone to her lips while gazing into his eyes, "but this seals the deal."

They spent most of the afternoon exploring the Rue du Rhône and its side streets. Despite being surrounded by the most elite clothing designers and watchmakers in the world, they were completely lost in one another. Sophie laughed when telling him about her mother, and cried while talking about her father. She told stories of her childhood, described her small childhood home, and shared secrets she had never shared before. And, of course, she talked about art. She described her favorite artists, told him about the many museums she had visited, and others that she dreamed of visiting. And Alie said very little. He just held her hand, content with every step, every word, and every breath.

"Can I ask you a question?" Sophie started.

"Of course."

"Do you ever get tired of me talking about art?"

"I don't ever get tired of you talking about anything," Alie responded while wrapping his arm around her and pulling her close.

"No, seriously."

"Seriously. I just don't understand it much, that's all."

"I feel sorry for you," Sophie teased.

"Why?"

"I just can't imagine not seeing what I see in a Pissarro or a Rembrandt."

Alie stopped in stride and took Sophie by the shoulders, positioning her in front of a store window of some Italian clothing designer neither of them could pronounce. "What do you see?"

Sophie curiously studied the display, and then answered, "Dresses that I could never afford and shoes I would never wear."

"Do you see art?" Alie probed.

"Art?" Sophie glanced at him, perplexed. "No, I see clothes."

"There are a lot of people, fashionistas and such, who consider this the highest form of art."

"Are you telling me that you think this…?"

"No, not me. Not at all," Alie insisted. "It's a bunch of silly cloth to me. But what some consider art may be rubbish to others."

"Okay, then, where is this art that you promised to show me?" Sophie inquired.

"That comes later," answered Alie. "But who knows, you may think it's rubbish."

"Oh come on, give me some credit."

"I just ask for an open mind, that's all." Alie leaned in to kiss her, but froze as something caught his eye over her shoulder. His eyes nearly tripled in size as he whispered, "Speaking of true art…"

Sophie turned to see whatever it was that deprived her of a kiss. "A car? Wow," she said, sarcastically. "Really? A car?"

"Ohhhh, Sophie, my dear." He slid past her, utterly mesmerized. "That's definitely not just *any* car."

"I suppose now you're going to tell me what kind of exotic supercar it is."

He gravitated toward the car like a moth hypnotized by a porch light. "That's a McLaren 650S Le Mans." Just as she predicted. Alie shook his head in amazement. "Unbelievable."

"Looks like something Batman would drive," said Sophie, less than impressed.

The sleek, jet-black machine sat empty directly in front of the Christian Louboutin boutique, with an audacious disregard for the traffic it was blocking. To Sophie, it looked less like an automobile and more like a spaceship. And it just screamed, "I am REALLY expensive!" Alie began circling the car, taking it all in the way Sophie did her ice cream. Just as he leaned in for a closer look, the boutique door flew open and out shot an exceptionally short man with spiked white hair and a skintight red t-shirt dotted with gold beads. He was followed by a scantily clad, lanky woman with arms so feeble that they could barely support the throng of shopping bangs that hung from them.

"*Arrêtez!*" the man shouted, motioning for Alie to back away.

"I am sorry, sir, but is this your car?" Alie stepped back, but did not take his eyes off the car.

"Yes," barked the Napoleonic owner, "and you are not authorized to touch it." He took an awkwardly aggressive step toward them, and Alie backed away with a grin.

"Excuse me, sir," snickered Alie. "I had absolutely no intention of touching it. I was just admiring."

"I'm sure you were," the man responded, "which you can do just as easily from over there." He strode past Alie and began loading bags into the car.

"Again, sir," started Alie, "we had—"

Sophie suddenly leapt in front of Alie and approached the open car door, much to the shock of its impish owner. "Actually, sir, we were just standing here thinking about stealing your car. But as we looked closer, we saw just how incredibly close the driver's seat is to the steering wheel, which would make for a very difficult get away, so we decided to pass. You have to weigh up the risks, you know." The man stared stupefied as Sophie gave Alie a sassy wink. "Come on, honey, let's wait until something better comes along. Oooohhh, look at that one!" She grabbed Alie's arm and pulled him down the street toward another, slightly less obnoxious car. Alie gladly followed in hysterics.

A block or so later, Alie caught his breath and said to Sophie, "Who *are* you?"

"What exactly do you mean?" Sophie asked.

"That's definitely a side of you I have not seen yet. Feisty!"

"Are you kidding me? I wasn't going to let that arrogant elf talk to you like you're a peasant."

"Well now," said Alie, "I'm officially beside myself. I have a feeling there's much more to you than I expected. I just hope we have enough time for me to find out."

Sophie's grin faded and she started walking past him, arms folded, down the sidewalk.

"Have I upset you?" Alie asked.

"No, not really," Sophie answered without looking back. "You just mentioned for the first time that topic we've both been avoiding."

Alie didn't have to ask. It was almost all he thought about; he just didn't know how to bring it up, or whether to bring it up at all. But the proverbial ten-thousand-pound elephant in the room—the obvious but unstated monster that neither of them wanted to face—was the fact that Alie's short time in Geneva was quickly coming to a close. Sophie had not had the nerve to ask exactly when he was leaving, and he had procrastinated telling her. But the more they avoided the subject, the more awkward it became. They both knew the answer wasn't good, so they naively did their best to pretend it wasn't coming. Sophie imagined that, somehow, he would miraculously be allowed to stay a while longer, at least until her semester ended. But she thought it was more likely that they only had, at best, a few more weeks. What Alie knew, but had not yet told her, was that it was actually only a few days—three, to be exact.

What made it worse was that Sophie had no way of knowing when they might see each other again, if ever. She had no plans of traveling to England any time soon, nor the financial means to do so. And even if she could hop across the pond, Alie was never really there anyway. Sure, England was his "home base", but for the better part of the past five years, he had bounced between Iraq, Afghanistan, and anywhere else his service to the queen carried him. So, with no real resolution to the problem, Sophie and Alie ignored reality, and the growing crater in their guts that accompanied it.

"Listen, Sophie, I hate to do this, but—"

"Tell me about that car," interrupted Sophie. She held his hand, but avoided his gaze.

"You…you want me to talk about that short guy's car?" Alie knew they couldn't avoid the topic for ever, but hated to ruin what had to this point, been a perfect day.

"Yes, please," Sophie said softly.

"Well, like I said, it's a McLaren—"

"No, I don't care what kind of car it is," Sophie stopped. She looked him directly in the eye and poked him in the chest. "I want to know why *you* reacted the way you did." The grin crept back as she kept pressing. "I'm starting to realize that I know very little about you, so I want to know why you turned into a kid in a candy store when you saw that car."

Alie stepped to the edge of the curb and looked in both directions. Sophie thought he was going to cross, but he just stood and watched for a moment, took a deep breath, and then said, "You were right; you really don't know much about me. But that's fine by me. I'd almost rather keep it that way."

Sophie grabbed his shoulder and spun his face toward hers. "Why would you say something like that?" she snapped. "I want to know everything about you, but you're like a little impenetrable box. Don't you trust me?"

"Trust has nothing to do with it, Sophie," he said while gently pulling her toward him and leaning in for a kiss. Except this time, Sophie stuck her finger square in the middle of his forehead and pushed him backward.

"Nice try, Romeo," she said. "You don't get to kiss me every time you want to avoid talking about something. What on earth is it about a dumb car that you can't tell me?"

"That 'dumb' car cost $280,000," Alie started.

"I don't care about the stupid car," Sophie interjected with an exasperated laugh. "I really, really don't." She grabbed his wrist and marched him to a bench and sat down. He was amused by her, but also afraid not to follow, so he took a seat. "I know it's only been a few days, but this feels like something more than just a fling—at least to me. *Talk* to me," she insisted. "Like, really and truly talk…about *you*." Her second poke to his chest emphasized, once again, that she was serious.

"Well, it's a McLaren 650S Le Mans…." He barely got it out before she slugged him hard in the arm. He laughed hard and leaned away from her, protecting his arm. "Okay, okay," he said, struggling to compose himself. There was clearly no getting out of this. He sighed, then stared at his shoes. "I just don't like talking about myself, I guess. My history is one that's better ignored than explored."

"I don't believe that," Sophie said. "Your past is just your past until you share it, and then it becomes your story. And every story is a masterpiece when told to the right listener."

He glanced at her for a second and shook his head, then fixed his gaze back on his shoes. "Well, okay then," he started, and then closed his eyes. "For me, cars were a means of escape."

"Escape? From what?"

"Life, I guess. You see, mine wasn't pretty, not at all." He stalled, and she slid her hand over his. This was clearly new territory for Alie. Where conversation was usually so easy between them, it always stalled with any mention of his upbringing. Sophie longed for him to let her inside.

"I guess I really had two ways to escape the hell of my childhood: martial arts and cars."

"Martial arts?" Sophie flashed a surprised smile. "Don't tell me you're some kind of karate master on top of being special forces? Yikes, maybe I shouldn't be punching and poking you."

Alie chuckled. "Not karate, although I did study that briefly, as well as several others. Battojutsu was my thing, and Kenjutsu." Sophie looked lost. "You've never heard of either of them, have you?"

"No, but I'm fascinated."

"Most people haven't." Alie continued, explaining that Battojutsu and Kenjutsu were ancient martial arts that heavily emphasized the sword and other long weapons. He described the hours upon hours that he spent in sacred dedication to the discipline of these arts, and how he would struggle sometimes for days to perfect a single move, frustrated with his mortal inability to move as fluidly and flawlessly as his mind. He also recounted that despite winning numerous awards and tournaments, not one of his family members asked him about his successes, much less went to watch him perform.

The practice of martial arts was very hands-on, personal. But cars were different, like a distant, unattainable fantasy. He had never performed well in school, but could recite engine specs on almost every sports car. Yet he was smart enough to know that such cars were far beyond the reach of a poor kid from lowly Shard End, England. So he learned to be satisfied with the glimpses into that world he got from perusing magazines, and occasionally sneaking into car shows.

"Hey now, maybe you shouldn't give up on your dreams so easily," Sophie said as she put her hand on his knee.

"Come on," Alie answered. "They don't exactly pay soldiers enough to buy something like that. I like to dream of those cars, but I'm a realist." He stood up and took several steps down the sidewalk, then stopped to see why Sophie didn't follow. "Let's keep walking," he suggested, "but let's get off this pretentious street."

They wandered off the glitzy Rue du Rhône and down some much less conspicuous side streets. At first Sophie pressed for more details about his past, but soon sensed that he had tapped out talking about himself. So they continued on down narrow stony passages, coming upon a modest courtyard at the base of the St. Pierre Cathedral. Sophie's pace quickened toward the stone steps that led past the imposing pillars and to the towering front door. Alie noticeably lagged behind. Sophie stopped on the bottom step and eyed Alie.

"Do you pray, Alie?" Sophie asked.

"Pray? Seriously? Never," he chuckled.

"Well, maybe you should." Sophie kissed him on the nose and started to pull him up the stairs.

"Aw, really? We have to go inside?"

"I promise I won't make you pray," teased Sophie as she dragged him up the stairs. "I just want to look." Sophie's voice turned to a whisper as she leaned into the heavy wooden door and slipped inside. Alie followed her into an imposing cavern of towering arches that resembled the rib cage of a massive stone dragon. Apart from several multi-colored, stained-glass windows and three large, looming chandeliers, Alie thought the inside of the church looked rather drab. Sophie, on the other hand, was fascinated. "Do you realize which church this is?"

"Some old Catholic cathedral, I'm assuming," muttered Alie.

Sophie shook her head. "Not Catholic," she explained, "not even a little bit." Several people occupying the hard wooden pews turned to inspect as Sophie's words echoed down the cold walls. They appeared to be waiting for the man in a white robe who was stirring behind the pulpit to begin, but he did not seem to be in any sort of a hurry. Sophie leaned in and whispered, "Notice the bare walls and lack of decorations, unlike a Catholic cathedral. They're like that for a reason. This is *the* heart of the Protestant Reformation. This was John Calvin's church." Sophie was clearly disappointed when Alie looked unimpressed.

"And...I'm supposed to know who that is?" shrugged Alie.

Sophie rolled her eyes. "Seriously? You're a caveman." The spike in her voice was met with more disgruntled glares from members of the congregation. She tugged him toward the back pew and forced him to sit. As the white-robed minister continued fidgeting behind the pulpit, Sophie explained softly how Calvin had been one of the prominent leaders of the Protestant movement that defied the Roman Catholic Church. She pointed to a roped-off, non-descript, narrow-backed chair toward the front of the church, and explained that it was Calvin's chair from which he gave sermons that influenced massive changes in Christian theology.

"But most importantly," Sophie continued, oblivious to the increasing volume of her voice, "this cathedral housed the altarpiece on which Konrad Witz originally painted the *Miraculous Draught of Fishes*." Even Alie knew enough to recognize Sophie's favorite painting. He didn't care so much about the painting itself, but loved how she lit up when she talked about it.

Sophie's bright eyes traced every inch of the cathedral's walls and ceiling. Alie, on the other hand, kept his eyes fixed on the floor. Sophie squeezed his hand. "You're fidgeting."

"Sorry. I just really hate churches."

"Why?"

"My mom made me go to church sometimes, and it always made me feel...uncomfortable."

"Because you don't believe?" Sophie asked.

Alie paused to think for a moment. "No, I mean I don't, but that's not really it," Alie reflected. "I suppose there was just something about the...the hypocrisy of my mother sitting in church that was more than I could handle." Alie hesitated while picking at a piece of skin on his thumb, but Sophie did not push him. "I remember her sitting between me and my brother, wearing a purple dress—the only one she ever owned—and us with our hair slicked wet against our heads, and thinking how just the night before she just watched as my step-father whipped us over and over with a switch." Alie's fingernail dug into his thumb, and Sophie could feel his breath quickening. "Once she stayed up late patching holes in our trousers, just so no one would see the marks on our legs."

Sophie's eyes burned with emotion. She leaned in close and took his hand. "Alie, I'm so sorry." She rested her head on his shoulder. Alie's breath slowed as they melted into one another. After several minutes of silence, the voice of the white-robed clergyman belted from the pulpit. As the rest of the congregation came to attention, Alie stood abruptly and walked out of the church.

． ．

Alie was much more relaxed as they walked along the waterfront where Lake Geneva poured into the Rhône River. The distant Jet d'Eau fountain spewed into the crisp evening air. Alie pulled Sophie close as she shivered.

"What about you, Sophie?" Alie asked.

"What about me, what?"

"Why do you choose to believe in a god?" He seemed unsure how to address the topic, but really did want to know. Sophie had never been particularly religious, or adhered to a specific system of beliefs; the question of whether God existed had never crossed her mind.

"There is so much beauty in the world, it can't just be random," she answered.

Alie shook his head. "I'm sorry, but most of what I've seen is ugliness," he replied, "and I've seen a lot of it. How could a god make us live in a place like this?"

Sophie stopped walking and said, "Come here." She turned his gaze toward the sparkling lakefront. "Why did you take me to the watch the sunset a few nights ago?"

"Trying to get a little nookie, I suppose," Alie snickered.

"Ha, ha," she said, rolling her eyes. "Seriously now."

"Seriously? Because I knew you'd love it."

"Why did you think I would love it?" Sophie pushed.

"Because I knew you'd think it was beautiful," answered Alie.

"And was it?"

"Yeah, I suppose," Alie said.

"Do you remember what you said about the sunset?"

Alie hesitated. "I said it was the second most beautiful thing I'd seen since arriving in Geneva."

Sophie smiled. "Don't you think it's possible that the ugliness in the world comes from people, not God?" She leaned back into his chest and he wrapped his arms around her, just as he had done before as they watched the sunset. "And that God gives us beauty to counteract the ugliness?"

"I dunno, Sophie," he whispered. "I thought I knew a lot until a few weeks ago, but now I just don't know." Sophie closed her eyes, wishing she could somehow ease his pain. For the thousandth time in the past few days, she wrestled with the thought that they would be apart in just a few days, and that she may never see him again. Maybe she was naïve to think that she could have any real impact on his world. But she selfishly hoped that a glimpse of true beauty, whether it be a sunset, a painting, or even just a kiss, would give him the courage to step away from the need to fight for a living and maybe, just maybe, find a way to be with her.

"Alie," Sophie said softly.

"Yes?"

"You don't have to sit in a church to find God," she said.

"What do you mean?" Alie asked.

"Well, I feel like I connect with him all the time in the museum."

Alie pondered this for a few moments.

Sophie backed away and leaned on a fence rail, watching him. "What about the karate studio?" she suggested.

"It's not karate…"

"Yeah, yeah, yeah. Whatever," Sophie giggled. "You know what I mean. Your fancy sword karate, whatever it is called. Wouldn't you say you connect with something there?"

"Kenjutsu," he said, amused by her playfulness. "And it's called a dojo, not a studio."

"Whatever, ninja boy," she quipped as she started bouncing in circles around him, jabbing him repeatedly in the chest.

Alie's eyes suddenly lit up. "And…believe it or not, there's one here in Geneva."

"Wait, what?" Sophie stopped bouncing and said, "There's a karate…or Kenjutsu studio in Switzerland?"

"Yep," Alie said, "and that's where we're headed." She squealed as he picked her up and carried her over his shoulder toward the Pont du Mont-Blanc.

. . . .

Alie's entire demeanor changed as he stepped into the dojo's front door and bowed. Sophie stayed outside momentarily, still finding it odd to see Japanese writing on a store front in Geneva. Through the exotic symbols painted across the window, Sophie could see that the dojo was empty except for a small Japanese man who had emerged from the back to greet Alie. Alie bowed again, and then the two began talking. During the conversation, Alie pointed toward the front door. The man gazed at the darkness outside the window, and then smiled at Sophie, motioning her to come inside. As she stepped inside, Alie signaled for her to bow, which she did awkwardly. The man dipped his head, and then retreated silently into a corner.

The dojo's interior was plain but spotless. Its floor was wooden, but almost entirely covered by a black mat. Several long white scrolls bearing minimalist Japanese characters hung from the walls. A selection of swords, both iron and wooden, rested neatly on two racks between the scrolls, with the largest blade suspended directly over the door. Alie circled the small room, examining each sword one by one with the same reverence that Sophie showed the masterpieces at the museum. After inspecting each sword with his hands behind his back, Alie started again, this time educating Sophie about the different weapons, their histories and purposes. Sophie maintained her distance, less interested in the swords than in observing Alie in his element. She had stepped into his world, and she was utterly fascinated.

After his second time around, Alie turned to the man in the corner, who seemed impressed by his knowledge. Alie motioned toward the top sword on the rack and the man nodded. As Alie respectfully removed the sword, the man reached for a knob on the wall that dimmed the lights, then slipped away silently into a back room.

Alie held the sword just inches from his face, moving it horizontally while examining every inch. He stopped halfway and grinned at Sophie over the blade. Then he swung the sword gracefully above his head, where he paused and inhaled deeply before methodically lowering the sword to his waste. Sophie's heart pulsated madly as she watched him flow from position to position, with deliberate pauses in between. As his movements danced somewhere between art and danger, she suddenly felt an irrepressible urge to be near him.

Sophie waited until he turned his back, then carefully took down one of the wooden swords. She took two steps forward and then stood with her feet together and the sword extended. He spun to find her peering at him down the wooden sword. They exchanged no words, but exchanged smiles as he walked to the rack and replaced his iron blade with a wooden one to match Sophie's. He returned to the center of the mat and bowed to Sophie without taking his eyes off her. Sophie playfully bowed back and said, "You ever been beaten by a girl, ninja boy?"

Alie laughed momentarily, but promptly transformed into a menacing frown. Sophie scowled back as fiercely as she could manage. Several seconds passed as they stood, frozen, fixated on one another. Just as Sophie opened her mouth to break the silence, Alie sprung forward to within inches of her. Sophie shrieked and fumbled her sword. Alie lost all sense of formality and bent over laughing. Determined to exploit his moment of weakness, Sophie quickly picked up her sword and lunged toward him. Alie instinctively blocked her charge with one hand and snatched her wrist with the other. He briefly lectured her with his eyes, then, in one swift motion, he disarmed her of her sword and took her to the ground. He sat straddling her, pinning her arms to the floor.

"Have you had enough, Ms. Caldwell," he beamed, "or would you like another go?"

"Lucky!" Sophie fired back as she squirmed stubbornly beneath him. He sprung to his feet and pulled her up with him. Then he chivalrously handed her sword to her and awaited her next move. Sophie swung wildly as he sidestepped and again gently swept her to the mat. She let out the first cuss word he had heard from her, followed by a blush. She got up and charged several more times, and several more times he dismantled her attack and took her to the floor. Alie helped her up for what he was certain would be the last time, and then leaned on his sword and watched her. Sophie momentarily channeled her inner swashbuckler and snuck one through, jabbing him in the ribs. Alie yelped and grabbed his side, Sophie immediately felt guilty.

"Oh man, sorry!" she exclaimed, her concern mixed with an accidental giggle. He immediately grabbed her arms with both hands and jerked her close to him, chest to chest. She squealed again, but he interrupted her by sneaking a kiss. As he started to back away, she grasped the back of his neck with both hands and kissed him passionately. The intensity of the kiss continued for several minutes until Alie froze. Sophie opened her eyes and saw that his eyes too were open. "Do you hear that?" he whispered, and looked over her shoulder.

A muffled whining sound rumbled from a distance, gradually rising as it crept closer. The noise intensified as the earth began to vibrate wildly beneath them. Within seconds, the humming was almost deafening as windows rattled and swords fell from the wall. Alie looked astonished as he pulled Sophie toward the door frame. The droning pulsated between a low growl to an almost earsplitting roar, and Sophie covered her ears. While she stood peering out into the frantic street, the sword hanging over the door fell. Alie caught the blade directly over Sophie's head as she ducked and screamed. And, just as suddenly as it began, the rumbling receded and the earth fell silent. Alie's chest rose and fell rapidly as he reached above the door and gently put the sword back in his place. As he did so, blood began to trickle down his forearm.

"Alie…you're bleeding," Sophie said, reaching for his hand.

"I'm okay." He opened the door and stepped away from her onto the sidewalk. "Let's go see if anyone needs help."

"Wait, let me have a look," Sophie insisted. She took his wrist as the air filled with panicked cries. People poured into the streets with dumbfounded stares. Alie wrapped his hand in his jacket and the two of them set off down the narrow street. They soon found that while many were shocked and frightened, there did not appear to be any injuries. As the streets calmed, Sophie asked, "What in the world was that?"

"I have no idea," Alie answered, still in a daze.

. . . .

Sophie sat next to Alie on the curb, examining his hand. She insisted that he needed stitches, but he refused. He was, instead, completely preoccupied with whatever it was that had just caused the city to shake like it was being tossed in a dryer.

"Was that an earthquake?" he inquired to no one in particular.

"I don't know," Sophie answered, "I've never felt one."

"Well I have, and that didn't feel like any earthquake I've ever felt," Alie said, scratching his head. They had both tried repeatedly to use their phones to check in with their friends, but nothing worked. When Sophie tried again to convince him to seek medical treatment, Alie brushed it aside, saying that Diggs could sew him up as well as any doctor. "Come on," he said, "let's go find them." Alie took several strides down the street before realizing that Sophie was not following. He turned and found her still sitting on the same spot on the curb, staring at the ground.

"Wait a minute…" she said softly. He got closer, wondering what she was up to.

"I'm waiting, I'm waiting. What it is?"

Sophie jumped to her feet. She suddenly started jogging down the street, trying to peer through buildings toward the western horizon. Alie followed. Once Sophie found a good view to the west, and saw nothing but black sky, she spun and faced Alie.

"I think I might know what that was," she muttered as a bewildered look crept across her face. Sophie recounted her conversation with the old man on the train, and his warnings about the underground sub-atomic Collider. Alie had heard of the Hadron collider, but didn't put much stock in the doomsday ranting of some stranger on a train. "I thought he was crazy at first, but he ended up being very sweet, and seemed to really know his stuff." She detailed his attempts to convince his organization that the collider was unstable, and how they repeatedly snubbed him before finally firing him.

"Let me get this straight," Alie paused, "all of this came from one conversation with this wacko, and you believe he might actually have the explanation for all of this?"

"I'm not saying that I do or don't believe him, or that I even have an opinion at all," Sophie answered. "But don't you find it just a bit interesting that I have that conversation, and a week later we're getting tossed around like popcorn?"

Alie shook his head while staring toward the black horizon hanging over the Jura Mountains. "Interesting yes, but significant? Not really.

But he does sound entertaining. Any chance you know where to find him?"

"No," Sophie shook her head. "He promised to visit me at the museum, but never showed up. I haven't seen him since."

"So you two were going to have a date?" Alie said with a sudden grin.

"Do I sense a little jealousy, Mr. Quin? I did mention that he was quite charming, didn't I?" Sophie stood and took Alie by the hand, pulling him down the empty street.

"Well, you're right about one thing," Alie said, "he sounds like a loony."

Chapter Sixteen

Virgil could sense that this conversation was going nowhere. He had carried on several such conversations with everyone from Rikku to the chief of police. No one really listened; they just stared at him like a lunatic. The man in the silky white robe was no different. In fact, he didn't even bother to stop lighting the stumpy candles that topped the brass candelabras posted around the cathedral's interior.

"Well, if he won't warn them, will he allow me to do it?" Virgil pleaded with the boy, who would then translate for the uninterested minister, who was only barely engaged in the conversation at all. Virgil had gone there hoping to find that the minister, tasked with caring for his congregation, would have a sympathetic ear. So far, that had not been the case.

"You mean you want me to ask him if he will let you preach to the church," the boy questioned. "I don't think he'll be too—"

"Son, you must understand the importance of what I'm telling you…and him…and your parishioners," spat a now-exasperated Virgil. The boy just stared back again without translating. Virgil was clearly getting nowhere. "Are you going to—"

"We don't have parishioners," the boy responded smugly. "Those are the Catholics."

Virgil shook his head. This was hopeless. "Okay, I get the hint," he said. "I'll be on my way, but please remember my words, especially if any of your people ask about that strange rumbling the other night. Please just ask him to consider it." Still, the boy gave no translation.

As Virgil nodded farewell to the boy, the minister stopped lighting candles for the first and only time during their visit and turned to Virgil. Looking Virgil directly in the eye, the minister said mechanically, in almost perfect English, "thank you so much for your visit, and may God bless your efforts."

Chapter Seventeen

Sophie stood dazed as a fierce desert wind pelted her face with grains of stinging sand. She struggled to catch a breath through the pungent, swirling smoke. Barren wasteland stretched out in all directions, the distant horizons interrupted only by scattered pillars of black smoke. Echoes of chaotic gunfire mixed with earth-pounding explosions, but from where they came, Sophie couldn't tell.

She was aware that she stood in some foreign place as war raged around her, but had no idea where or how she got there. She also knew she should take cover, but couldn't force herself to move. The bombs rocked the ground with a deafening violence that could crumble buildings, yet she just remained standing, watching and waiting for something, or someone she knew was coming. And then, she saw him.

At first, he was a gray silhouette, his arms pumping like pistons as he sprinted directly toward her. As the smoldering ash and smoke parted, she could make out his tan, military-issue boots, and then his desert-pattern fatigues. She was filled with anticipation as he drew near, expecting someone familiar, and hoping he would rescue her from whatever hell this was. The closer he got, the more powerful he looked, yet even a few feet away his face was completely indistinguishable. Then he stopped, just inches from her face, and she saw a soot-covered young man she did not recognize. He stared at her, expressionless, with dull grey eyes. She tried to say something, or even scream, but nothing came out. After a few seconds, he stepped squarely around her and again broke into a sprint, disappearing into the smoke.

Sophie's eyes moistened with desperation, but she could only manage to turn her head and again face the wall of smoke that now blinded the horizon from her view. For several minutes, she simply stared at the grey nothing. Then the smoke suddenly rippled and splintered as hundreds of soldiers sprinted toward her as if fired from a cannon. They rushed past her like a stampeding herd. She frantically tried to make out their faces, scanning each one as they raced by. But each soldier was identical to the one before him, and to the one who stopped in front of her: the same charcoal eyes, and the same dirty, expressionless faces. Somehow, she knew one among them was meant to help her, but couldn't remember who he was. She fought to clarify her memory, but with each wave of sprinting soldiers that passed, everything made less and less sense.

Then, as if summoned by some unheard command, the soldiers stopped abruptly and looked in unison toward the sky. A shrill hiss filled the air, getting louder and louder until it drowned out everything. But as hard as she tried, Sophie could see nothing in the sky except churning smoke. As she looked back to the sea of soldiers surrounding her, she trembled as she saw their faces, still looking skyward, frozen in terror, with eyes and mouths wide open in anticipation of—

Everything went white as a deafening boom ripped through the air. The ground quaked viciously beneath her. Completely blinded, Sophie reached out for something, or someone, to hold, but there was nothing. Again, she tried to scream out to this forgotten savior who she knew must be there somewhere, but could only produce short bursts of air from her lungs. When the blinding brightness finally gave way, Sophie saw hundreds, if not thousands, of soldiers leveled, face-down and still, all around her. An entire desert of bodies, lying motionless as swaths of smoke crawled over their corpses. But then something faint and distant called out to her, beckoning her to focus. She tried desperately to quiet her sobs and listen as her mind wrestled between two realities.

"Sophie! Sophie!"

Her brain pushed through the fog as the reality of soft hotel sheets enveloped her. Alie's shirtless silhouette stood before her in the moonlight, and it was instantly clear that she had been dreaming. As her thoughts began to thicken, her relief in seeing Alie turned again to confusion. Over Alie's shoulder, the moon hung framed like a painting in the open window. But she struggled to understand why the moon was dancing within the frame.

"Alie, why is the moon shaking?" she asked while rubbing her eyes.

"It's not the moon, it's the window," Alie answered. She realized that he was bracing himself against a chair and straining to look out the window. "It's happening again."

Sophie jumped to her feet and strode toward the window. "What's happening?" As she said it, she could feel the building swaying beneath them.

Alie held up a finger, shushing Sophie. "Do you hear it?"

"Hear what?"

"Shhhh!" He froze with his palm facing Sophie. She held her breath, and made out a low, whirring sound creeping just under the earth's surface.

"Just like at the dojo?" she whispered.

"Just like at the dojo," Alie repeated.

They stood motionless, listening to the humming as it rose and fell with increasing intensity. With each pulsating wave, the walls shook harder. Alie leapt to Sophie and embraced her, grasping the bed post with his other hand. Just when Alie's grip relaxed briefly, their entire world heaved upward beneath them, lurching and tossing them like rag dolls. And then all was still.

Sophie had crashed to the floor, followed by a lamp and an alarm clock from the bedside table. Her hip throbbed in pain, but she ignored it and reached for Alie. He had tumbled over the chair, but had already begun crawling toward Sophie.

"Are you okay?" he asked frantically.

"I think so. My hip hurts; I think I hit it on the corner of the bed, but it's fine."

"Are you sure? Let me take a look."

"No, really," she insisted, "it's fine." The room was completely dark except for the moonlight. Alie tried to turn on the lamp, but there was no power. Sophie dragged herself to her feet to prove she was okay. He sprung to his feet as well, and they cautiously made their way to the balcony.

People packed the streets as the night air buzzed with car alarms, panicked shouts and sirens. For the second time in just a few days, Alie and Sophie set out to see if anyone needed help.

. . . .

Sophie's limp worsened on the way back to the hotel, prompting Alie to insist on piggy-backing her up the stairs. Alie scaled the staircase effortlessly, even with Sophie clinging to his back. He rambled on about that night's mysterious events, but Sophie hardly heard him. Despite having just endured the second such unexplained, and highly unsettling phenomenon in less than a week, she couldn't keep her mind off her dream. The image of a thousand dead soldiers strewn across the desert played over and over in her mind. Even worse was the knowledge that there was someone among them she was meant to find, but could not. It was just a dream, she told herself, but felt it was something more.

"Do you think we're in danger here?" Alie asked as they simultaneously collapsed onto the bed. "You know, with these strange earthquake things going on?"

Sophie didn't respond, instead staring blankly at the ceiling.

"Sophie? You okay?" He rolled to his side and pushed her hair back from her forehead. "You seem kind of freaked out."

"Two days," Sophie whispered.

"Huh?" Alie propped himself up higher to meet her gaze. "What do you mean 'two days'?"

Sophie sighed deeply and closed her eyes, fighting to muster up courage. "You know what I mean, Alie. Or at least I think you do, or should." Alie flopped on his back, his fingers interlocked behind his head. As he lay silent, Sophie could sense his breath hastening, just as it had in the church. Before now, it was the only time she had seen him struggle like this, and he clearly didn't like it. She hated to be the one to make him suffer, but she worried that if she didn't bring it up, he would just disappear two days later and leave her to forever wonder what in the world had happened between them.

"Alie, are we just going to ignore the fact that you are leaving the day after tomorrow?" she asked softly. The profile of his face was outlined by the moonlight. Her stomach churned as she held her breath and waited for an answer. She had never even come close to feeling anything like this before, and couldn't bear to think that in just over forty-eight hours, it would be over. Despite what was coming, however, she thought that maybe, just maybe, she could survive him leaving if she knew that it was tearing him up as well, that he too would be counting the days until they saw each other again. But right now, her biggest fear was the possibility of *not* knowing; that was something she would never survive.

"The last thing I would ever want to be is one of those 'what-are-we' girls, especially so soon after we met," she continued. "But what am I supposed to do, Alie? Just pretend like the past few weeks didn't happen? Just act like my heart isn't being ripped from my chest when you get back on that plane? Like I didn't completely fall—"

"Don't say it!" Alie cried out as he sprung upward and sat on the end of the bed.

"Say what, Alie? The 'L' word?" She too sat up, determined to force the conversation if necessary. "You're scared to death that I'm going to tell you I love you, aren't you?"

"Please, Sophie," he growled as he leaned forward and buried his forehead in his hands. "Don't…"

"Don't what?" she shot back. "Don't ruin everything? Would that really be so bad, me mentioning the word 'love' in the same sentence as me and you? I know it's only been a few weeks, and in any other circumstances it would be crazy to talk about it so early. But…" She paused a moment to fight back the lump that was creeping into her throat. "But I just have to have something to go on when you leave. I just need to know what to tell myself at night when I can't sleep knowing you may be getting shot at. Or what about every time I walk by my favorite painting in the museum and all I can think about is you standing in that room behind me, watching my every move?" She crawled across the bed and reached for his shoulder as she whispered, "I just have to know when you get back on that plane, will I ever hear from you again?"

Alie rocked back and forth and shrugged her hand off his shoulder. He shot to his feet and retreated into a dark corner of the room. Sophie stared at him for several minutes waiting for an answer, but doubting it would come. She again fought her emotions, which with every passing minute of his silence were threatening to turn from frustration to rage.

"So that's just it?" she snapped. "Just a two-week fling. You got to hook up with the naïve American girl and then fly off to wherever, while I spend my days pretending to be interested in showing paintings to a bunch of flabby, sweaty tourists, when I'm really dying inside," her voice intensified, "all the while wondering if the reason I haven't heard from you is because you're dead, or just don't care?"

He shot forward from the shadows, and Sophie froze at the sight of the moonlight reflecting off his moistened eyes. He was trembling, with his fists clenched at his side. "Please stop!" he yelled. "If you had any idea, you would just stop."

"Just talk to me, Alie. That's all I ask," she pleaded. She took a step toward him, but he extended his hand, commanding her to stop.

"You want me to talk? Fine, here it is: I like you. I really like you a lot," he stumbled over his words, avoiding eye contact. "Who knows, maybe it is love. But I cannot afford to let myself fall for someone, especially for you. That's not a luxury I have."

"What is that supposed to mean?" she demanded.

"It means I have absolutely no control over where I will be next month, or maybe even next week. Hell, I don't even know where I will be the day after tomorrow. And if I did know, I couldn't tell you. How can I expose you to that kind of lifestyle?"

"I don't know, Alie," she answered. "I'm sure that would be hard, but I have to believe having you part time is better than not at all."

"It's not just that." He leaned over and gripped the table with both hands as if to steady himself. "What I do for a living is nasty, Sophie, worse than anything you can imagine." He turned to her and jabbed himself in his chest with his finger as his eyes bore deep into her soul. "I *kill* for a living, Sophie. Have you ever thought of that? When I show up, people *die*!"

Chills rippled down Sophie's spine. She knew what he was, and what that involved. And though she was not scared of him, she couldn't help but be moved when confronted by this side of him, a side that she knew must exist, but that she had not known until now.

"This guy you think you've come to know over the past few weeks, Sophie, it's not really me. This gentle...whatever you think I am..." The flimsy hotel room table creaked as he tightened his grip. "We're like beasts that they just plop down in the middle of Hell for a few days to devour whomever they label as the bad guys. Then it's off to some other version of Hell. Over, and over, and over."

"You don't have to be a soldier forever, you know," she said. "And then what? Might there be time for us?"

Alie released his grip on the table and closed his eyes. "That's not it exactly, well not everything." He glanced at her briefly and then collapsed into a chair. "I've tried to find a way to explain this to you, but I'm just not good at talking about stuff...about me."

"So I've noticed."

"I don't talk about my past, but I know that I owe it to you," he began with his gaze fixed on the floor. "Love is foreign to me. No one has ever loved me, ever. So I never allowed myself to love anyone."

"Well, this may be your chance," said Sophie, "and you're just going to throw it away because you're scared? Maybe it's right here, staring you in the face, and you're turning it down. Maybe someone out there is handing you something great to make up for before."

"Who? God?" Alie scoffed.

"Maybe."

"This is precisely why I don't believe," the words burst from inside him as indignation filled his face. "If that were true, if he really does exist, then why does he curse me? Why do others get to experience something amazing like this? But me? I find something, someone like you, only to have it torn from my hands a few days later."

"It doesn't have to be that way, Alie."

"Yes it does; that's how it's always been, Sophie." He leaned back and looked blankly out the window.

"Just because people dumped on you in the past, don't let that ruin this now," Sophie kept on, not willing to give in.

"You don't get it, do you?" he continued. "I closed that part off a long time ago. I shut it down. I used to pray every night for even the smallest sign that my mom gave a shit about me. I never got it. I prayed that my dad would come back, even for a little while, just to see what it was like to have a father. Never happened." Alie's voice cracked. "I asked God over and over to make my big brother pay attention to me, just to acknowledge that I exist. I hated him, but I would've given anything for just one sign that I meant something to him, that the pathetic childhood we were sharing made us connected in some way. But nothing."

Sophie couldn't hold back, was sobbing. She wanted to embrace him and show him love, but knew that as much as it hurt, he needed to get this out.

"So I built a big wall and hid behind it," he struggled to continue. "I made a conscious decision that love doesn't exist, at least not for me, and with that went any notion that there may be a god. And if he did exist, then I wanted nothing to do with him for putting me through all that." He paused and slowly walked to the window, leaning out into the night air. "So off I went to blow up stuff and kill Arabs. Perfect job for me, a guy with no heart, beyond feeling."

The silence in the room was excruciating. Sophie searched desperately for the right thing to say, but instead just sat on the bed, trying to dry her eyes with her sleeves.

"And then there's you," he said meekly.

"What?" she said, puzzled. "What did I do?"

"You went to a stupid club one night with your stupid roommates and just had to walk up to me and open your mouth and screw up everything."

She froze, completely dumbfounded. He was leaning against the window frame, talking to Sophie, but facing the stars. "You're the first and only person I have known in years, maybe ever, who I could love. And now, in two days, I'm gone, and that's it." His head drooped forward, his voice faint. "That's it."

"But it doesn't have to be," she pleaded. "It's only over if you give up." She strode toward him and grasped his bare shoulders. He turned and reluctantly took her by the waist as he shut his eyes. "So, don't give up," she added as she gently placed her hands on his face and kissed him with everything she had. He held her tightly and accepted her kiss for a moment, but then backed away slowly with a defenseless stare. Then he reached for his shirt and walked toward the door. "No, Alie, please," Sophie begged as he paused with his hand on the door handle. But it wasn't enough; he disappeared down the hallway and into the night.

Sophie rushed to the window, but never saw him. She thought about running after him, but what more could she do? Was there anything left to say? Or was he too broken? Would she have to face her shattered heart head-on and find a way forward without him? Knowing she would not sleep that night, she sat on the end of the bed, buried her face in her hands and cried.

Chapter Eighteen

Sophie nearly drove herself mad pacing back and forth from the balcony to the door, aching for him to return. But after waiting over an hour, she knew there was no use in staying. Plus, the hotel room had become suffocating and, if Alie wasn't coming back, she didn't want to be there either. But before she left, she searched the bedside table and found a small pad of paper and a miniature pencil. After trudging through several drafts that she crumpled and stuffed in her pocket, she settled on a simple, honest plea, and a final invitation:

> Alie,
>
> I think I've said everything I can say. If I thought I could tell you I love you and it would help, I would. If I thought it would help if I said I didn't, I'd do that too. I cannot fix your past, and I'm apparently not very good at the present. But that's not what I want; I don't want to fix you. I just want to be with you, whether it's the broken you, or the better you, or even the "real" you that you swear I won't like. I just want you, however I can get you.
>
> So if all that's left for me to do is beg, I will. I beg you not to give up. I beg you to remember me while you're away and promise that, when you return, you will at least try to see if we can love each other. I beg you please, please, don't give up. I know I won't.
>
> Love, Sophie
>
> P.S. In case you're willing to at least talk, I'll be at the Le Petit Marché tomorrow evening at 6:00 p.m. It would mean everything to me if you were there.

Time crawled, minute by excruciating minute, the next day at the museum. When she wasn't counting the ticks of the clock, Sophie watched raindrops trickle down the glass like tiny, gray snakes slithering toward the earth. The dreary morning imitated her mood, and did a fair job at keeping tourists away. Ms. Martineau, to her credit, mercifully left Sophie mostly to herself during the day. While finding a way to keep herself occupied would have probably done her some good, the likelihood of her concentrating on anything other than being at the cafe at 6:00 was dreadful, to say the least.

At some point in the late afternoon, Ms. Martineau found Sophie seated, biting her nails on the top step of the long staircase that descended onto the main lobby. Ms. Martineau flashed a grin that was equal parts patronizing and affectionate. When she asked if she could sit down next to her, Sophie responded, "Of course."

Ms. Martineau groaned a bit as she squatted, holding onto the rail before coming to rest on her backside next to Sophie. She put her hand on Sophie's knee and, after a long sigh, said, "Well, Ms. Caldwell, you're usually a dynamite worker, one of the best," she started with a grumble, which quickly turned to a chuckle. "But today, well, you're a dud."

"I'm very sorry, Ms. Martineau," Sophie began before Ms. Martineau nudged her with her shoulder.

"Aw, don't apologize, girl. We've all been there. Even I have fallen in love twice, and one of them loved me back," she chuckled. "But those are stories for another, less gloomy day."

"I'd love to hear them," Sophie whispered with her head bowed. She felt guilty, like she had been letting Ms. Martineau down the past several days. She wanted to apologize, and tell her how much she greatly appreciated her patience, but doing so would likely turn on the waterworks, and she wanted to avoid breaking down in front of Ms. Martineau at all costs.

"If this guy breaks your heart, darling, I'll track him down myself," Ms. Martineau said, shaking her finger.

"He's leaving," Sophie added softly. "Tomorrow."

"Aaaaahhh," Ms. Martineau replied, nodding her head. She wrapped an arm around Sophie's shoulders and squeezed. "Back to combat?"

"I think so." She only knew he would be gone and that, unless he miraculously showed up at the cafe in a few hours, she had likely seen him for the last time.

"You can't worry so much, Sophie," Ms. Martineau said. "If it's meant to be, fate will make it happen."

"I wish I could believe that," Sophie answered.

"Oh, believe it, mon chouchou. Never underestimate what the universe can pull off if it's meant to be."

. . . .

At 5:59 p.m., Sophie told the waitress for the second time that she was waiting for someone, and would not be ordering until he arrived. At 6:17 p.m., she repeated herself for the fourth time. This time of the evening, Le Petit Marché café was always bustling, and tables were at a premium. Unlike their usual haunt—the quaint COTTAGE CAFÉ—THERE WAS NOTHING QUAINT OR "PETIT" ABOUT the trendy Le Petit Marché. It was generally overflowing with the chic and ambitious, desperate to be seen sipping wine or the most expensive cup of coffee in town. Sophie did not particularly like Le Petit Marché, and ordinarily would not have chosen it for such a meeting with Alie. But the only other cafe name she could remember in the heat of the moment while writing the note was the Cottage Café, and the probability of running into her roommates there was just too risky.

Sophie had arrived early hoping to snag one of the outer tables that protruded onto the sprawling concrete plaza of Bourg-de-Four Square. The square sits at the convergence of a maze of narrow streets and picturesque buildings in the heart of Geneva's Old Town. After work hours, the plaza filled with shopping-bag-toting pedestrians and mopeds buzzing around café tables and the plaza's gurgling, marble fountain. Sophie hoped the outlying table would give her a strategic vantage point from which she would see Alie coming. But as of 6:21 p.m., she was still sitting alone, and it was looking like it would remain that way. The waitress had already given up, and she was getting dizzy watching the second hand on her watch. She plopped a coin down on the table and stood to survey the plaza one last time as she fought back tears. So, this was it, she thought.

She was determined to duck into the crowds and disappear into the city for the next several hours, if not late into the night. Wandering the streets like a brokenhearted zombie would surely be better than having to fend off questions from her roommates. But just as she slipped into the crowd, a hand grabbed her wrist and pulled her back.

"Not so fast," Alie whispered into her ear. He pulled her close as his lips touched her cheek.

"So fast?" Alie scoffed, pointing to her watch. "You're nearly a half hour late."

"I'm sorry. I was trying to find something . . . for you."

She wanted to be upset with him, but she was so happy he came that she just couldn't find it in her. "I thought you'd given up," she said.

"No, Sophie. Not hardly," he answered. "Please, can we sit?" The waitress watched them re-take Sophie's table and rolled her eyes. Alie sat directly across the table from Sophie and leaned forward, resting his elbows on his knees. Just hours before, he was a frenzied mess before vanishing from the hotel room. But now he seemed as if he was on a mission, with a look of laser-focused determination.

"So?" Sophie began.

"So, first I should beg your forgiveness," he responded.

"For what?"

"For last night," he continued. "That was selfish and immature, and I absolutely do not blame you for being upset."

Sophie sighed and shook her head. "I'm not mad."

"You're not?"

"I don't have time to be mad," she said. "*We* don't have time."

Alie understood. "You're right, as usual. We're sort of out of time, aren't we?" He leaned back deep into his chair and ran all ten fingers through his closely buzzed hair. "I know you already know this, but I feel like I still owe you some kind of explanation. My past, it…it's something that I haven't ever really tried to come to terms with. I don't really have the tools to deal with it, but that shouldn't be part of this."

Sophie reached across the table and said, "Alie, give me your hand." He placed his hand into hers. She gripped tightly. "Enough," she said boldly. "Forget about what happened last night, or years ago; we'll deal with that later. No more letting stuff from the past mess up the present. Tell me about us, right here, right now. Because if we can figure that out, I have faith that everything else will fall into place."

He smiled and closed his eyes, inhaling deeply as if he was refreshed by her suggestion. "Sophie, you're so good. All of the amazing things about you are all of the things that are missing in me."

"Then let's make this work," Sophie pleaded. She had no idea exactly how it would work, but all she needed was a chance.

"Okay, whatever it takes, but not here." Alie stood suddenly and said, "Let's go back to the lake front and finish this discussion. It's our last night, and I don't want to spend it trying to talk over this crowded madness."

"I would like that," Sophie replied as she got to her feet.

"Wait," he held his hands out, suggesting that she sit back down. "Wait here for just a moment. That something I wanted to bring to you is just around the corner. I'll be right back. Do *not* leave."

She grinned as he shot off into the crowd, and watched him vanish around a corner. After last night, she was tempted to not let him out of her sight. But she had to trust him, and would wait for him, no matter how long it took.

Chapter Nineteen

The late afternoon sun had dipped behind the buildings that walled Bourg-de-Four square, soon to disappear beyond the horizon. But as the daylight slipped away, Geneva's nightlife came alive. Sophie sat and waited for Alie to return while sipping from the sweet and acidic Orangina bottle she had ordered to pacify the waitress. She watched the passers-by with their deep shopping bags, some so big that she wondered if she could curl up and fit inside. She soon grew restless, so she pulled out the paint brush from her back pocket that had become rather uncomfortable pressed against the wrought-iron chair.

The bristles had worn down significantly over the years since her father died, with less than half remaining. Much of the burgundy paint had chipped away from the handle, exposing the bare wood underneath. The metal of the ferrule was dotted with rust spots and tiny dents. But it was Sophie's most prized possession, and it went with her everywhere.

She considered for a moment ghost painting the plaza, with its street venders and throngs of pedestrians. She imagined the look she would get from the waitress. But she didn't want to get evicted from her table, at least not until Alie returned. So instead she continued waiting, and twirling the brush between her fingers while starting at her drink, which sat nearly empty next to Alie's half-drunk beer. Her eyes danced back and forth between the two, momentarily entranced by the contrast between the tangy, pale orange Orangina, and the deep amber of his beer. The drowsiness from the lack of sleep the night before was setting in, making it hard to peel her eyes away. Something about the two liquids seemed strange, something beyond the contrast of colors that had her mesmerized. Her brain was slow to register, but she forced herself out of her trance to lean forward and take a better look.

Sophie wasn't touching the table, nor was anyone else, but the surface of Alie's beer was rippling as if shaken by an invisible hand. Sophie watched for several seconds as the tiny ripples grew in frequency. Her Orangina also began to slosh slightly against the side of the bottle. She looked at the people around her, as if to get some sort of confirmation that she was not seeing things. But everyone was too wrapped up in the banter at their tables. She noticed two tall glasses of wine on the table next to her, which were also rippling like tiny crimson oceans. Looking up, her wide-eyed gaze met the puzzled stare of a woman, who had simultaneously noticed Sophie staring at her table and the wine that was mysteriously agitating itself inside her glass. The woman seemed bewildered, and Sophie wanted to say something. But then her bottle began to rattle wildly against the metal tabletop.

A sea of gasps and shrieks travelled across the plaza as a rumbling slowly overtook the roar of the crowd. Some ran several steps and then stopped, as if they suddenly remembered the past two mysterious, earthquake-like events, and realized there really wasn't anywhere to go. Others grasped for something solid—the fountain, a chair, a light post. But most looked frantically toward the sky for no reason other than that they didn't know where else to look. The unnerving panic was palpable as reality set in: it was happening again.

The rumbling intensified like the last two events, but this time much more quickly and powerfully. It reverberated like an infernal siren between deep, subterranean growls and concentrated, piercing screeches. Glasses crashed to the ground as they bounced off the tables. Wooden shutters crashed repeatedly against the building walls, and flagpoles flailed violently as their flags popped back and forth.

Sophie jumped to her feet, searching hysterically for Alie, but struggled to stay upright as the earth beneath her swelled like it was breathing. She was horrified when she saw the first chunk of building fall and crash to the ground, followed by another, and another. People did their best to scramble away from the falling debris, but fell as they tried to escape. Sophie could see terrified faces, but couldn't hear their screams. The pulsating rumble had grown into a deafening roar, and Sophie desperately wanted to cover her ears. She didn't dare let go of her table, which was hardly stable enough to provide any security anyway. Sophie thought her ears might split open, and was about to vomit. She lost her sense of balance, and after nearly stumbling over the table, knew she must lay down or else she would pass out. Just as she grasped the edge of the table to try and lower herself, the jarring vibrations ceased and the earth stood still.

Chaotic sobs rang through the plaza as some screamed out for family and friends, and others for mercy from above. Sophie could barely muster a coherent thought as her head pounded and she struggled to find her footing. She forced herself to take deep breaths and concentrated on staying conscious. Her relief that the horror had stopped was brief, however, as she suddenly remembered that the rumbling had also paused briefly during the two prior events, before one enormous final…

In an instant, Sophie's mind fractured into a billion pieces. Excruciating pain tore through her like magmatic, electrical currents. She saw only severe and blinding whiteness. A shrill cry burst from within, as if it did not belong to her. Her mind then snapped back like a rubber band, into a sudden state of hyper-awareness, yet her body was unable to move. For a moment, time froze.

And then, as quickly as her body petrified, her muscles were liberated, and her body crashed to the earth. She watched it collapse beneath her like a mound of limp rags. Yet somehow her awareness hovered above, stunned to see her own lifeless body crumpled in a heap.

Sophie extended her two trembling hands. She recognized them as hers only by their familiar shape, but they felt completely foreign. Her silky skin was gone, replaced by steely gray flesh. She dragged her fingers across her arm and felt almost nothing, so she dug her fingernails in deep and watched as a smoky vapor rippled beneath her almost transparent skin.

Please, no. She couldn't be. Was she dreaming? Unconscious? Had something fallen on her and knocked her out, or had she fainted?

The bright color of her crimson jacket was evaporating before her eyes, slowly fading into an overcast gray-red, barely distinguishable from her blue jeans. The multi-colored lines of her plaid backpack hanging from her chair melted together into a monochrome mess. She ran her fingers down her thighs, making sure she still found legs inside of her pants. She noticed that somewhere below her knees, around mid-calf, her legs disappeared into the crumpled form of her body. Her body was still visible, lying in its unnatural fetal position, but now it looked like she was staring at it through a hazy looking glass. She lifted her leg, again revealing her foot. She raised both feet several times, and each time she lowered them, she was astonished to see them disappear inside of her body. She closed her eyes and took several deep breaths out of habit, but felt no air passing through her nostrils. She tried not to panic as she accepted the sickening reality that she was, without a doubt, no longer inhabiting her own body.

Sophie squeezed her eyes shut, terrified at what she might see if she looked up at the surrounding plaza. And for the first time, she became aware of the ghastly chorus of crying, shouting and moaning that permeated the air. She reluctantly opened her eyes and surveyed her dismal surroundings. Hundreds of ghostly forms checkered the plaza like a supernatural chessboard, with their motionless bodies strewn across the ground beneath them. Some knelt, rocking back and forth as they desperately pawed at the foggy outlines of their corpses. Others stood erect and threw their heads back as their shrieks echoed from the walls of the plaza.

The facades of the Palais de Justice and seventeenth-century bourgeois homes that walled the square now towered overhead like bleak prison walls, stripped of their previously charming details. The gray sky above displayed only a faint glow where the setting sun should have been, casting an ethereal shadow against the buildings. Only moments before, Sophie had caught a glimpse of the first star of the evening, but now the heavens above were obscured by a sinister haze. The floral fragrances that had danced on the breeze were also gone, replaced by nothing. Sophie could feel no wind, could smell no smells, and in the few moments between the groans and screams, there was no sound at all.

Sophie's eyes burned raw with emotion. She had been scared to make a sound, but could no longer hold back the sob that erupted from within her. But where tears would usually follow, none came. She buried her face in her hands, but immediately withdrew them, shocked to feel the cold, ceramic-like texture of her skin. She traced the contours of her face, which still felt like her own. Yet it was icy and almost completely void of sensation. Did she still look the same? Would she even be recognizable to anyone? To her mother and brother? To Alie?

Alie!

She frantically searched the sea of unintelligible faces, but none of them looked like his. In fact, none of them looked like anyone, or anything she had ever seen or imagined. Any distinguishing details were fading into blurred images that only barely resembled a human face. She saw sunken blots where eyes once were, and a withered cavity in place of a mouth that gaped open and shut as they spewed their cries into the night.

She knew what this must mean, but could not convince herself to accept it. This can't be happening, not now. Please, not now, not yet.

Sophie dropped to her knees and grasped for her body, only to see her hands disappear into its outline. Over and over she thrust her hands in and out of the shape of her body, but it did not move. She felt an indescribably magnetic pull toward her body, which only made her want to get closer. But no matter how hard she tried, it would not budge. She leapt over the body like a frog and crouched only inches from her face. "Wake up!" she screamed. "GET UUUUUUUUUUP!" Nothing.

Sophie then laid on her side just behind her back, doing her best to position herself in the same position that her body had taken after the fall. She raised her head several times to try and memorize exactly how it looked, and then slowly scooted herself inside its outline. The same powerful bond she had felt with her hands now flowed through her completely and, for a brief moment, she swore she could feel her lungs inflate as she frantically inhaled. She jerked her head upright, desperately hoping to not see her lifeless corpse beneath her. But there it was.

She tried again, doing everything in her power to make each inch of herself an exact replica of her crumpled cadaver, to disappear completely inside of her own form. After lying on her left side just inside her body, she craned her head backward until she was looking at the back of her own head. Then she pushed her face through her own head, searching through the inside of her skull to align her eyes, in whatever spectral, spiritual form they were in now, with her actual human eye sockets. For a second, she went too far, and the view beyond her face opened into the grayish light beyond. But she pulled back until her two faces, as best as she could tell, became one.

She lay still, silently struggling to somehow reunite with her flesh. She tried to block out the cries and groans around her and to force herself to connect, to feel like she had before, to force her chest to rise and fall like it had every minute of her entire life. She felt safer lying inside her body, as if it provided a momentary respite from the horror that surrounded her. And she was scared, so very terrified that when she rose, she would again find that her body had not moved with her. But she knew she couldn't lie there forever. She must force herself to get up, or else she would never know. After several motionless minutes, she began by twitching her finger. This time she would take it slow, hoping that small movements would allow the recoupling to take place naturally...although this was anything but natural.

Sophie bent and straightened each finger, one at a time, searching for some sign that her corporeal digits were following along. She couldn't feel anything different, but dared not raise her head for fear that she might disrupt her plan. So, she continued, meticulously advancing from finger to finger, and then opening and closing her hand entirely. She rolled her eyes downward, straining to catch a glimpse of her hand opening and shutting. But without moving her head, she couldn't look down, so she closed her eyes.

She gradually worked up the courage to bend her elbow and slide her forearm upward toward her eyes. Her arm was extended, elbow bent, with her hand suspended in front of her face. Something didn't feel right, but she forced herself to ignore it and hope instead. Before opening her eyes, she said a prayer to herself that when she did, she would wake up from this nightmare and see her delicate hand welcoming her back to the other side. She felt suddenly guilty as she thought how many times she had been ashamed of her hands—they were not particularly lady-like, with her nails chewed to the quick and all too often speckled with dried paint. But now she would give anything to have them back again. She thought of how comforting her father's paint brush would feel if she could just hold it again. And, even more, how it would be to feel Alie take her hand in his, not just once, but a thousand more times.

Please. I don't want to open my eyes if nothing has changed. Please, please, please. I'll do anything. Please let my hand be there, not the weird phantom hand, but my actual, real hand. Please. She opened her eyes.

The sallow, ashen appendage that hovered before her seemed even less a part of her than before. She slammed her palm into the ground in rage and lifted her head. She dragged herself to her knees and hunched over her cadaver. "Noooooooooooooooo!" she howled, far louder than the other cries she had heard so far that night. Her physical sensations were dulled, but the emotions—the desperation, the nauseating sorrow, the despair—were exponentially more intense than any she had ever felt before.

Please, no. Please. I cannot be…

Dead.

Please.

She had aggressively refused to accept any such thought, but it was becoming more and more difficult to ignore what was all around her. There was simply no other explanation.

"Somebody help, please!" Maybe if she screamed loud enough, her voice would carry through to the other side. Maybe someone would come along and give her CPR, or do something even more miraculous to rescue her. "Can anyone hear me? Help us!" She couldn't see anything moving on the other side. She could only see bodies, through the fading connection with the physical world, slumped over and lifeless like her own.

And where was Alie? He had made her swear to stay put at the table as he hurried off, only minutes before the quaking started. Now she had no idea what happened to him. Was he "dead" like her? Or did he survive the…whatever it was. Was he trying to find her? Could he find her? Would he recognize her frightful new appearance? Would she recognize him? As she looked at the other spirits in the plaza, which were barely even recognizable as human, she panicked as she realized there might be no way to identify one another. He might actually be there in the plaza with her, and she not know it.

"Alie!" she shouted, "Alie, can you hear me?" She examined the nearby distorted faces, searching for some sign that one of them knew her voice. Instead, she saw a huddle of four spirits who appeared annoyed by her screaming. She suddenly felt bizarrely embarrassed, although she wasn't sure why given the circumstances. Eight eyes, peering at her from barren cavities sunken into hollow faces, made her shudder. But she considered that if they appeared this way to her now, she must look equally horrific to them as well.

As terrified as she was, she wanted to see if it was possible to communicate. But the fear of leaving her body, even for a second, was overwhelming. There was the conscious, immediate apprehension of not knowing what would happen to her body if she stepped away. But there was something deeper: an intrinsic, indispensable union that made the thought of separation from her body seem wholly unnatural. She felt fiercely protective of it, but petrified that she really had no way to defend it if necessary. Regardless, leaving was not an option. Maybe she would muster up the courage soon enough, but not yet.

The four huddled-together… "people", for lack of a better word, continued to stare. They were talking to each other, somehow, but she couldn't make out the words, or even the language they were using. She waved her hand in their direction, hoping to suggest some sense of cordiality.

"Oh, so now I'm a friendly ghost," Sophie whispered to herself. "Like Casper. This is so damn weird."

She fixed her eyes on the ground, nervously determined to avoid their frightening stares. But as she tried her best to pretend like they weren't there, their awareness of her only intensified. One extended an elongated finger toward her while the other three started in her direction. Sophie was immediately aware that their strides did not match the distance they traveled and, before she could react, they stood just feet away. The shrill, indecipherable chatter pouring from their mouths surrounded Sophie, but she still understood nothing. Despite their ghastly appearance, Sophie didn't believe they meant her any harm. In fact, they were likely just as scared and disoriented as she was, but for reasons she did not understand, were apparently able to communicate with each other. Perhaps it was because they knew each other from before, and that connection continued on this side. Whatever the reason, Sophie envied them for at least having one another, while she was all alone.

The four of them fell suddenly silent as one reached out for Sophie, causing her to jerk away. As it leaned in a second time, she could barely make out a face peering through a misty shroud. This time, Sophie didn't move and, instead, watched its gaunt finger touch her shoulder. The sensation was faint, barely noticeable. But what did surprise Sophie was the slight puff of what looked like a bluish smoke that rose from her shoulder when the finger touched her, and then evaporated in an instant. She exchanged a perplexed look with the spirit, and it poked her again, this time significantly harder. A slightly larger wisp of grayish-blue smoke puffed, and then vanished as quickly as it appeared.

Sophie patted herself several times on the arm, but saw no blue vapor. She reached out and tapped the spirit stiffly on the shoulder. An almost identical cloud arose, and then it was gone. Sophie and the spirit exchanged looks, and Sophie managed a smile. After several silent seconds, a black hole opened in the spirit's face where a mouth should be, followed by a string of horrific sounds billowing from within. Unable to control her fright, Sophie jumped back and covered her face with her hands. She didn't know if that was supposed to be a sentence or a scream, but it was more than she could handle. She hoped that when she removed her hands from her face, the four spirits would be gone. But when she looked again, there they were, just standing there, completely still, staring at her.

She badly wanted to run away, but she just couldn't convince herself to leave her body behind. So instead, she tried to reason with herself. If they wanted to hurt me, or if they could hurt me, Sophie thought, they would have done so by now. But she simply couldn't stand to look at them any longer. So, at the risk of appearing rude—to the extent that such a thing even mattered anymore—she turned her back to them and crouched next to her body.

For some time, Sophie listened for the sound of the spirits walking away—or floating, or whatever it is that these beings do—but she heard nothing. She couldn't bring herself to turn around again and look, so she laid down next to her body, this time facing away from it. With her back to her corpse, she found herself looking directly at the marble fountain. It wasn't too tall, or too small. Before she thought it was quite lovely, yet somewhat unassuming stuck there in the middle of the hustle and bustle of the hectic plaza. But now it seemed to tower ominously over her and the bodies strewn across the square. Most of its ornamental details were dulled considerably in this phantom realm, but Sophie still found it to be beautiful, perhaps the only beautiful thing she could make out.

As she lay motionless, staring at the fountain, she tried to put some logic to everything that happened. She tried to recall everything she had ever been taught about the afterlife – Heaven, Hell, etc. She had spent her fair share of time in church, and had read even more about the diverse ways in which humans try and make sense of the spiritual and divine: Catholics, Protestants, Mormons, Adventists, and even Muslims, Hindu, and many other eastern faiths. She had never been overtly religious, but did have a deep curiosity about what made those religions tick. But at the heart of any religious movement or belief system was one central and fundamental question: was there some sort of life after death? Most religions didn't trifle with such a basic issue, taking that part for granted and moving on to much more profound and divisive topics. But, as evidenced by her talks with Alie on the matter, if you can't get past that central question, you can't really get anywhere when discussing spirituality, or the afterlife, or God.

Now, however, Sophie considered that there was obviously no reason to debate the existence of spirits or life after death. She was living proof…well, maybe not "living", but proof nonetheless. But so far, she was definitely not a fan of this newfound certainty of the afterlife. It was ugly, and dismal, and void of hope. She couldn't wrap her head around where she was, or what state she was in. Where were the pearly gates, or the light at the end of the tunnel, or God forbid, the fire and brimstone? She was certain this was not heaven, and as crappy as it was, it didn't quite seem bad enough to be Hell. She wondered if it was some type of purgatory-like place, a type of suspended existence stuck in between. Maybe she just had to wait here until something profound happened, like some sort of epiphany, or a judgment. Or perhaps if she did leave her body, she would be swept off to hell, or get lost in this spirit prison forever. If she had to remain here without her family and, of course, without Alie, it may as well be hell.

And what about her dad? If she were, in fact, dead, then was he here somewhere? Surely not. Surely a man as kind and loving as he was couldn't be banished to spend eternity in this miserable existence. He must have moved on long ago, far beyond to a heaven or paradise where he would spend hours playfully pestering the angels about Witz, and Pissarro, and Botticelli. Sophie's selfish side wished he would come pick her up off the ground and rescue her from this horrific reality. But, deep down, she really hoped he would never have to see this what had happened to her.

Sophie sat up and again searched desperately for Alie. She felt the same panicked sorrow when she saw no sign of him. The four spirits were gone, but the square was still scattered with hundreds of disoriented souls. Many, like her, were still sitting or lying next to their bodies. But some had since started to wander away. As she watched, she saw one in particular take a few steps away from its body, then turn back and drop to its knees next to its still corpse. After several minutes of shifting its eyes between the body and somewhere else, it tried again to stand and walk away, only to collapse again and crawl back. This went on several more times before it finally dragged itself away, disappearing around a shadowy corner. The separation was obviously excruciating to the spirit, and Sophie decided it must be far braver than she was. If she knew that Alie were there, somewhere, then perhaps she could force herself to leave. But not only could she not see him, she didn't even know if he too had died, or left his body, like she had.

She felt like any sense of hope was escaping her; she could feel it oozing out of her like molasses. But she couldn't help it. There was something about this place—or this existence—that resonated pessimism and sadness. She thought she may have been there several hours, or maybe a day, but there was no way to tell. She couldn't see the sun, the moon, or any stars, and couldn't really decide if it was getting lighter or darker. It wasn't like her to give in to hopelessness, but this was different. She feared she would never again recognize anyone, and that once she convinced herself to leave her body, she would be condemned to wander the earth like this forever.

And, of course, there was the gruesome reality that if she stayed, she'd be forced to watch her own body shrivel up and decay. In fact, she thought that rigor mortis had probably already begun to set in. Her muscles would be stiffening and her skin turning pale and beginning to sag. Even if she could figure out a way to reunite with her body, it was probably too late. Her body was likely too far gone. Yet despite having no desire to witness her body rot away, she still couldn't force herself leave. So she sat, and waited. For what, she didn't know. But she waited.

The misery came in waves, at times far more than she could bear. And when it came, she would scream out desperately, and nonsensically, for Alie. The logical side of her that was determined to hold on knew how futile it was to bellow out like a helpless lamb, but she couldn't help it. As the desperation crept in, crying out felt strangely like what she was supposed to do. So, she surrendered and let her cries gush out, blending with all the others. Her consciousness drifted in and out of a dreary stupor of disheveled thoughts and despair. She was occasionally aroused by a scream that managed to rise above the otherwise incessant droning, or a meandering soul that had wandered away from its body. But she would eventually descend back into the pitiful escape that she'd in the dark recesses of her mind.

After spinning her thoughts in circles for far too long, Sophie worried she would drive herself mad. So she again rolled over and stared at the fountain. Like before, its outline only barely contrasted against the monochrome building facades in the background. The tapestry of flowers that had dangled from the base of the fountain were now a colorless shadow. Sophie thought the previously charming fountain had become downright uninspiring and ordinary. But as she stared, something peculiar caught her eye. Draped along the periphery of the fountain's outline was a faint, oddly pleasing, crystalline silhouette that surrounded the marble structure like a translucent veil. Sophie thought initially that it might be some sort of ghostly aura, like the bluish vapor that appeared when she touched other spirits. But as she watched and forced herself to concentrate, she thought she caught a very slight movement in the glassy substance. She focused even harder, suspicious that it was just her imagination. Sure enough, the faintly sparkling outline was stretching very, very slowly away from the fountain, and oozing toward the ground. And, all at once, Sophie realized she was looking at water.

Duh, of course it was water, she thought. It was, after all, a fountain. But it was flowing so incredibly slow that it hadn't registered. In fact, its movement was so slow, it was almost impossible to detect. This had Sophie perplexed. Everything else in the plaza was moving at a regular speed—creepy and otherworldly sure, but not slow. But the water coming from the fountain inched along unnaturally and out of sync with the rest of her surroundings. Could it be that what she was watching was not water from the spiritual side, but instead from the physical world? Unlike the buildings, the chairs, and the solid fountain, the water was transparent and lustrous, like diamond droplets floating in the air, which made it difficult to perceive as being on one side or the other. But if she were, in fact, looking at water from the physical world, and if it really were moving so extraordinarily slowly, then that would mean...

Sophie jumped to her feet and scanned the plaza for a clock. She knew she had seen one before adorning one of the square's antique doorways, but had never really paid attention to it. But now she desperately wanted to locate it to see if her hunch could be true. If so, this could change everything.

She remembered the clock being pretty, but not necessarily very large. Still, it should not have been this difficult to locate. The ethereal nature of everything made it tremendously challenging to distinguish details in the architecture. But eventually she managed to focus on the basketball-sized circle above a now-obscured building entrance. Reading the hands on the clock, however, would be another challenge in itself. Despite squinting and craning her neck, she couldn't make out the position of the hands. She knew she would have to get closer.

Sophie glanced down at her curled-up body. It looked more and more pathetic every time she looked at it. Frail, comatose and utterly defenseless. Dead. Why couldn't she just admit it?

You're dead, Sophie. Deal with it already.

The more obvious it seemed, the harder it was to accept. Coming to terms with her sudden loss of mortality meant she would eventually have to detach herself permanently from her body. And walking away meant giving in to her own demise. But for the first time since all of this happened, she had a very faint glimmer of hope. She still had no idea how she might reunite with her body, but if her suspicion were true—if time were moving much slower in the physical world—then perhaps her body was not lost after all. Maybe this was the motivation she needed to actually walk away, to actually search for a way to make something happen. If she could find the right person, or say the right thing, or maybe even some kind of silly spell or something…maybe there was a fix to this insanity.

Turn away, Sophie. Concentrate on the clock.

She convinced herself to take two steps away from her body, and then turn her back. She fought with herself to ignore the invisible cords that she could have sworn were there, refusing to let her leave.

Do *not* look back. Focus. The clock, Sophie, the clock.

She took two more steps forward, and then noticed three spirits, kneeling perfectly still, watching her every move. They seemed to be entranced with her struggle, the way she had been with the ones before her. In a strange sort of way, she felt somewhat inspired by this audience, as if she were encouraging them to do the same.

One foot. Then another. Until you can see the hands on the clock.

Her pace quickened, just slightly. The edges of the clock face became a bit clearer with each step. The urge to turn and look for her body was strong. But she closed her eyes and took four more steps. Opening her eyes, she could make out the faint clock hands, but couldn't yet pinpoint their positions.

Come on, Sophie. Just a few more steps.

An abrupt surge of courage and determination sprung within her just as the thought of how ridiculous it was that she couldn't simply walk across a plaza. She gritted her teeth and took five large strides toward the clock as the hands became clear.

7:04 p.m.

So, there it was. Was that really so hard? Okay, maybe so, but she'd done it. She allowed herself to glance back toward her body, but kept her feet planted under the clock. It was time to figure this out.

Think Sophie, think.

She fought through the fog in her mind, wrestling with her distorted memories to remember when she had last checked the time. She knew the sun was setting when Alie told her to wait as he disappeared down an alleyway. And she recalled that he showed up late to...

6:00!

They were supposed to meet at 6:00 p.m., but she checked her watch at 6:21 and he still hadn't arrived. The distinct memory of the disappointment she felt was still with her, as was the thrill of him sneaking up and kissing her cheek.

"Whoa!" Sophie exclaimed as she began to connect the dots. If he arrived shortly after 6:21 p.m., and then they talked for a while before he left, and if it was now only 7:05 p.m., then that either means only a few minutes had passed, or an entire day...or two...or...

Her deliberation was shattered by a terrified shriek, unlike any she had heard yet. It ran up Sophie's spine with a chilled shiver, and was followed by another. They came from somewhere around a corner, and possibly down one of the narrow streets. Then came another, and another, until they blended together into a jumbled, spectral siren. The screams were dripping with unmistakable, blood-curdling horror. And they were getting closer.

Sophie couldn't imagine what might be coming, but it didn't sound good. Her instinct was to run back to her body, but she'd be completely exposed there. She looked quickly for a place to hide, but saw nothing. So, she backed away from the direction of the screams, terrified that it, or they, was about to emerge into the square.

They burst out of the alley and into the plaza as if shot from a gun—numerous spirits running in a panicked stampede. They scattered in all directions as soon as they entered the plaza. Some hid behind tables and trees, while others continued straight through, past the tables and fountain and into the alleys on the other side. Several even ran within inches of Sophie, and she could sense their fear as they passed. She didn't know what they were running from, but it seemed obvious that she shouldn't stick around to find out.

She again turned toward her body, trying desperately to locate it through the chaos. From where she stood, she couldn't distinguish hers from the others, so she quickly scrambled toward the fountain, knowing it was close by. She side-stepped several spirits that were crouching, terrified, next to their bodies. After reaching the fountain, she turned to get a better look. But before she could spot it, something else caught her eye.

A shadowy silhouette crept to the edge of the darkness, poking its hooded head out as if to survey the square. After jerking its head unnaturally from side to side for several minutes, it took two prowling steps into the plaza, paused, and then took three more. Sophie crouched slowly behind the fountain, peering around its base. From where she knelt, she could only make out a few details of the figure. It appeared to be draped in some sort of robe, with its head covered entirely by a hood that protruded extensively in front of its brow.

The figure wasn't large, but was frighteningly intimidating nonetheless. It walked upright like a human, but nothing about its movements was natural. It seemed to slither on two feet as it went from one body to the next, inspecting each one like a devilish scavenger. It passed some of the bodies with little more than a glance. But at others it knelt for a more thorough inspection, craning its neck to examine all sides of the corpse.

Sophie watched silently, moving only to duck her head each time the creature looked her direction. She didn't think it had seen her yet, but wasn't sure. She was too frightened to make a run for it, but also terrified of what it might do to her, or her body, once it reached them. She had no idea what it was, or what it was capable of, but it certainly didn't look friendly. Its head twitched back and forth erratically in between bodies, searching for its next target. Sophie tried to catch a glimpse of a face buried beneath the hood, but could make out nothing in the recessed blackness. Perhaps she could see more if she looked at it head on, but she wasn't about to leave herself exposed to that thing.

The creature eventually arrived at a pair of bodies that had collapsed almost on top of one another. A pair of spirits huddled closely next to the bodies, their eyes watching the creature's every movement. It ignored them at first, instead circling around the two bodies several times while eyeing them like a vulture eyes carrion. Each time the creature passed the crouching spirits, they cowered almost into a ball, but still didn't try to escape. After several rotations, the creature stopped and stood directly over the smaller of the two spirits, and the spirit ducked its head into its hands. The other spirit reached momentarily for the smaller one, but not before the demonic creature extended a foot and kicked the smaller spirit onto its side.

Sophie accidentally gasped out loud, and the head of the creature spun her direction. A pair of pale-orange, iridescent eyes flashed from within the hood like bike reflectors. They peered at Sophie for several unnerving seconds as it craned its neck back and forth curiously like an owl. She froze, mesmerized by the lure of the eyes. In that moment, the creature took an awkward step backward, threw back its head, and hurled a sickening scream into the air. The sound was nothing like Sophie would have expected. It was a foul, guttural bellow, reminiscent of a demented bullfrog. After pausing for a second, the creature let out another, even longer and deeper than the first.

Sophie dropped like a rock behind the fountain. She began to shiver at the sound, which was horrifically worse than anything she'd ever heard. It had seen her, and she was certain it would be upon her any second. She no longer had a choice; she had to try and escape. She crawled to the edge of the fountain and peeked one last time. To her relief, the creature wasn't moving toward her, but instead was plodding back toward the alley from which it came. She raised herself to one knee and tried to gauge the distance to the alley on the opposite side of the plaza. A wave of apprehension surged through her as she thought about running away from not only her body, but the place where Alie might come to look for her. But if that thing got ahold of her, she thought, all of that might not matter anyway.

She burst from behind the fountain in a dead sprint headed straight for the corner where Alie disappeared. Running felt strange, like her feet were less connected to the earth than before, which seriously affected her coordination. She had no plans as to where she would go once she rounded the corner; she just ran as fast as she could make herself go. Refusing to turn and look back, she kept her eyes fixed on the alley entrance and pumped her legs. She was only a few strides away when they rounded the corner.

Like an army dispatched from the gates of hell, a horde of dark beings marched out of the alley and into the square. Sophie's legs collapsed beneath her and she fell back onto her hands. She scooted away from the demonic mob as quickly as she could, but they advanced much more quickly than she could retreat. Unlike the wiry creature that had roamed the square moments before, these monsters were not hooded, although the details of their sullied faces were still quite obscure. And unlike the timid and decrepit movements of the hooded creature, these moved decisively and aggressively, as if they were set forth on some sort of wicked, preordained mission. They were almost on top of Sophie before they paused suddenly, as if they only just noticed her. For a brief second, Sophie locked stares with the one in front, who peered at her while leaning forward for a better look. It had no visible eyes, but through its eye sockets she could see smoky kaleidoscopes of blues, azures, and indigos somewhere within the demon's head. As Sophie stared petrified, it moved its mouth and a mix of vile noises spewed out. Its speech was terrifying and grotesque, yet had a metallic, almost musical tone. After it spoke, the others echoed similar, nauseating sounds.

She tried frantically to scramble to her feet. But almost immediately she felt her head jerk back as the blue-eyed demon grabbed a handful of hair. She reached upward for the demon's hand and dug her nails into its cold, steely skin. But the harder she tried to tear away at the demon's flesh, the louder and deeper it chuckled at her. It dragged her like a writhing, hooked fish across the square. Sophie's feet flailed to regain footing, but before she could, the demon hurled her like a rag doll against a wall. She didn't feel the immediate sting of pain like she normally would, but the brutal thud rocked her nonetheless as a concentrated rush of terror erupted within her, incapacitating her almost entirely.

She only dared to raise her head enough to peak at her surroundings. The demon horde had filled the square as they hunted the disembodied spirits like a cruel wolf pack. Some wore a sort of dark, sinuous clothing that flowed behind them like shadows when they moved, while others appeared naked. Large, brutish ones were scouring the plaza, picking off frantic souls one by one as they tried to escape. Some fortunate spirits got away, but most were herded and tossed like Sophie against the wall, where they huddled together in fear.

Sophie sat balled-up with her back to the wall for what seemed like hours, watching the demons scour the plaza. Several of them continued going from body to body, performing some sort of inspection as the hooded one had done before. Others trailed behind, keeping their distance, but with every bit of their attention focused intensely on the work of the inspectors. Occasionally, after spending an especially long time with one of the bodies, one of the investigating demons would summon others, and a discussion of sorts would ensue. After several minutes, the trailing creatures would erupt into a sickening brawl like manic hyenas.

As frightened as she was, Sophie cautiously studied the movements and tendencies of the demons. She would lift her eyes as stealthily as she could manage, careful to avoid detection. There seemed to be some sort of hierarchy among them. And there was a noticeable difference in intelligence and physical makeup. The movements of the ones inspecting the bodies more closely resembled humans, although not entirely. The creatures that followed behind them were clearly less cerebral, exhibiting the pack-like characteristics of dogs. Their movements were erratic and eerily unnatural, and many had oddly contorted limbs. And, of course, the enormous, ogre-ish brutes—like the one that had dragged Sophie by the hair—were the muscle. It was unclear if they were less intelligent than the others, or if they just understood the simplicity of their role: conquer, capture, and violently punish anyone who opposed.

And yet there were others that didn't fall into any of these categories. There was no mistaking that they were demons, but were less involved in the inspection of bodies and the capturing and terrorizing the disembodied humans. Instead, they appeared content to keep to the sidelines, like nefarious wallflowers waiting for their scraps, or simply enjoying the show. They were significantly less intimidating than the legion of demons that had initially overtaken the plaza. But they were also considerably less predictable, which complicated any possibility of escape.

Sophie's concentration was interrupted by thudding footsteps, and she suddenly realized she had been caught eyeing the demons. A creature snatched a handful of her hair and lifted her half-way to her feet. The creature hissed several unintelligible words only inches from her face as its rancid breath filled her nostrils. It smelled like piss, almost exactly. Its eyes were completely rust-colored, with no pupils and no whites, just solid balls of dingy-orange rotating within its sockets. More meaningless words spewed from its mouth as it scraped a fingernail down Sophie's cheek. She tried to turn her head away, but it pinched her chin and forced her to face him.

"Leave me alone, please," she whispered pitifully.

It perked up at the sound of her voice. "Ah, English is it then, love?" Her eyes widened and her back stiffened at hearing it speak English and, more surprisingly, that she could understand it. "What's wrong dear?" it cackled. "You look like you've seen a ghost." It threw its head back and let out a boisterous laugh, clearly proud of itself.

She wondered why it was that she could understand this demon's English, but couldn't comprehend anything from the other spirits. What kind of world had she entered where similar spirits couldn't communicate with one another, but the disgusting words of a demon were understandable? Perhaps this was hell after all.

The demon's countenance switched suddenly from playful to infuriated. Its eyes bored into her as its icy fingers slid around her throat, digging its claws into her neck. For the first time since leaving her body, she felt noticeable pain. It was not a familiar pain like what she knew in her human form. It came from somewhere different, from a deeper, more visceral part of her. But it was unquestionably pain nonetheless. She gripped the demon's hand with both of hers and futilely attempted to free herself. It snarled a low chuckle, amused at her struggle. After allowing her to squirm for a few seconds, it pulled her close and growled, "Perhaps we should have a little fun with you." Her toes scraped across the pavement as it pulled her by the neck away from the wall. Panic shot through her as realized this thing had singled her out, and she had no idea what it might do. She had to think fast and act now. But what? And how?

Just as the demon tightened its grip on her neck, a terrified shriek pierced the air and caught his attention. The creature's head snapped around toward the direction of the scream. Over the creature's shoulder, Sophie caught a glimpse of one of the large, hulking demons holding a dangling, trapped spirit high in the air by its leg. A second, slightly smaller spirit was crawling at the feet of the brute, screaming and reaching frantically for the soul that was flailing in the air. Sophie guessed that they were a couple, and realized that whatever was about to happen to the dangling one, the other would be forced to watch.

Sophie's demon was clearly torn between tormenting her and watching the spectacle. "Don't go nowhere, love," it hissed at her as it loosened its grip, "or you'll be next." He tossed her aside and joined the circle of demons egging on the brute. The dangling spirit belted out an excruciating groan from within the sinister crowd, followed by a helpless cry from his mate. Sophie instantly decided that she wasn't sticking around to find out what happened. She crouched in a sprinter's position, took one last took around to make sure no demon was watching, and bolted toward the nearest alley. Apparently, numerous other human spirits had the same idea. Like wild animals sprung from their cages, captive spirits sprang to their feet, as if on cue, and the plaza erupted in utter chaos. Sophie ducked and dodged her way through frenzied spirits fighting off pouncing demons as a hurricane of shrieks, snarls and growls churned the air. She was nearly trampled by frantic souls, twice getting knocked to the ground. She finally gave up on trying to flee on foot and dropped to her hands and knees, crawling around and over spirits and demons entangled in struggles on the ground.

Just as she thought she would break free, something snatched her by the right ankle. Her rusty-eyed captor had snagged her and was dragging itself closer. Its lips parted to reveal two interlocking rows of black teeth. Sophie screamed in agony as its nails sunk into her ankle like the bite of a python. Like before, the pain was unlike anything she had felt in the flesh, and coursed through her like lava seeping from her leg up through her spine. She tried to kick the demon's hand away with her other foot, but only succeeded in angering it even more.

"Naughty, naughty." The creature hissed while slithering onto its knees and extended his other hand toward her face. "Do I scare you, lit-tle…?" It pointed a gaunt finger at her face, and then grinned a sinister grin as its fingernail began to grow beyond its fingertip. The nail stretched slowly into a slender, silverish blade, stopping only inches from Sophie's eye. She whimpered as she tried to turn away, and the demon giggled. "You've got such pretty eyes, my love. Come let me have one."

The tip of the nail singed her cheek as it rested just below her eye socket. She closed her eyelids and threw her head back as far as it would go, but the blade tip followed her. For what seemed like an eternity, she waited for the blade to dig into her cheek. But something suddenly jarred the demon, and it pulled away. She opened her eyes just wide enough to see that another creature locked in its own squabble had tripped over her demon's legs. Rusty eyes turned and spewed some vile language at his offending accomplice, allowing Sophie just enough slack to slide a leg out. When the demon turned back to her and bore its blackened teeth, she promptly planted her heel as hard as she could into it mouth. Its head snapped backward, and she didn't wait around.

Sophie clambered away as fast as she could. Winding around one set of legs after another, she fled the demonic voice behind her. "Where'd ya go, lil' girl?!?" She wasn't even really crawling toward anything; she was just trying to get away from that awful voice. "When I find you, it ain't gonna be pretty!" Every part of her expected to feel the nails digging into her ankle at any second, or one of the brutes snatching her by the hair and lifting her off the ground. But still she crawled, looking for an escape. And as she did, her eyes caught a dim, golden light that crept through the crowd, just beyond the horde of demons. She had no idea what it was, but she was drawn to it. Something about it seemed to pierce through the pandemonium of the plaza, and begged her to come closer. She didn't pause to ask herself why; she just crawled as fast as she could. Strangely, she didn't sense that anyone else in the plaza noticed the light. But to Sophie, it grew brighter as she moved. Arriving at a slight opening in the chaos, she jumped to her feet and began to run toward the light. She still couldn't manage to see the source of the light; it was obscured by two brutes pulverizing some feeble spirits on the ground. Sophie cut immediately to her right, attracting the attention of one of the brutes. It spun as it took a swipe at her, which she just barely ducked. She didn't stop, dodging back left toward an opening, but then heard a voice as clear as crystal that rocked her to her core.

"Sophie!"

She gasped as the light snuck through the mass of demons. Her legs wobbled, and she staggered dangerously close to several of the devils, suddenly oblivious to the danger. Her head spun with a billion emotions, wanting to believe what she thought she heard, but incapable of sorting it out in her mind. She could no longer do anything but just stand there, completely vulnerable to everything in the plaza. She felt a warmth emanating from the glow baring down on her. A voice from within screamed at her to snap out of it and run, but still she just remained paralyzed. And then, from within the depths of the approaching light, Alie's hand reached for her.

Chapter Twenty

Alie stood before her, oblivious to the bright glow surrounding him. His head was on a swivel as he anxiously surveyed the surrounding horrors. Sophie was overwhelmed, and foolishly reached to throw her arms around him, but he pushed her away. "We have to go. NOW!" he screamed at her. He grabbed her by the wrist and pulled hard. "Run!"

Sophie's thoughts were still swimming, but her legs churned as fast as she could make them go. Running was still very awkward, with very little awareness that her feet were touching the ground. She almost face-planted several times, and would have had Alie not been dragging her so eagerly. Sophie didn't even bother to look back; she just focused on putting one foot in front of the other and let Alie do the rest.

As their escape took them down one dark street after another, the sensation in her legs evolved from unnatural and clumsy to a feeling of floating, as if her feet barely skimmed the street. Sophie noticed that the glow surrounding Alie seemed to dim and withdraw into him. But a sort of golden aura still illuminated his silhouette. Sophie wanted to ask him about it, but now certainly didn't seem like the time. He was clearly preoccupied with the getaway, and she was still focused intently on staying upright. She was really starting to get the hang of it when they turned a corner and saw three demons lurking ominously just down the street. Alie immediately jerked Sophie into a side corridor, which led them into a small, intimate courtyard.

Alie rushed her across the courtyard and stuffed her into a corner behind a bush. He then circled the perimeter several times like a sniffing dog checking for threats. Sophie trembled uncontrollably as she watched him move. After motioning for her to stay still, he disappeared for momentarily to make sure the demons had not followed, but returned soon, apparently satisfied that they were safe. For the first time since rescuing her, he let his guard down and grinned at her as he leaned against the wall. Then, with a smirk, he said, "Hey there."

Sophie let out a sob as she ran across the courtyard and almost tackled him. They crashed into one another in a ravenous embrace, and then kissed without stopping for much longer than they ever had before. Electric sensations rocketed through her, and she realized just how cold she had been up to that point. But with that kiss, everything was suddenly right. Things still didn't make sense, but they really didn't have to anymore as long as she was with him. Every kiss they had shared before was passionate, but this was otherworldly, almost beyond her ability to endure. But she did manage to endure it, quite well actually. And she looked forward to enduring quite frequently from that time forward.

"I can die now," she whispered through a broad smile.

"Uh, no, you can't," he answered.

"Well, I was obviously just being colloquial," she quipped. "But aren't we already…you know…"

"Dead? I don't think so." Alie spoke as if he knew something she didn't. "I mean, I don't think we are in the standard sense of the word."

Sophie eyed him curiously. "That's funny. I'm pretty sure I sat and stared at my lifeless body for the better part of…well, however long it's been since *IT* happened."

"Well, that's the thing. Whatever *IT* was that happened, I don't think it killed us." He leaned back, and then held his hand up between them. "We obviously aren't what we used to be, and I saw my body just like you did. But I'm just not ready yet to accept that we actually died. I think it was something else, something less supernatural, and more…explainable."

"Of course," she started, "you could never admit that something *spiritual* is happening."

He laughed. "Eh, I wouldn't say that. I'd be the most unobservant bloke on the planet if I didn't recognize that. In fact, after today, I'm pretty much open to whatever. But I've…"

Alie dropped to the ground instantly, and pulled Sophie with him as they were interrupted by shuffling sound overhead. He slowly backed them into a shadowy corner, and they both looked up to see a demon silhouetted against an ashy sky, creeping along the rooftop. It prowled back and forth, seemingly searching for something, or someone, but never spotted them. As soon as it moved on, Alie whispered, "We're not safe here. Let's go."

He led her through a maze of shadowy side streets and passageways, carefully checking around each corner before advancing. Several times, when they did see something, or when Alie simply had a bad feeling about a certain street, he would lead her up a staircase and down another, or even up an old fire escape to a clear passage across a rooftop. At one intersection, they crouched down behind some rather large flower boxes and watched and waited as various dark spirits rampaged up and down the adjacent street.

"You see that arched doorway several buildings down?" Alie leaned in and whispered. "That's where we're going."

Sophie saw what looked like an arch, but also saw six or seven demons between that doorway and where they were hiding. She also detected not only an increase in demonic foot traffic, but also a substantial rise in screams and commotion coming from the other end of that street. The commotion sounded a lot like what they had escaped from in the plaza. Surely he wasn't bringing her back there.

"Alie, where are we exactly?" He didn't answer, or even acknowledge her question. She pulled at his shoulder, trying to get his attention. "Why do I get the feeling we're going back to Bourg-de-Four Square?" The fear in her voice was palpable.

Alie spun on his knees and took her by the shoulders. "We're not going back to the square. Not exactly."

"Wait, WHAT?!?" her voice rose nervously, and Alie immediately pinned his hand over her lips. She closed her eyes and nodded, indicating that she understood. She continued, this time in a whisper, albeit a frantic one. "What do you mean 'not exactly'? I can't go back there, or anywhere near there. You don't understand what's in that plaza, the stuff that's going on there. It's literally hell. You didn't see what I saw."

"Yeah, actually I did." He took her gently by the hand, but she pulled it away.

"Well, I'm not sure what you may have witnessed in the few seconds before we made our break for it—which I'm very grateful for okay, but…" she was trembling so badly that she could hardly get the words out. "I just…you can't imagine the evil occupying that plaza right now. And if we go back, or if they find us, they'll do terrible things to us. If you'd seen it, you would understand and would be running the opposite direction as fast as I wish we were right now. Please, Alie. I can't."

"I did see it, Sophie. I saw it all."

"I don't understand," she blurted out, rather agitated. "You couldn't have. You weren't there…were you?"

"No," he tried to explain, but kept his eyes pointed down the street. "I was watching, from above. From a window overlooking the plaza." Alie lowered his eyes and stared at the ground for a minute. He kicked at some indistinct piece of garbage on the physical side, but it didn't move. The short amount of time that Sophie had spent with him since they turned was enough for her to realize that he was different than before. He was preoccupied, like he had entered a heightened state of awareness, possibly the way he did in combat. He seemed genuinely happy to see her, but had yet to really gave her his full attention, like the protective father of newborn prey on the lookout for a lurking predator. But in that moment, he briefly let his guard down and looked strangely disheartened, as if he had failed her somehow.

"Come on, Alie. Talk to me." Crouched behind a couple of boxes that didn't really hide them all that well, and with the prospect of heading back *toward* the plaza apparently on the table, Sophie's patience for trying to draw information out of him was immensely shorter than normal. "Now is definitely not the time for you to get all quiet and pensive on me, like back at the church. What's going on?"

"I saw it all," he whispered. "I saw them tormenting you, and everyone else. The huge ones picking those people up, and tossing them aside like rubbish. And the spirits of the people cowering before them, terrified of every move the demons made." He slow-motion pounded his quivering, clenched fists against his forehead as his words exited through gnashed teeth. "And I saw that slimy bastard putting his filthy claws on you." Alie looked suddenly down the street, as if he were hoping to see the rust-eyed demon.

Sophie reached for him and ran her fingers across the top of his head. "Hey, Alie, it's okay," she tried to sooth him, at least a little. "We're here together now, and we're going to get through this, right?"

Alie's eyes shifted back to the ground. "I know what you must be thinking, and it's the part that kills me." Sophie was thinking a whole lot of things at the moment, and couldn't quite pin down just one. Alie shook his head in anguish. "If I witnessed all this, why did I take so long to come and get you, right? I…Sophie, I…"

"No, no, no, Alie," she wrapped her arms around him and kissed his head. "It did cross my mind, but I never doubted you for even a second. I know there must have been a reason."

"I'm so sorry. I swear that I came as soon as I could." He extended his arms, and then his fingers, opening and closing his fists to try and calm himself. After grappling with several seconds of silence, he forced out the rest. "Our training teaches us to compartmentalize, to make decisions appropriate to the circumstances. My DS would badger me and my squaddies incessantly, almost to the point of tears, to get us to separate our emotions from our ability to use our brains. That was the only thing keeping me from jumping out of that window when I saw what they were doing to you. It was like torture, having to sit there and watch. But I knew that if I didn't wait for the right time, they probably would have captured me as well, and then we'd both be dead, or captured, or whatever it is that they are doing to those poor souls."

"Alie, you did nothing wrong," Sophie assured him as she snuggled close. "You have nothing to apologize for. Please know that. I owe you everything for what you did do." Alie never made eye contact, but seemed to calm down as she spoke to him. "But I do think we should seriously consider taking up this conversation somewhere else, preferably far from here." She tugged him by the elbow toward the direction they had come, which was deliberately away from the confounded arch doorway. But Alie didn't budge, and re-focused his attention back down the street.

She shook her head in disbelief. "But why, Alie? Why on earth would we want to go see all of that again?"

"You have to trust me. I need you to see something."

Seeing that there was no changing his mind, Sophie squeezed in next to Alie and peered down the alley. "Let me guess: we have to go through that doorway."

"Well, up some stairs and through a door or two, but yes, you're right."

She sighed. Why not, she thought. Even worse than the thought of going near that plaza was the thought of being separated from Alie again. She didn't really care where he was going; she was going with him.

Alie rose to a crouching position, which Sophie awkwardly tried to imitate. He pressed his hand firmly on her shoulder as they watched several black figures wander the alleyway. As they watched and waited for just the right time to make a break for it, Alie whispered, "Oh yeah, there's a closed wooden door in the archway that we'll have to pass through. Get ready."

"Hang on. What?" Pass through? What was he talking about? "Can we do that?"

"NOW!" Alie sprang to his feet and jerked Sophie up with him. Before she could formulate a second thought, they were out in the open and on a full sprint. She again had to concentrate on keeping her feet underneath her, which was not easy with thoughts of "how the hell am I supposed to pass through a closed door?" spinning in her head. She hoped he would yell out some instructions or something before they got to the door, but nothing came. Instead, his stride quickened as they neared the archway, followed by a sharp turn directly toward the center of the large, wooden door. She felt a firm yank on her wrist just before Alie disappeared into the door with a blue puff, followed by a…

WHAM!

Sophie's sat dazed, square on her butt, looking up at the closed archway door. Her face had pancaked against the wood, which seemed every bit as solid as it would have been in the physical world. Alie, however, had passed through like a hot knife through butter, and was nowhere to be seen. Again, a little tutoring on this whole passing-through-a-solid-door thing would've been nice before hauling her face-first into it at full speed. She likely would have been a bit more upset had there been more pain involved. It was still, however, more than just a bit jarring.

Finding herself suddenly very vulnerable out in the open, Sophie hopped to her feet and nervously looked around. Just as she did, Alie's face and upper body materialized through the door. "Well, that didn't work so well, did it? Come on, take my hand and try again."

"Thanks, but no thanks. Like you said, that didn't work so well last time." They shared a very brief, uneasy laugh, which they abandoned immediately with the recognition of the danger they were in. "How about instead you tell me how it is that you passed right through a solid door."

"It's only solid because you think it's solid," he answered. "From what I can tell, we are still somewhat contained by solid walls, but we can pass through windows and doors, windows being the easier of the two." He reached for her again and motioned for her to hurry as he looked both ways down the street. "But you have to convince yourself that the door is not a barrier. You have to believe you can do it."

Sophie shook her head and stretched out her hand. "This is so freaking weird," she muttered. A very light sprinkling of bluish dust scattered as her fingers tickled the wood, which seemed no less firm than before.

"You need to hurry, Sophie," he urged. "There's no time."

"I *know* that," she snapped. "Do you think it's easy trying to figure out how to pass through a solid object with your phantasmic head and shoulders sticking out telling me what to do? Why don't you disappear your face again and let me concentrate?" Alie vanished behind the door, and Sophie checked once more down the street before once again attempting the impossible. She pushed firmly against the door, which still didn't budge. She then closed her eyes and tried to remember some of the transcendental meditation techniques she learned in her semester of yoga class. That, too, did not work.

"Quit pushing against the door and just imagine it's not there," came the voice from behind the door. She wanted to tell him to shut up, but she didn't have any better ideas. She squeezed her eyes shut as tightly as she could and reached out again. This time, she felt an odd sensation as the tips of her fingers dipped into the old door, followed by her knuckles, the palm and of her hand, and finally her forearm. She could suddenly sense years of history woven into the grains of the wood passing over her, and thought she could hear the voices, all at once, of generations of people who had passed through the doorway.

"Alie, it's working," she said with astonishment. The wood had almost reached her elbow when the wail of a demon broke her concentration. Her eyes snapped open and she saw two quarrelling figures round the corner at the end of the street. They hadn't noticed her yet, but her panic made it impossible to focus. She again tried to push her arm through the door, but it was stuck. "Alie! I can't move. It won't go any farther!" On the other side of the door, Alie took her by the hand

and pulled, but her arm wouldn't budge. Her eyes darted back and forth hysterically between the approaching demons and the door. She was trapped between trying to remain quiet and wanting to frantically jerk her arm back and forth to free herself.

Alie stuck his head through the door to assess the coming threat. The look on his face confirmed her fear, and he pleaded with her to follow him through the door.

"I CAN'T," she blurted out, and the demons stopped motionless on the street. "Oh my…no, they see me. Alie, help me, please, help!" One of the creatures cocked its head sideways like a dog, trying to make sense of her. They were still half a block away, but would be upon her in seconds, especially if she couldn't get un-stuck. She was even more horrified because she knew Alie would dash out to protect her, and then that would be the end of them both.

"Hey, Sophie," his voice—which was way, way too calm—sounded from behind the door. He had stopped pulling on her hand, and instead had placed her hand on his chest. "Sophie, close your eyes and listen to me for just a sec."

She looked again at the demons, which were creeping in her direction. Was he crazy? Close my eyes and listen? What the—?

"Sophie, you have to trust me," he pleaded. "Just listen. Tell me again the name of that painting you like by that…that *Watz* guy."

That's it, he has officially lost his mind.

"You know, the one you showed me with the lake, and Jesus walking—"

"Are you nuts, Alie? They're coming, right NOW!"

"Sophie!" he barked. "Forget them and answer my damn question. What's the name of that painting?"

"What the hell, Alie? It's called *The Miraculous Draught of Fis*hes, by Konrad *Witz,* not…"

Alie's hand shot through the door and grabbed her shirt, then jerked her through the door with tremendous force. When she opened her eyes, she was stumbling toward the ground on the other side. Alie still held onto the one hand, and Sophie caught herself on the ground with the other.

"Now run!" Alie ordered as they both sprinted up a quick flight of stairs and around a corner. Sophie could hear hisses not far behind them, but Alie didn't slow down to check. She followed him around another corner and then up another flight of stairs. On the third floor, they ran almost the entire length of a dark hallway before he stopped in front of a dingy apartment door with a gaudy number 4 dangling just above a peephole. Alie wrapped his arms tightly around her and, after a very brief, apprehensive look, planted a very serious kiss on her. Her first thought was that it was perhaps the most bizarrely timed kiss in history, until she realized that he was falling backward through the door into the apartment, and taking her with him. They crashed to the floor on the other side.

"Well played, Mr. Quin," she whispered as she kissed him again. Both times he had managed to distract her, she passed perfectly right through the doors.

"Thanks, rookie," he grinned. "But we're not out of the woods yet. Get up. We may not have much time, and you need to figure out this door and window thing. And I need to show you why I brought you here."

. . . .

The view from the window was like a scene from the worst horror movie imaginable. From the shadows of the upper floor, Sophie leaned back into Alie's chest as he wrapped his arms around her, and they helplessly watched the terror below. Human spirits were lined up on their knees in rows, facing the wall, while the demons paced back and forth between them. There was no fight left in the spirits; they simply knelt with their heads bowed submissively.

"I don't think I can beat them," Alie whispered. Sophie turned and looked at him, completely baffled.

"Did you say *beat* them?"

"I don't think I can," Alie responded.

"Well of course you can't *beat* them," she said, her voice thick with wonder that the thought would even cross his mind. "Why would you even suggest something so absurd?"

She backed away from him just enough to take in his entire face, which was still bathed in a dim glow. She could read his eyes, and knew what was on his mind, and didn't like it one bit.

"You're actually considering fighting them? You can't be serious…right?" He didn't answer, instead staring down on the plaza.

"Alie?" She grabbed his chin and forced him to look at her. "Alie! Tell me you're not that crazy, or stupid."

He nodded his head and gently grasped both of her hands. "It's what I do, Sophie." She shook her head frantically and pushed away, but he didn't let her go. "You have to understand that my instinct is to fight to protect those who can't fight for themselves, no matter how nasty the enemy may be." He leaned toward the window, and then pointed at the imprisoned souls. "I may be their only hope."

"What hope are you talking about?" Sophie nearly shouted. "We don't even know where we are or why we're like this, except that right after *it* happened, these awful creatures showed up and basically brought hell with them. The human spirits aren't even recognizable as human, and those evil beasts are beyond horrifying." She turned and stepped closer to the window as her voice faded out. "So exactly what hope do you think there is?"

Alie pulled Sophie by the hand away from the window and sat her down on a bed. He knelt on the floor in front of her. "Do you recognize me?" he said.

"Of course I do, but…"

"Why?" He paused, and she tried futilely to come up with an answer. "Why do you think it is that you recognized me immediately, when I'm a spirit just like all the others, yet the others are completely unrecognizable? Have you thought about that?" She nodded her head, but still didn't have an answer. In fact, she had a million questions, not the least of which was why Alie was not only recognizable, but had been glowing from the moment he showed up at the plaza. She had been wanting to ask him about it, but they hadn't exactly had a quiet moment until now.

"Yes, I definitely recognized you right away," she answered, "and not only that…" She wasn't sure why, but she hesitated to mention the glowing, as if it were some kind of embarrassing condition. But Alie grinned in a way that hinted he might already know.

"There's something else, right?" he said.

"There's something about the way you…"

"Glow?"

She smiled back. "Yes, glow. Can you see it too?"

"Only when I look at you," he answered.

She didn't see that coming. "Whoa, what? Seriously?" She held out her arms and inspected them closely, but no glowing. In fact, she had been quite disheartened at the ghastly, lifeless shade that her skin had taken on. "But…"

"I think I might know why," he interrupted her. "You knew me straight away when you saw me, and even saw me glowing. I spotted you immediately in the plaza from this window because you too were glowing, at times downright beaming. When it got really bad and I thought you were in serious danger, you got even brighter. And those other spirits in the square, the ones that were screaming when the other was taken, they obviously knew each other."

Sophie stood up and peeked down onto the plaza, then spun back to Alie. "It's the connection, isn't it? If we had a connection with someone in the real world…"

"Then we still have that same connection here," Alie concluded.

Sophie nodded, and then took Alie by the hands and pulled him to his feet. "Kiss me," she said, "it's time to experiment." She kissed him with her eyes open, which was strange enough as it was, but became nothing short of fascinating as the light emanating from Alie doubled in intensity. "Open your eyes," she whispered, and felt him smile as she kissed him again. In those few minutes, the cold and despair faded away, replaced by a tender warmth that radiated through every inch of her. It was a perfect moment in what had become a miserable existence.

"Promise me something," she whispered. "Promise that you'll never leave me again. I don't care where you go or why, you never go without me."

He smiled, but said nothing. She could see in his face that he was troubled, which she did not like at all. She started to ask again, but Alie stopped her by pulling her backwards onto the bed. They held each other in silence as Sophie drifted off into something that resembled sleep. It wasn't a sleep brought on by fatigue, but rather by being perfectly safe and content in his arms. Her thoughts stopped racing and slowed into a dreamy stupor and, for a short time, she completely forgot everything that had happened.

. . . .

Muffled screams from outside tugged Sophie back toward awareness. She was immediately colder than before, and soon realized

Alie wasn't beside her. She felt an instant tinge of panic before rolling over and seeing him standing beside the window, staring in silence at the plaza. He didn't notice her, or at least didn't let on that he did. He seemed focused on whatever suffering was going on below; though powerless to stop it.

"Hey," she said softly as she rose to sit on the bedside.

"Hey," he answered without taking his eyes off the plaza.

"Is it just as bad as before?"

He didn't answer, instead waving her to come toward the window. "Come here. This is what I needed you to see." His voice was calm, but the way he said it made her stomach churn. When she joined him by the window, he pointed. "Look, over there next to the tables." Sophie saw a mob of dark figures, jockeying wildly for position to see whatever it was that was going on near the tables.

"What is it that I'm supposed to be looking at?"

"Just wait." She watched the throng of demons shuffle back and forth before abruptly turning their attention to the alleyway. A unified roar erupted as they scurried madly toward the dark passage, revealing what had them so intrigued. Three physical bodies were lined up neatly next to one another on the ground, their profiles still visible through the smoky veil that divided the corporeal from the spiritual realm. They were positioned uniformly on their backs with their hands crossing their chests, and their heads facing the same direction. Their orderliness was starkly at odds with the other vacant bodies scattered chaotically across the pavement. Sophie couldn't make sense of it, and tried to remember if she had previously noticed the three bodies before lying so neatly and out in the open.

"I don't understand. They couldn't have fallen that way," she said. "How did they get like that?"

"They didn't fall there," Alie answered. "They were placed."

"Placed? By what? The demons can't move a body, can they?" Just as she said it, something caught her eye that made even less sense. A vague, dark silhouette was approaching the three bodies in the physical realm. Its legs were outstretched, as if suspended in mid-stride. One arm was also stretched backward, dragging some sort of heavy object. Its upper body lurched forward, striving to haul the lumbering object. At first it reminded Sophie of the small statuette of a man hauling a

Christmas tree up a snowy hill that showed up on her grandmother's mantle every December. But then Sophie realized that this figure was grasping something much more sinister: the leg of a limp body being dragged like a sack of potatoes.

"Who…what is that?" Sophie gasped. "Why is there…I thought everyone on the other side was…" Alie touched her shoulder, but she was bordering on hysterical. Why was someone on the other side up and moving about? Didn't everyone else die, or at least detach from their bodies like she and Alie had? Had some people survived the event? And if so, what were they doing in the square moving bodies around? She watched and waited for the murky figure to reach the trio of tidily positioned bodies, but the advance never came, at least not that she could tell. Like the water in the fountain, the upright figure was suspended mid-movement in extreme slow-motion. Any indication of its labored heaving was only noticeable through concentrated observation over several minutes, and even then only barely. "Just like the fountain."

"What do you mean 'the fountain'?" Alie asked.

"Before you came, before the demons came, I was just lying there in the plaza watching the fountain." She pointed to the spot where she had laid. "The water is hard to see now, but it's there, and it's still flowing. Just barely. The drops hang in the air like they're frozen in time, like floating droplets of crystal. If you watch long enough, you can tell that it's moving, but only slightly."

Alie nodded as his mind churned, trying to put the pieces together.

"That's not all," she continued. "There's a clock, over there above the door. The slow-motion water made me think that maybe, just maybe, time in the physical world is moving much slower than here. Like time here marches on a completely different frequency than the other side. So just before the demons came, I went over to check the clock."

"And?"

"And according to the clock, only a few minutes had passed since *it* happened," she explained. "I'm not sure exactly how many, but it felt like I'd been lying there for hours, if not days. But the clock showed it had only been a few minutes, maybe a half-hour, tops. And the second hand was barely moving at all." She started to pace anxiously back and forth. "So that means…"

"That means there's still a chance…" Alie interrupted.

Sophie nodded, "that we could go back?"

"Maybe, somehow." Alie stared at the fountain, searching intensely for the floating water that Sophie described. "But it has to be before our bodies decompose which, until now, I had just assumed was a lost cause. But if what you're saying is true, then maybe not."

The image of the two bodies—one mysteriously upright and dragging the other—was dreadfully unnerving. But at the same time, it was, oddly, a sign of hope. Could it be that the upright figure had crossed back over, somehow finding a way to retake his body? Or did he come from somewhere else, somewhere far enough away that he was not affected by the event? With everything moving so slowly in the physical world, Sophie didn't think he could have come from far, definitely not outside of Geneva. Any why was he the only one? If some people really did survive in their bodies, then where were the rest of them? And why was this one dragging bodies around?

"So, is this what you brought me here to see?" Sophie asked.

"Not exactly," Alie responded. "Not everything."

"What else then?"

Alie pointed out a balled-up bundle of cloth at the feet of a short, rather portly demon, who maintained a good distance from the chaotic fray dominating most of the plaza. The fat creature stood naked, with one hand resting on its sagging gut, and the other holding a rope of some sort that extended from the heap of cloth on the ground. On either side of the tubby demon stood massive, juggernaut-sized creatures, apparently standing guard. More than once, another demon ventured too close, only to be immediately clobbered by one of the brutes. After observing and trying to comprehend the scene for several minutes, Sophie thought she saw the bundle move.

"Am I supposed to know what that is?" she asked Alie.

"I'm not even sure I know what it is," he answered, "but I need you to see it for yourself."

She was about to ask what was under the cloth when the fat one suddenly jerked violently at the rope, and the clump of rags stood up, revealing a pair of pale, scrawny bare feet sticking out from underneath. A pair of equally pale and pathetic hands poked out of the cloth and gripped the rope, which the fat demon had yanked taut, followed by a steady pull toward the mob surrounding the row of vacant bodies. As they approached, the massive bodyguards parted the crowd, quite brutally, to make way for the cloaked being and its plump captor. By that point, the horde had worked itself into a howling frenzy, almost climbing over one another in anticipation of something. But of what, Sophie couldn't imagine.

A particularly sinister-looking entity emerged boldly from the frantic mass wearing a crimson cloak dragging several feet behind him. Two other similar figures followed, both draped similarly in black cloaks. From their aggressive stride, to the submissive reaction of the others, Sophie guessed they must be leaders of some sort. They approached the fat demon with the rope, and a conversation ensued. A moment later, the black-cloaked leaders barked what appeared to be a series of orders at the horde, and the mass immediately parted, revealing the outlines of the three bodies on the ground. The crimson leader then snatched the rope from the fat demon and pulled the covered being closer to the bodies. The demon horde hissed and gobbed at the pale, pathetic creature, but dared not touch. The covered creature did not appear to put up any fight as it staggered clumsily toward the bodies. Once there, the crimson-cloaked demon grabbed the pale creature by the head and then let loose an agonizingly wicked scream directly into the creature's face. The scarlet demon then jerked the ragged cloak from the captive creature's body, revealing the frail, wretched being underneath. Its ashen-white skin was stretched thin over feeble bones. Two sunken eyes sat deep within its hairless head, which was disproportionately large for its body. Yet it was strangely more human than any of the other creatures in the plaza, appearing almost childlike and pure by comparison. The pathetic creature looked cold and disoriented without the cloak, but made no attempts to move, much less escape.

Sophie leaned closer to the window for a better look, but Alie quickly pulled her back to keep her hidden. "What is that thing?" Sophie whispered, but Alie didn't respond. "Are they going to hurt it?" Still, nothing from Alie.

The anarchic madness of the demon horde unexpectedly faded, and was replaced by a wraithlike chant that rose and fell in grotesque unison for several excruciating minutes. As the horrific sound carried on, the pale creature dropped to its knees and held its hands over its ears. It writhed onto its side, and then twisted onto its back, clearly suffering and fighting against some kind of inner torment. But eventually, it ceased to struggle and lay still. Just as the horde's shrieking reached its zenith, the pale being's head snapped up and its eyes locked onto the closest vacant body. It crawled slowly, its bony fingers scraping at the ground, until it was crouching directly over the body, its eyes just inches from the body's face. The pale creature then began to convulse in sickening spasms while its mouth moved rapidly, rattling off words that could never be heard above the deafening roar of the horde. Seconds later, the crimson demon dropped its scarlet cloak and stepped over the pale, crouching creature, placing its feet squarely into the outline of the vacant body. Then, as the horde howled in utter ecstasy, the demon closed its eyes, threw its head back, and laid backwards onto the ground directly on top of—actually *inside* of—the empty body. After a few minor adjustments, the demon had assumed the exact shape of the body. It remained perfectly still as the pale creature continued its hurried recitation, now inches from not just the body, but of the crimson demon as well.

"Oh dear God, no," Sophie muttered from beneath her hand cupped over her mouth. She reached for Alie's hand and squeezed it as nausea consumed her like a putrid wave in a rotten ocean. It all made sense now: the demons overrunning the plaza, the trio of bodies stacked side-by-side, the figure dragging the limp body in the corporal world, and the spine-chilling and grotesque ceremony that drove the horde wild.

"They're possessing the bodies!"

Chapter Twenty-One

"Sophie, please, you must remain quiet!" Alie pleaded as Sophie buzzed around the room with little concern for the volume of her outbursts.

"How am I supposed to do that?" she blurted hysterically. "How can we just sit here, knowing that our empty remains are out there, just waiting to be…*inhabited* by those beasts?"

Alie grabbed her by the shoulders, stopping her in her tracks, and placed a finger over her lips. "I don't know, but if you want any chance of getting our bodies back, you can't keep on this way." She nodded, and turned silently back to the window, searching the plaza again for her own body, worried that hers may be next. But she still couldn't make out anything more than the silhouette of a heap by the fountain that she thought may be hers. And, fortunately, there were no demons nearby, yet.

"Alie, we may not have much time," she whispered.

"Any ideas?"

"Well, I know your first instinct is to go all Rambo on them," she answered, "but I certainly don't think that's our smartest move." Alie peered out the window over her shoulder, as if he was considering the idea. "If that little scrawny runt of a creature is some kind of tool that allows them to take control of the bodies, then it seems to me that we should start with him."

"Agreed," Alie began. "But from what I've seen, they're not giving that thing up easily. We're not likely to get anywhere near it."

Sophie nodded. "Unless…" She peered out the window, surveying the plaza in all directions. "Unless we can create a distraction. A big one."

"Now we're talking," Alie grinned. "What do you have in mind?"

"I'm not sure yet, but whatever it is, it has to be big enough to allow one of us to grab that thing and get out of the plaza unnoticed."

"*Out* of the plaza?" Alie eyed her inquisitively. "How do you plan to use the little bugger outside of the plaza if your body is still *in* the plaza?"

Sophie was certain he wouldn't like her answer. "I just thought…" Sophie stammered, "I thought we'd start with you."

"What?" Alie exploded.

"Hear me out for a second," she pleaded.

"There's nothing to hear," Alie snapped back. "You actually think I'm going to leave you here alone with all of this? You're mad!"

"Alie, we stand no chance whatsoever of making anything happen inside that plaza with all of those monstrous *things* out there," she talked fast, and paced even faster. "But if we do succeed in getting ahold of that little puny magic thingy, we can send you back into your body, and then you can go take mine and carry it to somewhere else…somewhere safe."

The idea clearly enraged Alie, but he kept silent while maintaining his white-knuckle grip on a bed post.

"Sorry, Alie, but you know I'm right." Her eyes were suddenly gentle. She knew he felt helpless, and that helpless was something he didn't do well. "This may be our only shot, so we have to get it right."

"We can't," Alie said somberly.

"But, Alie, think about it, we—"

"We can't," Alie repeated, avoiding Sophie's gaze.

"Alie, what choice do we have? We'll never make it to my body, we have to start with yours."

"We can't," he hesitated, staring out the window. "We can't because it's gone."

"WHAT?!?" Sophie dashed across the floor and wedged herself between Alie and the window, forcing him to look her directly in the eye. "What do you mean 'it's *gone*'?" She grasped his shirt desperately with both hands. "Meaning you don't know how to get back to where it was?"

Alie shook his head and tried to turn away, but Sophie wasn't having it. She pulled him closer, her gaze demanding an answer.

"No, gone, meaning that I know exactly where it was, but it's not there anymore."

Sophie's grip loosened as her thoughts spiraled toward desperation. If Alie's body were taken, and not by him, then that means…

Sophie leaned her forehead against the window and closed her eyes. She tried to mold her thoughts into something productive, but they were cluttered by a flood of possibilities, all of them bad. What did this mean? Was Alie's body lost forever? Was there no way back? For either of them? She knew she should say something, but what? She hadn't exactly anticipated ever having the "sorry your body's possessed and you're stuck forever in the spirit world" talk with anyone, especially someone she loved. But she also couldn't just stand there like an idiot. She had to show him that they would keep going, together. So, she opened her eyes again to the twisted reality below them that had infested every inch of the square. And there, amidst the madness, two iridescent, rust-colored eyes were staring directly at her, smoldering as they watched her. Instantly she shuddered and stepped back from the window, reaching for Alie while calling his name. Alie leapt forward and took her place, searching the horde below, and saw them immediately.

"We have to go," he exclaimed as he grabbed her arm, "NOW!"

. . . .

They started back down the hallway toward the stairs, but were stopped immediately by the sound of movement coming from below. With no other choice, they turned and darted up the staircase. They passed the third floor and headed for what they hoped would be a fourth floor with better options for escape. But where a fourth floor should have been, there was only a single door with a sign that read "TOIT. PERSONNEL AUTORISÉ SEULEMENT". Sophie understood only enough to know that in the physical world, they weren't supposed to go through that door. But when you're a ghost, and when you're being chased by a marauding pack of who knows what, such signs are meaningless. She closed her eyes, but didn't break stride as Alie pulled her through to the other side, and found themselves on the roof.

The open air swirled with screeches from the horrific creatures on the streets below. Sophie didn't slow down to see if the demons had reached the rooftop behind them. Running still presented an uncoordinated challenge, but Sophie was gradually adapting to the way gravity affected her now. Jumping, however, was an entirely new challenge, especially when it involved clearing gaps between buildings. They were in full stride, with no time to gauge height or distance to the next rooftop. She just jumped with everything she had, looking down just long enough to catch a glimpse of the dark mob infesting the murky alley several stories below. She not only cleared the gap successfully, but did so several body lengths longer than necessary, landing even further than Alie. However, unlike Alie, Sophie's landing was far from graceful, sending her skidding face-first across the gritty rooftop. If she still had skin, she thought, her face would undoubtedly be a gravelly mess.

"You alright?" Alie asked with his hand extended.

"Sure, I guess," Sophie responded. "All but the ego."

"Good, 'cause we've got to keep moving." Sophie tuned into the menacing racket that was drawing closer and knew they couldn't slow down. Alie ran to the edge of the next building and peered over. "Come on, this one's a little wider, but we can make it," he said while backing up several steps. "Try and land on your feet this time."

Sophie followed him over another chasm between buildings, this time managing to land on her feet. She then cleared another, and then another, all without breaking stride. She was relieved when they reached a long stretch of rooftops that were all connected, with only some small walls and other obstacles. Sophie allowed herself to peek back several times, but saw no more signs that they were being followed. Alie must have done the same, as he slowed their pace from a mad dash to a jog. After several blocks of easily navigated, linked rooftops, they came to another large gap. The separation between buildings was wider than any of the others, and the opposite rooftop was significantly taller than the one on which they stood now. There was no way they would reach the other roof. There was, however, a rickety-looking catwalk hanging from the side of the opposite building about ten feet below the top, which was probably within reach of a very well-executed jump. But Sophie really didn't want to find out.

"I don't like the looks of that, Alie. Do you think we're safe to just climb down to the streets and take our chances?" Alie cautiously peered over the side of the building before answering.

"I don't know. There are still a few of them down there, and I still think we're safer up here."

Sophie looked again out over the alley toward the fire escape and fought off a sudden surge of vertigo.

"Any idea what would happen if we fall?" she asked.

Alie shook his head. "I don't know, but I don't intend to find out." He started to scan the sides of the building for a way down. "Maybe we should just get down long enough to cross the street and then climb back up." Sophie walked to the rooftop's edge to look for a way down, making sure not to reveal herself to any demonic eyes lurking below. She saw no way down.

Alie approached the opposite side of the roof, equally careful not to expose himself. Sophie watched as he crouched, slowly extending his head over the edge. But he suddenly lurched backward, barely dodging a black blur shooting up from below. Alie thudded onto the roof and he instantly rolled to his right, avoiding the large black mass that came crashing down next to him. A grotesquely sinister creature towered over Alie, its lanky, yet muscular legs spread in a fighter's stance, ready to pounce. Its body was completely black and bare, except for a ragged loin cloth that hung from its hips, and a swarthy hood wrapped around its head. Its gaze snapped back and forth between Alie and Sophie, as if trying to decide who was first. When it looked her way, Sophie could see one ominous, yellow eye illuminated underneath the black hood. The other eye was covered by something that resembled a patch, while its deformed mouth protruded from its face like the toothy snout of a dog.

Sophie froze at the sight of the creature, but Alie wasted no time. He landed a swift kick to its knee and then rolled once more before bounding to his feet. Alie's eyes were wide, but he showed no signs of intimidation as the demon stared him down and released a spine-tingling howl. Sophie, however, felt completely helpless at the thought of Alie actually trying to fight that thing. She frantically began looking around for some way to help, but how?

The creature snarled as it charged Alie. Sophie gasped as Alie met the demon's cry with a ferocious yell of his own. But just before impact, Alie dropped shrewdly to the ground, sending the charging demon tumbling across the rooftop. Its nails grated across the gravel as it slid to a stop just short of the edge. The demon sprang back to its feet in a rage. But just as it did, Alie's foot caught it directly in the chest, sending the monster flailing backwards over the edge and to the street below. Alie's momentum took his legs over the edge as his hip skipped off the ledge.

He caught himself by the elbow and swung his other hand over, searching for a grip. Sophie ran to help, but he screamed at her to stay back.

Alie grunted while struggling to hoist one leg up over the ledge, then the other. As soon as he was on his feet, he dashed toward Sophie while pointing toward the other building with the fire escape and yelled, "we have no choice, we have to jump!" He passed her on a dead sprint, expecting her to follow. And she did, watching him as he sailed across the open air and crashed into the fire escape. As she approached the edge, her mind screamed at her not to stop, but to jump with everything she had. But just as she reached the roof's edge, her eyes glimpsed the cavernous plunge beneath her, and her legs failed her. She collapsed just before jumping, crumpling at the edge of the building. She looked again down into the dark space below, and then across to Alie. His eyes filled with panic as he looked to the rooftop behind her. From the look on his face, Sophie knew she was about to regret not making that jump.

She turned to look behind her, and found the black demon glaring sharply from across the rooftop. It was back, and began to pace back and forth, never taking its gaze off of her.

"SOPHIE!" Alie's cry was desperate. She instinctively turned back toward the sound of his voice, and saw him perched in a crouching position on the fire escape. He was going to try and jump back.

"No, Alie, don't!" Sophie cried out. "You'll never make it." He did it anyway. Or at least he tried, but this time fell far short. She watched in horror as he plummeted toward the hard pavement below. But before she could see him land, or crash, the cold, gangly fingers of the demon grabbed her ankle and dragged her away.

"Shouldn't play too close to the edge, sweetheart." The demon's voice was grating and distorted, like it was talking through a rusty machine. It grasped her leg with the other hand and hurled her half-way across the roof. She landed like a ton of bricks, and immediately began to crawl away. She could try again to make it to the fire escape, but that would require her to run right by the demon. Or she could run back the way they came—across the long stretch of attached rooftops—but she didn't think she was likely to outrun the creature. Plus, that would take her away from Alie, and she wouldn't leave him, especially considering that he could be down there on the street seriously injured or…well not necessarily "dead", but something similar.

"So, it's *Sophie* is it then?" it muttered while walking along the edges of the building. It was clearly looking for Alie, most likely bent on revenge, and probably wasn't all that interested in her after all. If she timed it right, perhaps when it was distracted enough, maybe she could slip away, or maybe even push it over the ledge a second time. That would likely piss it off even more, but it may just shift its focus from Alie to her.

"And your little boyfriend," it grumbled on, still peering down impatiently to the street. "*Alie*, did you say? Where—"

"Looks like you're just a bit...humiliated, should we say, by that little tumble you took?" Sophie interrupted, surprising even herself at the level of sass she was willing to throw at this diabolical creature that could likely tear her to shreds. "Did somebody get its feeling hurt?" If pissing it off was the goal, then she had certainly succeeded. It was beyond terrifying and difficult to look at, but after everything she had seen lately, she was quickly getting used to terrifying. She backed herself to the edge of the roof and waited. She hoped it might become enraged and charge recklessly at her as it had at Alie, and that maybe she could use that to her advantage just as he had done. This was either moderately clever or amazingly stupid, most likely the latter. But it was really all she had at the moment.

The creature paused, shifting its focus to Sophie. It didn't charge or make any sudden movements as she had expected, but instead started very slowly toward her. As the demon's sleek black arms dangled at its side, it opened and closed its fingers repeatedly, and its fingernails extended to several times their prior length. It didn't say a word, instead bearing a mouthful of long, jagged fangs that hung like stalactites inside its snout. It was very clearly intent on making Sophie pay for her insolence.

But Sophie had no intention of letting it reach her; if necessary, she would leap backward blindly over the ledge and take her chances with the hard pavement below. By her calculation, the creature had looked several times exactly where Alie should have landed, and apparently didn't see him. So, Sophie was left to assume that he had either survived the fall, or had been carried away by other demons. Either way, his fate was no worse than what she was about to suffer.

Her legs were coiled, ready to spring backwards when something caught her eye behind the demon. Something had moved, but she didn't know what. The creature's large form blocked her view, and she didn't want to let on that something, or someone might be behind it. So she relaxed and let it come closer.

"I'm done playing with you," it snarled before snapping its jaws shut loudly. "You're wasting my time."

"You have somewhere else to be?" Alie's voice rang out from behind as he pounced violently on the demon's back. He squeezed one arm around the creature's neck and both legs around its waist, then jammed his other thumb right into the glowing yellow eye. The creature screeched as it stumbled backward, losing its balance. Alie's legs instantly unlocked their grip as he planted both feet firmly on the roof and used the creature's momentum to flip it backwards over his shoulder. It came crashing down onto the rooftop and let out another howl. In an instant, Alie was straddling the creature and pounding away at its face. Sophie was momentarily shocked at Alie's ability to not only fight this monster, but to apparently hurt it as well.

But the creature didn't stay down long. It grabbed Alie's forearms and sunk its claws in deep, causing Alie to scream in agony. The demon then launched Alie into the air and sprung to its feet just as Alie crashed down. Sophie screamed out for Alie and charged them with no idea what she might do when she got there. Alie yelled at her to stay back, but she refused to just sit and watch him take on the creature alone. She ran directly at the creature, shouting wildly the entire way, again hoping to provide some sort of distraction. And it worked, if only long enough to cause the demon to glance her way as Alie rose to his feet and kicked the creature squarely in the back before grabbing it by the hood and dragging it backward toward the roof's edge. The demon spun, flailing its arms desperately.

Sophie then either very bravely, or very idiotically, punched the demon directly in the back of the head. It spun again to grab her, but let go when Alie leapt again onto its back. This time Alie wrapped his arms completely around the demon's head and cranked powerfully on its neck. They staggered backward and arched its back while dragging its claws across Alie's head. Alie screamed out, but didn't let go. The demon snarled, gyrated, and took another clumsy step backward, but still couldn't shake Alie. One more step, and Sophie gasped at how close they were to the edge.

"Alie, let go!" she screamed. Alie's peeked at her over the demon's shoulder. There was a fierce, resolute look in his eye that Sophie had never seen before. For a moment, Alie looked every bit as savagely primal as the creature, and it was clear that nothing she could say would stop him.

The demon's claws thrashed behind its head and stabbed into Alie's neck. Alie torqued even harder on the creature's neck and arched backward, causing the creature to reach back with its foot one last time in search of better footing. But this time, there was none. The creature reached wildly for something to grab onto as the two of them tumbled backward over the roof's edge. Sophie let out a desperate scream and sprinted toward the ledge, expecting to see horror as she looked down. She watched the demon's body ricochet off several fire escape landings before splatting on the pavement. But then she saw Alie, lying flat on his back, looking up at her from the first landing only a few feet below. He flashed a peculiar smile, and rolled over to peer over the side in search of the demon. Its grotesque body lay distorted and still on the street. Alie rolled back over and looked again at Sophie, then burst out in deep, loud laughter.

"Well, I bet you never saw that coming," he blurted out.

Sophie sobbed and laughed simultaneously. "You're utterly insane," she said as she reached a hand down for him to grab onto.

He grunted as he gingerly reached for her hand. "Maybe," he grimaced. "Just crazy enough to kick that thing's ass." Sophie tightened her grip as he searched for the best way up. He was in obvious pain, but showed no visible signs of injury.

"Are you okay?" she inquired. He didn't answer, just kept searching for a footing. He hoisted one foot onto the iron railing, but then both froze at the sound of another nearby shriek. Sophie shivered at the sound echoing below. Something else was coming, and she wanted to be gone when it arrived.

Alie motioned for her to climb down onto the fire escape. "We're not safe here," he said. She agreed as her feet touched down quietly onto the landing. Alie looked into an adjacent window, then pulled Sophie into the humble kitchen of a small, one-room apartment where they stepped over two empty bodies crumpled on the tiles. Sophie shuddered as she passed the bodies on the way to a small living room, where they waited for the chaos outside to subside.

Chapter Twenty-Two

The screeching mob dissolved again into the night, giving Sophie and Alie the courage to venture out in search of safe passage to the plaza. They snuck from apartment to apartment, building to building, struggling to keep their bearings through a bewildering maze of hallways and corridors. Sophie felt lost most of the time, but knew they had to keep moving. Alie had managed to best a very nasty demon, but it was only one, and they didn't tend to travel alone.

So they trudged on, carefully and deliberately, checking every door and every hallway before entering. They jumped the gaps between buildings that weren't too far to jump—usually from window to window or ledge to ledge. And when the gaps were too far, they descended to the streets and crept across on foot. Several times they encountered other spirits, either holed up in their apartments or helplessly wandering the halls. Alie and Sophie tried repeatedly to make contact, but each time they found that, like the spirits in the plaza, their faces were just as grotesquely unrecognizable as their speech.

"We need to drop down here," Alie said as he and Sophie leaned out a window for a better look.

"Why? We can make that jump," she answered.

He backed away from the window and tugged her toward the door. "Just trust me on this one. I need to go down there."

They exited onto a narrow street that was empty except for a few benches and the remains of what appeared to be a quaint flower cart. Sophie followed Alie as he edged his way along the building facades, never letting his guard down. They ducked behind the flower stand as a lost spirit strolled by. After it passed, Alie stepped out into the street and looked at a scattered pile of something lying at his feet. Sophie drew closer and recognized the pile as a heap of flowers lying on the pavement. She stood next to him as he stared at the flowers, wondering what it was about them that brought Alie down to the street.

"They're beautiful and all, Alie, but there are probably better times to 'stop and smell the roses'," she chuckled as she leaned into him.

"They were for you," he confessed. His words jolted her and chased the smile from her face. They were just a simple bouquet of flowers, yet the sight of them suddenly stung Sophie so penetratingly. What should have been an incredibly sweet gesture was now an instant, painful reminder of their dreadful state of affairs. She stood over them, wishing she could pick them up, but knowing that there was no point in trying. She couldn't touch them yet there they were, taunting her as a cruel memento of how beautiful things once were, and how they may never be again.

"I…I'm sorry," she stuttered. "I didn't know."

"I was bringing them to you when *it* happened."

"So," Sophie hesitated, "so this is where you fell?"

Alie nodded, his eyes fixed on the flowers.

"But you aren't here," she said. "I mean *you* are, but…"

"It's not," Alie responded, very matter-of-factly. It was just as he said; his body was gone. The only possible explanation, as sickening as it sounded, was that his corpse had already been taken, which meant it was wandering around somewhere being piloted by some twisted, vile being. Of all the horrors Sophie had experienced since the incident, this was by far the worst.

"There's no sense in standing around and pouting," Alie said. "We have somewhere we need to be, and it ain't here."

. . . .

The plaza had emptied significantly since the last time Sophie saw it. Most of the horde was gone, leaving only a few stragglers to scavenge the square. Alie and Sophie scanned the plaza from the shadowy shelter of an alleyway, but their view of the spot where Sophie's body had fallen was blocked by the fountain.

"I can't see it," Sophie whispered.

"Neither can I," Alie agreed. "Stay here; I'm going to get a better look."

"No!" She latched onto his arm. "Not without me. I'm coming too." Alie began to protest, but Sophie was already several steps into the open, ducking behind benches and a retaining wall as she moved. With Alie on her heels, she managed to creep to a better vantage point where she could see beyond the fountain. But the spot where her body had lain was empty, with no sign of her remains anywhere. An involuntary whimper escaped from within her, and Alie immediately jerked her to the ground before the remaining demons detected her. He held his hand over her mouth and begged her not to make a sound. He then inched on his belly until he could see around the fountain and locate the demons. Once he was satisfied that they were still unspotted, he scooted back to Sophie's side and took her by the wrist, coaxing her to back to the alley.

But Sophie resisted. She was shaken profoundly by the absence of her body. They really had only one plan, and that was to find their bodies and somehow re-inhabit them. But that's awfully hard to do when there are no bodies to re-inhabit. She had thought that their biggest, and maybe only, advantage was the snail-like pace at which time was moving on the other side. But apparently their rooftop skirmish with the yellow-eyed creature, and the subsequent escape over and through buildings had taken much longer than she realized. It was at least long enough to give the demons time to either possess her body, or at least drag it from the square. Either way, she was sure it couldn't have gone too far, but had no way of knowing which way it went.

Alie tugged on her arm, again urging her with his eyes to retreat with him. She relented and scooted back in his direction. But after a few paces, an image of her father flashed like lightning in her mind, and she turned back. Her head swiveled back and forth between Alie and the fountain. She would follow him, of course. But she just had to check on something first. After mouthing "sorry", she dropped to her hands and knees and began crawling back to the edge of the fountain.

Alie watched in horror as Sophie repeatedly jutted her head out from behind the fountain, searching for the right time to make her move. He couldn't imagine what she was doing, but couldn't ask her without giving them away. So, he stayed crouched and panicked, prepared to fight if necessary.

Sophie disappeared behind the fountain, out of Alie's view. He slid silently behind a table until he could spot two of the demons, but couldn't make out Sophie. The demons were straddling an empty body, engaged in some sort of fierce debate that involved pointing, accusing and, eventually, shoving. Their quarrel quickly intensified to an all-out brawl, which Alie hoped would distract them from whatever it was that Sophie was doing. And it seemed to work, at least momentarily as the two of them crashed fiercely to the ground. One mounted itself atop the other, slashing and pummeling while other demons in the plaza closed in for a better view. The one on the bottom grasped for anything, and eventually managed to grab the other's throat before digging its claws deep into the other's neck while pushing its chin skyward. The demon on top howled in pain as its head bent backward. But then it froze suddenly, with its gaze fixed squarely in Sophie's direction. It had spotted her. The creature pointed an elongated finger toward the fountain and shouted a command. The other demons instantly turned from spectators to predators, snarling like a pack of hyenas preparing to rip its prey to shreds.

But before they could pounce, Alie leapt to his feet and charged directly at them, screaming like a maniac as he ran. The creatures stared at him, momentarily frozen at the strange sight of a human spirit coming straight for them. Alie glanced quickly over his shoulder and caught a fleeting glimpse of Sophie running the opposite direction toward the alleyway. When he looked back, he found that the demons were no longer focused on Sophie, but on him. Their rippling muscles twitched as they snarled at one another, and then at Alie. They gathered into a frenzied cluster as they readied themselves to intercept Alie's foolish charge. But it never came.

Half-way across the plaza, Alie grinded to a halt. His feet slid underneath him as he crouched and steadied himself on the pavement. Then he juked abruptly to his left and bolted into a passage that cut between two buildings. His plan was never to attack them, just to distract them. And it worked. Sophie had escaped, and now the demons were tight on his heels. He no longer had any plan whatsoever other than to run, and run fast.

He didn't allow himself to turn and look back. It would only slow him down, and he had no doubt they were there. Instead, he moved faster than he ever had, searching around every turn for some place to duck into without being seen.

He tore around corner after corner until he found himself sprinting down a wide street where a cluster of figures were gathered at the end of the block. It was too dark to distinguish whether they were demons or just more wandering spirits, but turning back or slowing down wasn't an option, so he rushed right at them. They appeared lost, huddled together like a blind, disoriented. As he drew closer, he could make out the same miserable faces of the lost souls from the plaza, and knew they were not demons. But he could also tell from their suddenly terrified expressions that they saw not only him, but the approaching demons chasing him. They started to scatter in a frenzy just as Alie plunged headlong right into the cluster. Still, he didn't slow down, barreling right through the middle of them. Just as he broke through into the open street on the other side, a figure shot out from a hidden corridor and smashed into him like a truck, driving him toward a closed door.

They passed right through the door, crashing hard into a wall on the other side. He was momentarily stunned, but forced himself to come to quickly, fully expecting his attacker to fight. But instead it lay crumpled at his feet instead, whimpering. The tiny entry hall was almost completely dark, but the figure was bathed in a dim light. He dropped to his knees and reached out his hand and reached for the light. His hand touched a head of soft hair, and he knew right way it was Sophie.

"Whoa!" she exclaimed in a half-cry, half-hack. "That was intense." She was trembling and breathing heavily, and about to speak again when Alie clasped his hand firmly over her mouth. Through the door he could hear the chaos of the crowd outside mixed with the sniveling demons that had almost caught him. But Sophie saved him. She had timed it perfectly, tackling him through the door and out of the sight at the exact moment he emerged from the crowd. By the time the creatures made it through the crowd, he was gone.

"I'm so sorry," she whispered, still panting. "They almost got you because of me."

"No, Sophie," he insisted, "you just saved me from them. That was brilliant."

"They were only chasing you because of me. I'm so incredibly stupid and selfish. I just had to…" Alie slammed his hand over her mouth again. The sound of raspy breaths penetrated the door. Sophie felt Alie's body tense just as a twitching, deformed nose poked through the door, followed by a snarling snout. With each breath, the tiny entry filled with a nauseating stench. Sophie clambered backward and almost over the top of Alie as they escaped around a corner, just as the creature poked its sinister head fully through the door. The putrid stink intensified as it inhaled and exhaled into the darkness. Sophie trembled, sure that it would sense them. But after what felt like an eternity, the breathing stopped, and the creature moved on.

A flickering light bulb drooped from the ceiling just a few feet down the hallway. Alie and Sophie crawled until they were huddled beneath the dimly illuminated ring of light beneath the bulb. They sat in silence. They had no physical bodies that could get tired, but were exhausted anyway. They couldn't keep this up—wandering around trying to stay hidden, and just barely escaping each time they were spotted. The only thing that had made sense to this point was to find their bodies and retake them, but that suddenly seemed hopeless. They were both overwhelmed by their predicament, and by the unknown future that lay before them.

"What now?" Alie whispered. Sophie shrugged, but said nothing. "If they have, in fact, possessed our bodies," he continued, "then we should be able to—"

"What happens if one of us dies?" Sophie interrupted.

"What do you mean *dies*, Sophie?" he answered. "You know that's not going to happen."

"I don't mean *die* like…you know…like when a body gives up the ghost type of dying…like we've apparently already done. But who knows? Who knows what happens if one of those things, or a lot of those things capture us? I'm pretty sure they're not going to want to hang out and play cards." The fear was thick in her voice, perhaps more than ever before. "It sure seems to me like they want to kill us. But is there some kind of *death* in this existence? Or something worse? Or are we just stuck here, destined to keep running forever?" She leaned her body away from his and turned to look him straight in the face. Her eyes were wide and intense. "Is this hell?"

Alie shook his head hastily. "Sophie, you can't talk like that," he exclaimed, seemingly irritated by her question. "We may be in a predicament, but I'm here, and so are you. By definition, that's not hell."

"Are you sure?" she responded. "Like I said, what if you die, or disappear, or whatever? What if we were reunited as just some kind of cruel set-up, only to be ripped apart again, but this time forever? *That* would be hell."

"As long as I am here," he insisted, "that will *not* happen."

"Over my dead body, right?"

Alie eyed her. Despair seemed to be tightening its grip on her, and it disturbed him.

"Sophie…"

"We can't just keep running, Alie. And *you* can't keep thinking you can protect me from them. I'm sorry, but it's not realistic." Her voice quivered, trying not to break. "You've seen them, with their fangs and protruding claws and disgusting faces. Most of them look like they were created to inflict pain, built for combat. And there are tons of them, and only one of you."

Alie's eyes narrowed as he leaned in close. His jaw tightened, and his countenance turned to steel as he looked past her into the darkness. His mind went somewhere else for a moment, and then he was back with her. For an instant, and the only time since they met, he intimidated her.

"Listen to me," he whispered with a fiery glare. "I have stared down the barrel of evil for most of my adult life. I have smelled the burning flesh of children set on fire just because of something their parents said. I have watched a woman's flesh peel from her bones after her husband doused her with acid, just because she looked at a man the wrong way. I have gathered the decapitated heads of so-called *infidels* and tried to match them to their bodies, just so their families could have something to bury." He paused and looked deliberately both ways down the hallway, and then back at her. She didn't dare say a word. "I've seen evil, Sophie. I've seen it as bad as it can get, and not from some silly, fantastical, otherworldly beast, but from one human being to another. So, if you think a set of glowing eyes and sharp teeth are gonna scare me, then you don't know me quite as well as you thought."

His words seemed downright insane, but she believed him. He really didn't fear those things. She watched him on that rooftop, and charging right at them in the plaza, and he didn't hesitate. Without him, she would have crawled into a corner and given up. But he had a way of changing things. He had told her once that the only thing he feared was losing her and, for now, that was going to have to be enough for her.

"But, Sophie," his eyes softened, but his grip on her hand was firm, "you cannot give up on me. I cannot do this alone. We need each other. I need you."

She nodded as she leaned back into him. "I know. I'm sorry."

"Stop apologizing, just say you're with me."

"I'm with you," she said. "And I love you."

"Me too."

They sat in a long, silent embrace, their bodies intertwined in the dim spotlight that dissected the otherwise dark hallway. With the noise and chaos gone outside, it was almost completely soundless except for the strange, hollow breaths that filled their own ghostly bodies. Since the event, she had not felt a heartbeat within her chest, nor Alie's, and she had no idea if there were still lungs of some sort inside of her. But she still felt the urgent need to suck in air and, when she did, her chest still seemed to inflate.

"Can I ask you a question?" she said, breaking the silence.

"Sure."

"The way you describe everything you saw in combat. It's terrible. Why would you keep doing it? Why go back, over and over again?"

"Hope." His answer was immediate.

"Hope?" she exclaimed. "Hope for whom? Or for what? How could anyone find hope in a place like that?"

"There are good people there, Sophie," he answered. "Lots of them. And if I can bring some sort of hope to them, in the face of everything they have to live with every day, then that's worth it to me. And if I can do that, then maybe there's hope for me too."

He shifted his weight to one side and slid his hand off her shoulder and behind his back. She wondered what he was doing. After a few seconds, his hand re-appeared.

"There's always hope," he whispered in her ear. Just inches in front of her face, Alie's hand held her father's paintbrush. Her body jolted as a sob exploded from within her. She could hardly control her emotions as she took the brush from him and caressed it with her fingers. It felt so familiar, so real. For a moment, it was as if she could feel her father there, prompting her to carry on. To not lose hope.

"Where...how did you get this?"

"I know," he answered tenderly. "I know you looked for it and you didn't find it. But I did. Just as I was charging like an idiot at those monsters, it caught my eye on the ground. I stopped and picked it up, then I ran. I just hoped I could get away from them so I could eventually give it back to you."

Sophie threw her arms around him and thanked him repeatedly. She then turned and leaned her back into his chest and extended the brush into the murky light cascading from the bulb above them. Alie rested against the wall, mesmerized by the beauty of her delicate hand caressing the empty space in front of them. He had no idea what image she was tracing, but he didn't care. He allowed himself to smile for a moment, and just sat and waited until she saw it.

She gasped suddenly, and then froze, staring at the brush. "Alie! Alie, can you see it?"

He laughed quietly. "Yeah, I see it."

Sophie held her other hand over her mouth, breathless, while moving the brush back and forth before her eyes. It wasn't easy to spot at first, but became more discernible once she knew what to look for. She swiped the brush to the left, and then watched in wonder at the faintly visible, yet identical silhouette of a brush dancing through the air, less than an inch behind her own. Back to the right, and the ethereal image followed, mirroring her brushstroke. Up, down, back and forth she whisked the brush, and the shadowy image followed, attached to nothing, yet never venturing from the brush in her own fingers. And when she stopped moving, it was as if the brushes combined into one, and the shadowy brush disappeared. The ghostly image of a floating brush was certainly unnerving, but Sophie knew that, ironically, it was her brush that was being manipulated by a ghost, and the floating image was a manifestation from the real, physical world. But how?

"What is it?" she pondered aloud.

"It looks like your brush."

"Obviously, but…what is it? And how?" She swiped again, this time playfully trying, unsuccessfully, to capture the phantom brush with her other hand.

"The best I can tell, it's from the other side," Alie answered. "But as for how, and why, and all that, I haven't the slightest idea."

Sophie held her brush a few inches from her eyes, examining it intensely. In the time since they were separated from the real world, however long that was, they had seen a lot, but never anything like this. Was she really controlling something in the physical world from her current state? And if so, why was it moving in sync with her movements, when everything else she had seen from the physical world moved so mind-numbingly slow?

"Alie, what in the world is going on?" she wondered.

"Well, I think you moving the brush here is causing the brush to move there."

"No, I mean, *all* of this," she responded. "Everything. The spirits, and the creatures, the darkness, and us? All of it. What's happening?"

Alie shook his head. He had no answers, and he wasn't so sure there were any.

"And why are we left to figure this out on our own?" she continued. "Is there even anyone to ask? Will we even be able to talk to anyone else, ever again? Or can we even risk going out with those *things* hunting us?"

"I told you before, Sophie, you can't give up hope," Alie insisted. "You have to stay with me." He squeezed her tightly. It was all he had to give her to try and make her feel safe. "If your father were here, what would he tell you to do?"

She turned to him, visibly shaken by his question. She stared at the brush in her hand for several minutes, deep in thought. Finally, she said, "Let's go to church."

That wasn't the answer Alie was hoping for, but he didn't have any better ideas. "Can I ask why?"

"Maybe like-minded spirits will go there," she answered, "and maybe the demons will stay away." She paused for a moment, glancing at the brush one last time before rising to her feet and returning the brush to her back pocket. "And maybe…well, maybe we'll find some kind of higher form of help."

Chapter Twenty-Three

A strange sky hung over St. Pierre's cathedral. Unlike the dismal, non-descript blanket of haze that had obscured the heavens since Sophie and Alie entered the spirit realm, a fiery glow crept through the clouds above the church, bathing the towering pillars and the plaza below in scarlet. Alie couldn't see the source of the light, and wondered if what they were seeing was the sun. The plaza extending from the church steps was both beautiful and terrifying, as at least a dozen creatures were roaming through the crimson hue. Alie had suspected it wouldn't be easy getting to the church, and it definitely was not; they had several close calls along the way. But he didn't expect the church grounds themselves to be infested with demons.

Once again, they found themselves hiding in the shadows, trying to figure out how to do the impossible. They would not only have to find a way to cross the courtyard unseen, but also pass through the door successfully without being pounced on or followed. As the demons paced the plaza, Alie struggled to come up with a plan that wasn't absolutely insane, but there simply wasn't one.

"Any ideas," he whispered to Sophie.

"Maybe." She didn't sound too sure.

"Any that aren't crazy?"

"Well, then no," she answered. "But that's never stopped us before."

Alie chuckled. "So let's hear it, then. What's your plan?"

Sophie rose to her feet and swallowed hard. She looked at Alie uneasily and said, quite a bit louder than she should have, "Have faith. What other plan is there?" With that, she turned and made a beeline for the church. Alie tried to grab her arm to stop her, but he was too late. She bolted right through the middle of the stunned creatures. The demons erupted into a frenzy, but not before Sophie had passed them and was closing in on the church steps. The two closest ones lunged at her, but missed. She cleared the steps in a single leap, spinning just before her back slammed against the towering, wooden front door. She had hoped to catch a glimpse of Alie just before passing through to the inside. Instead she stood pancaked against the door as the demons snarled at her with an infuriated rage. But despite their desire to tear her to pieces, they wouldn't step onto the stairs. They stayed on the pavement below, their eyes fixed intently on Sophie.

Alie was both shocked and ecstatic by this new phenomenon. Without thinking, he had taken several steps into the plaza to protect Sophie if necessary. Now that she was apparently safe, he found himself completely exposed in the middle of the courtyard behind a gang of very pissed off demons. But he could also see that they were completely preoccupied with Sophie, a fact that he planned to exploit.

Alie strolled nonchalantly to within a few feet of the demons and then shoved one as hard as he could, sending the creature crashing face-down onto the church steps. As the demon squealed, Alie vaulted himself past the crowd, his left foot landing squarely in the middle of the prostrate demon's back. He followed with his right foot on the back of the demon's head, smashing its face into the third step. He cleared the rest of the steps and joined Sophie at the front door. The demon doormat scooted frantically backwards away from the steps, its face mangled by its kiss with the stair. The demon mob was even more enraged now, but still wouldn't set foot onto the stairs.

"Well isn't that curious?" Alie chuckled as he and Sophie stood with backs to the church door watching the growling creatures pace back and forth at the bottom of the steps. "Do you suppose…" Alie took several steps back down the staircase, stopping just out of the demons' reach.

"Alie, no!" Sophie snapped. "Don't push your luck." But he couldn't resist. He stood his ground and stuck out an arm, then a foot, then an arm again, pulling them back each time a demon took a swipe at him. He taunted them shamelessly for several minutes while Sophie tried to figure out how to get into the church. She tried to open the large door, but it wouldn't budge. She knocked, pushed, kicked, and did everything else should could think of, but nothing changed. It was just as solid and impenetrable as it would have been in the physical world. Discouraged by the apparent failure of her church idea, she turned and again leaned against the door, this time sliding her back down its surface until she was sitting with her feet tucked underneath her. Alie had taken a seat as well, several steps down from Sophie, clearly entertained by the sight of hapless demons throwing their tenacious fits.

Sophie rested her head against the door, but the door felt oddly like it was pushing back. In fact, it was. Her feet slid slowly for several seconds toward the edge of the top step before she realized what was happening. The door was moving.

She sprang to her feet and out of the way as the door crept open. The demons retreated cowardly to the middle of the courtyard, still protesting. Alie also turned his attention to the hulking, dark entrance that had mysteriously opened before them. He gently pulled Sophie toward him and held her hand as they waited. After several seconds, a set of cautious eyes peered out from inside and studied the scene in the courtyard. A delicate, feminine hand holding a dimly glowing candle followed.

"*Qui êtes-vous?*" came a soft voice from behind the door. Sophie understood, but looked at Alie.

"*Nous sommes amis,*" he answered. "May we come in?"

The eyes hesitated and looked beyond them again toward the demons. Then they disappeared without another word into the darkness behind the door, followed by the candle. Alie and Sophie looked at one another. Sophie squeezed Alie's hand and then, for the second time in the past few days, pulled him into the St. Pierre cathedral.

The cavernous interior was almost entirely dark near the entrance. The massive door slammed shut behind them, echoing like a cannon throughout the hall. Gone were the vile rantings of the creatures outside, suddenly replaced by a chorus of curious voices buzzing from the opposite end of the church. Beyond the rows of pews, silhouettes mingled through rays of flickering candlelight emanating from the numerous candelabras scattered throughout the nave. Their faces were not discernible from a distance, but their movements and voices easily revealed that they were not demonic. Still, Sophie and Alie kept their distance, unsure as to exactly what they had walked into.

Rather than taking the obvious path right down the middle of the aisles, they stuck to the shadows on the periphery of the church, just outside the pillars. They ducked their way toward the opposite end of the church, slipping from pillar to pillar as they stole glimpses of the ghostly congregation. Their faces didn't appear quite as ghastly as the spirits in the square, and were of course a dramatic improvement over the demons. They seemed to not only recognize one another, but many huddled in groups and appeared to actually carry on conversations.

"Should we try to talk to them," Sophie whispered.

"I don't know," Alie answered. "I'm just fine where we are." He was clearly uncomfortable, just as he had been the last time they visited the church. This time Sophie wasn't sure if it was the church he didn't trust, or its otherworldly occupants. Either way, he was clearly in no hurry to join them. So Sophie stayed by his side, grasping his hand tightly and observing the intermingling spirits from afar. She was especially drawn to one in particular, a rather portly and oddly jovial entity who bounced from one group to another. While the other spirits spoke in a somewhat hushed, reverent tone, the voice from the heavy-set one was boisterous, almost to the point of being out of place. Several times he climbed a few steps toward the pulpit and delivered brief messages to the crowd. He would then continue moving throughout the crowd, who appeared to revere him as some sort of a leader or father-figure. Sophie couldn't make out what he was saying, but when he burst out in a hearty laugh that filled the hall, she jolted forward out of Alie's reach.

"Sophie, what is it?" Alie asked.

"There's no mistaking that laugh," she grinned. "I know him."

"Who? The chubby bloke?" She didn't answer, but instead darted from the darkness, weaving her way through the crowd until she stood directly behind him. His arms flailed energetically as he spoke with his back still turned to Sophie. But several others in the crowd had shifted their attention from the husky fellow to Sophie, which instantly made Alie nervous. He kept his distance, but not so far that he couldn't close the distance and snatch Sophie from the multitude if necessary. Sophie, however, didn't seem the least bit anxious as she reached out and laid her hand on the man's shoulder.

"Virgil? Do you know who I am?" She took a graceful step backward as he turned and eyed her from head to toe. Alie watched as his face transfigured from blurred to quite human, and then lit up revealing a wide grin.

"My goodness, my goodness! Sophie? Is that you?" He reached both hands out and gently placed them on her cheeks. He then immediately withdrew them and held a hand over his mouth. "My, my," he whispered. "It is! It is you, my sweet girl. The most beautiful American in Geneva is back, but this time she comes to me as an apparition, or a true angel even." He chuckled fervently as he clasped his hands onto her shoulders. "Who really cares what you are, or why you're here. I'm just glad that you are."

Sophie giggled and said, "It is very good to see you too, Virgil. I wasn't sure you would remember me."

"Well of course, my dear girl," he rumbled on. "How could I forget?" His eyes widened as a look of grave concern came over him. "Oh, but you must be so very put out with me," he said, quite troubled. "I failed to meet you for our date at the museum."

"Please, Virgil," she begged, "don't worry about that. It doesn't matter now. I just can't believe I found you."

"Yes, but please understand, I had a very good reason for missing our engagement," he continued contritely. "Please, let me explain."

She stopped him. "I would love to hear it, but first I want you to meet somebody." She turned and motioned for Alie to reappear from the shadows. For several seconds there was nothing, but then he emerged slowly and carefully. Their arrival had caused quite a stir with the crowd, which had gathered to inspect the new strangers. Unlike Virgil's, their faces were still unfamiliar. Like the spirits in the square, they still bore only a faint, unsettling similarity to that of a human. Virgil's face, on the other hand, was warm and welcoming, and entirely too cheery for an old man stuck in a dreary phantom world. Even Alie found him to be trustworthy, and began to let his guard down, at least a little.

Virgil threw an enthusiastic arm around Sophie and blurted out an introduction to the crowd, albeit a highly embellished one. He presented Sophie as "the loveliest and most talented authority on the arts that Geneva has ever known," and Alie, despite having never met him before, as Sophie's "tremendously fortunate, and formidable beau." After several additional sincere, yet slightly exaggerated pronouncements, Virgil led Sophie and Alie away and toward a more secluded area where the famed chair of John Calvin sat alone and unoccupied. That is, until Virgil plopped decisively down into the seat, which prompted a curious look from Sophie.

"Oh, don't look at me that way my girl," he sniggered. "What's ol' Calvin gonna do? Kill me?" He burst out into a roar, clearly pleased at his own wit. Sophie laughed as well, not so much at the joke, but at Virgil in general. He still wore the same tweedy coat over the same worn, hooded sweatshirt. Despite the hazy texture it took on in their current state, the sweatshirt was still tarnished by several faded coffee stains. And Virgil was still every bit as oblivious to his looks on this side as he was on the other. But he seemed delighted to be there, not one bit affected by what was clearly a tragic situation. When Sophie first mentioned their presence in the spirit world, he enthusiastically reacted, "I know, isn't it glorious?"

"Glorious?" She was astonished at his response. She shot a bewildered glance at Alie, who just shrugged silently. "How can you say that?" she fired back.

Virgil sunk contently into the hard-backed chair. "How? Well I can say it quite captivatingly, my sweet girl, because I am completely captivated by it."

"By what, exactly?" she insisted.

Virgil held up his arms and swept them around his head. "By all of it," he smiled as his gaze ascended, taking in the majesty of their surroundings.

Sophie stepped toward him, almost a bit desperately. "Virgil!" she snapped somewhat aggressively, which clearly surprised him. "Forgive me," she hushed herself. "I am sorry, but please explain to me," she paused and took a deep breath, "what it is about all of this that you find…glorious, or captivating, or not completely terrifying."

He grinned at her sympathetically, which did very little to calm her. She appeared ready to explode, but Virgil rose from the chair and took her by the hand, prompting her to take his seat on Calvin's throne.

"I understand you are scared, as most in this church are. But don't let your fear cloud your awareness of what's going on around you." He held out his hands in front of his face, wiggling his fingers spastically, and then lifting them jubilantly skyward. "What you have before you, my dear, is confirmation of my entire life's work."

This time it was Alie who cut in, "I am happy that you feel validated, sir, but that doesn't do a bloody thing to change the predicament we are in."

Virgil spun and snapped his fingers just inches from Alie's face. "Real knowledge is to know the extent of one's ignorance," he declared, snapping a second time for extra emphasis. "You know who said that? It was either Confucius, or my ex-wife," he squinted his eyes, trying to recall. Alie inhaled as if he had something to say, but nothing came out.

"We don't mean to be rude, Virgil," said Sophie, "but we have been through hell since, you know, *it* happened."

"The somatic fission?" asked Virgil.

"Somatic…huh?"

"Well, if you are referring to the event of recent days that resulted in you parting ways with your corporal form," Virgil explained, "then that is the name I have given it."

"So, do you know what happened?" Sophie probed, eager for some semblance of understanding. "We have so many questions."

Virgil inhaled noisily through his moustache, as if he were, for the first time, thinking very carefully about how to answer. "I have my hypotheses, most of which seem to be holding up. Ask away, and I will do my best to answer."

Sophie looked anxiously at Alie, who had decided he didn't mind Virgil, mostly for the entertainment value. But he clearly wasn't convinced that Virgil had any meaningful insight, or even much sanity for that matter.

"Where do we begin?" Sophie said under her breath as her eyes darted around eagerly, as if she was searching for some footing from which to articulate the millions of thoughts spinning in her head.

"With the obvious, I suppose," Alie answered. "Are we—"

"Dead?" Sophie blurted out.

Virgil shook his head and smiled slyly, as if he were already anticipating the question. "Dead? Oh no, my dear, not in the traditional sense."

"Traditional sense?" demanded Sophie.

"Well, death, in the 'traditional sense'," Virgil explained while retracting his hand inside his sleeve, "involves the departure of a spirit because its body, for one reason or another, is no longer capable of acting as a vessel for that spirit." His hand suddenly shot out of the sleeve, his fingers wiggling hastily, as if they had been set free. "In that sense, we have not kicked the proverbial bucket, as some say," he chortled while liberally flashing air quotes for emphasis. "Our spirits are free of our corporal forms, but not necessarily because of any incapacity on the part of our bodies."

"I don't get it," said Sophie, her gaze switching between Virgil and Alie, who sat with his eyes narrowed and mind churning. "I sat and watched my own body, and many others, scattered lifeless across Bourg-de-Four Square while spirits wandered helplessly. I just don't understand how that's not death?"

Virgil shook his head again. "Just because we don't understand doesn't mean that the explanation doesn't exist," he replied. "Do you know who said that? This one I am quite confident of…"

Alie warily rose to his feet, clearly annoyed by the conversation's lack of progress. "What does it matter who…"

"That one was Madeleine L'Engle," Virgil interrupted, oblivious to Alie's interjection. "Of that I am sure." He stroked his beard as his mind took a brief sabbatical, possibly to dredge up other bygone, barely useful quotes.

"Well, if we're not dead," Alie pressed, "then what, or where the hell are we?"

Virgil considered the question, then stretched out his legs and interlocked his fingers behind his head. "It's quite simply really. We are merely…stuck."

"Stuck?" Sophie asked.

"Stuck?" Alie added.

"Yes, stuck," Virgil continued. "Somewhere between the physical world and the place we're headed, had we actually died, that is."

"And where might that be?" asked Alie. "Heaven…or Hell?" Alie could hardly deny the existence of an afterlife anymore, but he was still clearly uncomfortable mentioning such things. Virgil clearly was not.

"Not hardly," Virgil responded. "To the extent that those places exist, you know, in the 'traditional sense'," he paused, again for effect, "we are nowhere near either of them, or even on any particular path to get there, or even anywhere at all, for that matter."

Alie continued to pace in front of Calvin's chair, stepping repeatedly over Virgil's feet "But I thought that's what was supposed to happen when you…" Alie paused, avoiding the word "died". "Well, you know, when we *exit* our bodies."

Virgil sighed. "No, that's what's supposed to happen when you *die*," he expounded. "Although my understanding is that it's not quite that…simple."

"Your understanding?" Alie eyed Virgil cynically. Why were they even indulging this eccentric old man?

"Yes, that's right," Virgil answered. "Based on my decades of research and analysis, of course."

"But is that understanding…biblical?" asked Sophie.

"It's science," answered Virgil.

"What's the difference?" Alie inquired.

"There's not one, not really," said Virgil. "At least, not…"

"In the traditional sense," Alie added while nodding.

"Right, my boy," exclaimed Virgil, unaffected by Alie's thick sarcasm. "You're spot on. For far too long humans have mistakenly drawn an absolute division between God and science, when they are really one and the same. For what is science, but the observation of the laws of nature? And what is God, but the creator of those same laws? Throughout history, mankind has stubbornly held onto a flawed belief that we have to choose between believing in a god, or in science, as if the existence of one disproves the other. Humans have arrogantly concluded that advances in science somehow disprove the existence of a creator when, in reality, they are merely tiny windows into the creator's work."

Virgil's words called for further reflection when the time was right. But time was something they just didn't have. "So, if we haven't died yet, is it possible to, you know, die here?" Virgil eyed Sophie curiously as she continued. "I mean, those creatures out there, they seem quite intent on seeing us, well, dead."

"That may be the most important question," Virgil stated, "and I'm afraid I don't have the answer. Remember, my dear, that the event caused by the hadron collider malfunction is rather unprecedented. So, there may not even be an answer, at least not yet."

"So where does that leave us?" she asked.

"The *where* is quite simple," Virgil answered while stomping his feet. "We're in Geneva, Switzerland. The same as before." Virgil stood and inexplicably thumped his chest twice. "The question you should be asking, my dear Sophie, is *how*?"

"Okay, then," Sophie responded, "how?"

Virgil looked around at the church's other occupants. Once satisfied, he took a seat directly between Sophie and Alie. After a deep sigh and a stroke of his thick moustache, Virgil began to dig into his favorite topic:

"Well, it should be quite evident by now that the *you* that you had come to know so well since birth was really made up of two parts: a physical body of flesh, and that which you call a spirit, a ghost, a phantasm, or whatever you call it." As he spoke, he again extended his hand and wrist out from his coat sleeve, and then wiggled his fingers. "Imagine a hand inside a glove. The hand is your spirit, and the glove is your body. Without the hand, the glove is essentially worthless. But with the hand inside, the glove comes to life. One fits perfectly inside the other and makes the other appear alive. However, if you remove the hand, it stays alive, but the glove becomes limp and lifeless. Once they are separated, the hand may feel cold or uncomfortable at first, but it will still live on without the glove."

"So, how does the hand get back inside the glove?" Alie inquired.

"Herein lies the dilemma," Virgil replied. "This is the same question that has been asked by every soul in this church, and I'm not sure I have the answer…yet. I have read quite a bit on the topic in years past, and I have my theories, but I don't believe I will have anything concrete until I observe the procedure myself."

"What procedure?" asked Sophie.

"It…it is difficult to explain." Virgil stumbled over his words.

"You used the word *procedure*," Alie said. "Does this *procedure*, by chance, look something like a ceremony or ritual involving, well, frail little white creatures?"

Virgil jumped to his feet, as animated as Sophie had ever seen him. "You've seen this?"

"Well, we're not exactly sure what we saw," Alie continued, "but it involved a squirmy little…thing, some chanting, and what appeared to be bodies coming alive and moving on the other side." Virgil looked as if he were ready to bolt from the church in search of what Alie described. He stripped off his coat and tossed it aside. He then ran his fingers on both hands through his hair in deep thought. "Where did you see this?" he demanded.

"In the plaza," answered Sophie.

"Bourg-de-Four?"

Sophie nodded while observing Virgil's sudden childlike

enthusiasm. Virgil thought intensely again for several minutes and then asked Alie to describe the creatures in very meticulous detail. Alie explained the pale, pathetic bodies, and the sunken eyes peering out from their bald, bulbous heads. He also described the eerie, rhythmic chanting and the small creature's disturbing transformation that followed.

Virgil's body stiffened as his face then took on a very ominous expression. "And then what?" he asked.

"We didn't see everything," answered Alie, "but it was enough. Another creature, a leader of some sort, laid down and assumed the form of an empty body."

"Did the body…rise?"

"Like I said, we didn't see everything. We had to leave," Alie continued, "but I can only assume that's what came next."

"So then it is true," Virgil mumbled and collapsed back into the chair.

"What's true?" Sophie insisted.

"The pures."

"The what?" Sophie probed.

"*Pueri sancti*," Virgil said ominously. "The pure children."

"They are children?" Sophie gasped.

"It is not known what they are," Virgil responded, "or how they came to be. They were named by their appearance which, as you describe, makes them look rather frail and childlike compared to their demonic captors. In Latin, the word for child is *puer,* P-U-E-R. The earliest known texts describing them are in Latin, where they are called the *pueris sancti*. This led scholars to refer to them as the pures."

"Scholars?" questioned Alie. "Do you mean that there are people who actually study this stuff?"

Virgil grinned and bowed his head. "In the flesh…well, I suppose not exactly," he chuckled. "But I have dedicated years of study to this *stuff*, as you call it. And much to the dismay of many of my colleagues in the scientific community."

"I remember now, on the train, you told me that you had just been…had just lost your job because of some controversy," said Sophie. "Is this what you were talking about?"

Virgil crinkled his forehead, trying to recall the specifics of the conversation. "Oh, yes, that is correct, my dear. I had only just been sacked from CERN, and was on my way to Lyon to compare notes with another researcher."

"Another paranormal researcher?"

"Doesn't seem so foolish now, does it, my boy?"

Alie didn't respond, and Virgil continued. "In fact, the scholarly study of para-existential phenomena has been ongoing for centuries, and by many brilliant and well-respected scientists. But it is also frowned upon heavily by most academics who dismiss it as merely fantastical ghost stories."

"I gotta admit," said Alie, "I was one of those, that is until I saw it with my own eyes. But isn't that science? The study of things you can actually see and observe?"

"Not necessarily. Take, for example, the theoretical study of the interior of black holes, which is a highly regarded scientific discipline despite no one ever having actually seen inside one," Virgil expounded. "And consider my former employer that has spent billions to study the Higgs boson, or 'God particle'—the one responsible for all this mess. Their work is considered by many as the greatest scientific experiment of our time, yet no one ever actually expected to see this so-called God particle. Billions and billions just to try and validate a hypothesis."

"So you don't believe the particle exists?" Alie questioned.

"Of course I do! I know it exists. I have known for as long as I can remember, and it didn't take a sixteen-mile-long tunnel and billions of dollars to convince me. You see, most scientists can only operate for so long on theories, or faith if you will. Eventually, it will drive them mad and they will seek out ways to prove themselves right, often very expensive ways. But if you so much as mention the possibility of an afterlife in the same breath as science, you are suddenly a pariah." Virgil paused and sighed aggressively.

"We need to know more about these *pures*," Sophie said. "Where do they come from?"

"The literature on the subject is quite inconclusive," Virgil explained.

"Literature?" Alie looked surprised? "Someone wrote a book on all this?"

"Books," Virgil answered. "And books, and books, and books.

Volumes and volumes. Entire libraries in fact. You just have to know where to find them."

"And where might that be?" Alie inquired rather skeptically.

"Some are here, some are there," Virgil replied, "but the vast majority are in Rome. The Vatican."

Sophie stood promptly as she hung on everything Virgil said. "What, exactly, are in the books?" she asked.

"The *how*," Virgil responded. "Consider again the hand and the glove, which could normally be slipped on and off at will. This is where the analogy differs from reality. The spirit and the body are joined by an extraordinarily strong bond at the most minute, subatomic level. As I said before, this bond is generally only severed when the body ceases its ability to function and, thus, house the soul. But when CERN's machine malfunctioned, the result, the rather ironic result actually, was a catastrophic and instant severing of these magnificently tiny bonds that bind spirit and body."

"And these bonds," Alie inquired, "are they the—"

"God particle," Virgil answered.

"Let me get this straight," Sophie interjected. "The same scientists, the ones who so adamantly reject the idea of an afterlife or a spirit world, set out to prove the existence of the very particle that holds the body and spirit together, and in doing so, created a disaster that caused the severance of the spirits from their bodies?"

"Exactly," exclaimed Virgil. "And if those nasty beasts roaming the streets out there have their way, the disaster will be much worse than losing our bodies."

"Do you mean that they will take them?" Alie asked.

"They will try everything in their power to do so," Virgil responded.

"Why?" Sophie probed. "What are they?"

Virgil stood again and surveyed first the crowd of souls clustered in the illuminated middle of the church as if he were protecting a great secret. "Well, humans often call them 'demons', whether it be from strange, supernatural encounters, or from simple folklore. But they are really nothing more than spirits, like us, but who never had the opportunity to inhabit a body."

"Whoa, like us?" interjected Sophie. "We've seen a lot of those things, and they're nothing like us."

"Not now. Perhaps they once were, but not anymore," Virgil explained. "After thousands of years of war and obsession, they have deteriorated into a miserable and grotesque species that hardly resemble us at all anymore. All of this over their blind fixation on one thing: the insatiable desire for a body. To us, it's routine, something we take for granted. But to them, it's a deep craving, like an addict and his drug." Virgil paused, raising one of his bushy eyebrows.

"At least, not until one of their pures helps them possess a body?" Sophie added. "But how?"

"I was hoping you could tell me," Virgil remarked.

"Just because we saw it," Alie said, "doesn't mean we have any idea what the hell was going on."

"But surely you must know," Sophie blurted out, "if there is a way for us to get back. Is it possible?"

Virgil turned his back to them and stared into a dark corner of the church. He was mumbling something, as if he were engaged in an argument with himself. After several minutes, he turned back to them, his face still perplexed, and said, "I need you to describe it to me again, the ceremony you saw in the plaza. I need every little detail you can remember," he hesitated again, exhaling a long sigh. "There are too many questions and not enough answers. I must travel to the archives and try to conduct additional research."

"You are going out there?" Sophie exclaimed. "Alone? Not a chance. You won't last a minute."

"That's why we're going with him," said Alie grimly.

"Nonsense!" said Virgil.

"No, Sophie's right," Alie answered. "You can't go alone. You'll never make it."

"I won't hear of it," Virgil insisted. "I'll not have you risking yourselves on my part."

"It's not just for you," Alie pressed on. "If going to all the way to Rome is what it's going to take to figure out how to solve this mess, then that's what we'll do."

Virgil continued pacing while shaking his head emphatically. "But I may not even find an answer," he said, "and even if I do, it will likely require the use of a pure."

Alie nodded as if he already knew that was coming. "If that's what it takes…"

"Alie, my boy, I applaud your extraordinary valor. But you must understand that the pures are the prized possession of the demons. They will guard them ferociously, all of them."

"Then I won't bother to ask," Alie said. "I'll just take."

"It's doubtful you can even get close to one," Virgil persisted. "And you certainly cannot fight them all."

Alie's eyes narrowed. "If that's what it takes—"

"Don't be ridiculous," Virgil scoffed.

"I have to try."

"Alie, you can't be serious," Sophie stepped in. "There's no way we can fight them all."

"I said *I* can try," he responded.

"Are you crazy?" Sophie cried out.

"Crazy?" he belted out. "What is it about this whole thing that isn't crazy?"

She reached for him, clearly distraught by his questionable fearlessness. "Okay, let's say I let you try. Even you said it before; you were fortunate to beat one of them. But what happens when you face two of them, or five, or a hundred? What happens if you lose? You act like you're invincible but, like Virgil said, no one really knows whether or not we can *die* here, and what happens if you do."

"Listen to me! I'm not gonna…" The words shot out of Alie hastily, and he caught himself and inhaled slowly. He put both hands apologetically on Sophie's shoulders. "You're right, we don't know, but I have to try. We can't just sit here, stuck for who knows how long? Maybe forever. You heard Virgil, this wasn't supposed to happen. We don't necessarily have a final destination, or an end in sight."

"Like Purgatory," Sophie whispered, turning her back to him and facing the darkness. The three of them stood in thick silence for several minutes. Their meeting with Virgil had provided some answers, but raised even more questions, none of which could be answered within the walls of the church. Alie was consumed with what he felt was a duty to keep Sophie safe, and to find a way to get her back into her body, while Sophie was fixated only on never again being separated from Alie. And Virgil was determined to seek out more information, as if the fate of everyone relied on his ability to find answers.

Virgil shot to his feet and announced, "Well I, for one, have had enough of pontificating over the hows and the whys. I've made clear my feelings on the two of you accompanying me but, if you insist, then let's be off."

"Wait," Alie said. "There's one more thing." Sophie felt his hand touch her lower back, and then lower until his fingers slid into her back pocket. She turned and saw him holding the brush out to her as Virgil looked on, puzzled. Sophie remembered that she too had intended to ask Virgil about her ability to move the brush on both sides, and immediately understood that Alie was asking her to show him. She retrieved the brush from him, and then glanced at Virgil. She lowered her hand to her side, then raised it again as a faint trickle of bluish dust followed. Virgil's eyes enlarged as he took a step forward, and then froze. Sophie's movements were modest at first, but then intensified into sweeping, dramatic strokes that captured the attention of others from the distant pews. As her motions continued to grace the air, the ethereal image of an identical brush began to materialize before their eyes, invading their spiritual space like a strange beacon from the other side. The image glided through the air, just barely trailing the brush in Sophie's hand.

Several gasps echoed through the church as the crowd neared, followed by an enthusiastic "Fascinating!" from Virgil. "The poltergeist phenomenon," he continued while coming even closer. "I've read much about this, but to see it with my own eyes…. Well, I suppose not really my own *eyes*, but you know what I mean."

"We think it's because she has such a profound connection with the brush on the other side," Alie explained.

"And you would be correct," Virgil nodded, now circling Sophie in awe. Others in the church also began to surround her, jockeying for a view. Sophie's arm did not stop moving, but her eyes watched Alie curiously, who had abruptly withdrawn from the crowd and taken a seat in Calvin's chair. He held his head in his hands as he stared at the floor for quite some time. Then, suddenly, he sprung to his feet and looked beyond Sophie and the crowd toward the front door.

"Sophie, wait here. I have to try something."

"No!" she screamed as the brush dropped again to her side. "No way! I will *not* be separated from you again. I'm going with you."

"It's too dangerous," he begged.

"I don't care," she insisted. Her face made it clear that there would be no argument.

Alie deliberated for a moment and then said, "Okay, then let's go. Virgil," he turned and faced Virgil, who was also clearly anxious to depart. "Will you please wait for us? I promise we won't be long, and then we can leave together. And I promise, with what I plan to bring back, we will be much better off."

Virgil protested initially, but then appeared suddenly calm. "Of course," he said, with a soft smile. "But please, please be careful."

Sophie hugged him, and then the crowd parted as she and Alie walked toward the door. Sophie turned to take one last look into the massive church and saw the multitude congregated between the pews, watching them as they stepped back out into the inferno outside.

Chapter Twenty-Four

The dojo. That's where Alie was so overwhelmingly compelled to go. Sophie couldn't imagine why he suddenly had to leave the security of the church and risk the nightmarish streets to get there, but she trusted him. After all, Sophie had felt strongly urged to go to St Pierre cathedral, and Alie didn't complain despite his strong dislike of churches. Perhaps he was headed for the dojo because it was his sanctuary, his St.-Pierre, where he felt the most comfortable in this madness. So, there they sat, huddled behind a parked car, waiting and watching the quaint street in front of the studio until they were sure they could enter unseen.

Sophie remembered how strange she thought it was to find a martial arts studio in Geneva, Switzerland. It no longer seemed odd, as her perception of "strange" had undergone a seismic shift in recent days. In fact, it seemed weirdly inviting from where she sat. The studio's interior was dark, except for a light from a back corner office casting a faint glow through the window.

As soon as Alie was confident that they were safe, they snuck across the street and glided through the front door without incident. Sophie almost tripped over Alie as he bowed just inside the entrance. She didn't bother to bow. The interior was the same, only much more cluttered. Almost all the swords that had hung on the walls were piled on the floor. That is, all but the sword above the door, which still hung exactly where Alie had placed it when it cut his hand. He stood below it with his back to Sophie, staring at the impressive blade that sat high on its perch. And, suddenly, Sophie got it. That's why they had come to the dojo. When faced with unrelenting threats around every corner, of course the warrior would go for his weapon. Something to even the odds, or maybe even tip them, if only a little, in their favor.

Alie reached for the sword, gently grasping the handle. But it didn't move. He stepped back and exhaled sharply while examining the blade from several angles. Then he reached again, but paused with his fingers just inches from the handle. Sophie watched his shoulders rise and fall as he breathed deeply before extending the final few inches. Sophie thought she may have seen it twitch slightly but, if it did, it was barely noticeable. He tried several more times, never losing his patience, but not making any more progress moving the sword. After multiple attempts, he turned and gave Sophie a blank look, then walked past her to the center of the room.

"I'm sorry, Alie," Sophie whispered, feeling helpless. Alie didn't respond, instead positioning himself squarely in the middle of the mat facing the door. He crouched momentarily, still eyeing the sword, and then sat with legs crossed and closed his eyes. The eerie silence made Sophie uncomfortable. She especially didn't like how frighteningly exposed they were to anything passing by on the street. "Alie?" she whispered to no response. "Alie?" Still nothing. So she withdrew into a shadowy corner, where she kept one eye on Alie and the other on the narrow view of the street outside.

Several minutes crept by, with no movement other than the slow rise and fall of Alie's shoulders. She noticed for the first time a slight flicker of the bulb in the corner. In her paranoid state, the flickering seemed like a massive neon sign advertising their presence. As Alie sat oblivious, Sophie's mind flooded with horrific scenarios. Her brain played trick after trick on her, as her thoughts turned harmless shadows into imaginary monsters. So, when something really did flash past the window, she almost convinced herself that it was nothing. But then came another, and another, and then several more: a crowd of panicked souls sprinting outside. They were only a blur, visible for just an instant. But that was all it took for Sophie to realize that something wasn't right. There were very few non-demonic spirits still on the streets, and those that were tended to avoid things that draw attention, such as running wildly in the open. Sophie feared that they would only do so if they were running from something horrible, and she was right.

Seconds after the last of the spirits bolted past the window, two dark silhouettes appeared, walking nonchalantly down the middle of the street. Sophie could hear them cackling to one another. As they walked, one turned its gaze to the dojo, and then did a double-take. Sophie caught a glimpse of faint neon-greenish eyes trying to peer through the glass. They didn't break stride, however, and before Sophie could catch her breath, they were gone.

"Alie!" she blurted in a half-whisper, half-yell.

She knew they needed to get out of there immediately. But still there was no reaction from Alie. Sophie had been determined not to disturb him, but now things had gone too far, and she couldn't just sit back and wait to be discovered. She had to go snap him out of it and convince him to leave. So, she inhaled deeply and took an apprehensive step toward him and away from the wall.

Just as her foot touched down out of the shadow, one of the figures reappeared in the window. Sophie gasped as she crashed backward out of the light. The same neon eyes, brighter now, glared into the dojo. Its head cocked like a curious dog, and a piercing screech rattled the window. A second silhouette appeared, and echoed the first with its own hideous howl. Sophie couldn't make out any details within their dark outlines other than their wretched eyes that bobbed and cocked as they scanned the inside of the studio. Sophie desperately wanted to scream out to Alie and beg him to come to. At this point, what could it hurt? They had to have seen him in the middle of the floor, completely unprotected and unaware. But Sophie didn't dare make a sound, and instead inched herself behind a pile of stacked-up pads, hoping the demons would lose interest and move on.

One of the creatures placed a gnarled hand on the window. An unnerving sound invaded the silence as it ran its claws down the glass. Sophie shivered at the sound, and wondered how Alie could remain tuned out. The grating stopped as the demon's hand rested on the glass, and then slipped through the glass into the dojo. The creature let out a second shriek and then leaned its upper body into the studio. The sound of its raspy breathing instantly filled the room. Sophie had to clasp her hand over her mouth to block an audible gasp from escaping. As she crouched out of sight, she felt completely helpless and guilty for hiding while Alie was in the open.

The second demon began its passage through the glass just as the feet of the first touched down inside. It was significantly smaller than the first, and unlike the other demons they had seen, its eyes didn't glow. It wore a greyish cloak draped over one shoulder, and a long silver rope was coiled around the other. The creatures stood side by side, gawking at Alie as their jaws snapped open and shut while spewing vile noises. They walked slow circles around Alie, hissing and eyeing him maliciously. Surely Alie must know they are there, Sophie thought.

After orbiting him several times, the demons stepped back, still staring. They appeared confused at Alie's lack of response. After what appeared to be a debate, one began to shiver, and then emitted a vicious growl. It's fingernails gradually extended like spikes from its gangly fingers. It took one ambitious step forward and—

"Hey!" shouted Sophie, no longer able to keep quiet. Both demons jumped backward and hissed ferociously. Their eyes searched the shadows in disbelief, and then locked on Sophie.

"Well, hello there," spewed the one with green eyes in an unfamiliar accent. "Come on out and let's have a look." Sophie knew she was exposed, but was too terrified to move her legs.

"Come out or we'll have our way with your boyfriend," growled the other.

Sophie slowly stepped out from behind the pads. Every inch of her trembled uncontrollably. The demons sized her up and then laughed raucously. They stepped aggressively toward her, and she felt herself crumble backward again to the floor. The gasp she had managed to hold in before escaped shamelessly, which prompted even further hysterical laughter from the demons as they advanced toward her. When they were just a step away, Sophie made out the details of their monstrous, grotesque faces, which were even more horrifying in the flickering light. The green-eyed one dropped to its knees in front of Sophie, completely obscuring her view of Alie.

Just as the creature leaned in, its silhouette was illuminated by a bright flash. The demons' heads whipped around, and in an instant the kneeling one was on its feet. Through its legs, Sophie saw Alie standing under the door where the sword had hung, which he now held in his right hand. His arm stiffened, extending the sword directly in front of his eyes. The demons began to snarl more ferociously than before, but Alie ignored them. Instead, he admired the sword in its entirety, running his left hand along the blade all the way to the tip. Alie's indifference toward them made the demons even more enraged, and they showed it by throwing a childlike fit, complete with stomping and screeching. Yet they didn't charge. Had they never seen a human spirit resist before? Or maybe they had never seen one take up a weapon. Either way, Sophie had a feeling that things were about to change.

After several minutes of their ravenous blustering, Alie still had not acknowledged the demons, which drove them absolutely wild. One finally mustered up the courage and advanced slightly toward him. Alie countered with an instantaneous and authoritative stomp of his foot, which rattled the floor beneath them and caused the demons to leap backward, almost stepping on Sophie. Alie's eyes were now locked on the demons like a vice. There was not an ounce of fear in his gaze, and Sophie thought she may have even seen a grin. He lowered the sword to his side, touching the tip to the floor. Sophie noticed, for the first time, the vague outline of the identical sword from the physical world lying on the floor next to Alie, its tip touching the tip of the blade in Alie's hand.

Alie took several methodical steps forward, scraping the tip of the sword across the floor. The image of the sword from the corporal world followed, sliding across the floor as he walked.

"What do you think you're gonna to do with that, boy?" snarled the green-eyed demon.

"Come here and find out," Alie answered, his voice hushed and hard, like steel.

A rumbling growl shot from the demon. "This isn't gonna be pretty, boy. You sure you want her to watch?"

With a swift flip of the wrist, Alie spun the sword and held it extended, pointing directly at the green-eyed demon. "Go to hell."

The demons screeched hysterically and charged. The green-eyed creature leapt like a cat, leading with its protruding claws. Alie dropped and rolled at the demon's feet, springing upward just as the creature toppled forward over him. As he rose, his foot jutted up into the jaw of the other demon, sending it staggering backward. The green-eyed demon looked shocked as it got back to its feet and spun, its claws swiping wildly at Alie, but he wasn't there. He was faster, and had anticipated its next move, slipping effortlessly to its side. The creature tried to shift its stance to strike again, but before it could recover, Alie's blade came crashing down in a flash. The demon's razor-like fingernails clinked like change as its severed hand fell to the floor. The creature cried out in agony as it stared in disbelief at the stump where its hand had been.

The other demon had been crouched and ready to rush Alie, but it froze at the sight of the amputated hand on the floor. Alie shot the shrinking creature a warning look before turning back to the now one-handed beast. The green-eyed creature drew back its other hand, but this time hesitated to make a move. Alie stomped heavily again and the demon jerked backward. Alie jabbed the tip of the sword into the severed hand on the floor, then lifted the skewered appendage into the air on the tip of his blade. He shot a brief glance at Sophie and grinned, then flung the hand at the green-eyed demon, which connected with a taunting thud into its chest. The demon shrieked as it withdrew frantically from the flying hand. It was both enraged and completely baffled, entirely unsure how to react. Exasperated, it fired a long, frustrated screech at Alie. Alie responded by plunging the blade deep into the demon's chest.

The creature howled a gurgling, grotesque howl and gripped desperately at the protruding blade while stumbling backward. Alie surprisingly let go of the sword and watched the demon struggle. He aimed another menacing look at the crouching demon, which didn't dare move. He then turned back to the green-eyed demon, which was still trying to remove the blade from its chest with its one remaining hand. The two stared each other down a final time. Alie took one sweeping step forward and raised his right foot, driving it powerfully into the demon's chest and sending it hurling backward. As its back crashed against the wall, the sword pushed forward, shooting handle-first from its chest. In one motion, Alie caught the handle and spun with the blade extended. The demon let out a final cry as its head toppled from its shoulders onto the floor. The creature's knees buckled, and its body crumpled at Alie's feet. Alie turned his gaze toward the second demon, which had absolutely no interest in tangling any further with Alie.

"Please, master," it pleaded. "There's no need. I will just leave the two of you—"

"What's the rope for?" Alie demanded.

The creature looked confused. "What? This?" It immediately removed the rope from its shoulders and held it out, offering it to Alie. "This is what you want? I'll make you a deal, you let me go, and it's all yours," the creature sniveled.

Alie laughed. "I'll make *you* a deal. I cut off both of your hands, and then I take the rope. Sound fair?" The demon didn't respond, instead shrinking even further away from Alie. Sophie, who had sat motionless while Alie carved up the other one, took the opportunity to get to her feet and stand behind Alie, far away from the demon.

"You okay?" Alie asked Sophie as he touched her face gently with his empty hand.

"Now I am," she said, still in shock at what she just witnessed. "But wow, that was...just wow. I'm glad you're on my team."

"So am I," Alie smirked as he looked over the dismembered demon that now lay strewn in pieces across the floor. "What do you think we oughta do with him?" he asked, nodding to the still intact demon crouched in the corner.

Sophie glared at the pitiful creature as it again began to beg for mercy. "I think maybe you should reconsider that deal," she answered, grinning slyly. Alie eyed her curiously as the demon shot to its feet.

"Yes, yes, reconsider the deal!" it exclaimed. "Listen to the lady. Spare me and the rope is yours, I'll be on my way and leave you two in peace." It took two tentative steps forward and held the rope out with both hands. Alie didn't look at the creature, instead maintaining eye contact with Sophie. Her eyes shifted between Alie's and the demon.

"But then again—" she said.

The demon shrieked as Alie's lips pursed. The blade swung overhead like lightning, and then ripped downward in a flash, cutting off both of the demon's hands. The rope fell to the floor, still gripped by the two charcoal-colored hands. The creature dropped to its back and screamed wildly as it held its two stumps in front of its face.

"Well then," Alie said, "what shall we do with that rope?" He proceeded to bind the demons' feet together like a roped calf, and then cinched the other end around the creature's neck, leaving just enough lead to be able to drag the demon toward the door. "I have a feeling we can make use of him later."

"What now?" Sophie asked as they approached the door. "Are we really leaving?"

"Yes. It's not safe here," Alie replied. "Too many windows."

"So *now* you notice," Sophie scoffed. "Wow, just wow."

· ·

They left the dojo intending to meet up with Virgil as promised. But dragging the bound-up demon complicated things. Even if they could quickly duck around a corner or vanish into a door when danger approached, there was a constant fear that their captive would scream out or otherwise give them away. Alie, of course, threatened to shorten its limbs even more if it were so inclined. But even then, Alie and Sophie simply didn't dare trust the creature. It was, after all, a demon.

So, when they did find themselves just around the corner from an approaching demon swarm, and still several blocks from the church, they had no choice but to plunge into the nearest passable door. This time it was a metal door that dumped them into the spacious, industrial interior of some type of warehouse. Inside were rows of boxes stacked on palettes stacked on boxes stacked on more palettes, forming a dark maze of way too many places for creepy things to hide.

"I don't like this," Sophie whispered, which induced a chuckle from the captive demon. Alie jerked sharply on the rope, and the demon stopped.

"I don't either, but what choice do we have?"

Sophie peer into the darkness, searching for a glimpse of another door or window on the other side of the warehouse, but she could only see more boxes. The only light inside came from above, which took several minutes for Sophie and Alie to decipher. The ceiling was dotted with tiny smudges of light that cut through the haze. As she stared curiously upward, she noticed the puffs that escaped her mouth with every breath.

"Hey, Alie, look." She let out a series of smoky exhales, which Alie imitated.

"It must be freezing in here," he said, "and we just can't feel it."

"But our breath still shows?" Sophie wondered. "Now that's just creepy."

Alie inspected the boxes more closely. Through a thin layer of frost, he could see the letters *GARDER CONGELÉ*. Keep frozen.

"This is a cold storage," Alie observed. "If we could find a way to get the bodies into here, perhaps we could prevent them from decaying too quickly."

"That's brilliant, Alie," Sophie said, "but first we need to find a way out."

Next to the entrance, a stairway rose to a catwalk that towered over the box maze and disappeared into the darkness. The debate over whether they should stay by the front door until the demons passed or venture further into the warehouse ended quickly when the chorus of shrieks and snarls outside rose to a dull roar. The only thing left to debate was whether they should brave the maze itself or take the catwalk. Sophie ended that debate before it began by quietly leading the ascent up the metal stairs.

Alie had to untie the demon's feet to make it up the stairs, but with Sophie tugging on the rope around its neck and the business end of the sword poking at its back, the creature wisely made it to the catwalk without a peep. From their perch high upon the catwalk, they had a much closer view of the ceiling overhead, much of which was made up of large windows. The tiny smudges of light that were only barely visible from the floor now revealed themselves to be stars peering in from a hazy night sky. The labyrinth of boxes below them, on the other hand, had almost disappeared into the darkness. If there were something, or a lot of things down there hiding and waiting for them, they would have no idea until it was too late. But they pressed on, scooting quietly across the grated metal panels that bridged the expanse to the other side of the warehouse.

"Hey, Alie," her voice quivered through the darkness. "Remember when I said that I'm glad you're on my side?"

"Sure," he responded.

"Well, I am," she hesitated, "but not just because of all of that touchy-feely stuff. That…whatever you did back there. I don't even know how to describe what I just witnessed. I mean, you completely diced up those two monsters like…cucumbers." The tied-up demon whimpered uneasily at her description.

"I warned you about me, didn't I?" Alie said. "That what you thought you knew about me is only part of the truth?"

"You say that like I'm supposed to be scared," Sophie responded. "You're a soldier, I get it. That's what you do. And you're good at your job. But what you did with the sword, those things had no chance, and it looked like it was easy. Am I wrong?"

Alie thought for a minute. He had never really considered whether it was easy or hard. It was just combat. Whether with guns or swords, same concept, different instrument. But she was right; this time was different. "No, I noticed it too."

"Well, that's not a bad thing, right?"

"It's…different," he answered. "And different can be dangerous if you're not prepared to use it."

"What do you mean, *different*?"

Alie stopped and stood on the catwalk. Sophie could barely make out his outline, but could see clearly the gleam of moonlight on the sword as he held it out to his side. "Free. Unrestricted. Like I'm moving for the first time after shedding a heavy weight," he explained. "When I let go of who I am, I become what I might be," he continued.

"I'm not sure I follow," Sophie responded.

"It's from an ancient Chinese philosopher named Lao Tzu, the father of Taoism," he explained. "Before, with Battojutsu, or most other combat training for the matter, I fared quite well against most everyone I faced. But the better and faster I got, the more I felt restrained by the physical limitations of my body." He paused, methodically waiving the sword through the moonlight. "But not here. Now, as soon as I can think it, I can do it."

To Sophie, this was puzzling. Could it be that Alie wasn't entirely out of place here? She was completely miserable in this spectral world, but it was almost as if Alie were in his element. He was beginning to realize not only that he had enhanced abilities, but that they were as good or better than the demons'. Or maybe what he said before was true: Sophie had only known one side of him, and was now trying to comprehend the other.

"Can I ask you something?" she inquired. "Are you scared of them, even a little bit?"

"No."

"Have you ever been? From day one?"

"I'm only scared that I will fail you," he answered softly.

"Well, based upon what I just saw," she said, "I have much to worry about, do I?"

"They're just bullies, easily preying on scared and disoriented souls. They're not used to fighting anyone but themselves, like dirty hyenas bickering over scraps."

Sophie turned and reached through the darkness, pushing aside the tied-up demon and placing her hand on Alie's chest. She touched his face softly and whispered, "But now the lion has arrived."

. . . .

"I sure hope that knot holds," Alie chuckled as he shoved the dangling demon, sending it swinging on the rope like a pendulum. Sophie and Alie had reached the bottom of the stairs on the other side of the catwalk without incident. The demon, well, not so much. About half-way down the staircase, Alie quickly untied the rope around its neck and attached it to the stair railing. Then he hurled the demon like a sack of potatoes over the side. And there it hung, suspended by its feet, upside down, while Alie and Sophie harassed it from the ground below. A faint blue light glowed through the window of a small office, partially illuminating the demon's shifting, iridescent eyes.

"I think we can help each other," Alie declared while prodding the tip of the sword into the demon's chest. "We need each other right now, you and me. I'm assuming you have some very valuable information that if you were so inclined to share, well, could sure help out your situation."

"Yeah? And what is it you think I need from you?" the demon gurgled.

Alie laughed sarcastically. "Well, in case you haven't noticed, your current situation is a bit, let's say, precarious. I'm holding a very sharp blade that is itching to cut something," the demon gulped as Alie slid the sword's tip down to its chin. "And you just happen to be hanging from a rope that needs some cuttin'. If I were you, I'd be making sure this blade is cutting rope, and not something else."

"He doesn't really need both of those feet," Sophie joined in. "Couldn't we just tie the rope to one, and do away with the other?"

"Okay, okay!" the creature burst out. "What is it? What do you want to know?"

Alie grinned. "Atta boy. Let's start with this: where's your mate?"

"Mate?" the demon asked. "What do you mean, mate?"

Alie drew closer. "You know. Your comrade that I sliced up back there. Where is he?"

The demon looked even more confused. "You...you saw him. He's scattered all over the floor."

"I know where his head is, and his hand, and the rest of him. But is that it? Is he done? Or does he go somewhere else, you know, after he…lost his head?"

The demon's eyes bulged and it began to squirm, as if that were a question it didn't want to answer. "I dunno. I just dunno."

"Odd reaction," Alie said while beginning to run his finger up and down the blade. "Maybe I should help you go and find out."

"No, no, no," the demon insisted. "I swear, I don't know. None of us do. Heaven, Hell. There's no way for us to know what happens to us if we're, you know, ended."

"Then what's your purpose?" Sophie inquired. "Why do you exist?"

The demon's face contorted at her question. It snarled at her viciously until Alie lifted the sword as a subtle warning. "Why do I exist?" it barked. "Why do *you* exist? Why does any of this exist? Why do you trifle with such foolish questions?"

Sophie glanced at Alie, trying to figure out this dangling monster. It was hardly a pleasant chat they were having, but she agreed with Alie that they should try and take advantage of it while they had the chance. "What about the pail, puny creatures?" her interrogation continued. "The hooded ones that you drag around by ropes?"

The demon was instantly enraged by the question. "What about them?" it snapped. "What do you think you know about them? They are *not* for you and your kind!" The demon was writhing wildly in the air, suddenly desperate to escape.

"Well then, have we touched a nerve?" Alie chuckled. "What is it about those little things?" Alie got closer to the swaying demon, which snapped its jaws at him. "And what exactly were you planning to do with this rope?"

The demon's convulsions increased as it snarled and jerked violently. "They are *NOT* for you, you putrid filth!" Alie's patience abruptly ran out and he swung the sword in a high arc before bringing it downward with a vigorous swing. The demon squealed as the flat face of the blade connected with a thunderous clap on the side of its head. Its writhing and swinging came to a sudden halt, after which the demon frantically rubbed its handless stumps all over its head to make sure it was still there.

"Now then, let's be a little more civil," Alie said. "We were asking about the little pale creatures, and you were about to tell us everything we want to know."

The creature continued to hold its head, now emitting a grimacing whimper. It wheezed heavily, but still said nothing. Alie drew back the sword again, but Sophie reached and gripped his forearm, halting his swing. She stepped in front of Alie, and very close to the hanging demon.

"What do you think?" she addressed her question to Alie, but never took her eyes off of it. "Should we let it in on our little secret?" Alie didn't respond, but the demon paused its ranting and listened intently. "I mean, if we are still going through with the plan, we may need…"

"What plan?" the demon howled.

"…it's help." Sophie finished.

"What plan?!?" it insisted.

"Go ahead then," Alie played along.

Sophie leaned in even closer, as if she were sharing a deep secret. The demon's nose twitched anxiously. "What if I told you," Sophie paused, letting it hang out there, "that we know how to get one?" The creature cocked its head like an odd bird as it studied Sophie's face. "One of those frail little creatures we were talking about. We know where to find one."

"LIARS!"

Sophie didn't flinch. "Perhaps," she spoke softly. "Or perhaps we found one curled up in the kitchen of a quaint, little house, just a few blocks from here." She eyed the creature with a slight grin. "You wonder why the swordsman here didn't chop you up like he did your friend? Perhaps it's because we thought we might need you, you know, to help us make use of the little frail thing."

The demon's face was just as enraged as it was riveted by Sophie's every word. "I don't believe you," it grumbled.

"Very well then," Sophie jumped to her feet. "Cut its head off," she said, motioning to Alie. "We'll need the rope."

"Wait! Where? Tell me where it is!"

Sophie closed in to within inches of the demon's face, not letting on that its rotting stench turned her stomach. "No," she responded sharply. "It's our turn to get some answers, or you lose a head, and we go back to the little creature."

The dangling demon nodded its head rapidly, suddenly in

agreement. "What do you want to know?"

Sophie backed away gladly and looked to Alie, who took her place. "Why the obsession over the feeble, little creatures?"

"The obsession's not with them, you see," it replied. "It's with what they can do."

"And what's that?"

The demon's face twisted into a sinister grin. "Inhabit," it hissed.

"Bodies?" Alie inquired.

"Yes," the demon answered lustfully. "Bodies. Sweet, previous, human bodies." Sophie's stomach turned again.

"So, you prey on people's vacant bodies, taking them as your own?" Sophie asked with a disgusted look.

"Only if we're lucky," it answered. "You asked me why I exist, why we exist? Well, that's why. We dream of someday knowing what it's like to have one."

Sophie and Alie looked curiously at one another. "Why?" Alie inquired. "They're quite imperfect you know. Why the fascination with having one?"

"Easy for you to say, having had one and all. But to never…to hunger, to taste, to feel, to touch…pleasure. But to be deprived for all eternity, while you and your abominable kind get to partake…" It made a gagging sound.

"So, what are the pale ones?" Alie continued, "and why do you need them to possess a body?"

"They are uncontaminated, and ancient," it explained. "A race entirely different from ours, but weak and submissive in their current state."

"Current state?"

"It is said that they were not always this way," it continued. "But it is the only way I have ever seen them."

"Where do they come from?" Sophie asked.

"Unknown," it answered. "I only know where they are kept."

"Kept?" said Sophie.

The demon was suddenly angry. "They are *not* for you!" it screamed. "And you will never know where."

Alie tapped the tip of the blade twice sharply on the floor. "We will if you ever want to see one again."

The creature bore its fangs and tried futilely to reach the rope tied to its feet. "Argh, what's the use," it grumbled. "You could never get to them anyway. They are guarded, protected by legions, far greater than your puny sword." It paused, taking several shallow breaths. "Ours are in the city you call…Pa-ris." The name of the great city sounded labored and unnatural on the demon's tongue.

"Paris?" Sophie sounded shaken. "Where?"

"Underground," it snarled.

"Underground?" she wondered.

"The catacombs," Alie said somberly. It made sense. Beneath the exquisite, timeless beauty of the great City of Light was a vast network of ominous tunnels containing the skeletal remains of millions of dead Parisians. The skulls of countless, nameless deceased line the walls, stacked from floor to ceiling like morbid brickwork. There is perhaps no place more fitting in all of Europe, if not all the world, for a multitude of demons to call home. "So, all of you come from the catacombs?"

"Not all," it replied. "There are others. But we, yes."

"Others?" asked Alie. "Others like you, who also use the pures?"

"They are *NOT* for them," it bawled, offended at the suggestion. "They are filthy, rotten souls, unworthy, and they are *not* for them." It held very still for a moment, in great concentration until it muttered, "or for you."

"So that is why they are guarded?" Alie said, thinking out loud. "Not against human spirits, but other factions of demons?"

"Against all filth," the creature hissed. It continued to hang motionless as Alie paced, concocting some sort of plot to seize a pure, which to this point was the only way they knew of to re-take their bodies. They didn't currently have one stored away in a kitchen, of course, but the demon didn't know that, and fortunately was gullible enough, or dumb enough, to go along. But that still didn't help them to actually get their hands on a pure, which were apparently guarded constantly by hordes of demons. Sophie sat cross-legged and alternated her gaze between Alie and the demon. The creature's newfound, uncharacteristic calm made her nervous, and even more so when she noticed its head twitching and eyes shifting sneakily back and forth. She was about to bring it to Alie's attention when the silence was broken by voices approaching outside, demonic voices.

"Alie?" Sophie whispered.

"I hear it," he responded, holding out his hand to signal for silence. The demon began to fidget, and Sophie sensed that it knew very well what was coming. Alie sensed it too, and handed Sophie the sword while eyeing the demon. "If that thing makes a sound, remove its head." He then turned and disappeared behind a stack of boxes.

Sophie felt a rush of panic without Alie present, but she wouldn't let it show. It was just her and the demon, which was watching her with a predatory stare. She hated when Alie vanished without first telling her where he was going. But only seconds later she saw his silhouette rise atop the wall of crates. She watched him shuffle along carefully until he neared the faint outline of a window, where he peered out covertly onto the street below. Then he disappeared again as the hum of voices grew louder. Alie emerged shortly after from the maze of boxes.

"They're coming," he announced. "A lot of them."

"And now, you shall die," the demon laughed.

"Not if they don't know we're here," Alie responded, taking the sword back from Sophie. The demon gulped again audibly and fell silent. The look on Alie's face made it clear that there was something more. "And they have a pure."

"Are you sure?" Sophie gasped. "What do we do?"

"Wait a minute," the demon piped up. "I thought you already had one." Alie looked at the demon, and then at Sophie before they shared a brief laugh. "LIARS!" it screamed.

"So, what do we do with him?" asked Sophie.

Alie thought for a moment. "We take him. I have a feeling he may still be of use."

. . . .

"You have to trust me on this," Alie had insisted. She thought it was suicide, either for him, or her, or both. It had nothing to do with trust; she hated being apart from him. Like always, she begged him to reconsider his plan, to consider something that didn't involve them separating. Now she was alone again, huddled behind the banged-up remains of a car that had apparently crashed through a store window when its driver ditched his body. And Alie was dragging the pitiful creature by the rope across the rooftop of the warehouse.

From where she hid, she had a fairly good view of a large group of demons rioting over a group of lifeless bodies. The scene resembled the gathering in the plaza, only quite a bit smaller. There were a handful of the brutish, hulking beasts keeping watch, a pack of raucous underlings whipping themselves into a frenzy, and two slightly more civilized ones donning long, dark robes. And there, on the fringe of the horde, was an oddly malformed individual holding onto a silverish cord that was fastened to a bundle of squatting cloth. Alie's plan involved her somehow getting her hands on that little bundle and disappearing without being seen or captured. In his limited explanation of said plan, there were instructions to stay still until he had attracted the attention of the demons, and a promise that if something went wrong, he would fight his way back to her. It sounded like absolute madness to her, but he insisted that they had no other choice, and had to act while they had the chance.

When the demon pack had taken their places, they started their eerie, rhythmic chant. As the wicked rite amplified, a flicker of movement caught Sophie's eye. High above the demons, Alie's head poked up from the roof of the warehouse. She was quite sure that no one else had noticed, but she still couldn't control herself from shaking. Knowing that he was fearless, almost to the point of insanity, was making her crazy. But what choice did she have? He was going to do what he was going to do, and she was left to just hang on for the ride.

Alie waited for the moment when the feverish shouting turned to a dull rhythm, and then stood completely upright in full view. He gripped the rope in one hand, and held the sword high above his head with the other. Still the entranced horde didn't notice him, so he began to shout while clanging the blade loudly against the metallic roof. A sudden hush fell over the horde as Sophie's heart stopped. For what seemed like an eternity, the demons tried to contemplate what they were seeing. Alie yelled out again, this time jerking upwards on the rope to reveal the ensnared demon. The demon immediately began to squeal like a baby piglet, which prompted a buzz from the crowd. Sophie watched the distorted being that was holding the rope connected to the pure. It had taken several inquisitive steps forward, but still held tight to the cord.

Alie yanked on his rope again, and then kicked his captive demon from behind, almost sending it tumbling over the side of the warehouse. A sure plummet to the crowd was halted by Alie's grip on the rope, which resulted in the demon being suspended, leaning out at an angle several stories above the horde. While the demon's arms flailed desperately, Alie hacked at one of the arms just above the elbow. The creature screeched horribly, which set the horde into an absolute tizzy. Alie hauled the demon back from the edge, but only to take a second, brutal swipe at the arm. He then leaned out again, holding the severed arm above his head and yelling something at the horde before tossing the arm off the roof.

The demons recoiled from the arm as it landed in their dead center. They appeared stunned as they examined their comrade's detached appendage at their feet. But their bewilderment turned quickly back to rage as several began to search for a way up the side of the building. Some hunted for something to grip onto, while others simply jabbed their claws into the walls of the warehouse and began to scale upward toward Alie. Sophie checked the pure's captor again, who was now gyrating hysterically as the horde focused on Alie.

Alie's head disappeared for several seconds, and Sophie hoped he had wised up and decided to run. But, of course, he had something much more dramatic in mind. He reappeared, only this time hoisting the writhing demon above his head. He roared a barbaric roar to the demonic audience below, then hurled the helpless creature downward. Its plunge took out several of the climbing demons, sending them all crashing downward in a screeching mass of flailing arms and slashing claws. They collided with the pavement with a ghastly thud, just as others started up the warehouse walls. Sophie looked frantically for Alie, but he was not there. She then looked back to the bundled up pure, and saw only the mound of cloth crouched in the middle of the street. Its misshapen keeper had given into the urge to join the crowd in its assault on the human intruder who had blasphemously interrupted their ritual. With their attention fixed madly on revenge, and their backs turned completely to Sophie, it was now or never.

No longer hindered by her awkward, ghostly stride, Sophie sprinted with tunnel vision toward the hunkered heap of cloth. Just to her left was an unassuming doorway back into the warehouse. She hoped she could make it back to the door before something spotted her, and that the pure was equally capable of passing through the door. Her feet slid out from underneath her as they grinded to a halt just past the bundle of cloth. She had been moving so fast that she almost overshot the pure. She grabbed clumsily at the silver cord, her feet already in retreat before she managed a good grip. You've only got one shot at this, Sophie, she chastised herself as she tugged desperately, urging the delicate creature to follow. She glanced back just in time to see the pale, fragile feet appear beneath the rags, followed by the creature toppling over on its side. Terrified, she looked around quickly for any searching eyes, and then darted back to help the pure back to its feet. She tugged again, only slightly less forcefully than before, this time pulling with her back toward the door so she could keep an eye on the apprehensive little creature. Its spindly feet stumbled forward, nearly tipping over a second time. They finally began a semblance of a stride just as Sophie looked up and saw the infuriated eyes of the pure's captor, standing and watching her attempt to steal their most precious possession.

The contorted demon's warped lips parted and spewed out a hellish, earsplitting distress call. Sophie threw the rope over her shoulder and lunged toward the door, no longer caring if she had to drag the wretched pure on its limp legs behind her. But it didn't collapse, instead keeping up rather efficiently as she barreled toward her escape. The demonic alarm belted out a second time as she plunged through the doorway with a vice grip on the cord, hoping with everything she had that the pure followed. And it did. In fact, she stumbled clumsily into the darkness, headlong into a stack of boxes. But the pure remained upright and unaffected, except for the ragged cloth, which apparently stayed outside. A pair of gleaming, angelically blue eyes nervously scanned the dark interior of the warehouse. Sophie noticed the cold mist pour out of its nostrils with a first exhale, but didn't wait for a second. She leapt to her feet and pulled the pure into the labyrinth of crates and boxes. Before she had feared the unseen inside the maze, but it was the seen that now compelled her into the unknown.

She stumbled along, crashing repeatedly into the walls of crates that blocked her from the other end of the cavernous warehouse. Her heart sank as she heard the cries of an unknown number of demons, which were now inside and hunting her. After so many blind turns, she lost track of direction, and prayed she was not headed back the way they had come. She looked up at the glass ceiling, searching for something to guide her to the other side. Instead she saw dark silhouettes stalking her from the catwalk. Everything within her wanted to collapse into a dark corner and hide, but she had to press on. If she stopped, the demons would undoubtedly find her, and she had to reach Alie somehow. So she kept dragging the pure through the darkness, rounding every corner hoping for the exit.

Just when she thought she would never escape, a final corner gave way to an expansive opening. It was the only thing between her and a faintly lit exit sign above the door. Her chest pounded as she looked out from the obscurity of the maze, knowing she and the pure would be completely exposed once they made a break for the door. But she did it anyway, sprinting with the pure in tow. As they closed in on the exit, movement caught her descending from the catwalk. Before she could change directions, a dark form crashed violently into her, sending her tumbling across the cold floor. She sprang back to her feet almost immediately, but was empty-handed. A black form stood ominously before her, breathing heavily as it held the cord with the pair of unsullied blue eyes attached to the other end. Sophie cowered as a colossal brute of a demon came barreling down the stairs a second later. Then a third dropped down from a stack of crates, and Sophie knew there was nowhere left to go.

The one holding the cord blurted some indecipherable orders to the brute, and the colossal beast started toward her. She tucked her head into her arms and waited for its massive hands to snatch her up, but her anticipation was interrupted by a sharp, grotesque grunt, followed by a massive thud. She looked up and saw the brute lying headless on the ground. Flashes of silver shimmered through the darkness and the second demon's scream turned to silence. Alie stepped into the pale light that streamed down from the glass above, and stood before the remaining demon. It didn't move, as if it were waiting for its inevitable fate. Alie obliged the creature, and in an instant, only the pure was left standing with wide eyes.

Sophie ran to Alie, wrapping her arms tightly around him. He held her close, never taking his eyes off the pure. The frail creature only looked on curiously at their embrace, which they had to cut short. They were by no means safe, so they poked their head through the exit door and checked the street outside. Thankfully, it was empty, but wouldn't be for long. So, they bolted across the street and into another mysterious doorway, and then through many more before finally resting.

Chapter Twenty-Five

Sophie once again found herself separated from Alie. But this time she was not alone. She shared a small, cheaply decorated living room and an awkward silence with the uncloaked and mostly unresponsive pure. Their getaway from the horde had taken them through numerous lifeless buildings and darkened halls, from houses to offices to obscure passageways, all in search of somewhere to hole up while their pursuers scoured the city. Alie had been gone an hour or so, insisting over her fierce protests that he venture out solo in search of their missing bodies while Sophie stayed hidden with the pure. She knew that keeping the pure unseen was an absolute necessity, and Alie certainly was much faster and more effective by himself than with all three of them. But that still didn't ease the sting of yet another parting. Her vow to never separate from him had again proven frustratingly unattainable.

So now Sophie sat on some stranger's couch, curiously observing the enigmatic, pathetic little creature. It stood in the middle of the room, rigid and expressionless, staring blankly into a corner. For the first time, Sophie was able to study it in some light, which revealed just how strange of a being it truly was. She decided that it couldn't be any taller than Kevin, her little brother. Its paper-thin skin stretched gauntly over protruding bones, topped by a hairless, bulbous head that appeared ready to tumble off its scraggy neck at any moment. But despite its sickly form, its face was surprisingly much more human-like than any of its captors. And set within its sunken sockets were two azure, beaming eyes that seemed completely out of place attached to its pale body. They looked like they could be ripped from its head and sold as exotic jewels.

Sophie never heard it make a noise. It just stood, staring, oblivious to her and apparently everything else around them. She couldn't help but be troubled that their hope for escaping this dreary existence rested entirely on this pathetic creature. They weren't even sure what it was, or how to use it, or even exactly what it was supposed to do. They just knew that they were currently on one side of mortality, and wanted to get to the other. And, so far, this scrawny little thing was the only thing resembling a link that they had seen.

It was well into the second hour since Alie's departure when the pure abruptly snapped out of its comatose-like state and looked unnervingly at the front door. Its unexpected jolt startled Sophie, who had essentially slipped into a daze. The pure was staring intently at the door, and Sophie was staring intently at the pure, wondering what caused the sudden alarm. It was then that she heard the first hint of a commotion from the stairs down the hall. The sound of stewing demons swelled as they went door by door, clearly searching.

She slid quietly off the bed and looked for a place to hide, certain they would pass through the door at any second. The modest apartment had few options for hiding, but she did manage to find an antique wardrobe with room for one inside, and possibly two if they squeezed. But despite her gestures to the pure to hurry and join her, it didn't move. Instead it stayed put, as if its oversized, clumsy feet were nailed to the floor. And its stare didn't stray from the door for a second, not even to acknowledge Sophie's pleading.

The menacing racket outside reached the door to their unit, and Sophie stiffened. If they came through now, her hiding place would be completely useless. They would not only recapture the pure, but would soon find her as well, and their entire plan would be spoiled. But at this point, if she moved or so much as made a peep, they would know she was there. So all she could do was wait.

The door rattled, and the voices outside snarled, but nothing came through. The door handle rattled several more times, followed by more snarling, but still nothing passed through the door. Sophie checked the pure's eyes again, which still had not budged. She noticed that its gaze was intense, but not necessarily scared, as if it were caught up in deep concentration. But its expression didn't flinch. This carried on for several more excruciating minutes before the demons gave up and moved on.

When Sophie caught her breath, she snuck softly out of the wardrobe and tip-toed back to the couch. The pure had returned to staring expressionless at the blank corner, as if nothing had happened.

"Hey," Sophie whispered. "What was that? Did you do something?"

It didn't respond, not even a flinch acknowledging she was there. "The silent type, huh? I get it."

. . . .

"I'm telling you, Alie, it did something to prevent those things from coming through the door." Her voice quivered as she filled him in on her near-encounter with the prowling demons. Sophie was doing her best to piece together the story as they snuck their way again through the city.

Alie looked skeptical. "But it just sits there like a daft stump."

"Yeah, trust me, I know," she replied. It felt awkward talking about the pure right in front of it, as if it weren't there. But, as always, it appeared completely oblivious to anything but Alie tugging on the rope around its neck. "I watched it do nothing but stare at the wall for hours, except for the few minutes that the demons were trying to get in. Then it was as if it woke up and focused strenuously on the door until they left."

"Well, let's hope it can work some more magic when we get to where we're going," he responded while warily inspecting the open space across the street.

"And where's that?" She was terrified what the answer might be. But rather than answer, Alie pointed to a modest patch of lawn dotted with quaint benches and manicured shrubs. Just beyond the grass was what looked to Sophie like a vast ocean of dreary nothingness stretching out for miles before disappearing into a black horizon. After struggling to decipher exactly what it was, Sophie realized she was looking at Lake Geneva. She sadly remembered the last night she and Alie shared together on the lakefront watching the setting sun dazzle the sky. But this time, the lake was a dismal, never-ending sea of gray.

"Can you see it?" Alie whispered, pointing at something on the lawn. Sophie strained to distinguish one nebulous shape from another. She didn't recognize what Alie was referring to until two dark figures stepped from behind a tree and stood directly over it, gawking while Sophie strained for a better view. There on the ground was a body lying on its back, its hands resting across its chest like a dormant vampire. She didn't want to admit it to herself, but she knew what this must be. With the help of a few parked cars and a large, abandoned bus, she crept closer as the contours of the body became recognizable. It was her.

She instantly became both excited and sickeningly apprehensive.

She knew the goal all along had been to find a way back into their bodies. But she also knew Alie had insisted that, given the option, she would be the first to go, no matter how hard she fought against it. It was one thing to be separated from him, but to be caught on two different sides of mortality was simply unacceptable.

"And yours?" She knew the answer before she even asked.

Alie shook his head, and then led Sophie and the pure up into the bus. He had heard Sophie's emphatic protests about her going first many times. But unless they were lucky enough to find both bodies in the same place, they would have to go with whichever one they happened to find first, and then hope that person can locate the other. It just so happened that Alie did, in fact, find Sophie's first, and only Sophie's.

"Listen, Sophie," he pleaded, "we have to try it. I don't like it any more than you do, but this may be our only chance." She didn't respond, instead burying her head into his chest and choking back a sob. Everything about this felt wrong, and horrifying. What if they got caught? What if it didn't work? What if it did? Would her body even work anymore? And what would she find back in the physical world? Would she be alone in a city littered with deserted bodies?

"So now what?" she asked.

"We each have a job to do," Alie looked out over the park from a bus window. "Mine is to create a distraction, and yours is…"

"By yourself?" Sophie protested.

"I only see two of them; I'll be fine," he insisted. "You'll have a good view from up here of everything around us. When you're sure their attention is completely on me, and that there are no others, you're going to have to guide this thing over there, to your body. Hopefully then it will take over and do its job."

"This is insanity!" she snapped while nervously wiping away tears.

"You're right, but it's gonna work," Alie grinned. "It has to." He handed her the rope secured to the pure's neck and took a long, hard look outside in all directions.

"But what do I do once I'm on the other side?"

Alie reached for her, gently placing a hand on the back of her head, and then pulling her close. "Find me." The look in his eyes was ridiculously and inexplicably confident. It was the opposite of everything Sophie was feeling, and she was almost upset with him for how easy he made this look. "Remember, you won't be alone. I'll be right here, beside you, wherever you go." He elegantly withdrew the sword and squeezed its handle, and then again scanned their surroundings.

"But, Alie…" At this point, her words were frivolous. "Please, not yet."

"It's now or never, Sophie." He again squeezed her tight, and kissed her one last time. "You can do this. *We* can do this. Trust me." He flashed a final reassuring smile, and then his face transformed from tender to lethal. "I've gotta go. I've got a scrap to pick."

She felt empty as he bounded out of the bus and down the sidewalk. She was terrified that she might never again hear his voice or feel his touch. She watched as he slipped from one parked car to another, until he was a block away. Then he stood quickly, in full sight, and haphazardly crossed the street onto the far end of the lawn, no longer caring if he was seen. From the inside of the bus, Sophie couldn't hear much. The demons in the park, however, apparently had no problem hearing the ruckus Alie was creating. Their attention shifted abruptly from her lifeless body to Alie, and they started toward him in a swift stride.

Alie didn't let up. Sophie could see that he had set the sword down on the ground, and was bouncing around while taunting them. Occasionally he glanced around for others, but then carried on with his carrying on. When the demons had gotten to within a few feet, he snatched the sword from the ground and held it, cocked and loaded, ready for a fight. Sophie desperately wanted to stay and watch to make sure he was safe, but she knew she could not. After searching intensely once more for any sign of lurking creatures, she led the pure down the bus steps and onto the street. One final check later, and she gave the rope a stiff tug before dashing across the street and onto the lawn.

Sophie glanced quickly to her left and caught a glimpse of what looked less like a fight, and more like Alie toying with two outmatched and ill-fated creatures. Her strides across the lawn were hampered by clumsy strides of the gangly and frail pure. She half-ran and half-staggered to where her body lay, giving her the first up-close view of it in what seemed like a long time. At first glance, it looked almost peaceful, as if Sophie should feel guilty for disturbing it. But upon further inspection, Sophie saw what appeared to be disturbing changes in her face. Her cheeks appeared slightly gaunt, her lips pursed, and eyes eerily sunken.

There's no way this isn't going to suck, Sophie thought as she knelt next to her body. She wasn't sure why she had expected the pure to just automatically cooperate and kneel with her but, true to form, it just stared blankly into the distance as if she weren't there.

"Hey," she called out in a half-whisper, half-shout. When it didn't budge, she tugged on the cord, nearly toppling it over. But once it gained its balance, it just continued its numb-minded stupor. "Hey, magic creature thingy!" This time she jerked the cord while simultaneously kicking it in the back of the knee. Its scrawny leg buckled, bringing it to the ground like a sack of brittle bones. On its hands and knees, it finally made some semblance of eye contact with her. So she grabbed its distorted head and torqued it until its eyes were pointed directly at her body. The creature froze almost immediately, and its body became completely rigid. For a moment it remained completely still, and Sophie worried something was wrong. Was this not going to work without that strange, demonic chant? Should she start reciting something sinister and rocking back and forth? If this thing refused to perform, she thought, their plan was over before it started.

And then, all sorts of weirdness began.

The pure's shoulders and head began to spasm, its already bulging eyes appearing to protrude even more than before. Its arms tweaked and twisted as it inched closer to the body, almost as if it wanted to fight against the compulsion to do what it was driven to do. Eventually, its movements metamorphosized into a rhythmic rocking. A hideously bizarre string of overlapping noises discharged from its mouth that made Sophie feel sick. But as much as she wanted to run away, she realized what was about to happen, and moved into position to re-take the same prostrate form as her body. Her chest pounded as strange sensations began to rush over her. Just as she gave in to lay her head back completely, a shrill scream pierced through the pure's commotion and seized Sophie's attention. It was coming from Alie's direction. She cocked her head and could see Alie still dealing tediously with the same two demons. But beyond Alie she saw several others approaching from behind.

"Alie!" She sat up suddenly as the panic-induced scream escaped her lips. As soon as it did, she knew she might just have ruined everything. Alie's head whipped around and, from the other side of the park, she could the dread in his face. His two opponents were also staring at her in a sort of fuming disbelief. The pack of demons that had been sneaking up on Alie froze as well, also focused on Sophie and the pure. A horrifically deformed one reared its head back and spewed a devilish cry, and all of them tore off into a mad dash directly toward her.

Sophie slammed her head backward onto the grass, trying to take the exact shape of her corpse. Just as her back hit the ground, the bizarre sensations began again to rush through her like tiny, electric pinchers.

Hurry! Please hurry!

She couldn't help but glance in the direction of the stampeding demons. One by one, the creatures in back fell as Alie and his slashing sword pursued from behind. But there were too many of them, and they would overtake her before Alie could finish them off.

Come on, you strange little beast! Faster!

She straightened her head to once again match the exact position of her body, and the sensations increased. She knew she must fight the urge to look again toward the coming demons, regardless of how close they were. She forced herself to close her eyes and concentrate, although she had no idea if concentrating would even help. The pulsating rhythm of the pure's unintelligible mantra swelled from a child-like voice to a commanding roar. She expected a sprinting demon to crash into her and the pure at any second. But she still wouldn't allow herself to look. Just as the intensity of the chanting and the throbbing shockwaves reached their zenith, she caught the image of a demon in full stride in the corner of her eye.

She stiffened from head to toe, ready to receive the monster's attacking blow, but nothing happened. The demon froze in mid-stride. And so did the demons behind it, and everything else. The jolting waves that had been ravaging her stopped, and there was suddenly silence. She tilted her head for a better view, and could see the same barrage of demons still in full stride, but completely immobilized. And there was Alie, fighting like an enraged animal, but also frozen in time.

She looked down toward her feet, expecting to also see the pure motionless. But it was gone. Standing in its place was a massive being, entirely different than any she had seen before. She only saw him for a brief instant—less than a second. But his immensely broad shoulders and tightly squared jaw made an instant impression. His skin was a chrome silver, almost like a lifeless statue. But there was no doubt that he was very much alive. He had long hair as black as the night sky that contrasted almost unnaturally with his metallic skin. His face was completely expressionless, but he stared directly at Sophie, or maybe even into Sophie.

And just like that, he vanished, as did everything else around her. In its place was complete and total blackness. And pain. More severe and intense pain than Sophie ever imaged one could experience. She couldn't see or hear anything. But she screamed anyway.

Chapter Twenty-Six

She felt as if she'd been sucked through a vacuum into the jaws of a massive python, as it simultaneously crushed her and ripped her apart with razor-sharp fangs. Every attempt to move brought the pain of a million stinging needles over her body. She tried to gasp, but it felt like a 10,000-pound weight was crushing her chest. The suffocating pressure made it almost impossible to breathe, or even move. But the need for air finally forced a breath.

Sophie continued to fight, one breath after another, feeling like her lungs were filled with pudding. Her head throbbed, and her ears felt like they would explode with each heartbeat. For what seemed like forever, she could do nothing but writhe helplessly on the ground in agony. She could barely manage a cohesive thought, other than pleading, over and over, that the pain would subside. Through the torment, she could make out the sound of screaming, as if it were coming from the other end of a long, hollow tunnel. But, suddenly, she realized the screaming was her own. She told herself to concentrate on the sound of her own voice, and follow it like a beacon back to sanity.

What was happening? What was causing this suffering? Was she being attacked by something?

Her thoughts returned to the demons that were rushing toward her while she was lying in the park, trying to re-take her body. Did they get to her? Was she being tortured? As unbearable as this anguish was, she would not be surprised to learn that she had been dragged to Hell.

Breathe in, Sophie. Inhale, exhale. You must breathe.

Her chest fought against her struggles to take in air, like a new balloon fresh out of the package. But as her lungs continued to expand, the excruciating stabbing sensations slowly turned to tolerable tingling. With more breaths came slight improvements in her ability to twitch a finger, wiggle a toe, or flutter an eyelid. She tried to open her eyes, but felt as if her eyelids were glued together. She tried harder, forcing them apart, and immediately clamped them shut again to protect them from a thousand stabbing rays of sunshine. She tried to swallow, but felt as if her throat were filled with crushed glass. She tried again, and her mouth began to sweat hot, acidic bile. She knew what was coming, and that it was really going to suck.

Her muscles hurt like they were ripping from her bones as she lurched to her side and vomited violently. She was unable to do anything other than lie there and heave repeatedly onto the ground, not caring that she was lying partially in her own puke. When the heaving stopped, she rolled onto her back and concentrated on the rising and falling of her chest.

A warm stream of tears flowed down her temples and into her ears. It was the only warmth she could feel on her otherwise frigid body. The shivering set in as her teeth chattered and her rigid muscles convulsed. Her thoughts had coalesced enough to recognize that she had succeeded in re-entering her body, but now she feared that doing so was a huge mistake. In the unknown amount of time that her corpse had been vacant, her heart had not pumped blood to her body, her lungs had not expanded, and her muscles had stiffened and maybe died without oxygen. Could the effects be irreversible? If so, was she going to die?

Death would mean leaving her body again, but this time on different terms. Would she be sent somewhere else? Would Alie be there, or get there eventually? Or would she be separated from him permanently? She didn't know, and didn't want to find out. So, she convinced herself to fight.

She rolled back to her side, sucking in oxygen painfully through her parched mouth. She managed to force her eyes open again, if only for an instant. Then the second time for an instant longer, and again and again until she could stand to have them open long enough to take in her surroundings. She was overwhelmed by the vividness of the colors and the clarity of everything. She felt sad to think that she'd almost been in the dismal spirit realm long enough to get used to the dreary way it was.

She forced herself to flop onto her stomach, her chest now completely soaked in the puddle of vomit. But she did manage enough strength to hold her head up out of the filth. A blanket of emerald-green grass stretched out before her, and beyond the grass she could see through an iron fence and all the way across Lake Geneva. The sight of water caused her badly dehydrated body to scream out for a drink. She strained her neck to look both right and left for some other source of water, but there was none. She pleaded with her right arm to move, to reach out in front of her, and finally succeeded in grabbing a handful of grass. She held on tight until she could fling her left arm in front of the other, grabbing a second handful. Then she mustered up everything she could to drag herself several inches, just far enough to clear the pile of puke before her face dropped like a rock onto the lawn. Everything in her wanted to just lie there motionless, but she forced herself to extend her arm another time. As she inhaled, she took in the smell of fresh grass and soil, and found the strength to prop herself up onto her elbows. Pain shot through her shoulders like they were being skewered by a hundred forks, but she just kept telling herself that unless she forced herself to move, none of this was worth it.

She dragged herself several more feet before her head collapsed again. And then a few more, this time convincing her legs to bend and kick, putting together something that resembled a very pathetic crawl. But she was moving, little by little, toward the waterfront. Beyond the grass, she could see that she would have to cross a wide street before confronting a short metal fence. In her current state, it was everything she could do to slog gruelingly, inch by inch, across the soft grass. Crossing the unforgiving asphalt, and then lifting herself somehow over the fence seemed impossible. But she knew that without water, she wouldn't be able to function much longer.

When she finally reached the edge of the lawn, she hung her chin over the jagged curb that dropped into the street. If the traffic were running like normal, her head would be crushed like a grape. But like the empty bodies, the cars that had previously buzzed around this city sat scattered and lifeless. The abrasive asphalt grated like sandpaper on Sophie's sensitive skin. Every tiny bump and pebble dug like broken glass into her forearms, hands and knees, making her struggle across the boulevard feel like crossing the Sahara. But she made it. The last few feet required her to clench the iron fence with both hands and pull with every ounce of strength left in her, but she made it.

All that separated her now from the lake was the rather short fence that would have otherwise not been much of an obstacle at all. But in her current state—stomach-down, face resting uncomfortably between two iron bars, and tears streaming down her cheeks—it may as well have been the Great Wall of China.

Sophie stretched her hand upward, reaching for the top of the fence, but came up short. She tried again, but it was just beyond her reach. She crumpled to the pavement, completely exhausted. Another wave of nausea surged through her, and she braced herself for the heaving that would follow. But as her stomach constricted violently, nothing came out. She keeled over as her arms gave out, and her head dropped with a thud onto the hard sidewalk. For a moment, she thought she was going to pass out. But instead, she found herself on her side, her cheek pressed against the pavement.

Compared to the cold concrete, the grass in the park looked soft and inviting. There was one spot in particular, beneath the shade of a large tree, that she imagined would be especially comfortable. A charming red bench decorated the base of the tree, but Sophie thought she would instead opt for the velvety lawn, if she could ever make it over the fence and to the water and back, that is. Her eyes glazed over while staring at the enticing scene, until movement just beyond the park snapped her out of her daze. She lifted her head to try and focus, and her stomach churned as her eyes confirmed what she thought she had seen.

A man was standing on the sidewalk on the other side of the park, looking directly at her. He was rather ordinary-looking, with tan pants and a dark, navy shirt. But the way he stared blankly terrified her. How long had he been there, watching her struggle across the lawn, and then the street? And what was he doing there? She had expected to be alone. But then she remembered that she was not the first to cross back over and occupy a body. Others had been taken already, although not necessarily by human souls.

She shivered at the realization that she was likely looking at a body possessed by something that didn't belong to it. Although the appearance of the demonic creatures prowling the spirit world was far worse than this bizarre fellow watching her, she was much more disturbed by its wicked, unnatural presence. She was also frightened by the realization that if he wanted to inflict harm on her at that moment, there was absolutely nothing she could do to defend herself. Should she try again to lift herself over the fence? Or was she better off keeping completely still until this mysterious person decided, hopefully, to move on.

After several more minutes of the man standing motionless, not flinching in his gaze, he suddenly turned his back and began looking in all directions. He took several very awkward steps in one direction, his eyes still scanning intently. Then he turned, nearly toppling over in the process, and took several more irregular steps in the other. His strides were beyond strange. He appeared to be just falling forward, with his feet barely catching him before he face-planted onto the concrete. He stopped again, still nervously surveying his surroundings. When he appeared satisfied that whatever it was he was looking for was not there, his gaze turned back to Sophie, and he started staggering directly towards her.

Panic tore through her as she realized it would take less than a minute for him to reach her, and she could barely crawl, much less run away. She curled her legs up under her body and pressed one hand as hard as she could on the pavement. It felt like she had a truck on her back, but managed to bring herself to her hands and knees. She glanced quickly back toward the mysterious man, who was still advancing clumsily across the lawn. She reached out and clenched one of the bars with trembling fingers and pulled franticly, begging her muscles to not fail her. Her body rose just enough to allow her other hand to reach the top rail. She felt herself tipping backward as her equilibrium begged her to abort. But she stubbornly grabbed the rail with both hands, refusing to fall. She pulled long enough to drop an arm over to the other side, and then collapsed with her body draped over the fence like she'd been hung out to dry.

She looked back to find the man already several steps into the street. He would be upon her any second unless she succeeded in flinging herself over the fence. But, for the first time, she caught a glimpse of where she would be landing, and it certainly wasn't what she had hoped to see. Where the stone wall dropped to meet the lake water below, there was a pile of jagged rocks. And from her vantage atop the iron fence, the drop suddenly appeared much higher than she had remembered. The thought also entered her mind that if she could only barely move, how could she expect to swim? Perhaps she was better off taking her chances with this unnerving gentleman who was apparently so eager to meet her.

When he was just feet away, he opened his mouth and tried to speak. What came out was a sort of ghastly, incomprehensible noise that again turned Sophie's stomach. He reached out toward her, but stumbled before reaching her shoulder, crashing face-first onto the concrete.

When he lifted his head, streams of crimson blood were flowing from his nose into his mouth, and his eyes were rolled back into his head. Yet he still struggled to his feet and reached again for Sophie. That made up her mind; she was going swimming.

With one desperate heave, she flung her other leg over the rail and fell to the rocks below. Her hip hit first, smashing down onto a sharp edge. Her head followed, bouncing off one rock and then another until her groans were choked by a mouthful of water. For several seconds, she didn't know which was way up or down. But her hands finally found the mossy rocks jutting up from the shallow sludge below, and she felt her way back up toward the light above.

As soon as her head breached the surface, the cool air stung an open cut on the side of her head. Soon the minerally taste of blood invaded her mouth. She gripped the jagged rocks and tried to steady herself as the water lapped rhythmically against her back. Once she felt a little bit stable, she dipped her mouth back into the water and drank. Actually, she chugged, one swallow after another, choking several times in the process. She was fully aware that the water wasn't clean, and that she would likely pay the price later. But at that moment, she didn't care.

The man was still above her, staring down like a hawk from behind the fence. He hadn't followed her over the railing, perhaps wisely. But as Sophie started shimmying down the rock wall toward a large dock surrounded by lavish boats, he stayed directly overhead, not taking his eyes off her. She didn't know where she was headed, or how she would find a way out of the water. But she did know that this thing seemed intent on being there when she did.

After feeling her way several hundred yards down the stony shoreline, she was completely exhausted when her hand finally touched the fiberglass hull of a sleek vessel parked at the dock. She grabbed tight onto an anchor rope and closed her eyes as she tried to find the strength to stay afloat. She wished desperately that when she opened her eyes, the man would be gone. But he was not. Just like before, he was watching her. She knew she had to try and swim around the back of the boat to escape his sight, but was terrified that letting go of the rope would mean sinking to the bottom. But once again, she didn't think she had a choice.

The man became visibly agitated as Sophie arched her back and flattened out on the surface of the water. She began pulling herself along the side of the boat and away from the shore. He paced back and forth along the railing, eyeing her like a panicked dog. She eased along, her nose taking in air as it skimmed just above the surface, until she reached the back corner of the boat. Her hand felt along a wooden platform extending off the stern until she grasped the cold metal of a ladder. With her hand gripping tightly to the top rung, she raised her head above the surface as she again searched for enough strength to pull herself upward.

Somehow Sophie managed the impossible climb into the boat. But as soon as she felt the cool deck on the bottom of her feet, her vision blurred, and then went black. She woke up face-down on the floor of the boat, her head throbbing. She had fainted, with no idea how long she had been there completely vulnerable and exposed. She popped up and searched frantically for her creepy pursuer, but didn't see him. Her legs quivered feebly beneath her as she staggered toward the boat's edge for a better look. The long dock that jutted out from the lake's edge was empty, and there was no sign of anyone on shore. There was little chance she would be able to climb gracefully from the boat down to the deck, so she was likely facing another painful plunge and brutal landing. But compared to her crash onto the jagged rocks, and everything else she had been through that day, the flat wooden planks really didn't look so bad.

Sophie succeeded in landing on the dock without bouncing off and into the water, but only barely. The sun warmed her face as she rested briefly on her back. She deliberated whether to try and stand and walk the length of the dock, or just stick to crawling to avoid the very real possibility of toppling over into the water. She rolled over onto her stomach to evaluate the path to the shore, and saw him waiting at the other end of the dock.

There was no longer an iron fence separating them, or water, or anything but a lengthy stretch of wooden slats. She searched frantically for an alternative escape route, but she knew she could never make it back onto the boat, and didn't care much for the prospect of going back into the water. Plus, if he went in after her, and managed to get ahold of her, he may just drag her helplessly to the bottom.

His steps were clumsy, but deliberate, just like before. His eyes never strayed from her, and she wasn't even sure that he blinked as he scooted down the dock. She estimated that it would take him twenty steps to get to her, maybe twenty-five. Either way, she had very little time to devise any sort of plan that didn't involve running, climbing, swimming or fighting. That essentially left her to choose between striking up an improbable conversation with a possessed stranger, and praying for a miracle. Unless…

Sophie spun cumbersomely onto her back with her legs pointed toward the shore. By the time she got herself situated, he was no more than ten steps away. By her estimation, he had been on sensory overload since taking possession of whoever's body it happened to be inhabiting. Over the past several hours, or days, or however long had passed, it had experienced an entirely new array of previously unknown feelings, sensations, pleasures and pains. But there was one thing Sophie was pretty sure it had yet to experience. Until now.

Crunch!

Just as the man took his final step and began to lean over toward her, Sophie raised her foot and swiftly kicked him square in the crotch. He bellowed deeply and hunched over trying to catch his breath as his knees buckled. He choked twice, and then tumbled toward Sophie. But just before he collapsed onto her, she tucked her knees to her chest and caught him with her feet, diverting his fall over the side of the dock and into the lake. A cool, refreshing splash of water doused Sophie's face as the man disappeared beneath the surface. She rolled to her side and looked over the edge of the dock, and there he was, looking up at her from several feet below the surface. His hand was extended, reaching up from the deep.

She felt a hint of guilt as she thought about the poor soul who used to belong to this body that she just watched sink to the bottom. She may have sent him plunging into the water, but it wasn't her that possessed his body, and it surely wasn't her who caused this catastrophic mess in the first place. This was all the more reason to try and figure out if there was some way she could help, beginning with finding Alie's body and bringing him back.

She grasped the side of the boat and struggled to her feet. She changed her mind about crawling to the end of the dock. There would be no more crawling today. She would stand, and she would walk.

JOSH DEERE

Chapter Twenty-Seven

A ghost town. That's what kept repeating in Sophie's head. Like the old boomtowns of the American West, or Detroit's abandoned, factory-worker neighborhoods, the regal, bustling city of Geneva had become, in an instant, an empty shell of its former self. Just a few days, or even hours before, it was in the upper echelon of world-class cities. But it had become an eerie necropolis of stalled vehicles and lifeless corpses, scattered mercilessly across the city's streets and sidewalks.

Sophie walked down one of her favorite streets that she had walked many times. But this time it felt like it took an eternity to go just a few blocks. Some of those blocks required her careful navigation around mounds of heaped-up bodies. Others were desolate, except for maybe a single crumpled corpse or the tiny body of a helpless child limp in the arms of a parent. The only thing worse than trudging past the empty bodies were the occasional run-ins with those that weren't empty. She tried to stay as far away from them as possible, as they lumbered along with their unnatural strides. When they did see her, Sophie tried to impersonate their peculiar walk and mannerisms, hoping to possibly blend in. But they still stared relentlessly, and sometimes even followed her. With her feet mostly back underneath her, she felt pretty confident that she could outrun them, but they were unnerving nonetheless.

Her quest was as clear as her determination: she would find Alie's body no matter how long it took. But where would she even begin? The last they checked, it was definitely not in the plaza, nor in the alleyway where Alie had left it. So, with no real idea where to start, she set a course for her apartment. She felt that she needed to see what was inside, although she was afraid what she might find.

It had been just a few chaotic, but fantastic months since she lugged her overstuffed luggage up the same, stale staircase to her unit. She had since gotten to know, and even grown to love her outrageous roommates—yes, even, for the most part, Bridgette. The same fluorescent light was still flickering in the hallway, and the same cheesy novelty map of California still hung on the outside of their door. But an unnerving silence hung in the air, and her stomach churned as she gripped the cold door handle.

Sophie pushed the door open slowly. She expected to find something horrible inside, but still gasped at the sight of her sweet roommate, Liz, balled up on the carpet next to the couch. There was a paperback novel propped open on the couch next to a blanket, Liz's cell phone, and an overturned cup of coffee. Sophie knelt beside Liz and sobbed as she touched her graying cheek. She had never felt so helpless in her life. She desperately wished she could move the body to the cold storage warehouse, or at least somewhere it would be better preserved. But she couldn't, so she leaned over and kissed Liz's forehead, then gently covered her body with the blanket.

Sophie noticed the television was on, but there was no sound. A news anchor was talking with a grave look on her face as aerial images of Geneva scrolled behind her. Sophie dove for the remote and turned up the volume, but the anchor spoke in French. She could make out a few words intermittently— Geneva, bodies, reports, Hadron, military— but was left guessing at the rest. She turned to another channel, only to find it was out of service. She tried another, and then another, and found the same. In fact, she found only four stations functioning, all of which were broadcasting reports in French about Geneva.

Sophie searched the rest of the apartment, but found no one else. While standing in the kitchen, she realized she'd been teetering all day between nauseous and starving. So she proceeded carefully to dig through the refrigerator for something she could stomach. After only a few minutes, however, the feelings of sadness and guilt swarmed her, and she just couldn't stand to be there any longer. She found her backpack and filled it with two apples, a semi-stale loaf of bread, and a bottle of water, and then set out again while fighting back tears.

She spent the next several hours roaming Geneva's desolate boulevards and pathways, searching the vacant faces of countless corpses, and hiding from the wandering, possessed bodies. She still hadn't decided what she might once she did find Alie's body, and hoped she would somehow be instantly inspired when she did. Strangely enough, she actually hoped his body had been occupied by some foreign spirit, as opposed to lying empty and decaying in the sun, or being picked at by scavenging birds. Either way, she needed to find it as soon as possible. But so far, she had found nothing.

Sophie used to love the magical, final hours of the day in Geneva, when the sun slipped behind the jagged horizon and the sky faded to dusk. But on that evening, the setting sun only brought the dread of facing the night alone. She knew her re-acquired physical form would soon grow tired, and she would have to find somewhere safe to sleep. She had passed by the church while scouring the city. But without the advantageous skill of passing through solid objects, she had no way of getting inside. She also considered the museum, but knew it too was probably closed. She was terrified that she might run across Ms. Martineau's body, which she thought was more than she could handle. So, she settled on the dojo, thinking that it was where she would feel closest to Alie.

The door to the dojo was wide open, and the lights were on. This troubled her. She didn't see anyone inside through the windows, but would still have to search the back offices. She slipped through the front door and quickly turned off the lights so as not to attract anyone else, then locked the door behind her, never taking her eyes off the dark hallway leading to the back. She immediately noticed that the collection of blades that had gracefully adorned the walls before were scattered chaotically across the studio's floor, with several of the racks ripped from the walls and smashed on the ground. She reached uneasily for the sword above the door—Alie's sword—but it was gone. So she slid silently along the wall, trying to reach one of the other swords. But as she drew closer, something shuffled in the back, followed by a loud crash. Sophie froze and listened as one of the doors down the hall creaked open.

. . . .

He stood only inches from her face, but knew she couldn't see him. She was frozen, and visibly nervous, standing alone in the dark with her hand gripping the sword's handle like a vice.

He had followed her for what felt like weeks, or months, or even longer. Time had essentially lost its meaning as it just barely crawled along. He spent most of his time perched on the rooftops, looking down on her, or sneaking from building to building to avoid the hordes of demons roaming the city, always watching her through the windows.

Sometimes, when nothing else was around, he would walk out into the street and stand next to her, remembering what it was like to touch her, or feel her breath. And he would whisper in her ear, hoping that somehow she could hear him, or at least know he was there.

He had spent countless hours waiting for her to walk a city block, or just watching her take a drink. And he watched in agonizing horror each time she came across one of the wandering, possessed corpses. He would scream desperate warnings at her of coming dangers that he could see long before they came into her view. But he never left her, not for a minute. He had become her ghost story, determined to haunt her every movement until they were together again.

It wasn't long until the demons figured out where to find him. He could only hide for so long. Eventually they learned to follow the nebulous outline of the blonde-haired girl, showing through from the other side, and her sword-wielding protector wouldn't be far behind. Over time, he earned a reputation among them, having destroyed many demons bold enough to challenge him. They had stubbornly tried to hunt him, only to find that they had become the hunted.

He followed her into the dojo, and long before Sophie heard the mysterious noises from the back office, Alie knew what was there. The creature clumsily carried a sword, which it hardly even knew how to hold, much less use. But it was a sword nonetheless, and Alie knew that Sophie had no business being there.

Over what felt like an eternity, Alie moved back and forth between the back office and the studio, whispering to Sophie a thousand times that she needed to leave. Several passing creatures saw him through the windows, some of which recognized him and wisely moved on. Others stupidly entered the dojo, soon to find themselves minus an arm, or even a head. But he stayed, trying maddeningly to communicate with her, the way he'd done with every other danger she had faced back in the physical world.

. . . .

"On second thoughts," Sophie whispered to herself, "I think I'm done here." Something didn't feel right, and she didn't see any reason for sticking around to see what was causing such a ruckus. She had nearly crippled the thing on the dock, and made her escape in the process. And she had fared fairly well since then, mostly avoiding any run-ins with the unsavory roamers. But she thought it better to leave the sword fighting to Alie, so she snuck out of the dojo without being seen. She did take the sword with her for the time being, but had something else in mind for protection that she wouldn't find in a karate studio.

Sophie had passed the police station on Rue Rothschild many times during her time in Geneva, often receiving a friendly wave or a nod from the idle officers watching the world pass by. Sophie wondered just how busy they actually were. She'd heard that there was occasional crime in Geneva, but had never actually seen one. But on this trip by the station, there certainly would be no smiling policemen moseying along their casual patrol. In fact, outside of the station's glass and metal façade, the sidewalk was empty. Through the large windows, Sophie could see the bodies of several staff workers slumped onto their desks, and a few officers collapsed on the ground.

It felt strange to walk unimpeded into a police station and past the front desk, and even stranger to root through the pockets of the lifeless officer crumpled on the floor. Once again, she had one of those "I can't believe I'm actually doing this" moments as she delicately slid the black pistol out of the officer's holster. She gripped it like it was some sort of foul, toxic artifact that needed to be handled both carefully, and at a distance. She'd ever even held a gun, much less fired one. But then again, she'd never shared city streets with demons draped in stolen carcasses.

Sophie gathered several guns and spread them out like a firearm smorgasbord across the receptionist counter. She planned to spend a while figuring out how to work each one, and then choose the one that best suited her. But just as she picked up the first one, something caught her eye from the street. She dropped like a brick behind the counter, waiting several minutes before raising herself up just enough to take a peak. A snarly face with squinty eyes was plastered against the glass. Its mouth was moving like it was talking as it tried to get a look at what was inside. It didn't appear to notice her, and she remained frozen, praying it would leave. Then another silhouette appeared in the darkness next to the first. After a brief conversation of some sort, the second one leaned into the light, revealing its face. Sophie got a good look, and almost collapsed.

Her eyes filled with tears at the sight of Alie's face. She was both happy to see him in one piece, and furious that something else was walking around inside of his body. She wanted to charge out the door in a rage, but didn't move until she was comfortable that they didn't see her. She slid slowly to the floor and carefully undid one of the officer's gun belts, which she draped over her shoulder before creeping back to the entrance. Alie's body and its sidekick apparently lost interest and disappeared down the dark street. Sophie snuck out into the night not far behind.

She caught up to them two blocks later, and then spent another block anxiously wondering what to do next. She couldn't exactly walk up to them and politely ask for Alie's body back. And, of course, she didn't want to do anything to damage the body. Nothing she could think of seemed like a good idea, but she wasn't about to lose his body now that she'd found it. So, she just went with the obvious.

"Hey!"

The two creatures looked shocked as they turned and saw her standing in the middle of the street. By the looks on their faces, it was clear they knew she wasn't one of them. They eyed her inquisitively, and then exchanged words in a strange language. The short one soon began to cackle out a disturbing laughter as he walked toward her. Alie's body followed shortly behind. As soon as they started toward her, Sophie held out the pistol, hoping to warn them against coming closer. It didn't work. She really didn't want to pull the trigger, especially aimed at Alie. But what was she supposed to do if they didn't stop?

"Watcha gonna do with that, love?" spat the stubby sidekick.

"You have something I want," she answered, trying to keep her voice from shaking.

"Oh, I bet I do," the other one chortled out of Alie's mouth. He stepped closer, much, much too close. His face was there in front of her, but his eyes were not. Sophie was powerless to do anything but stand there trembling. He took another menacing step toward her, sending her stumbling backward. She dropped her grip on the gun and stumbled backward. Alie's body leapt forward and snatched the pistol from the ground. Then, with a devilish grin, Alie's arm raised and pointed the gun right at Sophie's face. The other one began to cackle as the demon with the gun peered down the barrel at Sophie. "Say hello to my mates on the other side for me," he grinned.

Click. Click. Click.

"Oh yeah," Sophie said. "Sorry, I couldn't figure out how to put bullets in that one."

Her finger squeezed the trigger of the slightly smaller, but easier to figure out pistol she had pulled from the officer's holster. The gun lurched violently, jarring her and almost causing her to drop it. But she held on, and fired another shot. The sidekick's legs buckled and he dropped to his knees, holding his stomach. He looked up at Sophie in disbelief, and then bellowed out as the agonizing, unfamiliar pain racked its borrowed body. The one occupying Alie stepped back in shock, looking suddenly helpless at his comrade, and then at Sophie. She rose to her feet, and then said confidently while pointing the gun at Alie, "You too, on your knees." But he didn't move, still staring at her like a wild animal trapped in a cage. "I'm pretty sure there are a few more of those left in here," she said, insistent, pretending that it wasn't hard to aim a gun at Alie. "Should we find out?"

Alie's knees bent and the creature took its place next to the other, which had collapsed in a blubbering mess as a crimson stain grew beneath him. Sophie held the gun on him while approaching warily. The demon's eyes watched her curiously through Alie's face. There was obviously something going on in its mind as it tried to figure her out, and Sophie feared it would be onto her soon. Was it too obvious that she would not shoot him? She wasn't going to wait to find out.

"Sorry about this, Alie, wherever you are," she whispered just before pulling her fist back and clocking Alie's face square in the nose. His head snapped back as pain shot up her arm. She had never punched anyone before, and it hurt much worse than she'd ever imagined. The demon held Alie's hands over his nose as blood trickled down his wrists. Unable to come up with any better ideas, she'd hoped she could knock him out, and then maybe that would cause it to loosen its grip on Alie's body. Instead, she'd just pissed off an evil demon inside the body of an elite Special Forces fighter. With Sophie unwilling to pull the trigger, she was out of options, and the demon knew it.

"Pull the trigger, why don't ya." He then placed his fingers gently across the top of the gun and pulled the barrel into Alie's forehead. "You're not gonna do it, are you?" he taunted her. "You're not gonna do anything." The stubby sidekick gurgled out a bloody laugh from its fetal position on the concrete. She tried to stand firm, but he was right. She wasn't going to pull the trigger. She couldn't.

. . . .

A crowd had gathered around Alie. The air grew heavy with angry snarls. But like hyenas surrounding a thick-maned lion, no one dared charge him head on. He paced circles around the nearly motionless image of Sophie in a stand-off with his possessed body. For what felt like numerous agonizing hours, she had held the gun on Alie's body.

"Do it, Sophie! Pull the damn trigger!"

He knew it would mean that his body would be lost. But it would also mean she would be safe. He also knew that it didn't matter how much he screamed; she would never do it.

But something had changed, something in the face and the posture of the demon occupying his body. The fear was gone, and he had turned into the aggressor. His hand was inching upward toward Sophie's outreached arm. Alie's instinct and years of combat training made it clear; the demon was going for the gun.

An infuriated shout burst from within him, first aimed at the demon confronting Sophie, and then at the horde of malevolent souls surrounding him. "How do I stop it?" he screamed. The crowd roared with laughter as their collective nerve grew. He knew they were waiting for the right moment to rush him, and if it weren't for Sophie's current predicament, he would beat them to it. "Somebody tell me how to stop him or I will annihilate all of you!" They only laughed louder and became more hysterical.

Alie fought back the panic and forced himself to breathe deeply. He sat down on the ground at Sophie's feet. For several minutes he watched the mob of demons waiting to tear him to pieces. Then he closed his eyes, concentrating on the sacred breathes filling his chest. The sound of the demon horde intensified, signaling that they were coming. He couldn't just sit there for long, and he knew it. He had hoped to be able to quiet his mind, if only for a second, to reach for some inspiration. Instead, he felt a hand on this shoulder and sprung to his feet with the sword ready to strike. But it was not the hand of a demon on his shoulder. It was the pure.

He had stashed the pure in a closed room in what he hoped was an inconspicuous building while he followed Sophie. He had returned numerous times, fearing the demons would find the it while he was away. He had never anticipated that the pure would wander off, especially to come looking for him. Now the scrawny, pathetic-looking creature had slipped past the demonic crowd and was standing before Alie, gripping his arm tightly with its dangly fingers. The pure's presence amplified the mob's fury, especially the sight of it touching Alie. Several of them shot forward in a mock-charge, only to retreat cowardly into the crowd. Alie was on full guard, the sword cocked in his arm as he spun repeatedly, ready to intercept anything that dared make the advance. It wasn't only himself that he had to protect now; he must keep the demons away from the pure.

The pure, on the other hand, was apparently oblivious to the danger. It tugged gently on Alie's arm, pulling him back toward the confrontation between Sophie and Alie's body. The pure then looked Alie squarely in the eyes as it reached out and wrapped its fingers around the neck of Alie's body. Alie stared for a second, bewildered by whatever it was that the pure was trying to signal to him. Then he imitated the pure and bizarrely reached for his own neck. He felt nothing but air, but did his best to mold his fingers into what he thought was the size and shape of his throat. The pure then laid its other hand on Alie shoulder, and the demon mob hushed. Almost instantly the sensation of flesh and strained tendons materialized within his grip, and Alie dug his fingers into not his own throat, but the throat of the demon that possessed his body. He realized immediately what had happened, and he squeezed and jerked furiously at the demon's neck with everything he had.

. . . .

Alie's fingers touched her hand as the demon gripped the gun's barrel and began to pull. She held tight to the grip, but kept her finger off the trigger. Her mind was swimming, but her body was helplessly frozen. She stared into the now-empty recesses of what used to be Alie's eyes that bore into her with an unfamiliar malevolence. And then those eyes rolled back into Alie's head and went blank.

Alie's body stiffened as his head flailed backward unnaturally. His hands scratched rabidly at his throat for a second, and then his body went completely limp and collapsed onto the street. Sophie gasped and dropped to her knees, taking Alie's head in her hands. She knew right away that whatever was inside of him was gone. But how?

"Alie?" she screamed out, looking everywhere for some sign of him. "Alie!?!" And there, for a brief second, Alie's face appeared before her like a vapor peering through a wispy veil. And then it was gone. Vanished, leaving her aching for more.

"Sophie," a distant voice whispered like a feather on the wind, fading into oblivion.

"Alie? No!" she shouted. "Don't go." But it was too late.

Chapter Twenty-Eight

Sophie was overcome by intense sadness brought on by the feel of Alie's lifeless body in her arms. The ecstasy of feeling his skin against hers was overshadowed by the emptiness of his corpse. Part of her just wanted to hold him and hope for his resurrection, but she knew that it wouldn't be long until the other possessed beings wandered onto their street, leaving both of them vulnerable.

She gently laid his head onto the concrete before scrambling to her feet. Then she began to pull on his arms, trying to move him out to somewhere safe. But Alie's dead weight was too much for her, especially with her strength so diminished. She looked around for some other way to move him, and saw an abandoned flower cart. She thought it would be impossible to lift him on top of the cart, but after much effort, and adding several accidental bumps and bruises to Alie's body that she would apologize for later, she managed to wedge his body into the gap beneath the upper bin and the wheels.

The roaming occupied bodies that she passed on the streets were clearly suspicious of her. As a blonde, dainty girl doing a bad impression of a possessed person, she was already a curious anomaly. But pushing a large wooden cart covered with floral arrangements, she stuck out like a lighthouse in a storm. Many of them shouted at her in strange tongues, while others followed her. She tried in vain to remain inconspicuous, but it was hopeless. She knew where she wanted to go, but began to truly fear that she wouldn't get there. So she started into a jog, then into a run, struggling to guide the lumbering cart toward the cold warehouse.

As she picked up speed, it felt more like the cart was pulling her than she was pushing the cart. Of course, that meant that slowing down to turn a corner came with a great deal of effort. Twice the cart almost flipped over, and once she was certain a wheel was going to come off when she crashed into a curb. But she managed to turn the corner onto the street that ran in front of the warehouse with the cart and, more importantly, Alie's body in one piece. The trio of possessed bodies loitering down the block, however, were a different problem.

Fighting exhaustion, Sophie spun the cart and lurched back around the corner and out of their sight. But when she peeked back around the corner of the building, she saw them already in a quick stride toward her. She leaned her body back into the cart, willing it forward from a slow crawl to a lurching walk, and then eventually back to a jog. She glanced behind her just in time to see the three demons stumble around the corner in their still awkwardly occupied bodies. She pumped her legs harder, heading for the next corner. It wasn't the route she'd planned, but if she could keep a fast enough pace around the building, then perhaps she could circle it entirely and escape into the warehouse's massive sliding door before her pursuers saw her.

The cart whipped her around another corner, giving her a look down the next road. This one was going to be interesting. There, standing in the middle of the road, was another lone, occupied cadaver. The look on its face revealed that it was every bit as surprised to see Sophie as she was to see him, especially with her mobile flower shop on wheels barreling straight towards him. He re-situated himself and stumbled toward Sophie's oncoming cart. He was apparently either determined to get his hands on her, or really, really wanted some flowers. Either way, it was quite clear that she stood no chance of stopping in time to avoid a collision, and even less of getting the cart going again in time to escape the three others that were following her. So, she tightened her grip on the cart's handle and pushed even harder. A second later the cart was rocked by a loud thud, followed by a vicious jolt that launched the cart's right side upward as the wheel ran over the man in the road. Between the first wheel and the second, the cart dumped almost half of its flowers onto the street. Sophie glanced down as she leapt clear of the waylaid body, and saw the carnage that was left behind. He was still "alive", but definitely not in the same shape as before, with a few limbs now situated quite differently than before.

But she didn't stop. Even with the cart now hobbling on a rickety wheel that she seriously feared was about to fall off, Sophie couldn't afford to slow down. She checked to make sure that Alie's body was still there and, amazingly, it was, except for a wayward arm dragging on the ground. Sophie gave the cart a hard shove and then ran alongside it while bending down to flop the arm back into the safe compartment. Then she re-grasped the handle just in time to round corner number three of the warehouse. Now onto the fourth and final corner, all the while praying no one was there.

Sophie maneuvered the hulking cart around the last corner just as the three pursuing demons rounded the third. She pushed with everything she had until she reached the massive sliding doors. She pulled back on the cart's handle just enough to slow it down to a steady roll, and then sprinted ahead to slide the door open just wide enough for the cart to pass through. A rush of frigid air escaped the warehouse as she turned and readied herself for the cart. It was charging mightily toward her, with no time to get out of the way. So she vaulted herself on top of the cart, crashing down into the not-so-soft bed of flowers, and taking in a mouthful of stems and petals in the process. She then flopped off the back and dashed toward the door. There was no time to look down the street to see if she was in the clear, so she closed the door and hoped they hadn't seen her.

The dark, frozen interior of the warehouse made Sophie's skin crawl. The last time she was there, they were being hunted by the grotesque demons, albeit in the spirit world. Now she was alone with Alie's body, which she was in charge of keeping safe. Bringing it to the warehouse was her best option, she thought, in hopes of slowing down the inevitable decomposition. She grabbed onto both of Alie's hands and dragged him out from beneath the flower bin, and then heaved with the little strength she had left until she had moved him to a hidden spot behind a wall of crates. She slowly rolled the cart back toward the entrance, hoping to block the door if the demons tried to enter, or at least slow them down. She sincerely hoped they would pass right by and leave them alone. But if they didn't, she had an entire gun belt of bullets waiting for them.

Several minutes passed and the door stayed closed. She crouched silently behind the crates next to Alie and waited. She could see almost nothing except for her crystallized breaths rising into the moonlight beaming down through the giant skylight above. When they were spirits holed up in this same building, the moon and stars appeared to be little more than smudges of light peeking through the window. But now she could make out the sharp edges of a full moon, looking down on her from its silvery perch in the heavens. As she stared through the glass, she realized just how exhausted she was, and felt every piece of her body that was throbbing from the exploits of the day. She leaned to her side and rested her head on Alie's leg. She would just close her eyes for a minute while listening for any incoming dangers, but wouldn't allow herself to fall asleep.

. . . .

This time the faces were different. She stood where she'd stood before, with the thunderous explosions erupting all around her. But the burning pellets of sand that had once stung her face like a million wasps had transformed into icy droplets of freezing rain.

Sophie was shivering uncontrollably when the soldiers broke through the towering wall of smoke in front of her. She expected the first one to run past her as he'd done before, but it did not. Instead it stopped abruptly, just feet in front of her. Like before, its face was indistinguishable at first, barely even resembling that of a human. She watched as the other soldiers burst from the smoke and into the open toward her. Just like the first, they didn't pass her by, instead breaking off their charge just feet in front of her, and then joining the ranks of the others as they fell into formation. Their bodies were rigid and their lines taut and unflinching as the frigid raindrops pelted their faces. Sophie studied the sea of sopping wet faces, and saw the same drab, emotionless expressions as she'd seen before. But as she searched their faces, they simultaneously turned their gaze toward the soldier standing directly in front of Sophie. She too looked back to the first soldier that had stopped in front of her, and saw that it was Alie.

Her heart leapt as he flashed her a warm grin. Her hand reached for his, but the sky was suddenly ripped open with an ear-shattering blast. The ground beneath them bubbled in a violent upheaval, sending Sophie toppling over onto the frozen ground. She lifted her head to search for Alie, but was blinded by black, swirling smoke. She could hear him coughing somewhere in the blackness, but he didn't answer when she screamed his name. Just as she reached into the smoke, another explosion caused the ground beneath her to erupt again, tossing her into the air like a rag doll.

. . . .

The smoke dispersed and the explosions ceased, and Sophie's

thoughts fought their way back to reality. Her teeth were chattering, and her limbs were stiff as she lay unprotected from the frigid air. Just as she realized she was back in the warehouse, she felt Alie's body convulse beneath her as it was shaken by a roaring cough. Sophie sprung to her feet and studied Alie from head to toe. His face was twisted into an agonizing grimace as he gagged and struggled to find a breath. He twitched and writhed beneath her as Sophie looked on in horror.

"No! No, not again!" she yelled at his flailing body as it fought against being reanimated for a second time. Sophie dropped to her knees next to the body and grabbed its shirt with both hands. "Leave him alone!" she screamed while shaking him violently. "There are a million bodies here. Not him! Leave him alone!"

Sophie scrambled to her feet as Alie's body continued to gasp for air. She searched for something to tie him up before she was again faced with the dilemma of how to protect herself against something she couldn't harm. She ran to the flower cart, digging through the bouquets in search of some extra-long pieces of twine, but found none. She then turned and started feeling her way through the darkness, searching for anything that might work. But just as she tripped over an unseen pile of rubble, she heard a voice rattling faintly from Alie's thrashing body.

"Sophie?" the voice choked out.

She froze and listened for what she thought she'd heard.

"S-s-s... Sophie?"

She sprinted back to the body, and found it squirming as its chest inflated and collapsed spastically between choking and hacking. Sophie straddled Alie's chest and bent over, skeptically taking his face into her hands as she looked into his eyes. The blank, soulless presence that had unjustly seized his body was gone. Instead, she saw the eyes that she'd known, and loved, fighting to come back to life. It was Alie.

"Alie, listen to me," Sophie dropped back to his side and lifted his head onto her lap. "This part's gonna suck, but don't fight it. Just trust your chest to rise and fall like it's programmed to do." He wheezed loudly while clutching his chest. "Breathe, Alie. You gotta breathe." His eyes squeezed shut and his chin twitched rapidly as he struggled for some regularity in the inhaling and exhaling. He opened them again and focused on Sophie's face. She took him by the hand, and he clinched hers fiercely as he took in a first deep, clear breath.

"That's it, Alie. Keep going."

She did her best to comfort him, knowing the hell he was going through. But she hoped his re-entry might not be as bad because his body had at least been recently mobile. When the heaving came, she was waiting for it, and rocked him onto his side so he didn't choke. But he didn't vomit like she had, instead dragging his fingernails across the cold floor as his body painfully convulsed.

"Alie, you need water. I'll be right back." She thought her best chance of finding a water source would be in the warehouse's office, which was on the other side of the building, through the winding maze of crates and boxes. She thought of braving the dark labyrinth again, but decided that it was probably quicker to go up and over the catwalk. She moved quietly and quickly over the grated platforms that stretched over the maze, and returned within minutes with a painfully inadequate used coffee mug full of water.

She found Alie already on his hands and knees, groaning as he struggled to recover far too quickly. She bent over and helped choke down the water.

"Slow down, Alie," she ran her fingers down his back as she tried to comfort him. "We have plenty of time."

"Yeah," he spat out, "but they don't."

"Who?" Sophie asked.

"On the other side," he answered, and then collapsed back onto the concrete floor.

. . . .

Just as Sophie had expected, Alie's transition back into his body was easier than hers had been, but was still rough. She was ecstatic to be reunited with him, but it still pained her to see him struggle. She was used to seeing him radiate strength and confidence, so she hated to see him barely able to walk. But despite his dilapidated state, he refused to rest. He was shaking his arms and legs repeatedly, trying to speed up his recovery, as if he were in some sort of a feverish hurry to get somewhere.

"So, what now?" she asked.

"We've got work to do," he mumbled.

"What do you mean?"

Alie stumbled across the cold concrete floor, not stopping until he was grasping the handle of the sliding warehouse door with both hands. He hunched forward, leaning his head against the door while exhaling gusts of frosty breath.

"You might not want to open that," warned Sophie, assuming he was unaware of the possessed wanderers outside. Alie shot her a fierce look, and then grunted heavily while hauling the massive door across its tracks. The golden hue of the morning sun was just beginning to spread across the city. Alie stepped out into the street and looked to the sky, taking in the sun's warmth. Sophie hurried out behind him, looking frantically for possessed bodies, but they were alone.

"Sophie, come here," Alie said, reaching for her with a pale grin. "I suppose I should give you a proper kiss, shouldn't I?"

She had to steady him at first, but he pressed his lips to her just as firmly as he'd ever done. The feeling of his arms wrapped around her—his real, actual, in-the-flesh arms—was miraculous, and his lips even better. At that moment, she selfishly wanted nothing more than to run away with him, far from Geneva, and the bodies, and the hell they'd experienced. More than anything else, she wanted to get as far as possible from the huge atom collider that Virgil said caused the catastrophe in the first place. But she wasn't surprised to learn that Alie had other ideas.

"Can you help me wheel that big cart out here?" Alie asked before walking back toward the warehouse entrance.

Sophie eyed him in disbelief. "What exactly do you think we're going to do with that?" she inquired, dreading the thought of trying to shove that stupid thing around again.

"I know, you have sort of a…love-hate relationship with that thing," Alie chuckled.

"Love? Hate-hate is more like it. That thing almost killed me several times," she grumbled.

"I know. I saw the whole thing." He laughed again. "And in slow motion…*very* slow motion. But we need it, at least until we can find something bigger and better." He paused for a moment, and Sophie noticed a sadness in his face. "Sophie, we have to find my guys—Diggs, Redwine, Harris. We must get their bodies to the cold storage. And your girls too, and then as many others as we can get. That's the only way they'll have a chance."

Somehow Sophie knew that was coming. What could they do? With only two of them, and hundreds of thousands of bodies spread all over the city, how could they hope to even make a dent?

"We have to try," was Alie's answer. "Even if we can only save a few, we have to do what we can," he insisted, trying to drag the cart back outside even before Sophie could assist him. He tugged strenuously, only managing to rock it back and forth a few times. On the third attempt, his legs gave out and he collapsed.

"I should have known you'd be so eager to help," said Sophie as she knelt to help him to his feet. "But you need food, and more water. We both do."

"Sophie, there's no time," Alie answered.

"There has to be. We're worthless like this. We need our strength." With a large heave, she lifted him up and began to guide him toward the door. "Plus, maybe we can find a phone and call for some help."

They soon found a suitable eatery without any unwanted run-ins. The plan had been that Sophie would cook up something while Alie searched for supplies. But there was something about stepping over bodies on the way to the kitchen that squelched their appetites, even as famished as they were. So instead they stuffed an abandoned backpack with several loaves of bread, cheeses, sausages, and a few bottles of water. Just before leaving, Alie noticed Sophie staring vacantly at a telephone hanging on the wall. She reached for a second, but then withdrew her hand and continued to stare.

"Sophie?"

She glanced at him, and then back at the phone. "It seems surreal almost," she said softly. "The fact that maybe I could pick up the phone and call my mom."

"Why don't you try it and see?"

Sophie shook her head. "What do I tell her? Hey mom, everything's going great here at my semester internship," she quipped. "I'm learning a lot about curating, and I met a great boy. Oh, and I died the other day, and then came back to life. And now I'm just hanging out here in a city full of limp bodies and others that are possessed by demons."

"But you know this must be all over the news," Alie added. "She must be worried sick."

"I'm sure you're right," Sophie nodded. "But if I talk to her, do you really think she'll be any less worried? Or okay with me sticking around so I can help drag bodies into a cold warehouse? Hell no. She'll freak out and demand that I get on the next flight home." Sophie reached for the phone again, taking the receiver in her hand. "But I wonder…"

She held the receiver to her ear, and immediately her eyes widened.

"*Bonjour?*" A female voice spoke immediately on the other end of the line. "*Bonjour, est-il quelqu'un? Bonjour?*" Sophie was surprised to hear the voice instead of a dial tone. She held the receiver away from her, unsure if she should respond. Alie took the phone and answered the woman.

"*Bonjour,*" he said. "*Parlez-vous anglais?*" There was a long pause on the other end, and then Sophie heard a male voice speak up. From the sudden change in Alie's expression, Sophie could tell that he was military. Alie gave his name and rank, and explained that he and Sophie were stuck in Geneva. When the male voice pressed for more information, Alie paused, struggling to find a way to explain it without sounding crazy. But there wasn't one.

As the conversation progressed, Alie became more agitated by the interrogation he was forced to endure, unable to provide any answers that didn't prompt more questions. When he said that what they really needed was manpower to help move the bodies, the man inquired as to why Alie was alive and everyone else wasn't. When Alie explained that there were some others walking the streets as well, and that they could be dangerous, the man's overly accusatory question was why should he believe that Alie wasn't dangerous too. Before long it became quite apparent that Alie was getting nowhere with the man, and he hung up mid-sentence.

"We're on our own," he said while heading toward the front door. "We need to find a truck, or a van or something, and we need to do it soon. I have a feeling that the guy on the phone is the first of many headed this way who won't be too understanding about what's going on here."

"And what if they do come?" Sophie asked.

"Oh, they'll come," Alie nodded.

Sophie swallowed hard. "Well, then what?"

"Then we'll deal with it."

"Wait," Sophie was clearly perplexed. "What exactly do you mean 'deal with it'?"

"I mean we will worry about it when they get here." Alie slung the backpack over his shoulder and headed toward the door. But Sophie quickly snatched him by the arm.

"So that's it? That's the plan? We're just going to stack dead bodies by the truckload into cold storage until whatever…military force, or whatever that was, shows up and decides what to do with us?" Sophie shook her head and looked out the window. "I'm sure nothing could go wrong there?"

Alie all but ignored her and continued toward the door.

"Wait, Alie," she insisted. "I really would like to…"

"There's something else," Alie cut her off without making eye contact. "Something I wasn't sure I wanted to tell you." Sophie fell silent, troubled by his tone. Alie looked away, fidgeting uncharacteristically before speaking again. "I saw Cammie."

"What? Where?" Alie hesitated again, but Sophie pushed him. "What do you mean you 'saw Cammie'?"

"On the other side," he responded, his voice swathed in dread.

"Why…why didn't you tell me before?" Sophie paced frantically, chewing on a fingernail. "Where…did she see you? Did you talk to her? Did she…"

"Sophie, it wasn't good." He leaned against the wall, looking momentarily vulnerable.

"What do you mean, it wasn't good?" Her voice elevated as she demanded that he fill her in. "Alie…tell me what you saw!"

Alie's eyes lowered, struggling to explain it to her. "One of those things had her," he stammered. "One of the big ones." Sophie clasped her hand over her mouth. "I tried to help her," Alie continued, "to do something. But I couldn't get close. There were too many of them. I wouldn't have stood a chance."

Sophie bit her lip and struggled to stay calm. She turned again to the window and rested her forehead on the glass. Her head was swimming, trying to make sense of what to do. Just a minute earlier she was sure they should try and help with a few bodies, but then get as far away from Geneva as possible. But as she pictured Cammie being dragged through the streets by a monstrous beast, she knew they couldn't leave. In fact, she was sure of something else, something that seemed like pure insanity: they had to go back. They had to find a way back to the spirit world. They couldn't just leave Cammie behind, or the rest of their friends, or really anyone for that matter. For the first time since all of this chaos began, the thought burned inside her that there had to be some reason she and Alie had not only survived the demons in the spirit world, but had managed to find a way back into their bodies. For all she knew, they were the only ones who had made it back, and knew how it was done. It was as if they had a responsibility, a mission to do what they could to help. It was a responsibility she didn't want, but one that she couldn't escape. She sighed deeply and swallowed hard as she turned back to Alie.

"You know what this means, right?" she uttered.

"Yes. One of us has to go back," he responded, knowing she would fight against his answer.

"*One* of us?" she barked. "No! Not a chance."

"It has to be this way," he persisted softly, yet firmly. "At least until we find someone to help. One of us has to move bodies while the other gets a pure to perform the ceremony." He stepped closer. "I've seen what they do to the other spirits. We can't let that happen to our friends. You *have* to find their bodies while I try and find them on the other side."

Sophie knew what he said was true, but that didn't make her hate it any less. In fact, she hated everything about this entire mess. But it was the mess they were in, and she was in it with Alie, come what may. So, she stuffed the last few supplies into the backpack and headed for the door, making no attempt to hide her displeasure.

"So, now what?" she grumbled.

"Now?" Alie cocked his head as if he were considering the options. "Now we're going to take a little trip to CERN, to see if we can't get a little tour."

"You mean to turn the machine back on?" Sophie had assumed the massive Hadron collider was destroyed, but maybe not. Maybe it had just been shut down after failing, and could be re-started so that it could malfunction again. It sounded crazy, but what didn't at this point?

"Unless you know of some other way for me to jump back out of this body of mine," Alie answered. "Without actually dying, that is."

"But if the collider blows again, won't that send both of us back?"

"Not if we can get you far enough away first. We'll drive until we've reached the edge of the blast radius, then I'll drop you off. And I have to get back even more quickly."

"And then what? Where will you go?" The dread in Sophie's voice was palpable.

"Paris."

Sophie's face turned pale. She knew what that meant. "The catacombs?" Alie nodded. "But, why?"

"I learned a few things while we were apart," Alie explained. "Remember that a lot of time passed for me while you were here alone. *A lot* of time. I mostly stayed close to you, but out of sight. But I also hunted demons. In fact, I became quite good at it." His voice was soft, but with a calm and unmistakable finality. As he spoke, Sophie wondered self-consciously, as she had many times before, if he was meant to be here. Was it his destiny, or something like that, to protect the helpless and hunt the demons? And was she just in the way, slowing him down? She didn't mention it to him; she knew he would have nothing of it, even if he knew it too.

He went on to describe that the more demons he hunted and slew, the more difficult it became to stay hidden. He had gained, or perhaps earned, a reputation among them. "I didn't pursue the demons just for the sake of terrorizing them, although I must admit I took a fair amount of pleasure in doing so. I made a point to learn from them as well. I studied them. And I captured and interrogated, much like we did with the dangling creature in the warehouse."

Sophie tried hard to remember exactly what was said during the banter with the demon hanging from the stair railing. She could recall some talk of the catacombs, and that it became violently defensive when they mentioned the pures. But beyond that, it was just a whole lot of snarling and pitching a fit.

"So, what else did they tell you?" Sophie asked.

"That these demons aren't the only ones. There are others, entire armies of them. Enemy factions made up of thousands of demonic souls, all fighting over who controls the pures. And all this because they are obsessed with one thing: taking a body."

"What about the pure you used to cross back over?"

"I'm sure they took it, and that it's being guarded more heavily than ever. Plus, we're gonna need more than one."

Sophie watched as Alie stood reverently over the vacant body of a fallen police officer. "There is apparently a heavily guarded place, deep within the catacombs, where they keep the pures locked up."

"And you're going to march right into this heavily guarded, underground demon fortress and bust these pures all by yourself?" Sophie forced an exasperated chuckle. "You gotta admit, Alie, that even for you that's ridiculous."

"That's precisely what I'm going to do, only not by myself."

"Even if you found the others—Diggs, Redwine and Harris—it would be suicide," she insisted. "You'd need an entire..."

"Army." Alie looked up from the floor with his trademark determination burning deep in his eyes. "That's exactly what I plan to get."

"And where, pray tell, do you plan to get that?" Sophie squawked, her frustration growing quickly at what seemed like Alie's craziest plan yet, which was saying a lot.

"The enemy of my enemy," Alie paused while stepping briefly out of the shadows, his face partially illuminated by a thin ray of moonlight, "...is my friend."

Either his meaning wasn't clear at first, or Sophie's brain couldn't imagine that he would suggest something so preposterously absurd. "Alie?" She wanted to scream, but instead clinched her fists and spoke slowly. "What...do you mean?"

Alie too spoke slowly between deep, concentrated breaths. "Several years ago, the boys and I were assigned to support a regiment of British Regulars who were bogged down in a conflict with a stubborn village of poppy farmers. They were proud and wanted a fight, but we elected to wait them out, trying to avoid unnecessary bloodshed. But after several days of worthless negotiations, we were getting impatient, and they were getting trigger happy. Just as things really started to break down, a bloodthirsty band of Taliban militia came roaring over a hill. Those villagers hated us, no doubt, but had been terrorized by the Taliban for over a decade." Alie nodded his head with a slight grin. "In almost an instant, we became the villagers' best mates. They let us into their village and we repelled the Taliban, with a little help from the Royal Air Force, which the poppy farmers enjoyed graciously. It's funny how quickly the negotiations turned after that."

"But, Alie," she snapped, "these are *demons* we are talking about. *Demons!*"

"Yes, among whom I have apparently become a known commodity. If they are half as hell-bent on gaining access to those pures as we think, then I am quite valuable to them, either as a trade, or as a hired assassin. Either way, I get in."

"You're insane," Sophie blurted out. "This has got to be the worst…"

"Then let's hear a better idea," Alie retorted. Sophie wanted to answer, but had nothing. "In the meantime," Alie kept on, "our friends are being subjected to who knows what by those things." He reached for Sophie, placing his hands tenderly on her shoulders. "You used to speak to me of having faith. Well, faith isn't really faith until it's all that's left between you and the impossible, right?"

"There's faith, and then there's insanity, Alie," she whispered.

"Well, sometimes you need a little bit of both." Alie made one last sweep in search of supplies, and then treaded carefully onto the street outside. "And now to find a fast way out of the city."

Sophie's head was spinning as they ventured back outside. But she managed to respond to Alie, her voice still barely above a whisper. "You want something fast? Leave that to me." She started down the street, but stopped immediately at the sight of two upright figures a block-and-a-half away, watching them. Alie tugged on her sleeve to go the opposite direction, but Sophie instead reached inside her bag and pulled out the pistol.

"Wait, can you please take this?" She held out the gun, eager to be done with it. "I know it's not your sword, but it'll have to do."

Alie accepted the pistol and handled it like it was part of him. "Hey, just because I prefer a blade doesn't mean I don't know what to do with this." His hands worked the pistol naturally into a flurry of snaps and clicks. Then he aimed it, locked and loaded, down the street toward the silhouettes. Sophie reached out, placing her hand gently on top of the gun, prompting Alie to lower it.

"There will be time for that, plenty of it," she said. "For now, let's go find you some speed."

Chapter Twenty-Nine

The passenger door on the rickety delivery truck was missing its handle, and was held shut by a frayed bungee cord. The contents of the cab, including Alie and Sophie, were getting tossed around like coins in a dryer. Sophie, who had insisted on driving, giggled every time she had to violently jam the gear shift into gear. Surely this wasn't the "speed" that Sophie was referring to, Alie thought. They had searched various vehicles in vain for keys before stumbling upon the truck with its driver slumped over the steering wheel and the keys still in the ignition. Many of the other cars were either missing drivers, had crashed into something while driving, or had just run out of gas. But the truck was sitting parked and ready in the delivery lane of a bakery, ready for the taking.

However convenient the truck may have been to commandeer, it was a nightmare to drive, especially while trying to navigate the eerily littered streets of Geneva. Several times Sophie had to stop and allow Alie to get out and drag a body or two out of their path. Alie suggested stacking the bodies in the truck, but Sophie explained that they would soon be leaving it behind for something more "fitting". Alie wasn't sure what she was talking about, but decided to remain silent and find out.

Alie's eyelids grew heavy as Sophie piloted the noisy truck away from the dense city center. He finally gave in and let them close as the first sliver of the morning's sun peeked over the horizon. The truck's jostling had eased from obnoxious to tolerable once they had escaped the stops and starts of the city. One moment Alie was drifting off thinking how the truck felt like it was going to tip over when Sophie turned a corner, and the next he was awakened by squealing brakes.

"Where are we?" Alie muttered, trying to clear his head. Through the truck's dirty windows, he saw that they had stopped just a few feet from a massive glass building. He also noted that Sophie didn't bother with any formal parking etiquette; she literally drove right up to the front door.

"You once told me that you dreamed of driving one of those exotic, expensive sports cars, but thought you never would," Sophie said, looking up at the towering, colossal structure. "Well, we need something fast, so now's your chance."

Alie's expression morphed from confused to astonished. For a moment, all the fierce, calculated bravado that defined him slipped away, replaced by child-like wonder. Just a few days earlier, he had mentioned that Geneva's annual International Motor Show was scheduled to begin in a few days. She remembered feeling sad that he was going to miss it by a day or two. Now she smiled at the sight of Alie looking up in awe at the gigantic canvas banner flapping in the breeze above the entrance, announcing the show's grand opening. Alie took Sophie by one hand and tugged on the first of a long row of glass doors with the other. It was locked. He tried the next one, and the next, but none of them would open.

"I don't suppose it would do us much good to knock?" he said while studying the doors for a way in.

"Look," Sophie said, pointing to the banner. "It says the show closed at 5:00, and the collider malfunction happened later in the evening. By that time, it must have been all locked up."

Alie backed up and scanned the building's façade. "We could start walking around looking for an open door".

"I've got a better idea," Sophie responded as started back toward the truck. That was when Alie witnessed Sophie do the most un-Sophie-like thing he'd seen her do to date: She cranked up the truck's tired engine, grinding the noisy gears into a sharp turn away from the building. The driver-side window rolled down, and Sophie said, "you may wanna stand back." Then she jerked the gears into reverse and inelegantly let off the clutch, sending the truck's hind end lurching backward until it crashed like thunder through the glass doors. Alie stood in shocked silence as shattered glass cascaded over the sides of the truck. Sophie looked at him with a wide, proud grin, and then shoved the truck into first gear one last time before jutting forward.

"I...I don't..." Alie mumbled through an amused chortle. "I'm speechless."

Sophie exited the truck and tossed the keys onto the driver's seat. As she approached Alie, she said, "Oh the things I'll do for you. Now let's go shopping."

"Isn't that stealing?" Alie chuckled.

"Only if there's someone here to catch us," Sophie quipped.

"Good point."

They stepped carefully over the glass and through the make-shift entrance, and into the hall's vast interior. "No…way," Alie whispered, taking in the enormity of what lay before him. In a space big enough to easily house several soccer fields, and then some, cars were lined up in every direction as far as the eye could see. In fact, Sophie's view only extended so far into the darkened exhibit hall through the dimmed lighting that cast long shadows over the rows of cars. But other than the cars and extravagant displays, the hall was eerily empty. Sophie strained her eyes in search of roaming bodies, but saw nothing.

"Shall we?" Sophie asked, nudging Alie with her elbow.

"We shall," he answered before starting down the first aisle. Sophie let him take the lead, following just steps behind as he moved from car to car, reverently reciting aloud some sort of exotic statistics about each one. After walking half the distance of the first corridor, Alie made a significantly longer stop in front of one particularly striking machine, and then stepped over the velvet rope that was supposed to serve as a barricade. He circled the car once before announcing that it was an "Aston Martin DB11." That didn't mean much to Sophie, but it was sleek, bright yellow and a convertible, and it was gorgeous. That was good enough for her.

"Can we take that one?"

"Not likely; not unless you happen to have a key," Alie replied while opening the driver's door and sinking into the plush cockpit. He closed his eyes and inhaled dramatically with a guilty smile as he caressed the steering wheel. "Despite what Hollywood may have you believe, it's almost impossible to hotwire any car manufactured since the mid-eighties."

"Well, that sort of limits things," Sophie said, looking around for something from an earlier era.

"Not at all," Alie answered. "There's plenty of speed from the good ol' days." He drew in a final, lustful breath from the interior of the Aston Martin, and then exited. He stood on his tiptoes in front of the car and strained to see further into the shadowy vastness of the exhibition hall. "If that's what I think it is," he uttered, "I may have found just the thing."

He led her deeper into the hall, ignoring rows of velvet rope barriers, past one dazzling, exotic car after another. He finally stopped under a large, yellow sign displaying a black stallion reared up on its muscular hind legs.

"Ferrari," Sophie whispered.

"Ferrari GT4 Berlinetta Boxer to be exact," Alie expounded. "The fastest car of the 1970s. And maybe, just maybe, susceptible to having its ignition hacked." The candy-apple red beauty sat defiantly on its haunches like a proud alpha. Alie found the car unlocked and knelt reverently next to the driver-side door before removing a military-issue pocket-knife-type device from his jeans pocket. Sophie watched curiously as his head disappeared into the dark space under the steering wheel. For several minutes, he tinkered, grunted, cussed and pried away at the underside of the steering column. Then a beefy, motorized roar erupted from within the bowels of the car, causing the floor beneath them to rumble. "Bingo," Alie announced. "You wanna drive?"

Sophie laughed sharply. "Not a chance! I'll enjoy the ride."

She slipped into the passenger's seat while he was removing a row of velvet ropes. He took his seat behind the steering wheel, and then revved the engine several times before inching forward out of the car's resting spot. The car rumbled and hummed down the aisle, between rows of cars, and toward the distant light at the shattered entrance. As the Ferrari crept along, the headlights produced fleeting flashes of brilliant colors eerily reflecting off the surfaces of the cars. Despite the bizarrely fabulous experience they were sharing of sneaking an extremely expensive, vintage Ferrari out of a massive collection of exotic treasures, Sophie couldn't help but feel sorrow. To her, these priceless cars, sitting empty in a giant, darkened hall, represented the hundreds of thousands of vacant bodies strewn across the city. Like the cars, each one of those bodies was a precious work of art, but was worthless when left empty and abandoned.

The sun seemed especially bright as the Ferrari's tires crunched over broken glass and into the daylight. Alie continued to maneuver gently around Sophie's battering-ram truck and other obstacles on the sidewalk. He looked sick as the underside of the car scraped the top of the curb as he carefully dropped into the parking lot. But that was where he left any sense of precaution behind in a smoldering, rubber-burning cloud of smoke. Like a wild mustang escaping its corral, the car launched forward in a furious eruption of power and grace. Alie pushed the legendary vintage motor to its limit as they jetted from the parking lot back onto the roadway. Within a few terrifyingly awesome seconds, they were flying down the highway, weaving in and out of the cars stalled on the road.

For a brief, nearly magical moment, Sophie almost forgot the reason they had pilfered the car in the first place. The windows were down, a cool wind was whipping her hair wildly, and Alie was driving an obnoxiously expensive car as fast as it would go with a child-like grin on his face. She tried to block everything out and take in the perfection of it all. But she couldn't escape the nausea of knowing that they were on their way to try and enact a plan that, at best, would mean that she and Alie would again be separated for who knows how long on different sides of mortality. It was probably the most insanely ridiculous plan of all time. But it was, in their bleak situation, all they had.

As with everything else wonderful about her time with Alie, the trip to the CERN facility went by much too quickly. Alie's driving didn't help. Within a few short minutes of turning onto the Route de Meyrin, the peculiar domed structure of CERN's large, wicker-ball-esque reception building came into view. There was no sign of any space-aged, apocalyptic equipment, or even an indication of the sixteen-mile tunnel that was apparently hidden beneath them; just the wicker globe and a scattering of unassuming, white buildings. Sophie expected more security. But the only thing separating the entrance from the road was a wide-open, woefully inadequate gate with no security features in sight.

Despite the lack of traffic, or anything else on the road for that matter, Alie took special care when parking the car out of the roadway in a delivery lane. He took Sophie's hand reassuringly as they walked in silence toward the unwelcoming door at the base of the bizarre sphere, not knowing what might be inside. Sophie thought it likely that they would find nothing, and that they stood about as much chance of turning the monstrous machine back on as they did of sprouting wings and flying away. But she kept her mouth shut as they opened the front door and stepped into CERN's world.

Inside the Globe of Science and Innovation, Sophie and Alie stepped into an otherworldly exhibition of sleek displays and space-aged, automated presentations. Atmospheric lighting bathed the otherwise dark interior in a mystifying indigo glaze, while blips of light danced across the rounded walls leading up to the hemispherical ceiling. The spectacle was beyond impressive, and beautiful. Unlike the auto show, the exhibits inside the globe were running at full capacity. But like the auto show's exhibition hall, the interior was eerily vacant.

Around every corner and behind every futuristic display, Sophie anticipated being pounced upon by some blood-thirsty, possessed soul. Shadows and dark corners were bad enough, but there was something significantly more disturbing about being at the place where all of this apparently started. What if the possessed ones were attracted to this place, like evil, zombified flies drawn to a nucleophysical flame? She squeezed Alie's arm as they snuck through the azure-tinged darkness in search of some sort of door or passageway that would take them away from the extravagant visitors' area, and into the bowels of the facility. But after numerous failed attempts at opening doors, all of which either led to bathrooms or broom closets, or were just simply locked, it became quite apparent that they weren't likely to find what they were looking for.

"I'm not so sure we're going to find a way in inside this place," Alie muttered. "At least, not in here."

"You're right. You won't." A voice answered from the shadows. Sophie screamed and nearly jumped out of her shoes. Alie instantly stepped in front of Sophie and, in a flash, aimed the gun into the darkness.

"Show yourself," Alie growled, his entire body suddenly tense.

"I'm not hiding."

"Don't move," Alie whispered to Sophie. He inched forward slowly with the pistol's sights trained firmly on the direction of the voice. "I'm armed, and will not hesitate to shoot."

The voice chuckled. "Then you could save me a bullet."

Alie froze. Did this mean the voice was armed? Sophie wanted to scream at Alie to back away immediately. She was about to lunge at him when the sound of something scraping across the floor stopped her.

It was the gun. It slid to a halt at Alie's feet, just before Alie kicked it toward Sophie. Alie backed up slowly as a silhouette appeared in the indigo glow.

"Welcome to CERN," the man muttered.

The figure was unassuming at best. He wasn't particularly tall, and of a noticeably slight build. His posture was rather slouched, with a hand resting on a display counter as if he were holding himself up. The other hand clutched the neck of a nearly-empty wine bottle. His salmon-colored button-down was only half-tucked into his slacks, and he was wearing argyle socks with no shoes. "If you're looking for a tour," the man jeered, "I'm afraid we're closed."

"Who are you," Alie demanded, "and why are you here?"

"I'm a walking dead man, that's who," the man replied. His accent was northern-European, maybe Finnish. And he spoke like a man defeated. "And why am I here?" He chuckled. "Punishment, I suppose." He suddenly hurled the wine bottle into the dark, and it exploded against a wall. Alie leapt backward and tensed his grip on the gun. But the man only stumbled backward as well, gripped his forehead, and groaned. He was clearly drunk.

"I knew someone would be coming soon enough," the man stammered. "But you're not exactly what I expected. What are you, UN? Red Cross?" Alie didn't answer, and was clearly still sizing this guy up. Ignoring his previous instructions, Sophie stepped in front of him, close enough to smell the booze on the man's breath.

"None of those," she answered. "We're just…trying to help."

The man's demeanor changed. He stood up straighter and eyed Sophie skeptically. "What do you mean *help*?"

Alie again went on the defensive and extended the pistol past Sophie, but she placed her hand gently on top of the gun and lowered it. "Easy, Alie. I don't think he means us any harm."

"He's a strange chap hiding in the dark with a pistol and a wine bottle in a city where no one's supposed to be alive," Alie grumbled. "Pardon me if I find that suspicious."

"If no one is supposed to be alive," the man interjected, "then how do you explain the two of you?"

Sophie looked at Alie with a grin and quipped, "Good point. How *do* you explain the two of us?" Alie returned the grin, but just shrugged.

"Unless you've got a key to the interior of this place, I think we'll just let the explanations stop here," Alie insisted.

"A key?" the man erupted. "What on earth for?"

"Please, sir, tell us if you have any affiliation with CERN," Sophie pleaded. "We don't have a lot of time. We need access to the collider."

At this the man's eyes widened, and he took a step back. "You don't have a lot of time…for what?"

"Again, that's none of—" Alie started.

"We're going to turn it back on," Sophie interrupted.

"Sophie!" Alie blurted out.

"What!?!" The man snapped out of his intoxicated stupor and appeared outraged. "Are you insane?" The man took several more wary steps back, acting like he was looking for a way to escape. "Do you have any idea what this thing can do?"

"More than you could ever imagine," said Sophie.

"It has killed thousands," the man shouted, outraged. "Maybe hundreds of thousands."

"Yes, we know," responded Sophie. "And we may know how to bring them back."

He stood for several seconds, silent and bewildered. And then he burst out in howling laughter. "So, you are insane, then."

"Perhaps," said Alie. "Crazy times call for crazy measures. Let's get out of here, Sophie."

He tugged at Sophie's arm as he started to back away, with the gun still aimed at the stranger. The man didn't move, but continued to bark at them as his shape faded into the darkness. "You'll never get in," he shouted. "And even if you did, are you stupid enough to think you could turn it on yourselves?"

"We're stupid enough to think a lot of things," Alie answered, not stopping his retreat.

The man did have a point, but not one they hadn't thought of already. They had discussed it several times, and even argued about how they were supposed to turn on the most sophisticated piece of scientific machinery on the planet. Alie had mentioned, jokingly, that there must be a manual somewhere. But unfortunately, without some sort of miracle, that really was all they had to go on.

"He's right, you know," Sophie said to Alie. "We stand no chance. We should have found Virgil and made him come back with us."

"What did you say?" the voice roared back to life from within the darkness. His silhouette reappeared, this time running toward them.

"Stop!" Alie commanded while Sophie behind him. The man ignored Alie's warning and got close enough that Sophie feared Alie would pull the trigger.

"Who did you say?" the man demanded. "Who should have come back with you?"

"Why do you ask?" Sophie stepped forward, only to be blocked by a side-stepping Alie. "Oh, cut it out," she snapped. "Put that stupid gun away, would you?" She stepped again toward the man, who looked like he was about to hyperventilate.

"I thought I heard you mention a name," he continued. "Someone you say should have come back with you."

"Virgil?" Sophie uttered cautiously, as if she were protecting the name.

"Virgil! Yes, Virgil," the man cried out while clapping once, and then pointing a trembling finger at her. "This Virgil, you say, he is a scientist?"

"Yes, a rather hairy, unkempt one," answered Sophie.

"That's him!" The man burst out into a loud sob and buried his face in his hands. "Tell me, please, how do you know Virgil? Have you seen him? Is he okay? Is he…you know…dead?"

Sophie hesitated and looked at Alie, who appeared somewhat exasperated, as if he had completely lost control of the situation. She turned back to the man, who was waiting in a frenzy for her answer. "He has, well, passed on," Sophie said as the man gasped, "but he's fine."

"What do you mean he's *fine*?" the man retorted, quite frustrated. "How do you know he's *fine*?"

Alie touched her on the shoulder, but she carried on. "Because, sir, we've seen him."

"But I thought you said…"

"Not here, sir," Sophie responded. "Not on this side. On the other."

"But…but you…how?"

"Because we, too, were, well, *dead*," Sophie continued. "But now, well, we're back."

"Ta-da," Alie jeered, and then turned his back on the man for the first time and appeared to head again toward the entrance. The man's mouth remained open, but no sound came out. Sophie began to withdraw toward the door as well, but kept her eye on him. He reached toward them while taking a few clumsy steps. When he finally exhaled, an unrecognizable bellow rose from within his gut.

"I'm sorry, sir, but this ship appears to be sailing," said Sophie, nodding toward Alie. "He's not much for chit-chat."

"Wait," the man begged. "What if I *can* help you?" Sophie stopped. "What if I do have a key?"

"We're listening," Sophie replied. "But you've got a lot of explaining to do." She glanced back at Alie, who too had stopped, suddenly very interested in what the man had to say.

"I suppose we should start with introductions," the man suggested, his voice quivering.

"I suppose *you* should start with your name," Alie responded.

"Very well," said the man. "My name is Rikku Laine, but most people call me Rik."

. . . .

Alie and Sophie followed Rik out of the giant sphere, across a courtyard and through the first of a series of doors, each of which required Rik to swipe a card and enter a code. He was quiet at first as they walked, and visibly nervous. But after being prompted several times by Alie, he began to open up. In fact, he not only opened up, he proceeded into a very long, drunk confessional, tears included, about his involvement with CERN, and how he and his colleagues had completely ignored Virgil's repeated warnings. He credited Virgil over and over again with brilliantly predicting the catastrophe, and expressed overwhelming regret for the way he had dismissed Virgil, who he called his friend.

He also begged Sophie and Alie for more details about their journey to the other side, especially about Virgil. But they purposely held back details, promising to deliver only after he kept his promise to get them inside. They did, however, interrogate him intensely about his role in the collider disaster. In particular, they demanded to know how he had managed to survive the event unaffected, while the rest of the city clearly did not.

"That is the question that's haunted me ever since," Rik responded. "I don't know the science behind it at all, but somehow those of us deep within the facility weren't affected."

"Those of *us*?" Alie jumped in.

Rik stopped abruptly, but didn't turn around. His head lowered as he faced another closed door. He fiddled with the card in his hand, clearly uncomfortable with Alie's question. After a deep sigh, Rik turned and put his back to the door.

"You should know," he began, still looking at the floor, "that what's behind this door is not likely what you're expecting." This was met with a stare from Alie, leaving no doubt that Rik must open the door. Rik nodded, and entered the code. But before opening the door, he signaled toward Alie's gun and said, "You'd better put that away. We're not alone."

As Rik yanked open the heavy steel door, busy voices echoed from somewhere down a long corridor. The door slammed behind them, and the voices immediately hushed. As Sophie and Alie followed Rik down the confined metallic walkway, they quickly discovered that what Rik had said was, in fact, true: they were not alone. CERN workers were scurrying like frantic ants throughout the tunnels, stopping only briefly with surprised eyes when they first noticed Sophie and Alie. But then they carried on, chattering with one another and on walkie-talkies in multiple languages. Rik pushed past the workers without greeting them, or even acknowledging they were there.

After what felt like a mile-long trek through the cramped corridor, Rik stopped just short of a long glass window. He stretched out his hand behind him, halting Sophie and Alie before they came into view of the window. "If you really want to turn it back on," Rik whispered, nodding toward the window, "here's your chance."

Sophie crept forward and peeked through the glass. Inside was an intimidatingly large conference table, littered with empty coffee mugs and scattered papers, and surrounded by a very tense gathering of important-looking people arguing, if not yelling at one another. Behind them were several large screens, some tuned to news channels, others running a constant stream of what appeared to be some sort of data. Behind the screens was a massive whiteboard covered in formulas, calculations, and the like. As Sophie surveyed the unnerving scene, she inadvertently locked eyes with a very unpleasant-looking bald man with a craned neck and a protruding Adam's apple, who then nodded toward the window. Sophie jerked back, but not before several sets of eyes around the table saw her.

"Who are they?" Sophie asked uneasily. But before Rik could answer, the door to the room flew open and the vulturesque bald man stuck his very grumpy face out to investigate.

"Rik?" the man snapped, clearly surprised to see him. "What are you—"

"We need to talk," Rik said, and barged right past him into the room. Alie followed Rik's lead, followed by Sophie. A diverse assortment of emotions was slathered on the faces of those around the table, none of which were good. Sophie expected Rik to start into some kind of explanation, or at least an introduction, but he said nothing. After several moments of awkward silence, a visibly hostile woman impatiently shrugged her shoulders.

"Well?" she said.

"Well?" Rik mimicked, addressed directly at Sophie and Alie.

Alie stepped forward, and instantly snapped into a decidedly more formal tone. "Greetings mam, gentlemen. My name is Corporal Alisdair Quin of the British 22nd Special Air Service Regiment, D Squadron, Mobility Troup. We apologize for the interruption, but we have some information that we believe to be critically important to your…discussions." Alie's greeting was met with blank stares, but he carried on unfazed. "I assume I don't need to tell you all that has happened out there, that the streets are littered with lifeless bodies." He paused for a reaction, but still got nothing. "These bodies, well, they—"

"Who sent you?" the hostile woman demanded.

"Yes, what exactly is the SAS doing here?" inquired another impatient fellow with a refined British accent.

"My, um, *colleague* here and I, have reason to believe that…" Alie paused, swallowing uncomfortably, "that they can be brought back."

The incredulous eyes continued to stare in the excruciatingly painful silence, until the vulture finally piped up and said with hearty disdain, "This? You interrupted us for this?" he scolded Rik. "Get these idiots out of here!"

"Wait, please," Sophie pleaded. "Just hear us out." She placed a gentle hand on Alie's shoulder before moving past him until she was almost leaning on the table. "I'm sure that you are all brilliant scientists, or whatever you are. And I know that none of this is going to make much sense to you," her voice trembled as she struggled to maintain her composure. "But in light of the recent, catastrophic events that, with all due respect, apparently came from this place, the least you could do is listen for a minute."

A thin man with a wispy beard and a ponytail leapt to his feet. "Enough of this drabble," he shouted. "We've got an entire squadron of UN troops headed this way, followed undoubtedly by a horde of media who are going to want answers. And we are wasting our time listening to these…fools?" He stormed past them and out the door, disappearing into the tunnels. After a few additional seconds of awkward silence, the vulture followed.

"The rest of you, I beg you, please hear me out for one minute," begged Sophie.

"Sixty seconds," the woman ordered. "Not a second more. Go!"

Sophie glanced at Rik, who stood aside rather aloof, almost as if he was just along for the show. And then she looked to Alie for some assurance. He nodded his encouragement, and she continued.

"Like I said, I'm sure none of this will make much sense, but you must ask yourselves if any of this does. I beg you, for just a moment, consider the possibility that maybe, just maybe, you don't know everything there is to know about what happened when this machine down here malfunctioned." Sophie pointed to the door behind her, but every eye in the room was still on her. She inhaled sharply, reaching anxiously in her back pocket for the brush. "Those people out there, whose bodies are scattered across the street. Well, they're not really…dead. At least, not exactly."

"What do you mean they're not dead?" the woman demanded, bordering on irate.

"It's very difficult to explain, but much of it we learned from someone who I believe you all know." Again, she tried to swallow, but her mouth was beyond dry. "Virgil?"

The woman gasped, and the remaining men in the room rocked forward in their chairs. "Virgil?" one of them exclaimed. "You have seen Virgil? Where?"

"Yes, we've seen him," Sophie continued. "We have, but not on this side."

"On this *side?*" the woman snapped. "What do you mean this *side?*"

"I mean this life, this existence, you know, mortality," Sophie struggled.

The woman scoffed. "Do you mean to tell me—"

"She means to tell you we saw Virgil in spirit," Alie interrupted. "In fact, not just saw him. We had quite a conversation with him." The collective looks on the faces around the table made it very clear that they thought Sophie and Alie were lunatics.

The woman stood up and motioned to Rik. "Are we done here?" she grumbled with a sigh as she shooed Sophie and Alie out of her presence.

"I told you it would sound crazy," Sophie said. "But ask yourselves, how is it that we know about Virgil? And that he predicted this disaster? And how is it that we beat everyone else here? The UN, the military, the media?"

The woman looked at Rik, who just shrugged sheepishly. "But you're not..."

"Dead? A ghost?" Sophie responded. "You're right. My, uh...this SAS soldier standing next to me, who you already met, he and I, well, we came back."

"Came back?" The woman snickered before re-taking her seat, clearly unimpressed by Sophie's paranormal account. "And what exactly is it that you and your soldier colleague want?"

Sophie leaned over the table with her knuckles pressing into the cherry-red-stained surface. "Well, ma'am, we need to go back."

"Back? What is that supposed to mean?" the woman queried.

"We, um," Sophie stammered. "We need you to turn it back on."

The entire room exploded at Sophie's request. Some shot to their feet in rage, while others just rolled their eyes. The woman leading the conversation stayed seated, but raised her hand and said, "I believe you're well past your sixty seconds, miss. Be on your way, or I will have you escorted out," the woman insisted.

"But, ma'am..."

"Get out!" the woman insisted, pointing an angry finger at Sophie.

Sophie started to react, but Alie stopped her, interjecting, "Very well then, we'll do it my way." In a flash he snatched Rik by the back of his collar and withdrew the pistol. Shoving Rik forward until he was leaning over the table, Alie buried the muzzle of the gun into the back of

Rik's neck. The room filled with gasps, followed by heated threats aimed at Alie. But Alie ignored them, only barely raising his voice while insisting that someone turn on the machine immediately, or else he would start by covering the table with Rik's brains, and then continue until everyone in the room was dead. Sophie was shocked, but truly doubted that Alie would actually pull the trigger. Then again, Alie had warned her several times that there was an almost unrecognizably brutal side to him, and she had more than once come to see it for herself. Either way, she did her best to not show any sign of weakness or doubt as Alie maintained his menacing grip on Rik.

"You wouldn't," the woman grumbled through a fiery glare.

Alie cocked the hammer back on the gun. "Try me."

She jumped to her feet, sending her chair crashing against the wall behind her. "There's a small army of UN troops heading this way as we speak," she screamed. "You'll spend the rest of your life locked away in prison, labeled a terrorist…if you're lucky enough to walk out of here alive, that is."

Alie's lips pursed as he stared intensely at the defiant woman. She clearly wasn't easily rattled, at least not by Alie's threats. So Alie stepped it up a notch. He raised the gun just inches above Rik's head and pulled the trigger. The blast shook the conference room walls, and a baseball-sized hole opened up in the middle of the table as splinters covered the terrified onlookers.

"Gyah!" Rik screamed. Like Sophie, he clearly hadn't considered Alie's threats to be real, until now that is. Even Sophie wasn't so sure anymore.

"The next one will be through his skull," Alie warned. Whatever bravado the woman may have had a few minutes earlier had disappeared. Like the rest of the attendees, she was now clearly rattled. But still no one moved. "One, two—" Alie continued.

"Enough!" A distraught, British voice blurted out from the back of the room, and a silver-haired man stood slowly, relying heavily on a bamboo cane. "Everyone stop pretending to be so astonished. We all know what we were planning to do anyway. This fellow has just provided the excuse we needed."

Alie leaned forward with his head cocked. The look on his face matched the confusion Sophie felt. "Excuse? For what?" inquired Alie.

"Oh, shut up, boy," the old snapped. "You come in here waving that pistol and making threats like a fool; you're certainly not entitled to any more explanation." He nodded and shook his cane at one of his significantly younger colleagues. "Daniel, you know what to do. Initiate the protocol."

"But, sir," the young man protested.

"Do it," the woman acquiesced, her disdain for Alie evident. "What choice do we have?"

Rik let out a long, exasperated sigh, and Alie jerked him away from the table and back out of the room. A crowd of people had gathered in both directions, gawking as the young man led the group away from the conference room, followed by Alie with the gun still buried into the base of Rik's skull. The group walked silently past several groups of dumbfounded onlookers, and down several hundred yards of cold, sterile tunnels before shuffling into a darkened doorway. The young man flipped on the lights, revealing a sprawling control room housing a considerable collection of monitors, screens, and other technical equipment covering numerous tables grouped into four large, circular stations. The group spread out among the four stations and went to work. For more than ten minutes, Alie and Sophie watched as the screens came to life, filling the room with bleeps and whirs until the group began calling out a cadence of technical jargon, some in English, and some in French.

"LHC?" a voice called out.

"Systems appear calibrated and functional," came the answer from another.

"SPS?"

"Ditto. Synchronization anticipated as usual."

"PS Complex?"

"No visible anomalies. Normal reactions. Acceleration imminent."

"And TI? How does everything look?"

"Under the circumstances, manageable."

The woman slowly approached Alie and shook her head. "This one's on you," she grunted, and then took a seat before burying her forehead in her hands. Seconds later the entire underground structure began to emit a whining hum, mixed with the whirring startup of the ventilation system. The corridor outside filled with alarmed voices and the sound of feet clanging feverishly up and down metal grates. Several people peered into the control room, and some even tried to open the door, which Alie had locked behind them.

Alie leaned over to Rik and whispered, "Now what?"

Rik shot him a curious look. "What do you mean, 'now what'? This was your idea, not mine."

"Is the collider running properly?"

"It depends on what you mean by *properly*?" Rik answered. "It obviously wasn't running properly before, and we just turned it on for the first time since, so I'd say it most certainly is not working *properly*."

"But will it continue to run if no one turns it off?"

"It will continue to run until it's turned off, or until someone triggers one of the emergency shut-off switches," Rik explained.

Sophie watched nervously as Alie focused his gaze on the floor, trying to piece together their next move. The two of them had come to the CERN facility with very little more than a ridiculous idea to turn the machine back on. They hadn't counted on meeting Rik, and definitely didn't anticipate finding such a large group of CERN's workers and higher-ups still inside. In fact, Sophie didn't expect to find anyone at CERN, at least not anyone upright and alive. So whatever scheme, or plan, or idea that they may have had en route from the auto expo had quickly turned to little more than just winging it.

"If we leave, they will undoubtedly turn it right back off," Sophie said.

"And if we stay, the next blast may not affect us, which means I can't get back to the other side," Alie responded.

"Evacuation," Rik said timidly.

"What?" Alie questioned. "What do you mean?"

"We can initiate the evacuation protocol, which will trigger alarms directing everyone to abandon the facility," Rik explained. They spoke softly while Rik kept a cautious eye on the rest of the room. The others manning the stations were shooting wary glances at Rik and Alie, clearly suspicious of their stealthy conversation.

"Can you start this evacuation protocol on your own?" asked Alie.

"I believe so," answered Rik.

"Very well then." Alie stepped forward and raised his voice. "Everybody out!" he commanded while waving the gun in the air.

"Hands off the keyboards, and get out." Everyone looked at him in disbelief, which made him even more demanding. "Move! Now! Get out!"

One by one the CERN crew filed out into the hallway, where they stopped, dumbfounded, while Alie followed with the gun still pointed at them. He shut the door behind him, with Sophie and Rik still inside. No one said a word as they stood helpless on the walkway, waiting for Alie's next command. After several fretful minutes, the shrill sound of an alarm shattered the silence. As the siren blared, Alie caught a glimpse of the woman, whose face showed that she now understood where this was going.

"OK, everyone, to the nearest exit," Alie ordered.

"You can't be serious," protested one of the group members.

"Oh yes I can," Alie insisted. "Now, move!" The group continued down the walkway, ducking periodically to avoid low-hanging valves and conduits that stretched like steel veins through the collider's interior. As they walked, other escaping CERN workers caught up with them from behind, seemingly unaware of Alie and his pistol. And just behind those additional workers were Sophie and Rik.

They eventually made a turn down a brighter and wider hallway that led away from the droning purr of the collider, and toward a reinforced steel door. When the door was opened, sunlight poured through. Sophie's eyes struggled to adjust, even more so when they stepped out onto the lawn that sprawled between them and the wicker-sphered visitor's center.

The CERN workers formed a line on the lawn like school children, waiting for further instruction from Alie, who no longer appeared as hostile as before. In fact, standing there on the lawn holding a pistol he didn't intend to use, and staring down a bunch of world-renowned scientists, Sophie thought he looked uncharacteristically helpless, at a loss for what to do next. He looked at her as if to say, "How did we get ourselves into this?" She wished she could project a better sense of certainty, but she too wasn't quite sure where to go from there. They had just conspired to hold hostage an entire team of who's who in nuclear physics, and forced them to turn on a machine that could cause who-knows-what to happen. At this point, taking their chances with the hell they faced on the other side of mortality didn't sound quite so bad compared to the trouble they had stirred up in the here-and-now. And, to make matters worse, the CERN group seemed to be quickly catching on to Alie's hesitation, like predators sensing weakness in their prey.

Chapter Thirty

Alie and Sophie stood speechless before the CERN group, like a spaghetti western showdown. A bead of sweat started at Sophie's hairline and trickled down her cheek. The sun's heat seemed to intensify exponentially with each nerve-racking moment. Sophie watched the eyes of the crowd shift suddenly from Alie to somewhere beyond the welcome center. Sophie turned to see what it was, and her heart sank.

Just outside the fence lining the road, a caravan of avocado-colored Humvees was rolling to a stop. A band of machine-gun-toting soldiers poured out of the vehicles and headed straight for the gate. The arrival of the soldiers prompted a rejuvenated confidence in the CERN crowd, which began to dissolve in front of their eyes as they headed toward their approaching liberators.

"Alie, we gotta go," Sophie pleaded. The look on his face showed that he absolutely agreed. The first of the band of soldiers rounded the welcome center, guns half-raised, as Sophie and Alie headed the opposite way. But they had taken only a few steps when the CERN crowd started screaming and pointing frantically at Sophie and Alie. Sophie couldn't make out exactly what they were saying, but was pretty sure it wasn't particularly flattering. When the soldiers lifted their guns, that left little doubt.

"Should we run?" Sophie whispered.

"It's too late for that," Alie replied. "Don't say a word. I'll handle this." He tossed the gun and dropped to his knees. Sophie reluctantly did the same. The soldiers approached cautiously, their guns all trained directly on Sophie and Alie. Sophie thought she might pass out. The soldiers shouted orders in French and motioned for them to lay down face-first on the ground. Sophie's eyes filled with anxious tears as her face pressed against the cool grass, and she willingly put her hands behind her back.

"Alie?" He didn't respond, at least not to her. He began speaking quickly to the soldiers in French, who shouted back, first in French, and then in English.

"Who is she then?" One barked. Sophie looked directly into Alie's eyes, their faces only inches apart on the grass.

"She's my hostage," Alie answered, his eyes still fixed on Sophie. "I kidnapped her too."

"Alie, no!" Sophie screamed, just as one of the soldiers buried his knee into Alie's back. "That's not…"

"Don't move, mademoiselle!" shouted another, his words only barely recognizable through his thick accent. Sophie felt him pressing squarely in the middle of her back, holding her firmly to the ground. She and Alie had gotten out of a lot of tight spots together, but she couldn't imagine how they would get out of this one. Her mind raced with a million panicked thoughts of Alie being taken from her at gunpoint and locked away somewhere where she would never see him again.

"Please, you must listen to us," she screamed. "Let us try and explain." But even as she said it, she knew it would be impossible to explain their unexplainable story. And not a single one of them paid any attention to her.

She called out to Alie as well, but she could only see the back of his head, which was oozing blood from an open gash.

"Alie! Look at me please!"

Alie groaned as the soldier's knee dug deeper into his back.

"Stop it! You're hurting him," Sophie pleaded. But again, her words disappeared into the chaos. More and more soldiers arrived, several walking alongside a Humvee that had found its way past the gate and around to the back side of the visitor's center. Its front tire stopped just inches from Alie's head before he was jerked up and dragged toward the back of the Humvee. Sophie tried to wiggle to her feet, only to be flattened again by the soldier's heavy hand. She screamed again. But her cry, as loud as it was, was inexplicably drowned out by an ear-splitting humming boiling up from inside the earth. Her head suddenly felt as if it would split open. She saw the soldiers staggering about, many holding their heads in their hands.

"*Quel est ce son?*" a soldier growled. Sophie's fingers, which were buried in the grass, began to quiver. The vibration continued up her arms and into her chest. Her eyes fixed on the delicate, cottony wisps of a fragile dandelion poking through the lawn. It was trembling like a twig in a terrible storm, and Sophie immediately knew what was coming.

"No," she whispered.

The humming turned to a sickening roar, bringing instant blackness. Sophie struggled to lift her head, but it felt like it weighed a thousand pounds. The pain of a million needles shot up and down her spine, and her eyes burned like they were on fire. A string of drool hung from her bottom lip as her mouth filled with a burning, metallic taste that made her gag. For what felt like an eternity, her mind danced somewhere between agony and confusion. As soon as her thoughts began to reshape, she noticed something was tugging on her wrist. She looked up, and there was Alie.

"Come on, Sophie, get up," he was urging desperately. She tried to formulate words, but nothing recognizable came out. Her eyes spun again into a blur, and then the blackness returned. Her mind crept back again seconds later, and she realized she was being carried. Her sputtering brain perceived Alie's sturdy arms cradling her as he staggered toward the road. Sophie glanced back over his shoulder and saw the uniformed figures scattered across the lawn next to their guns. Some were just beginning to come to and struggling to get up, while others were completely still.

"Put me down," Sophie whispered.

"But we have to move, like now!"

"I can make it," she insisted. The sharp stabbing shot up through her feet as they touched the ground, and she almost collapsed. But she managed to stay upright, stumbling back around to the front of the welcome center. Each step was a little less painful, and soon she was running, albeit awkwardly, toward the front gate. Two soldiers who had been standing guard in the gateway were now crumpled side-by-side on the ground, writhing and gasping as Sophie and Alie bounded over their bodies and into the street. The red sheen of the parked Ferrari came into view, just a few hundred feet away, as the first of many shouting soldiers rounded the CERN sphere. The soldiers looked stunned, only barely able to remain upright, but still clearly determined to not let Sophie and Alie get away.

Sophie flung the passenger door open and jumped into the seat. Alie was fidgeting desperately with the underside of the steering wheel when the soldiers started to pour through gate and into the street. Sophie's heart sank when she saw the loaded Humvee round the sphere as well, barreling toward the street.

"Hurry up, Alie," she pleaded. "We're not gonna make…"

The engine roared thunderously to life. An instant later, the tires squealed like mad banshees as Alie jammed the car into gear and freed the clutch. The Humvee crashed through the half-closed gate, sending sparks flying as it took aim directly at them. Alie jerked the Ferrari into a wild one-eighty and pointed it back in the direction of the city center. But the Humvee closed in on them in a flash. Within seconds, it was on their back bumper. Sophie braced herself, expecting the massive vehicle to pulverize them. But just before impact, Alie slammed the pedal to the floor and the Ferrari took off, quickly putting distance between itself and the Humvee. Sophie's head slammed back against the seat as Alie cycled through the gears, swerving nimbly around vehicles scattered across the roadway.

"Turn right up here, onto the A1," Sophie shouted. "We can lose them in the tunnel."

Alie glanced at her and nodded, then shifted downward, causing Sophie's head to nearly slam into the dash.

"What are you doing?" she screamed.

"Hold on," he commanded, and decelerated dramatically to nearly half the speed as before. The Humvee, on the other hand, didn't slow down. It plowed ahead, catching up to them quickly, and again almost ramming into their back bumper. As it closed to within a few feet, Alie again buried the gas pedal into the floor. The car exploded into an eager sprint, with the Humvee again losing ground. Sophie looked back just in time to see a soldier lean out of the passenger window and aim a large, black rifle at them.

"Alie!"

The Ferrari swerved suddenly across two lanes, just barely sliding onto the off-ramp. The Humvee's brakes wailed as its tires smoked and skidded rowdily, struggling to keep a grip on the asphalt. Two of its tires briefly rose off the street and then came down with a thud as the monstrous machine fought to redirect itself toward the off-ramp. It finally managed to point in the direction of the escaping Ferrari, vaulting over the curb and taking out two signs in the process.

The Ferrari's tires peeled around the curve and onto the A1

motorway, dancing between motionless cars as Alie pushed the motor to its limits. Within seconds of climbing onto the A1, the road disappeared into the blackness of the Vernier tunnel. Alie flipped on the lights and zoomed into the darkness. The engine's roar was even more intimidating within the shadowy confines of the tunnel as they buzzed past numerous cars, sometimes just narrowly snaking between tight gaps. Sophie held her breath. Fluorescent lights hanging on the tunnel walls whipped rhythmically past them as they buried deeper into the dark. But another light in the side mirror caught Sophie's eye, and she spun around to see the Humvee's headlights in pursuit. She turned back to Alie and grabbed his arm.

"I see them," he said. "As long as we have a clear path, they'll never catch us."

Sophie looked back just as the Humvee plowed through two parked cars, lighting up the tunnel in a shower of sparks. It violently sideswiped another, then another as its hulking body struggled to navigate the narrow spaces between cars. Sophie turned back just as the first hint of sunlight began to creep around the next turn. But just as the end of the tunnel came into view, Alie slammed hard on the brakes. A mess of cars clogged the exit, blocking their escape. Alie skidded to a stop just feet from the first of the stack of cars, and jumped out of the Ferrari while screaming at Sophie to do the same. She threw open the door and followed him onto the heap of stalled vehicles. The Humvee was still lumbering through the twisted metal not far behind. But it was what they saw up ahead that made Sophie cry out.

Less than fifty yards from the tunnel's exit, the road was completely blocked by a small army of Humvees and other armored vehicles forming an unbreakable wall across the roadway. The road's shoulders were narrow, and just beyond them was nothing but thick, impenetrable brush that thwarted any possible escape. Sophie's legs froze as she stood atop the cars with no idea where to go or what to do. She watched in a trance as the Humvee from the tunnel hurled maniacally toward her. Her stupor was broken by Alie's frantic shouting.

"Sophie, get up that hill, now!" he yelled as he pointed toward the weed and brush-covered incline that rose steeply just to the side of the tunnel. That's crazy, Sophie thought. But there was no time to weigh it out in her mind. She leapt from the cars and sprinted toward the thick weeds, expecting Alie to follow. She scampered clumsily up the hill, but turned back at the sound of shouts from the soldiers. They were manning massive guns mounted on top of the vehicles that formed the barricade. A terrified scream erupted from within her as she saw Alie standing directly in the middle of the road, staring into the tunnel. The soldiers from the barricade continued to hurl threats and commands at him, which he ignored with his back turned defiantly toward them.

"No, Alie, no!" she screamed as she started sliding back down the hill. Alie looked at her and shook his head, commanding her to stay where she was. He stood like a lunatic, staring down the Humvee charging toward the tunnel's exit like a locomotive. Behind him, a whole host of guns was aimed at his back, just waiting for him to make the wrong move. Alie glanced over his shoulder at the soldiers scattered across the blockade and touched his index finger to his forehead before offering them a modest salute. Two of them looked at one another, completely bewildered in an instantaneous moment of confused silence. And then the Humvee erupted from the tunnel like a missile shot from the snarled, twisted end of a colossal cannon. Glass and mangled steel exploded across the roadway as the Humvee lost control and crashed into the railing on the opposite side of the road, narrowly missing the spot where Alie had stood. But Alie was not there; he was running directly toward Sophie, signaling for her to follow him through the billowing smoke and back into the tunnel. To do so seemed insane, but not any less insane than everything that had happened to them over the past hour, so why the hell not?

Sophie plunged into the wall of smoke pouring from the tunnel and immediately felt an intense heat directly to her right. She closed her stinging eyes and followed the sound of Alie's coughing while feeling her way along the concrete wall. Alie called out to her frantically and repeatedly in between wheezing coughs. But his cries were soon drowned in the menacing shouts of soldiers, who must have been just behind her, about to enter the tunnel. She opened her eyes for an instant to try and see, but was overcome by the intense pain of smoke in her eyes and lungs. She stumbled forward, struggling for breath just as Alie's hand grabbed hers and pulled her into the clear.

"Move, Sophie!" he begged. "Cough all you want, but move your legs. I think it will still run." What will still run? She opened her eyes again and tried to see through the pungent haze, but couldn't make out anything but the orange flicker of flames. The side of her face felt like it was melting, but her feet continued pounding on the hard surface as Alie yanked her further into the darkness. She felt him place her hand on something large and metallic, and quickly realized it was a car door. She felt blindly for the door's handle, but no matter how hard she tugged, it would not open. She felt's Alie's uncomfortably strong grip on her leg, and instantly she was off the ground. He thrust her feet through the busted-out side window and into the interior of the car. She slid down into the leather seat just as Alie found the driver's-side door.

"They're right behind us." Alie cranked up the Ferrari's engine, but there was clearly something wrong. The engine's components grinded unnaturally, as if they were fighting against one another. It had clearly suffered significant damage when the Humvee tore its way out of the tunnel, but just how much was impossible to see in the darkness.

Alie grunted heavily as he forced the engine into gear. The car bolted backward and then sputtered for a moment before spinning to face the other end of the tunnel. Alie released the clutch to the sound of a loud bang, and the car bucked forward awkwardly before launching into a thrashing gallop. Sophie felt the underbelly of the car shimmying violently as it lurched away from the heat of the flames, and away from the soldiers charging through the smoke. The stabbing in Sophie's eyes began to ease, and she turned around to see the silhouette of a soldier raising his rifle.

"Get down!" Alie screamed as he shoved her head toward her lap. She tucked into a ball just as the back window exploded. Shattered glass scattered throughout the inside of the car, and Sophie panicked as she looked to see if Alie was okay. He looked back at her and nodded. Through the recurring flicker of fluorescent lights passing outside the car, she could see the protective rage building in his eyes. Her heart pounded relentlessly as the car jerked between gears and fought to carry them to freedom. But she could tell by the look on Alie's face as he checked the rear-view mirror that they weren't in the clear yet.

They exited the tunnel headed back toward the city just as smoke started to gush out from underneath the hood. "Oh, come on!"

"So, what now?" Sophie asked. "Where do we go?"

"Well, the way I see it, we have two choices. We would be foolish to go back toward CERN, so we either go straight to the airport, or back into the city."

"That's not exactly sticking with the plan. You know, going back *into* the city."

"I think that plan just changed, whether we like it or not."

Sophie looked at him with worried eyes. With heavily armed soldiers pouring into the city from seemingly every direction, and no way to know which roads, if any, were open for an escape in their crippled car, they were essentially trapped. Plus, if the collider were still running, it might not be long until another event happened that would once again turn everything inside out.

"The cold storage," she exclaimed. "We have to get to the cold storage." She trembled at the realization that they could both soon be back in that awful world, trying to survive the onslaught of demons hell-bent on destroying them. But she also knew they would go together, which made it just a tiny bit more bearable.

Alie, on the other hand, appeared even less optimistic. He pounded furiously on the steering wheel and let fly a feverish string of cuss words, some British, and some rather international. He then jerked the car again toward the ramp that ascended upward toward the overpass that led back into the heart of Geneva. They approached the red light at the top of the ramp, but Alie didn't stop. Sophie looked over her shoulder as he made the turn and saw a massive armored vehicle, quite larger than a Humvee, barreling toward the off-ramp. She looked back over the other shoulder toward the road to CERN, and saw two more Humvees parked and facing their direction just several hundred yards away. Her stomach turned as they both began to roll ominously toward them.

She felt the sudden urge to vomit, or to faint, or both. She searched for something to grab onto to steady herself, but apparently they didn't think of such things back when they made this car. So she slid her hand into her back pocket, searching like a child for comfort in her father's brush. But it wasn't there. She cried out as she frantically searched each of her pockets, and then the seat and floor of the car's interior. But it was nowhere.

"Alie, the brush," she muttered, realizing that to him it may sound silly. But to her, it was a tragedy, one that seemed to strip away any sense of hope she had left.

Alie slammed the gas pedal to the floor again, and the Ferrari did its best to respond, growling like a sick tiger as smoke continued pouring out from under the hood. Sophie closed her eyes and tried to will the car forward, hoping it would at least be fast enough to keep them ahead of their pursuers. As Alie pushed on, Sophie caught glimpses of the countless bodies scattered throughout the city's roads and sidewalks and, occasionally, the upright, occupied corpses that wandered the streets. Even more disturbingly, she saw at least two groups of soldiers carefully searching the city blocks, one of which was nervously confronting a possessed wanderer with guns raised. They watched curiously as the smoking Ferrari chugged noisily past, and then left the strange wanderers to join the pursuit.

"Can we lose them?" Sophie asked.

"I don't think so," Alie answered while glancing again in the rearview. "I think we'll be lucky to even make it a few more blocks."

"Then what?"

Alie squinted as he grinned at her. "We negotiate."

Sophie laughed despite the craziness of it all. Alie was good at a lot of things, but negotiating didn't seem to be one of them. She took his hand and held it close to her chest.

"I don't want to die, Alie," she said. "But I would rather that than we get separated and thrown behind bars in some international prison for the rest of our lives. Plus, we always seem to find each other, don't we, on this side or the other?"

Alie raised her hand to his lips and kissed it firmly. "We're not going to die, Sophie. Not on my watch. We're going to make it out of this. I'm not sure how yet, but we will."

"I know we will," she replied, not really believing it as she said it.

She watched through moist eyes as they rolled back into the center of the city that she had grown to love, a city that she had once, in a naively optimistic way, begun to almost feel was made for her. She watched the modern, industrial buildings scroll by beneath a dreary, overcast sky, then fade into rows of château-style architecture. She admired the multi-colored shutters and flower boxes that uniformly dotted the building facades. She looked up sadly at the melancholy gargoyles perched atop the gothic buttresses of the cathedral Notre-

Dame de Genève. And she listened for the rushing of the Rhône's waters beneath the famed Pont de Mont-blanc, with the Jet d'Eau fountain bursting heaven-ward in the distance. And, finally, she squeezed Alie's hand tightly as they plowed down the Boulevard Emile-Jaques Dalcroze, where her beloved Musée d'art et d'Histoire peered down upon them. She lost it, sobbing uncontrollably. Putting her head into her hands, she refused to look anymore as they sped past the museum and toward the miserably cold confines of a warehouse where they would hide, and wait to willingly sacrifice their own bodies. And for what? Sophie could only barely remember.

"There it is," Alie whispered as the tall, steel-paneled walls came into view. Sophie glared loathsomely at the structure, which suddenly seemed to embody everything that was so horrifyingly wrong with their situation.

"Are they still behind us?"

"We may have lost them around that last turn, but only for a minute I'm sure." Alie slowed briefly to survey the surroundings, then brought the car to a stop directly in front of the warehouse's massive sliding doors. "We must hurry," he insisted as they both leapt from the car. The clamoring motor protested their sudden stop as Alie jammed it into neutral and began to push on its backside until it was rolling, vacant, down the descending boulevard. They sprinted to the warehouse's doors and heaved mightily until they opened just enough for them to disappear inside.

The air inside seemed even more frigid than before. She wanted to scream out her anger at having to be stuck inside this insidious place again. But, like he always did, Alie pressed forward into the impending darkness, leading her away from the danger outside. After easing themselves through rows of stacked crates, Alie pulled her into a corner, where he lowered her to the ground and wrapped his arms tightly around her. She nestled into his chest with her ear pressed to his heart.

"Man, the lengths you'll go through to get me alone in a dark place," she whispered.

"You have no idea," he chuckled.

As they waited, they looked up through the skylight and watched the gray clouds roll by. Sophie could hear the faint sound of the Humvees rumbling outside, but it was hard to distinguish from the constant drone of the warehouse's fans. She fought the cold as long as she could, but soon was shivering beyond her control. Alie tried his best to warm her, but he too was starting to give in to the effects of the frigid interior. So he stroked her hair gently as he squeezed her.

"Sophie," he whispered.

"Yeah."

"I can't remember if I ever told you…" He choked on his words, sounding more emotional than she'd ever heard him.

"I know, Alie," she whispered. "Trust me, I know."

"I know, but you deserve to hear it." She rolled toward him and felt his warm breath tickle her face. He cleared his throat, and then said, "Sophie, I love you. With all my faults, and insecurities and weaknesses, I never thought I would feel that way about anyone, much less actually say it. But I do." He paused for a moment, and Sophie tried to kiss him. But he placed two fingers gently over her mouth and stopped her. "I…I'm sorry I have failed to keep my promise to see you to safety…"

"Nonsense!" she blurted out as her body stiffened. "I don't want to hear that from you, not at all."

"But it's true," he insisted. "We should've left here when we had the chance. Whatever it was that gave us the miracle of returning back to life—God, the universe, or whatever—also gave us the chance we needed to survive this and escape. And like a fool, like a reckless, bloody fool, I led you right back into the middle of it."

This time she covered his mouth before saying, "I love you too, Alie, so don't take this the wrong way…but shut up! You did what you did because it was the right thing to do, and possibly risked your own life in doing so. And I followed you, gladly and willingly, like I always will. It doesn't matter if we go back to that…that place, or to the depths of hell. I'll go with you. Always."

He wiped a tear from her cheek with his finger and kissed her softly. She could feel every part of his body pressed to hers, and smiled as the coldness and fear disappeared into the dark. She closed her eyes, ready to face whatever may come, and gently fell asleep.

. . . .

"Sophie. Sophie," Alie whispered as he shook her awake. She immediately recognized the urgency in his voice.

"What's wrong?" she answered out loud, but he instantly clasped his palm over her mouth.

"Shhh, don't speak," he whispered. "They're here."

She listened for the unwelcome sounds of boots clicking on the cold concrete. But instead they clanked on the catwalk above. Alie silently rose to a crouch for a better view. But as soon as he did, he shifted back into the shadows. The beam of a flashlight pierced the darkness from above, illuminating a wall of boxes just feet from where they hid. A second beam followed, then a third, as the catwalk creaked under the weight of multiple people. Sophie could feel Alie start to panic as he searched for a way out. She knew that if they made a dash for the entrance, they would undoubtedly run directly into them. But if they stayed where they were, they would be found in less than a minute. Their only chance was to break the other direction toward the back of the warehouse. Alie looked at her one last time and took her by the hand. She nodded back, and scrambled to her feet. They rushed into the open, hoping to be miraculously unseen. But less than three steps into their escape, the air filled with shouting as numerous beams of light converged on their position. They stood in the open, exposed and out of places to run. Within seconds they found themselves face-down, once again, their eyes just inches apart as they stared helplessly at one another and waited to be taken away.

Chaos erupted as the soldiers surrounded them, guns drawn, and shouted a slew of French commands. She didn't move, trying to take in what might be her last look at Alie. Her hands were tied behind her, and pain ripped through her shoulders as she was hoisted upwards by her wrists. She watched in horror as Alie screamed at them in French and struggled to get back to his feet. He made it to his knees before the butt of a rifle crashed down on the back of his head. His body dropped limply to the floor, and Sophie screamed.

They carried her by her arms and legs, like a bound pig, away from Alie and into the maze of boxes toward the giant sliding doors. She begged hysterically for them to listen to her. But they tossed her mercilessly into the back of a truck, which she shared with two soldiers who held her down with their boots. She struggled to get a last look at the warehouse entrance, but the weight of the soldiers kept her motionless as the truck began to roll away.

"Please, *s'il vous plaît,* listen to me," she pleaded through frantic tears. "You can't do this! Please!" But the more she pleaded, the harder the boots dug into her back. She finally gave up when she heard the rush of the Rhône beneath them. Her cheek bounced ruthlessly against the bed of the steel truck bed as her tears formed tiny puddles of mud in the dust.

Alie was gone.

Chapter Thirty-One

"Who is he?" The man's breath smelled like bologna and cigarettes, and he let loose tiny spit droplets when he was particularly agitated. He was, at that moment, particularly agitated. He didn't start out that way, but after a couple of hours of screaming questions and threats at Sophie, with almost no response from her, he'd worked himself into a thick-tongued frenzy. As far as Sophie could tell, he was the only one of the soldiers in their group who spoke English, albeit with a very strong French accent. He had threatened to hit her with his one arm, or to kick her, throw her in prison, and even put a bullet in her head. But despite his tough talk, he had yet to do anything other than make a lot of noise.

"I'm going to ask you one last time! What's his name?"

His stubborn determination was impressive, Sophie thought, but even more obnoxious. He'd been at it for hours, pouring on his incessant barrage of questions about Alie. They apparently weren't too interested in knowing anything about her, as they asked little more than her name. She told him her name was Brittany, which he apparently accepted without question. It was clear that they considered Alie to be the real prize, and Sophie thought they must be eyeing him as some sort of terrorist with a connection to the Geneva catastrophe. Regardless, she wasn't giving them anything, content to return his relentless bullying with a vacant stare.

Since leaving the warehouse, the truck had bounced its way back toward CERN, but stopped short of the visitor's center. They parked somewhere near the outer edges of the airport, where they were soon joined by several other military vehicles and men in uniform. When the others arrived, those sharing the truck bed with Sophie graciously took their feet off her back, and harshly propped her up so captain bologna breath could berate her. Every few minutes or so, one of them would come up with a different question for Sophie not to answer, which they would convey to the English speaker, who would then proceed to bark it at her. She knew that, ultimately her refusal to answer questions wouldn't really matter. But, for the moment, it just felt good to be a bitch.

One of the translator's particularly jarring tirades was interrupted when a younger soldier approached and handed him a piece of paper. He hopped down from the truck bed and snatched the paper, reviewed it, and then glanced at Sophie with a devilish grin.

"Alasdair Quin." He said it with a sense of spite, as if he'd prevailed in some sort of cruel game. "Tell me, Miss Brittany, who is Alisdair Quin?" Hearing his name spoken by the one-armed interrogator made her nauseous, and even more determined to make things difficult. She knew Alie's identity wouldn't likely remain a secret for long, but it wasn't going to come from her.

"You've got the paper, sir," she mocked. "Why don't you tell me."

This just made him chuckle, and then show her the words on the paper in a flash before crumpling it up and tossing it into the truck bed, out of Sophie's reach. He shook his head at her one last time, and then stomped away to join a garish gathering of his comrades. From what Sophie could tell, they looked like they were preparing to gear up and head out to another location. Whether she would be going with them, or hauled off to some confined location, was impossible to know, especially with her extremely limited French. But with her tied up in the truck bed, there wasn't much she could do about it anyway.

She spent the next half hour struggling to decipher what little she could hear of their banter, as well as the constant stream of chatter coming from the radios. She thought back to when her father bought her a pair of cheap walkie-talkies for her seventh birthday. Sometimes after she'd been tucked into bed by her mother, he would let her talk to him from her room until she fell asleep while he painted in the basement. She couldn't remember what happened to those walkie-talkies, but she would give anything to hear his voice coming through one of them now.

"I'm sorry, Daddy," she whispered to herself. "I don't know how I got myself into this, and I have no idea what to do now."

The soldiers appeared to have all but forgotten her now. All except the captain, that is, who continued to glance creepily at her over the shoulders of the other soldiers in his entourage. She really didn't wish any harm on any of them, not even the off-putting captain. After all, they were only doing their job, and likely had no idea what they were dealing with. How could they? Even if she tried to explain everything to them, it would just be a waste of time.

She watched curiously as one of the soldiers held up his radio to his ear, then showed it to another, who also lifted it to his ear. The second soldier suddenly jerked it away as a painful scowl twisted across his face. Sophie could hear it too from a distance—a shrill sizzling sound coming from the radio. Soon the same sound was coming from all the radios, and it was getting louder and harder to tolerate. The soldiers shared a look of confusion. And that's when the rumbling began.

Sophie first noticed the squeaking of the truck's shocks, and then the bouncing of the truck itself. The vibrations of the truck bed soon became violent to the point that she was being tossed uncontrollably. Her hands were still tied behind her back, so she had no way of stopping herself from crashing repeatedly against the side of the bed. Her face was taking quite the beating when she felt a strong grip on her ankle, and then a sturdy tug. She looked down and saw the captain sliding her to end of the truck bed. His face had turned from arrogant and gruff to that of a frightened child. With almost no balance of his own, he struggled to help Sophie to her feet. As soon as her feet touched the ground, an intense shockwave caused the earth to swell beneath them.

"What's happening?" he pleaded. "Something tells me you know." Oh, how things had changed so quickly, she thought. Two minutes ago, he was her captor, and she was completely at his mercy. Now he was begging her for some understanding. She knew exactly what was happening, and how to go about responding to his questions. But she also knew he wouldn't like the answers.

"Cut my hands loose," she demanded.

"But, I—"

"Do it now!"

He fiddled around with a small knife and managed to cut the nylon zip-tie that bound her wrists, although he did prick her a couple of times in the process. She immediately grabbed for the truck to steady herself, then rubbed the painful marks left on her wrists. The captain looked around frantically at his fellow soldiers who were still scrambling to make sense of what was happening. Once she somewhat had her bearings, Sophie reached out and grabbed him by the collar and pulled him closer. Only a few minutes earlier, he would have never tolerated this from her.

"Listen to me very carefully," she insisted. His panic-stricken eyes were locked onto hers as she spoke sternly. "Something is about to happen, something you will not enjoy one bit. When it does, everything you see, hear and touch is going to be very different."

"Www…what do you mean?" he fumbled. "What's going to happen?"

"Shh. It's too late for that," she continued. "Shut up and listen. You're not going to recognize anyone or anything. But when it does happen, someone will be there, right in front of your face, trying to talk to you."

A loud pulsating buzz was rising and falling, making it very difficult to hear Sophie's words. "Who?" he shouted. "Who will be there?"

"I will be," Sophie answered. "I will be that person. You must remember!"

He was completely perplexed. Sophie smiled at him and patted him on the shoulder for some reassurance. Then she laid on her back and placed her hands over her chest. He watched her curiously as the droning sound became almost deafening. She glanced casually up at him and yelled out, "Don't forget!" and then closed her eyes. A few seconds later, she opened them again and shouted, "Oh, and you're probably going to want to lie down." She closed her eyes again and then waited with a grin.

The captain tried to say something else, but the words were shredded by an excruciating, subterranean roar that erupted from somewhere beneath them. Lightning shot through Sophie, followed by a piercing kaleidoscope of screams coming from all directions. The screaming splintered into a million pieces, all repeating simultaneously like a maddening chorus of broken records. Sophie cried out in agony as the sensation of being ripped apart ravaged her body. Somewhere inside her was the conscious thought that this would be over in a second. But it seemed like a lone rational thought fighting to be heard amongst a shroud of splintered cries for help. Her last, feeble strain of logical thought felt as if it was slipping away for good when she suddenly felt herself suspended off the ground, with seemingly nothing holding her in the air. The instant insecurity of weightlessness caused her arms to flail and feet to feel for some place to land. But her thoughts soon crystalized back to reality, and she felt the same sense of exponentially intensified awareness that she had the last time. Her ears filled with the pitiful whimpers of a hundred suddenly disembodied soldiers whose entire reality just turned inside-out. As she looked to her right to try and spot the captain, the momentum caused her entire body to start to roll in the air, like a skewered pig rotating over a fire pit.

She spun until she was looking face-down, floating several feet above the corporeal image of her now-empty body. She immediately felt the familiar sadness of observing her own helpless form from the wrong side of mortality. But she also knew she was on a mission, with no time to waste mourning her supernatural predicament. She reached out a hand toward the ground beneath her, and abruptly crashed to the earth.

The captain was bent over on his knees, just a few feet from her. He was alternating between staring incredulously at the pasty, unfamiliar hand that had sprouted from where before there had only been a stump, and trying in vain to grasp at his body that was crumpled underneath him. Sophie took her first extremely awkward step since ditching her body for a second time, and almost came crashing down from the bizarre sensation of her ghostly feet trying to reconnect with the earth below. During her last foray into this existence, it had taken her a very long time to get used to the dramatic change in sensations from the physical to the spiritual world. This time, however, the synchronization happened much more quickly.

Things didn't go quite as smoothly for the captain, however. He was all kinds of messed up when Sophie reached him. His face was distorted and barely identifiable, but she immediately recognized his brusque mannerisms and knew it was him. She placed her hand carefully on his shoulder, and a cloud of smoky-blue vapor puffed into the air. The captain jolted like a startled child. He looked at her like she was a monster as he scrambled backward across the ground.

"Oh, captain," Sophie chuckled, "if you think I'm scary-looking, you're *really* not gonna like this place." Rather than continuing to advance toward him, which was apparently terrifying, she opted to slowly take a seat on the ground. She hoped doing so would signal that she wasn't a threat. After staring at her in disbelief for several minutes, he opened his mouth. He was instantly surprised at the sound of his own voice, and repeated several words aimed at no one in particular. Several noises and words later, he looked back at Sophie and tried again. She still didn't understand him, but at least this time recognized the sounds as human. "Do you remember me and what I told you, captain?" she replied slowly but firmly.

He squinted apprehensively while studying her. She continued talking to him, not necessarily to make him understand, but just to try and make a connection. His men were in various states of frenzy all around them, but the captain remained locked on Sophie, visibly searching for something buried inside. After several minutes of disjointed attempts at communication, Sophie stood and walked slowly toward him. This time he didn't flinch or back away as she knelt and took him by his newly formed hand.

"Do you remember now?" she asked. He nodded, still visibly shaken. "I need your help," she continued. "You and your men, please. Can you help me?"

He struggled mightily to eke out his words. "Where are we? What happened?"

"I know this is all crazy, and I can explain. But we don't have much time. Can you start trying to gather your soldiers?"

He nodded again and then looked down at his body. "Are we...dead?"

"Not exactly," Sophie answered. "And I think we can reverse this; you know, make it back. But we must move now."

The captain rose to his feet and took a step before falling forward again to the ground. He caught himself with his two hands, and then laughed out loud. Sophie helped him sturdy himself as he tried again, this time achieving five or six steps before nearly toppling over.

"You're doing much better than I did my first time," Sophie declared.

"Well, you said we don't have much time," he grumbled while still trying to move forward. "It looks like you're in charge now, so what choice do I have?" The captain continued to trudge toward the figure closest to them, who appeared bewildered while crouched over his body. They both approached him, and he too cowered away. But when the captain called out to him, he stopped moving and listened.

"Touch him," Sophie whispered. "Take him by the hand." The captain approached and reached out reassuringly. He spoke to him again as he grabbed his hand, and the frightened, dazed look quickly faded into recognition. They both stood and embraced one another as Sophie watched. She was amazed to see that as soon as the man recognized his captain, she also saw the distorted features of his face disappear into recognizable, human form. And when he looked at her, she could also see him soften at the sight of her. The fear was definitely not gone, but he appeared resolute, and Sophie could work with resolute.

Soon the two soldiers connected with two others, and then four more, and then on and on until the entire group was coming together and embracing one another. Their chatter, although in French, was welcoming to Sophie. It was the only time, other than the church, that she'd seen a group of human spirits banded together. They came together quickly, finding strength in one another, despite their dreadful circumstances.

After several minutes, the captain shouted boldly above the stir of the crowd, calling everyone together. They immediately gathered around him as he climbed onto the truck bed. He spoke to them briefly before pointing to Sophie, signaling for her to join him. She hesitated, but he insisted. So she climbed up next to him and looked out over the assembly of uniformed spirits, who were bathed in a faint, azure glow. She felt hope, for the first time in way too long, as they waited for her to speak.

"What should I say?" she asked the captain.

"Why don't you start with explaining what the hell just happened?" he answered.

Sophie hated public speaking worse than almost anything in the world. She would almost rather go back and fight every creature in the Bourg-de-Four Square than stand up and give a speech. But she knew she had to get back to the warehouse and find Alie, and she liked her chances of getting there much better with a hundred eager soldiers than on her own. So she swallowed hard and stepped forward, trying her best to look confident.

"Um, well, hello everyone," she started. "Sorry about, you know, your bodies." Wow. Really inspirational, Sophie. She looked sheepishly to the captain, who was eyeing her curiously.

"You want me to translate *that*?" he asked.

"Um, maybe not," she said. She shuffled her feet and looked out over the top of the crowd toward the city. A sinister grey fog hung over the city's center, obscuring any view of the water and the mountains beyond. She knew where the warehouse should have been, but couldn't see it. She reminded herself what was at stake, and that she didn't have time to spare. And then she propped her foot upon the side of the truck bed and projected her voice toward the soldiers.

"I'd like to say I have all the answers," she shouted, "or that I even understand some of this." She paused as the captain echoed her words in French. "But I don't. I do understand what you think you saw when you arrived at the CERN facility…" Another pause, and another translation. "But please understand that I'm not the bad guy. And that guy who was with me, he isn't either." She stopped and pointed toward the city as the captain repeated in French. "In fact, that guy is a highly decorated British Special Forces officer. A soldier, just like you." The captain continued the translation, this time looking at her incredulously as the crowd murmured. She nodded to him and then continued. "Now, if you've been looking down at your feet and wondering whether that really is your body crumpled at your feet, I'm sorry to tell you that it is." The captain hesitated but she nodded and said, "we have to tell them."

The captain's translation drew a disturbed grumble from the crowd, but Sophie pressed on. "But you must listen to me when I tell you there's a way back. This isn't my first trip here, to this spirit world I mean. But I found a way back, and I believe you can too." She paused again, waiting for the translation, but the captain said nothing. She looked at him, and he returned her gaze with a grin.

"They understand you," he said.

"What? How?"

"I don't know," he replied. "But they do."

She looked out at the throng of troubled, yet resolute faces hanging on her every word. Her anxiety instantly doubled. She couldn't even begin to imagine how she was expected to rally a group of troops, much less under these circumstances. As she stood with a vacant stare, one of the soldiers raised his hand like an eager school child. She knew his question before he even asked it.

"Are we—"

"Not exactly," Sophie cut him off. "I suppose it depends on your definition of dead. It is true that you're now in spirit form, and are no longer inside your body. But not because you died. The giant underground machine at CERN malfunctioned and caused the separation of your body and your spirit. When you arrived at CERN and started chasing us, we were just trying to fix it."

Several other hands shot up, but Sophie interrupted them as well. "I'm sorry. I really would like to explain everything better. But the truth is that we're running out of time to help you, and every other lost spirit wandering around Geneva. And that soldier I was with when you were chasing us, he may be the key to reversing all of this, and he's in serious danger." Mentioning Alie emboldened her. She stood a bit taller and raised her voice. "I guess what I'm saying is...I need your help."

Sophie went on to explain the demons and their plan to possess as many bodies as possible. And she explained the pures and the process of re-inhabiting a body. Finally, she recounted the demons' brutal treatment of the other spirits in the city, and especially what she experienced in the plaza. Her description of the horrors she witnessed prompted a sudden metamorphosis in the soldiers. They were no longer frightened, displaced souls. Their eyes narrowed and jaws clenched, as if their fear was displaced by a higher purpose. They were warriors again.

"You won't have any weapons, and some of them do, and most are very scary," she warned the captain.

"We've seen worse," the captain replied, unconcerned. "Let us worry about that, you just point the way."

Sophie led the march down the long boulevard that eventually became the Pont du Mont-Blanc, the largest bridge in Geneva. She was exhilarated by the site of the small army following her and the captain. Ahead she could see the city drop off into the water, and the beginning of the bridge spanning the convergence of Lake Geneva and the Rhone River. The bridge was lined on both sides with a striking array of flags stretching from one end to another. On a sunny day, the flags would pop in the breeze just above the heads of pedestrians stopped to take in the view of the towering Jet d'Eau fountain and the lake beyond. But on this grey, bleak side of mortality, the flags were stiff and suspended in the air, while an ominous fog hung over the opposite end of the bridge that led to the old town. And that was exactly where they were headed—into the old town to the warehouse, where she hoped to find Alie.

As they approached the bridge, the captain grabbed her by the forearm and told her to wait. He held his hand up and the soldiers stopped immediately. He then stared across the bridge and into the fog, studying intensely the several cars and busses that dotted the bridge's roadway. Sophie looked too, but didn't see anything, at least not at first. She could tell by his face that something concerned him, and he watched, motionless, for several minutes. Sophie grew impatient and finally asked him what was wrong.

"Do you not see them?"

Sophie looked again, straining for some sign of whatever it was that he saw. She could faintly make out the other side of the river where the boulevard disappeared into the outline of buildings that rose from the bank, and the still, black water below them. And she could see a handful of empty bodies scattered on the bridge's walkways, but nothing that would cause the kind of alarm on the captain's face. Unless…

Her heart sank like a rock. Through the murky haze, they began to materialize like the preface to a nightmare. A horde of them.

The captain barked out a command, and the soldiers gathered into a tight formation behind him. Sophie could sense the raw fear saturating the group, but they didn't budge.

Sophie focused on a gangly silhouette standing on top of a bus on the opposite end of the bridge. She watched as it stood erect and craned its neck, trying to get a better view of Sophie and her band of fighters. Then another emerged from the shadows, followed by another, and then another. The stone-faced soldiers surrounding Sophie didn't flinch at the sight of the first demons, but when the shape of the first of several massive brutes emerged, they almost turned and ran. But the captain continued to shout out rousing commands, galvanizing his men to stand their ground. Over his cries, Sophie could hear the devilish bellows of the gathering horde as they too rallied their sinister legions.

"We're weaponless, my brothers," the captain roared. "But our own souls may depend on what we're about to do, as well as the souls of many innocent people. We have no choice; we must fight!"

Sophie turned and inspected the brave band of strangers who, only a few hours earlier, were ferociously pursuing her and Alie. Now they were willing to fight for her, even at the risk of an unknown fate. "I'm not going to lie," she shouted, "those things are pretty ferocious, and many have long, nasty claws and teeth." Several of the soldiers swallowed uneasily. "But their weakness is their impulsiveness, like playground bullies. It makes them reckless, and sloppy, and stupid. I have personally seen one person—the Special Forces soldier I told you about—defeat several of them one-on-one, even without a weapon. You do stand a chance, but only if you're smart."

The captain's shouts overtook Sophie's as he struggled to drown out the screeching of the demonic mob. His men responded valiantly to his unwavering fearlessness. He turned and started walking swiftly across the bridge. But when Sophie started to follow, he held his hand out and said, "I'm sorry, but you must stay back."

"No! I can't," Sophie pleaded. "I have to—"

"You have to *survive*. That's what you have to do. You have to survive and find this soldier of yours, and then you have to fix this!" Sophie's face showed her disapproval, but he insisted. "Wait for us to create an opening, a way through. And then you must run to the other side, and then don't stop running until you've found him."

The captain's look made it clear that this was the way it was going to be. Then he turned one last time to take in the sight of the advancing horde, and then broke into a jog, and then a feverish run. Sophie crouched behind a pillar as the soldiers passed her like charging stallions. She anguished at the thought of staying behind and hiding, like a coward, while the soldiers ran unarmed into a battle that, for many of them, would mean their doom. But she also knew she really didn't have much to contribute to the fight. And, regardless of the outcome, finding Alie really was the most important thing she could do.

The two armies crashed together in a torrent of excruciating cries and bloodcurdling screams. The soldiers' fearlessness was extraordinary, but it wasn't enough. They were no match for the demons' dagger-like claws, or the monstrous brutes that were three times the size of any man. One soldier climbed a brute like a tree, only to be snatched off its back by the brute's beefy hand, and then effortlessly dismembered. Sophie watched another soldier manage to pin down a demon and pound several fists into its screeching face. But seconds later another creature skewered the soldier with its elongated claws, and then lifted him high over its head with a triumphant howl.

Sophie felt an immediate, intense guilt for guiding these men to their slaughter. But then remembered the words of the captain, imploring her to survive the battle and find Alie. If she did not, if she gave up now, the sacrifice of the soldiers would be pointless.

She waited for some sort of break in the chaos—a way through, like the captain directed. But it never came. In fact, the longer she waited, the worse things got. Any tiny opening that might allow her to sneak through closed as quickly as it opened.

She looked downriver to see if she could possibly make to the next crossing, but she would be exposed for far too long trying to reach the next bridge. She also considered jumping into the water and trying to swim, but knew she'd be easily spotted. The only other option was turning back, which really wasn't an option at all. So she decided to stick with the original, foolish, impossible plan, and crept out onto the bridge to try and sneak closer to the melee while waiting for some sort of opening.

Sophie managed to get close enough to the chaos that she could smell the nauseating stench of the demons. She tried to stay hidden by crouching behind the very few benches and trash containers on the bridge's walkway, but it was in vain. She was clearly visible and available for any demon who may look her way. She knew that every second she stayed on the bridge, she was ripe for the picking. So she swallowed hard and waited for any brief, miniscule sign of a gap in the carnage. As soon as a rift formed long enough for her to see the gloomy smog of the opposite bank, she took off.

Sophie was six steps into a sprint when a massive brute, with two soldiers wrapped like pythons around its neck, came crashing to the concrete and completely blocked her route. She skidded to a halt as she frantically scanned for another option. She darted toward another opening, only to watch it vanish. And then another, with the same result. Completely out of options, she hunched as low as she could and scampered into the fray, searching desperately for a way through.

Just a few steps in, a pair of strong hands snatched her from behind. She instinctively began flailing and kicking, trying to break the hold. But the familiar voice in her ear caused her to pause.

"Forgive me," said the captain, "but this can't be your fight. You must go and find him."

"But wait, I don't—"

Before she could finish her protest, he hoisted her into the air and over the side of the bridge. Suddenly, she was plummeting face-first toward the river below. Her arms jutted out, expecting to feel the sudden rush of a chilly current as she broke the surface. But it was unlike anything she could have anticipated. She didn't feel any splash or icy, refreshing flow. Instead, she was sucked into a blackened world of muted, gurgling sounds. The water felt oily and smelled rancid. She could feel the strength of the current pushing her downstream, yet the water was just barely moving. She looked around for something to grab onto, but just sank, very slowly, until she felt the slimy silt of the river's bottom. She latched onto a large rock at first, hoping to stabilize her fall, but soon realized that she could dig her feet into the slime below and stand in the current with surprisingly very little effort at all. She had been holding her breath out of habit, and waited for the familiar ache of breathlessness to set in. But it didn't come; she never felt as if she needed to suck in air.

Looking up, Sophie could barely see the hazy contour of the sun peeking down through the surface. Below and all around her were just faint shadows in different shades of black, distorted by the slow-motion flow of the river. She knew the river must not be all that deep, but it felt like she was a mile below the surface. For several minutes, she took in the surreal scene surrounding her and tried to figure out what her next move should be. She tried briefly to push off from the river bottom and swim, but her efforts were useless, as she found herself being pulled, albeit very slowly, downstream. So she allowed her feet to settle back down on the bottom, and then turned in the direction of what she thought was the riverbank that would eventually lead to the old town. Her feet slogged along, one lumbering step at a time, through the grimy bottom until she found herself scaling up a mound of slippery rocks leading toward the surface.

With her eyes and ears just barely above the surface, she peeked in the direction of the bridge. What she saw was heartbreaking. In the time she'd been below the surface, what had been a lopsided battle had turned into a massacre. She could only make out a few soldiers still standing, surrounded and outnumbered by the ravenous demons closing in to finish them off. One of the brutes was standing at the edge of the bridge, holding a limp soldier in each hand, like rag dolls, looking down into the water. With little more than a flick, it tossed one into the water, and then held up the other, which was still twitching. Sophie waited in horror for the monster to toss the other body, but instead it paused and looked out across the surface, and then directly at her. Sophie slipped below the surface in a panic and waited, hoping it hadn't seen her. She stayed low and deliberated whether it was riskier for her to try and stay hidden below the surface, or to quickly scramble up the riverbank and make a run for it. She couldn't see anything from under the water, but imagined the raging demons rushing down the banks to fish her from the water and tear her to shreds. She finally decided that attempting an escape was better than staying below the surface, not knowing whether they were coming for her. So she raised her head above the surface again, just high enough to get a glimpse. There, standing on the bridge, staring directly at her, were a pair of rust-colored eyes.

Sophie clambered wildly up the rocks and onto the street that lined the river, no longer caring how noticeable she might be. Just as she managed to reach dry ground, she saw the first of numerous demons dashing off the bridge and right at her. She quickly scanned the lavish store fronts on the opposite side of the street until she found a gap in between buildings, and ran like she'd never run before toward the opening. The air filled with screeches and howls as she sprinted into the alleyway. She didn't dare take time to look back; she could hear the mob of creatures stampeding into the narrow corridor behind her. She prayed as she ran that the passageway wasn't a dead end. But even if she could escape the alley, then what? Could she actually find the warehouse before getting caught? And if she did find the warehouse, what would she do then? Even if Alie were there, he stood no chance against the large army of demons pursuing her. Her chances of survival seemed to have gone from slim to hopeless, and she might be bringing doom to Alie in the process.

The hisses and roars of the horde were deafening, and she knew they were closing in. As she turned what she hoped would be the last corner before escaping from the narrow corridor, she took a quick glance behind. The scene was horrifying. The bulk of the creatures were barreling through the alley directly behind her, while others had climbed the buildings and were running across the rooftops, screeching like banshees. As she made the turn, she looked down a long street, thinking it might be the last she ever saw. There was simply no way she could keep up this pace for another block. And yet the demons were only getting faster. Her feet pounded out a few more desperate steps before something grabbed her ankle and pulled her downward. Then the street disappeared, and everything went black.

She crashed hard to the ground, but not the same ground on which she'd been running. She knew she'd fallen, but just not to the street. Somehow, she fell *through* the street, and crashed quite painfully into a dark, wet world below. Looking up, she could barely see two small holes peeking up to the grey sky above, and the faint outline of a manhole cover. When the stench hit her like a brick, she realized that she was in the sewer.

"You can kiss me later, when we don't stink. But for now, run!" She could only see his silhouette, but Alie's voice was the best sound she'd ever heard. Before she could respond, he was tearing down the slender tunnel leading away from the manhole and toward a dim, distant light. Sophie was right behind him, her feet splashing through the putrid stream of drainage that flowed the length of the tube. As they ran, the enraged cries of demons seeped down from the street above into the tunnel. She assumed it wouldn't take long for them to figure it out, and they would soon fill the sewers looking for her. Hopefully she and Alie would be long gone by then.

"Alie, where are we going?"

"Back to the warehouse," he answered. "My body is there, and so is a pure."

"But doesn't that mean—"

"That they're trying to take my body? Most likely, but not if we get there first."

The maze of tunnels snaked on for what felt like an eternity. In every dark corner and around every bend, Sophie was sure that sharp claws would snatch her. But considering the situation she'd just escaped, this was definitely an upgrade.

"Shhh," he whispered while slowing long enough to listen for sounds coming from the dark behind them. "They're in the sewers." Sophie could hear them too; their snarls reverberated down the concrete tunnels, signaling that they were on the hunt. Alie yanked her back into an all-out sprint, but the louder the vile commotion got, the more difficult it became to tell where it was coming from. Just as Sophie was sure the demons would round the last corner and spot them, Alie skidded to a halt at the base of a ladder. He practically flew up the rungs before peeking carefully at the scene above. "It's okay," he said, and Sophie followed him up and out onto a familiar city street.

They were standing directly in the middle of the same road where she'd found the flower cart. That meant they were close to the warehouse, but were also completely exposed in a place with a high concentration of demons, with more on the way. Sophie nodded toward a wooden, double-doorway that led into what looked like an old pub. Without a word, Alie followed her through the doors and into a room filled with tables, barstools, and old newspaper articles pinned to the walls. Half of the tables were still draped with the bodies of lifeless patrons face-down in their spilled drinks. Seated in one booth that she found particularly disturbing was a young couple who had been preserved almost perfectly in their upright positions, with only their heads drooping on raggedy necks. If she allowed herself to think about it, the overwhelming air of sadness permeating everywhere, and everything was almost too much. Instead, she forced herself to focus only on where they were headed next, which was through the swinging door into the kitchen, and then up the dark staircase in the back.

They continued pushing forward, winding up more stairs and through obscure hallways before leaping to the next building. The air outside echoed with the sickening furor of hundreds of enraged demons. But for now, Sophie and Alie were undetected. They stopped inside a small office where Alie peered warily out a window.

"We're here," he said. Sophie moved quietly next to him and peeked. They were directly across the street from the warehouse, and as far as she could see, they were alone.

"Now what?" Sophie asked.

"The longer we wait around, the greater chance they'll find us," he answered. "We need to cross the street straight away."

"But, that doesn't really answer my question," Sophie persisted. "I understand we're going to the warehouse, but then what?" Alie didn't respond, instead staring blankly out the window, so she continued. "Whatever plan we had, once upon a time, was completely trashed when the soldiers showed up and blocked us from leaving the city."

"We had no choice, Sophie."

"I agree. You know what they say about the best-laid plans. But everything depended on me staying in my body while you sneak around as a ghost. That's clearly not gonna happen anymore. Which brings me back to my question: now what?"

Alie still didn't answer immediately. He paced the floor while rubbing his head. He was clearly agitated, and Sophie realized he was likely just as unsure as she was.

"I'm sorry, Sophie, but I just don't know anymore." He answered without looking her in the eyes. His voice cracked with palpable emotion as he continued. "I know I'm supposed to have a plan. But I honestly have no idea what we're supposed to do. All I know is that we're in here, my body is in there, and I can't get you back in your body unless I re-take mine first. So, I'm going into that warehouse, one way or another."

Sophie drew near to him and placed her hand on his chest. "I'm sorry, Alie. I didn't mean to place this all on you."

"But it *is* all on me," he snapped. "I promised to keep you safe, and to get us out of this mess, and so far…"

"So far we're alive, and we're together," she interjected. "Nearly every plan we've tried has failed, but we're still here. Maybe, just maybe, we aren't meant to follow a plan. Maybe we just need to have…you know, faith."

"What other plan is there?" he whispered.

They held each other in silence for several minutes more. Then he took her by the hand and led her quietly out the door and down to the bottom floor. They waited for some sign that the demons were nearby, but none came. So they snuck across the street and, very carefully, approached the warehouse door. Inside they could hear the foul noises of quarreling demons.

"We can't go through the door," Alie whispered. "We wouldn't stand a chance. I need to see inside."

"What about the skylight?" Sophie responded. Alie nodded, and they cautiously slipped around the corner where he boosted Sophie up onto the ladder to the fire escape. They climbed slowly and deliberately, determined to make as little noise as possible. Once they reached the top, they scurried carefully across the metal rooftop toward the window that dissected the roof, and opened up into the building's icy interior. Moving inch by inch, they slid until they could peer down through the skylight. Sophie gasped at what they saw.

"Those bastards," Alie snarled. His body was directly below them, situated almost perfectly on its back with hands resting at its side. A circle of demons surrounded the body, most of which were rocking back and forth while reciting their dreadful chant. Standing just inches from Alie's head was a robed figure that rose above the others. Sophie couldn't see its face, but its powdery hands jutted out from bulky sleeves, and held one end of a silvery rope that disappeared into the demon crowd. The creature's head was veiled by a swarthy hood that hung heavily over its eyes, completely obscuring its face. But with its every gyration, the hood rocked in and out of a dim beam of light streaming down through the skylight. In between rocks, Sophie could see the chiseled contours of Alie's illuminated face. It looked as if, at any moment, his eyes would open and look directly at her.

"You know what this means," Sophie whispered.

Alie nodded. "It means we're out of time." He brusquely rose to his feet and looked in all directions before pointing to the north. "Can you make it back to the church?"

"What?" Sophie blurted out. "Why?"

"You have to," he insisted. "Get back there and wait for me. I will get there as soon as I can, and with your body."

"Are you insane? I told you—"

"I'm sorry, but there's no time for discussion," he insisted. "I have to get down there and…"

"No!" she shouted. She couldn't hold it any longer. Alie stiffened and quickly scanned the rooftops. Sophie started to try and explain herself, but Alie held out his hand, telling her to stay quiet. He crouched and scooted toward the edge of the window, just barely peeking into the frigid chasm below. As soon as he did, his head snapped back, and Sophie knew that whatever he saw wasn't good.

"They know we're here," Alie snapped, and then immediately headed back toward the fire escape. As soon as he reached the edge, a tempest of frenzied shrieks erupted from below. Alie hopped down onto the fire escape, and then motioned for Sophie to do the same. But just before she could jump, a pack of demons rounded the corner in a furious wrath.

"Alie!"

He leapt back onto the roof and screamed for her to run to the other side. She sprinted across the rooftop, her steps reverberating like tinny drumbeats into the space below. The cries of creatures climbing the fire escape were answered by similar cries a short distance away. Alie hurdled the skylight in stride, and Sophie followed. As they approached the opposite side of the roof, Sophie expected to see Alie soar right off the edge toward another rooftop. Instead, he skidded to a clumsy stop, with Sophie almost crashing into him. She looked out beyond the warehouse and saw a very large rift between them and the next building, far too wide for a jump. And, even worse, the horde of demons from the sewers had answered the other's cries, and were racing down the street right toward them.

They spun to see the first of the ascending demons slither onto the rooftop. The second vaulted high into the air from the fire escape and onto the roof, even more menacingly than the first. Alie turned to run toward the back of the warehouse, but before Sophie could follow, a twisted, elongated arm crept over the edge like a spider. The being that followed was the most hideous she'd seen yet, and its other grotesque arm dragged two more demons up with it. Sophie turned back to the ledge behind her and saw the swarm already scaling the walls like a rising infestation.

They were trapped.

Alie screamed something incomprehensible at Sophie, and then charged toward the demons coming from the fire escape. He again cleared the skylight, but only in time to see six more demons climb onto the roof. He would be slaughtered within seconds, and Sophie screamed at him to please stop. He turned back to her with a look of helpless terror, and then switched his gaze repeatedly between the demons and her. Sophie ran toward him too, ignoring his pleas for her to stay away. There was nowhere else to go except to him.

The demons howled with sick glee as Sophie crashed into Alie and he wrapped his arms around her. His head continued a frenzied swivel as the creatures poured onto the roof, surrounding them. Alie backed her away hopelessly until Sophie's foot bumped the window's edge. She looked back into the warehouse's cold abyss and saw only the faint

image of Alie's face and the feeble outline of a pure kneeling next to
him. She looked back to Alie, who too was looking down at his body.
Sophie looked back at the ghastly faces of the demons as they advanced,
ready to pounce like wild dogs. Sophie looked again to Alie, who was
staring deep into her tear-flooded eyes. She felt his fingers dig into her
shoulders and squeeze her tightly.

"Sophie," he shouted. She could barely hear him over earsplitting
screams of the horde. He shook her powerfully until she was focused
only on him. "Look at me, Sophie, not them. You know I love you,
right?"

She nodded as a sob exploded from within. She opened her mouth to
try and say something back, but no words came.

"It's okay, Sophie. I know." He looked down through the glass one
last time, and then said, clearly, "Sophie, I *will* find you."

"What?" she shouted.

The glass exploded into a million pieces, glistening like gems in the
steely rays of light streaming down from the desolate sky above. They
burst through the skylight, falling in what felt like slow motion as the
shards surrounded them on the way down. Alie tightened his grip on her
as they plunged, and for a fleeting instant she felt his familiar, protective
warmth. Their bodies spun as they fell, just enough for her to catch a
glimpse of numerous demon heads peering down through the shattered
window above. And then…

Thud.

Her back slammed violently to the floor, with Alie smashing down
on top of her. Pain shot through her like lightning as she hacked
desperately for a breath. She threw her head back and gasped, and saw
the pure's dazzling eyes staring directly into her, only inches from her
face. She tried to sit up, but a pair of powerful hands pinned her back to
the floor. Alie was on top of her, and wouldn't let her move.

"Alie, what are you…" That was when she realized she was lying
directly within the contours of Alie's body. "No! No, no, no!" she
screamed, but he wouldn't let her move. A demon sprang onto Alie's
back and sank its serrated fangs into his neck. He howled in pain, but
still wouldn't let go. Sophie fought against his grip as much as she
could, but it was useless. She looked again at the pure, whose feeble lips
were snapping rapidly open and shut as a flurry of unfathomable noises

flowed from its mouth. "Please, Alie, don't do this," she cried, knowing that he wasn't listening. More demons continued to pile on him as the hooded one screamed out and jerked the rope around the pure's neck. But it was too late.

Her thoughts began to swirl, and then melt together into an insane mess. The sucking came first, as if she were being squished through a tunnel half her size. Then came the excruciating stabbing sensations, all over her skin, and the feeling of a thousand fishhooks forcing her lungs to expand and contract. She arched her back as the pain throttled her, and reached out for Alie. But her arms grasped only frigid, empty air. The shrieks of the demons were gone, and so were the iridescent eyes of the pure dangling over her. She rolled onto her side as the dry heaves set in, and saw that she was alone in the warehouse.

"No," she whispered through an agonizing cough. Her back smacked painfully again onto the floor as her body convulsed. Through teary, blurred eyes she looked again toward the skylight. But the glass was perfectly intact, holding back a light rain that trickled down from the heavens. And then he appeared, a perfect vision of Alie that materialized through the veil dividing their worlds. His face was twisted into a violent scream, but it only came through as a harsh whisper. The faint words were almost unintelligible, but she thought she heard him say "catacombs". His body was wrapped in the slithery arms of demons that were dragging him away from her. She reached for him a final time, and then he was gone.

Sophie collapsed and choked back a sob. She buried her face in her hands, and suddenly recognized the rough callouses scratching her cheeks. She held out her arms, and saw Alie's hands before her eyes. She looked down past the hands, and saw Alie's boots attached to her feet. She ran her hands all over her body, and felt nothing but Alie. She stroked his buzzed hair on top of her head, and the chiseled forearms she had first noticed when he was sitting alone in the booth. She was alive, resurrected back into a body, but it was not hers.

Sophie rolled again onto her side, and then tucked into a fetal position. Everything seemed completely hopeless. At the very best, Alie had been carried off to suffer in the demonic lair deep within the catacombs in Paris. But for all she knew, he also could have been dragged to the depths of Hell, where she would never find him. She was completely alone and helpless. Virgil may have answers, but he had slipped off into the spirit world to apparently read spirit books. And the captain and his soldiers had most likely been wiped out completely. And now she inhabited the very body of the person whose memory would haunt her every time she looked in the mirror. She couldn't even pick up the phone and call home, or ask for help.

She clutched Alie's white t-shirt with his hands and squeezed her eyes shut, wishing that the CERN collider would cause that massive black hole Virgil had talked about and end everything, once and for all. But through Alie's thin t-shirt, she felt a very slight, pulsating sensation. She pressed his hand harder to his chest, and felt the rhythmic thad-ump, thad-ump. It was his heart, beating within her, stubbornly urging her to keep going.

Fighting against everything that made her want to quit, Sophie flopped over onto her hands and knees, sucked in two very long breaths, and stumbled to her feet. Her head throbbed as she struggled to stay upright. She was shivering uncontrollably, with Alie's teeth chattering painfully within her mouth. She stumbled toward a wall of crates and grabbed on to steady herself. His lungs were still straining to take in air, and she had to stop every few steps to keep from passing out. She was turning the corner toward the exit when a faint gasp from the shadows caught her attention.

A crumpled pile of something was squirming just beyond the edge of the darkness. It began to wheeze unnaturally, and then a human hand shot from the shadows and reached into the light. Sophie drew cautiously closer until she could make out the outlines of several bodies stacked into a heap of discarded flesh, all of them lifeless except the hacking being struggling to reanimate itself. For a brief moment, she hoped against the impossible that somehow it would be Alie, but its unnatural writhing and twitching gave it away. It was not human, which could only mean one thing.

An immediate, untamed wrath filled her as she bounded across the floor and seized the wrist of the waking creature. She dragged it into the dim light and took hold of its head by the hair. She paused to take a long look at Alie's powerful forearms and hands, one of which was now latched firmly around some unfortunate stranger's neck that just happened to now house a demonic intruder. Its eyes were bulging as she applied pressure to its panting throat.

"What are you?" she yelled, just inches from its terrified face. She shook the body viciously. "You'd better speak now! What the hell are you?" Still it didn't answer, but just continued to tremble and stare at her in horror.

"All right then. Welcome to my reality, you son of a bitch," she growled. "You're about to experience whole new levels of pain." With just a tad more pressure, she was confident she could crush its larynx, and then watch it thrash on the cold concrete as its first breaths became its last. In fact, that was just the first of a million unholy things she imagined doing to this wicked creature. But a little bit of sanity snuck through her rage to remind her that, perhaps, like Alie, she could take advantage of this opportunity to see if she could torture some information out of it.

She released her grip on its throat and took another handful of hair in her left hand. Then she cocked her right fist back and shouted, "Where is he? Where are they taking him?" The creature quivered in her grasp with a look of complete confusion on its face. Its lips parted just barely, but only a wisp of air snuck out. Any miniscule amount of patience she may have had for this creature was instantly exhausted, and Sophie brought her fist down like a hammer, smashing the creature square in the nose.

"Tell me where he is!"

Pain shot up from her knuckles and through his arm, and it felt good. A stream of crimson started to gush from the stranger's nose. Fear resonated from its woozy eyes, and its mouth opened again, only to emit another strange, alien sound. She raised Alie's balled-up fist again, this time cocking it even further behind her, and prepared for another strike. The creature whimpered and turned its face away, its hands shooting up to try and guard against another blow. Just as she was set to rain down a second time, a bizarrely familiar voice escaped the creature's throat. It was reciting the ethereal chant that she heard come out of the pure just before she was sucked into Alie's body.

She released her grip and the body dropped to the floor. She sat back on the concrete and stared at the creature in disbelief. It quickly scampered away from her, and then huddled in fear against a large crate.

"You're not a demon at all, are you?" she said. "You're a pure."

The creature eyed her with a sense of distant understanding, but said nothing. After watching her suspiciously for several minutes, it began to paw harmlessly at the air in front of its face. Its chest rose and fell with very deliberate breaths as it concentrated on the sensation of cold air entering and exiting its newly acquired, human lungs. When Sophie finally shifted and began to rise to her feet, the creature cowered again.

"It's okay. No more beatings," she said. "At least, not as long as you behave."

She walked over to a junk pile underneath the stairs and retrieved a long steel chain. She returned to the creature and draped the chain over its neck, then tied what she hoped would be an effective knot.

"You're coming with me." She gave the creature a tug, and it scrambled willingly to its feet. She began to lead it toward the exit when a faint whisper of a sound caused her to pause. The creature looked at her curiously as she closed her eyes and listened to the darkness. Somewhere amongst the whir of the cooling fans, she thought she heard the sound of a hundred foul voices screaming out in infuriated protest. Sophie listened, and then smiled.

"That's right, I've got your pure!" she shouted. "And if you harm Alie, I will kill it. And then then I will come for you!"

The ghostly shrieks intensified, but then faded into the chilly blackness of the warehouse as Sophie led the pure outside. With a mighty heave, she slammed the massive sliding door shut behind them.

Chapter Thirty-Two

Sophie returned to the third-floor apartment to find the pure still sleeping like a baby on the couch, its chain still firmly fastened to the dingy radiator on the wall. It had refused a blanket several times, seemingly content to lay uncovered on the soft cushions. Sophie had barely slept, peering out the windows and pacing the unit's small interior until she could no longer stand it, and she ventured out into the early dawn hours.

She had found the strength of Alie's body extremely useful in loading up her body, and the body of the captain and several of his men, into a butcher's truck before transporting them to the warehouse. She also went back to the police station, found a pen and blank paper, and wrote a long letter explaining everything that had happened, and the need to preserve as many bodies as possible. She then taped it to the front door in the hope that someone would find it and read it. Whether they would believe what it said was now beyond her control.

Then Sophie made one last stop by the dojo, where she bowed before entering, and then picked up something she thought might be useful.

She returned to the apartment with a bag of groceries. She wasn't sure if it was the savory smell of scrambled eggs that woke the pure, or the clanging of the borrowed pans. It remained huddled on the couch and watched her curiously as she rummaged through the kitchen, and then sat down to eat her breakfast. She glanced occasionally at the small mirror hanging on the wall where she saw Alie's face looking back at her. She talked to the image in the mirror like a crazy person, and then chuckled at the American accent coming from Alie's mouth. After taking down a rest of her breakfast and some orange juice, she stood from the table.

"Shall we?" The pure looked at her strangely, but continued playing with its chain as if it were a shiny toy. Sophie approached him and reached into the small paper sack in her hand. "Here, you'll like it. It's food. It's called a strawberry."

The pure fumbled the strawberry in its hands awkwardly before copying Sophie and inserting it into its mouth. It licked the fruit awkwardly, then held it in its mouth until the strawberry started to dissolve. Once the flavor kicked in, the pure slowly started to mash the strawberry between its teeth until red juice trickled down its chin.

"You'll need the energy. We've got some traveling to do."

With a tug, the pure followed her out the door of the apartment and then down the stairs. They stepped out onto the empty street, and Sophie looked up and closed her eyes to feel the warm sunlight on Alie's face. She clutched her chest and felt his heart beating strongly inside her. She adjusted the sword strapped to her back, and then looked once more at the pure, who was stuffing strawberries into its mouth. Then she turned toward the northwest, and toward Paris.

ABOUT THE AUTHOR

Josh Deere is an author, attorney, consultant and speaker. He comes from a long line of storytellers, and fervently believes that a good story has the power to change lives. In addition to his law practice and ongoing writing projects, Josh consults with attorneys and other professionals about strategies to reinvent their practices and careers.

More importantly, Josh is a husband to an amazing woman who is WAY out of his league, and a father to three fantastic sons who think their father is a huge dork. He and his family are lucky enough to live in Colorado, where they love to fish, hike, camp, and sneak around haunted hotels in Estes Park.

www.joshdeere.com

Don't Forget to Leave a Review!

We'd love it if you'd leave a review for Purgatorium at:

https://www.amazon.com/dp/0578600668

https://www.goodreads.com/book/show/48750981-purgatorium

https://www.barnesandnoble.com/w/purgatorium-josh-deere/1134947188?ean=9780578600666

Thank you!